PENGUIN CLASSICS

THE GOLDEN ASS

APULEIUS (we do not know his other names) was born about AD 125 in Madaura or Madauros, a Roman colony in North Africa, now Mdaourouch in Algeria. His father, from whom he inherited a substantial fortune, was one of the two chief magistrates (*duouiri*) of the city. For his education Apuleius was sent first to Carthage, the capital of Roman North Africa, and then to Athens. During his time abroad he travelled widely, spending some time in Rome, where he practised as a pleader in the courts. While detained by illness on his way home at Oea in Tripoli, he met and married the wealthy widow Pudentilla. This was at the instance of one of her sons, whom he had known at Rome; but other members of her family objected to the marriage and prosecuted Apuleius on various charges, principally that of winning Pudentilla's affections by magic. Their accusations were brilliantly, and it would seem successfully, rebutted in his speech *De Magia* or *Apology*, delivered in or shortly before AD 160. He appears to have spent the rest of his life in Carthage, where he became a notable public figure, holding the chief priesthood of the province and receiving other public honours.

The age in which Apuleius lived was that of the Antonine emperors Antoninus Pius and Marcus Aurelius, described by his contemporary the Greek sophist Aelius Aristides in his oration *To Rome* as a period of unexampled prosperity and felicity, a verdict echoed by Gibbon in the opening chapters of *The History of the Decline and Fall of the Roman Empire*. It was an age in which success in public speaking offered a passport to fame, and Apuleius owed his contemporary reputation to the mastery of language deployed both in his many display speeches, of which we have excerpted specimens in his *Florida*, and in the Neoplatonic philosophical writings which earned him a statue in his native city. Of these the most important which survive are *On the God of Socrates* (*De Deo Socratis*) and *On Plato and his Doctrine* (*De Platone et eius Dogmate*). An imposing range of other writings in both prose and verse we know of only from fragments and references in other authors. The modern world knows him best as the author of the great serio-comic novel *The Golden Ass* or *Transformations* (*Metamorphoses*), which he is generally thought to have written after his return to Carthage. He probably died about AD 180.

E. J. KENNEY is Emeritus Kennedy Professor of Latin in the University of Cambridge. He was born in 1924 and was educated at Christ's Hospital and Trinity College, Cambridge, of which he was Scholar and Fellow. In the Second World War he served in the Royal Signals in the United Kingdom and India, being commissioned in 1944. From 1953 to 1991 he was a Fellow of Peterhouse, Cambridge, where at various times he held the offices of Director of Studies in Classics, Senior Tutor, Librarian and Domestic Bursar. His publications include a critical edition of Ovid's amatory works (1961; second edition, 1995) and editions with commentary of Lucretius' *De rerum natura III* (1971), Apuleius' *Cupid and Psyche* (1990) and Ovid's *Heroides XVI–XXI* (1996); and he is currently preparing a commentary on Books VII–IX of Ovid's *Metamorphoses*, to appear in a five-volume edition of the entire poem. In 1968 he was Sather Professor of Classical Literature at the University of California at Berkeley; his lectures were published in 1974 as *The Classical Text* (Italian translation, 1995). He is a Fellow of the British Academy and a Foreign Member of the Royal Netherlands Academy of Arts and Sciences. He is a past President of the Joint Association of Classical Teachers and of the Classical Association, and is currently President of The Horatian Society.

APULEIUS

The Golden Ass

or *Metamorphoses*

Translated with an Introduction and Notes by
E. J. KENNEY

PENGUIN BOOKS

PENGUIN BOOKS

Published by the Penguin Group
Penguin Books Ltd, 80 Strand, London WC2R ORL, England
Penguin Putnam Inc., 375 Hudson Street, New York, New York 10014, USA
Penguin Books Australia Ltd, 250 Camberwell Road, Camberwell, Victoria 3124, Australia
Penguin Books Canada Ltd, 10 Alcorn Avenue, Toronto, Ontario, Canada M4V 3B2
Penguin Books India (P) Ltd, 11 Community Centre, Panchsheel Park, New Delhi – 110 017, India
Penguin Books (NZ) Ltd, Cnr Rosedale and Airborne Roads, Albany, Auckland, New Zealand
Penguin Books (South Africa) (Pty) Ltd, 24 Sturdee Avenue, Rosebank 2196, South Africa

Penguin Books Ltd, Registered Offices: 80 Strand, London WC2R ORL, England

www.penguin.com

First published 1998
Reprinted with revisions 2004

038

Set in 10/12.5 pt Monotype Bembo
Typeset by Rowland Phototypesetting Ltd, Bury St Edmunds, Suffolk

Printed and bound in Great Britain by Clays Ltd, Elcograf S.p.A.

ISBN-13: 978-0-140-43590-0

www.greenpenguin.co.uk

Contents

Acknowledgements

For various advice and information generously given I am indebted to Dr James Carleton Paget, Dr Gillian Clark, Professor John Crook and Dr Emily Gowers.

My most fundamental debt, however, is a very old one, to the framers of the Cambridge Classical Tripos as it was in 1946–8. In those days Part I had no syllabus of prescribed texts, and its unstructured character encouraged the discursive exploration of Greek and Latin literature. Unprompted, I then first read *The Golden Ass*, as its author intended, for pleasure; a pleasure which, half a century later, it has been a delight to renew, and which I hope this translation may help a new generation of readers to share.

Abbreviations

OCD   S. Hornblower and A. Spawforth (eds.), *The Oxford Classical Dictionary*, 3rd edn. (Oxford, 1996).

OLD   P. G. W. Glare (ed.), *Oxford Latin Dictionary* (Oxford, 1982).

Introduction

Apuleius is the most whimsical of authors and is a law to himself. H. E. BUTLER

. . . the [Golden Ass] *is a puzzle.* J. J. WINKLER

Apuleius is determined to confuse us. M. GRANT[1]

I

What is conventionally termed the Prologue[2] to *The Golden Ass* ends with an apparently straightforward promise of entertainment in store. *Lector, intende: laetaberis* – 'Give me your ear, reader: you will enjoy yourself.' That promise is amply fulfilled. This is the most continuously and accessibly amusing book that has come down to us from classical antiquity. But in *The Golden Ass* appearances more often than not turn out to be deceptive, and there is a good deal more in this short Prologue than immediately meets the eye.

The two words *intende: laetaberis* are more suggestive than they seem. *Intendo* connotes directed effort; the reader is to be *intentus*, attentive, serious, switched on.[3] The coordinate structure of the Latin phrase stands, as often, for a conditional clause: *if* you give your mind to what follows, you will be made happy. The implication is that the amount, and possibly the quality, of the reader's enjoyment will depend on the degree of attention brought to bear on the book. What has preceded, however, is calculated to puzzle the really attentive reader. The Prologue begins with an address to some unidentified person in a chatty and informal style suggesting a conversation already in progress: 'Now (to get down to business), what I am going to do . . .'. First we are promised 'a series of different stories' strung together in a 'Milesian discourse'. This points to a collection of tales of the kind associated with Aristides of Miletus (*fl. c.* 100 BC): anecdotes, more often than not scabrous, culled from the illimitable subliterary repertoire of traditional popular storytelling and embellished for an educated audience. This class of literature was not considered edifying. After the battle of Carrhae in 53 BC the victorious Parthians were, or affected to be, scandalized by the discovery of Aristides' *Milesiaca* in the baggage of the defeated Roman army (Plutarch, *Life of Crassus*, 32). According to the author of the life of Clodius Albinus in the *Historia Augusta*, that emperor was criticized for frittering away his time on 'his countryman Apuleius' Milesian stories and other literary trivialities' (*Historia Augusta*, 12. 12. 12). This is 'amusing gossip',[4] which will 'charm the ear'. However, this anodyne programme is immediately qualified by the following request not to 'scorn' Egyptian paper written on with a sharp pen from the Nile. These disparate stories, it seems, have some sort of Egyptian flavour and are in some way pointed (see 1.1 and note). Moreover, they have after all a common theme, metamorphosis, transformation of men's shapes and fortunes.

At this point a voice is heard asking *Quis ille?*, 'Who is this?' We may well retort the question: who is supposed to be asking it? The writer himself, anticipating the reader's curiosity? The reader, in words put into his mouth by the writer? A third party? The possibilities, given more particularly that ancient scribal conventions knew nothing of quotation marks and such devices, shade into one another: the blurring of identities which so much preoccupies critics of *The Golden Ass* has begun. The answer to the question is not altogether precise. Corinth, Athens, and Sparta together make up the speaker's 'ancient ancestry', but their respective parts in his formation only emerge later (1.1 and note). The verb used to describe his Latin studies at Rome is ambiguous: *excolui* can mean, not merely 'cultivated', but 'developed', 'improved', 'adorned'.[5] Such apologies for insufficiency prefacing a book or a speech are commonly disingenuous, as the following comparison with the trick-rider shows this one to be. This collection of stories, it is insinuated, is to be a stylistic *tour de force* by a Greek who can teach native Romans a thing or two about how to handle their own language.

But one more surprise is in store. In two crisp words we learn that what is about to unfold is a single tale, *fabulam Graecanicam*, 'a Grecian story'. It seems that after all this is not some sort of anthology of anecdotes, but one story translated or adapted from a single Greek[6] original.

The reader is for the time being left to wonder – and wonder has been promised as well as pleasure – about this apparent discrepancy. That will eventually be resolved when *The Golden Ass* turns out to be both these things. For the surprise that is ultimately in store not even the most attentive of first-time readers can have been prepared. Clairvoyance rather than concentration would have been needed to foresee that.

2

We have not long to wait for the first of the promised metamorphoses. The figure of the author, manipulating with almost insolent assurance his diverse literary materials and the two languages of which he is self-proclaimed master, now fades into and is lost in that of a narrator, the hero of the *fabula Graecanica* – the plaything of Fortune, the slave of his passions, controlled by the events of the story which as author he had purported to control.[7] He identifies himself as one Lucius – though his name is only revealed casually towards the end of book 1 [8] – a young man of good provincial family from Corinth, on his way when the story opens to Thessaly 'on particular business'. This proves to be an obsessive interest in witchcraft (for which Thessaly was famous); and it turns out that his hostess at Hypata, where he is bound with letters of introduction, is a renowned sorceress. With the help of her maid Photis he obtains access to her devil's smithy, where by mischance he is changed, not as planned into a bird, but into a donkey. Before he can get at the antidote to the spell, which is to eat some roses, he is carried off by a gang of robbers; and the tale of his ensuing adventures, misadventures, and narrow escapes from death as he passes from one owner to another takes up the rest of the first ten books of the novel.

The narrative is bulked out by stories heard by Lucius both before and after his metamorphosis, making up some sixty per cent of the text of books 1–10. This is the 'Milesian' element heralded in the Prologue, but an attentive reader will perceive that there is more to it than 'amusing gossip', though that is how Lucius himself invariably accepts it. These stories are clearly intended to form an integral part of the literary structure of the book, providing what is in effect a commentary on the experiences, sufferings, and final deliverance of the hero. Their allegorical character (using the word in its broadest sense) is most obviously evident in the tale of Cupid and Psyche, set off from the rest by its length, elaborate literary texture, and central placing in the narrative framework (4.28–6.24).[9] This is yet another surprise: the implicit undertaking to combine 'different stories' and a single 'Grecian story' is fulfilled in a way which their separate mention at the two extremes of the Prologue could hardly have led any reader, however attentive, to expect.

3

In order to tell his story, Lucius must survive his adventures and regain his human shape. It required no excessive ingenuity on the author's part to contrive a plausible opportunity for him to find the prescribed remedy, for by the end of book 10 it is once more spring and roses are available. It is now that events take the most startling turn of all. With the last of his series of owners Lucius has apparently fallen on his feet. Thiasus ('Mr Revel') discovers by chance that this ass of his possesses almost human tastes and intelligence, and 'trains' him to display his capabilities in public. A rich woman falls in love with him and bribes his keeper to allow her to spend a night with him. This is a great success, and when Thiasus gets wind of it he decides to exhibit Lucius in the role of lover in the games he is about to hold at Corinth. On learning of this and of the atrocious crimes of the woman who is to be his partner in the spectacle, Lucius despairs. Confronted with what he sees as the ultimate in degradation and fearing, reasonably enough, that the beasts in the arena are unlikely to distinguish between the innocent and the guilty parties, he decides to make a break for freedom. He escapes and prepares to spend the night on the seashore a few miles from Corinth. So ends book 10, with the hero in a state of physical and spiritual prostration.

To him at this nadir of his fortunes rescue now comes, in a way that the most percipient and attentive reader could not have guessed. He suddenly awakes from sleep to see the full moon rising in all her unearthly brilliance from the sea, and prays to her for deliverance.

Nothing has prepared the reader for his instant conviction[10] that here is his salvation, that she – invoked simultaneously as Ceres, Venus, Diana, and Proserpine – is the supreme governing power of the universe and that she and she alone can save him. This unexplained revelation comes, as is the nature of revelation, out of the blue. The goddess answers his prayer, not in any of the guises under which he has invoked her, but in one that subsumes and transcends them all. After enumerating the names under which she is worshipped throughout the world, she discloses her real identity: Isis, truly venerated under that name in Egypt – and the mind of the reader is immediately transported back to the mysterious hints in the Prologue.[11] She promises him release from his sufferings and gives him exact instructions for achieving it: in return he is to devote the rest of his life to her service.

All goes according to plan. Lucius is duly restored to human shape, receives a public lecture from Isis' priest on the significance of what has happened to him, and is initiated into the cult of the goddess. He moves to Rome, undergoes further initiations, and the end of the story finds him an apparently respectable member of society, simultaneously pursuing a secular career as a successful barrister and following a religious vocation as a shaven-headed official of an ancient priestly college. The emergence of the story into the light of common day finally reveals the nature and purpose of the over-arching metamorphosis from which *The Golden Ass* itself has emerged, and, so to say, gives the literary game away. Lucius has turned out to be a mask for the author himself, his story taken over, as will appear (below, §4), and allegorically transformed so as to illuminate an (ostensibly) actual spiritual experience, just as centrally within the book the tale of Cupid and Psyche is taken over and transformed to illuminate his own fictional case (see below, §9). The distinctly prosaic note on which the book ends, anticlimactic as it may seem after the excitements that have preceded, is functionally motivated, a deliberate underlining of the author's intentions.

Nevertheless the sense of anticlimax continues to nag. The first fifteen chapters of book 11 constitute the longest sequence of consistently elevated writing in the novel, writing as brilliant and compelling as anything in Latin literature. That glory of revelation and rebirth tails off into a workaday account of successive initiations and the shifts to which Lucius has to resort to meet the necessary expenses. The demands of God and Mammon, however, are finally reconciled when, under the special protection of Osiris, he is enabled to work up a flourishing legal practice. And so, to adapt the famous though possibly apocryphal dictum of Thomas Gaisford, Dean of Christ Church, Oxford, we see that 'the advantages of serving Isis and Osiris are twofold – it enables us to look down with contempt on those who have not shared its advantages,[12] and also fits us for places of emolument not only in this world, but in that which is to come'. Is this really what Isis meant when she prophesied that under her protection Lucius would 'live gloriously' (11.6)?

4

A book which began by seemingly promising nothing but entertainment, with only the faintest of hints that some reading between the lines might be required, has abruptly, and without anything that can reasonably be called warning, modulated at its end into fervent religiosity tempered by meritocratic self-satisfaction. To some critics book 11 has seemed too loosely attached thematically to the first ten, and too sharply contrasted with them in tone and feeling, for *The Golden Ass* to be convincingly defended as an integrated literary whole. A work in eleven books is in itself an anomaly: the preference was for even numbers or multiples of five. The author could perfectly well have incorporated the 'extra' element in a ten-book structure; the 'Isis-Book' draws attention to itself by being, literally, extraordinary, *extra ordinem*. Ideally the problem ought perhaps to be tackled without reference to anything but the book as we have it. That view is expressed robustly by George Saintsbury:

Origins . . . and indebtedness and the like, are, when great work is concerned, questions for the study and the lecture-room, for the literary historian and the professional critic, rather than for the reader, however intelligent and alert, who wishes to enjoy a masterpiece, and is content simply to enjoy it.[13]

However, in this case it happens that, whether fortunately or unfortunately, we do possess a good deal of information external to *The Golden*

Ass, both as to its author and as to its sources, models, and literary congeners. This is something we can hardly affect to ignore. In attempting to arrive at a proper appreciation of the author's genius and the merits and failings of his creation, and of what it has to say to us, that material cannot be left out of account, even if examination of it raises more questions than it answers.

The Milesian element in *The Golden Ass* is referred to twice in the book, once, as we have seen, in the Prologue, and again in a facetious authorial apology for reporting an oracle of Apollo in Latin verse. This latter allusion, however, is opportunism of a kind one soon learns to recognize, prompted by the fact that the oracle in question is the one at Miletus (4.32 and note). There is nothing remotely Milesian about the story of Cupid and Psyche. The *fabula Graecanica* we can identify. Transmitted among the works of the Greek satirist Lucian (*fl. c.* AD 165) is a piece entitled 'Lucius or the Ass' (*Loukios ē Onos*; henceforth *Onos*). This is a first-person narrative by one Lucius, who is changed into an ass by a spell which miscarries and after various adventures is changed back again: a version of our story lacking certain episodes, most notably that of the Festival of Laughter, the stories heard or reported by Lucius, Cupid and Psyche, and the Isiac sequel. The close correspondences between *The Golden Ass* and the *Onos* leave no room for doubt that they derive from a common original (see Appendix). What this was we learn from the *Bibliotheca* of the Byzantine scholar Photius (*c.* AD 850), who records having read both the *Onos* and another book distinct from it called 'Various tales (or books) of Metamorphosis by Lucius of Patrae'. Photius' testimony, when critically examined, is less precise than might be wished, but there is general agreement that

(i) *The Golden Ass* is an adaptation and the *Onos* an abridgement of that lost work (henceforth *Met.*).
(ii) The *Onos* is not, as it stands, the work of Lucian.
(iii) The ascription of *Met.* to 'Lucius of Patrae' is due to confusion on Photius' part between author and fictional narrator.
(iv) *Met.* may have been by Lucian, though several other candidates have been proposed.[14]
(v) Most or all of the material in *The Golden Ass* that does not figure

in the *Onos* did not figure in *Met.* either. It is hardly conceivable that Cupid and Psyche can have done.

The chief question mark is that hanging over book 11 of *The Golden Ass* and Lucius' 'conversion'. In the *Onos* Lucius, now restored to human shape, again presents himself to the lady whose favours he had enjoyed as an ass and is humiliatingly rebuffed because his genital equipment no longer measures up to her requirements. Some have thought that this broadly farcical denouement has replaced an original ending on a more serious note which served as model or inspiration for book 11 of *The Golden Ass*. There is little evidence either for or against this hypothesis, which is a good example of the type of explanation to which scholars resort from an ingrained reluctance to believe that any classical writer ever thought of anything for himself. There is no solid reason to withhold from our author the credit of originality as regards the way in which he chose to round off his book. Whether the result of combining this and the other disparate elements – the cautionary tales and Milesian stories, Cupid and Psyche, and the rest – in the framework of the ass-narrative can be considered successful is another matter. Certainly the whole undertaking was an ambitious one, like nothing else in the way of prose fiction that has survived from classical antiquity.

5

Most readers probably feel that down to the end of book 10 the story hangs together well enough. Though loose ends and minor inconsistencies abound,[15] where the author has not taken sufficient pains to dovetail the added material into the original fabric, the reader is irresistibly carried along by the sweep of the narrative and the narratives within the narrative. This is the secret of the classic novel,

the trick of maintaining an even flow of narration, steadily moving on no matter how thick and rich it may be. If a man can do this instinctively – and, let me add, very few men can – then God intended him to be a novelist.[16]

There is no doubt that God intended the author of *The Golden Ass* to be a novelist. The book is indeed 'thick and rich' with interwoven matter, but the weaving is done with skill and *élan*. This is particularly evident in what has been called the 'Charite-complex' (4.23–8.14), in which the fates of Charite and Tlepolemus, Cupid and Psyche, and Lucius himself are integrated into a complex counterpoint.[17] It is only now and then, as in the case of the tale of the delinquent slave (8.22), that a story is casually tossed in simply because it seemed too good to lose. In general the inserted stories and episodes significantly reinforce and illustrate the main narrative and the characterization of the hero.

Of the inserted episodes preceding Lucius' metamorphosis that of his involvement with the Festival of Laughter, his encounter with the 'robbers', and his public humiliation in his spoof trial for murder (2.31–3.18) has provoked much discussion. It can be read as a warning of what is in store for him if he persists in his obsessive interest in witchcraft: it is a mistake on the part of Photis, the sorceress's apprentice, that leads to the unplanned metamorphosis of the wineskins and its sequel, and it is to be a second mistake of hers that precipitates the disaster of Lucius' own transformation. The mockery which he suffers during the 'trial' is then a foretaste of his lot as an ass, proverbially a subject of ridicule for ugliness and stupidity. There are obvious technical flaws in the conduct of the story (3.13 and note), and it is difficult to know how exactly to interpret the manifest irony of Byrrhena's invitation to Lucius to 'provide a diversion' (2.31 and note). She is a more ambiguous character than Abroea, her prototype in the *Onos*; is she, like Milo, a willing party to the deception?

The other inserted episodes and stories in books 1–3 are, in contrast, transparently cautionary, reinforcing the warning explicitly given by Byrrhena (2.5). Read or reread in the light of the priest's homily after Lucius' retransformation (11.15), they can all be seen as underlining his – proleptically asinine – perseverance in the courses that ultimately cause his downfall. Of the stories that he hears as ass, that of Cupid and Psyche stands in a class by itself and calls for separate consideration. The others constitute a running commentary on the world of which he is now a feeling but inarticulate spectator. It is in fact the same world as that which he formerly inhabited when he was a privileged individual who would contemplate life *de haut en bas*. Now he sees it from below and is duly appalled by what he sees.

6

Provincial life in second-century Greece as depicted in *The Golden Ass* is in many ways so anarchic, legally, socially, and morally, that it is natural to question the historical accuracy of the picture, and to ask whether the writer has taken the novelist's freedom to create his own world – a travesty or caricature of reality – to enhance the impact of his narrative and to point the moral of his book. No more than poets are novelists bound to tell the truth –

> oh, creative poetic licence
> Is boundless, and unconstrained
> By historical fact –[18]

and *The Golden Ass* was not written as social history. However, unlike most of the Greek romances, but like the *Onos* and Petronius' *Satyricon*, the setting of the book is firmly contemporary, and as far as we can tell from the available evidence would have been recognized by contemporary readers as broadly realistic.

There is no doubt, for instance, that outside the larger centres law enforcement in the provinces of the Roman Empire was by and large of the do-it-yourself order.[19] Large landowners policed their estates themselves with their own retainers; it is the insensate rage of the tyrannical plutocrat rather than the arbitrary nature of his conduct that would have seemed exceptional (9.35–8). Brigandage, prominent in the plots of other romances and central in that of *The Golden Ass*, was a fact of life, controlled, in so far as it was controlled, by *ad hoc* punitive action (7.7) rather than by systematic policing. In point of fact the only effective police were the soldiers at the disposition of the provincial governor. Hypata boasts a town guard (3.3), but in the absence of government troops the city was evidently powerless to curb the activities of the local Mohocks (2.18). This may be a case of authorial inadvertence, but rings true in the light of what Juvenal has to say about street crime

xviii

in Rome itself some half a century earlier (*Satires*, 3. 278–314). Whether a court other than that of the governor was legally competent to try a Roman citizen [20] on a capital charge is debatable, but many contemporary readers may have been no more certainly informed than modern scholars on such points, and it would probably have occurred to few to think about a question which the hero himself does not raise. Nor again would most readers stop to wonder why the doctor in the trial of the evil stepmother delays giving his crucial evidence until the very last moment (10.8), instead of aborting the proceedings at the outset. That would indeed have spared the innocent defendant much anguish, but it would have deprived the reader of his pleasure. Court-room scenes were a standard feature of ancient romance precisely because of their dramatic potentialities, and the essence of drama is suspense.

It is against this on the whole recognizable background that the inserted stories in books 8–10 are projected. They present a grim composite picture of a world motivated by deceit, spite, greed, and lust. Increasingly it is the themes of adultery and murder, often by poisoning, that come to predominate. The colouring of the picture is self-consciously literary: so the story of the incestuous stepmother is acknowledged as lifted from Greek tragedy and embellished with allusions to the Latin poets (10.2 and note). Nevertheless it will not do to write them off as too literary and too highly coloured to be credible. A glance at a typical morning's newspaper headlines suffices to make the point: infidelity and murder, often in bizarre circumstances, are as much part of the fabric of everyday life as they were eighteen centuries ago. The mother whom Juvenal, ironically expecting to be disbelieved, arraigns for poisoning her own children (*Satires*, 6. 629–46) actually existed, and there were others like her. When he proclaims that

> Posterity can add
> No more, or worse, to our ways; our grandchildren will act
> As we do, and share our desires. Truly every vice
> Has reached its ruinous zenith,[21]

he no doubt exaggerates the peculiar wickedness of his own age, but what he says would have corresponded, as such portrayals still do, with contemporary perceptions. The scene of moral chaos of which Lucius,

INTRODUCTION

willy-nilly, is a fascinated and revolted spectator and in which he is forced in the end to participate, formed part of the mental furniture of the age. It is to escape from this nightmare world that, quite unexpectedly, he throws himself on the protection of the saviour goddess Isis.

7

In the *Onos* Lucius manages at the eleventh hour, when he is actually in the theatre and about to perform his act, to snatch a bite at some roses and regain his human shape. This he accomplishes without divine assistance, but the intervention of the governor is needed to save him from possible untoward consequences (54).[22] In *The Golden Ass* the role of the governor is taken by Isis, the implication being that only under her special protection can the reverse metamorphosis be safely achieved. But why Isis? In the popular consciousness as interpreted by the Greek writer Artemidorus (*fl. c.* AD 175) in his handbook on the interpretation of dreams, Isis and other Egyptian gods stood for salvation of those in extreme peril (*Onirocritica*, 2. 39). That of course cuts two ways: in invoking her protection Lucius might appear to some to be a credulous victim of superstition. Credulity has all along been one of his leading characteristics and has contributed heavily to his downfall. Will he fare any better as a devotee of Isis than he did as a devotee of witchcraft?

The beauty and the fervour of the language in which his experiences and sentiments are described may seem to rule out irony, or they could conceivably be taken to underline it. Striking correspondences with historically attested cases, particularly that of St Augustine, can be cited in support of the thesis that this is the authentic narrative of an actual conversion – that this is autobiography. For the effect that the sight of the full moon has on Lucius, Nancy Shumate has compared what was felt by the former Black Panther Eldridge Cleaver, also on a Mediterranean seashore.[23] This is not an isolated instance. At the age of fourteen Gerald Brenan underwent a similar experience, though it ended less dramatically than Cleaver's, which culminated in a vision of Christ. This was at Dinard on the coast of Brittany:

Going into my bedroom one night after dinner I discovered the full moon pouring in through the double windows and filling the little box-like space with its light. It seemed to be distending and pushing apart the walls with its brightness, to be filling the room, the bed, the cupboard to bursting. I stood gazing at it for a moment. Then, stepping out onto the balcony, I looked down on the long glittering path it had laid on the water and heard the waves splashing softly far below. All at once a feeling I find it difficult to describe came over me – a sense of some enormous force and beauty existing around me: a presence, a state that promised unspeakable delight and happiness if only I could join myself to it. But I could not so join myself. I was my ordinary self, carried suddenly into an over-charged, over-resplendent world. For a time I stood there, overcome by the sheer transcendency of the spectacle, then gradually the impression faded and I went away.[24]

Brenan's vision in fact has more in common with Lucius' than does that of Cleaver; particularly interesting is the suddenness of his 'sense of some enormous force and beauty existing around me', which closely parallels Lucius' instant conviction that what he sees is a manifestation of the goddess whose power controls the workings of the whole universe (11.1). Even more interesting, perhaps, is the contrast between Lucius' voluntary submission to the dominion of the goddess and Brenan's stalwart refusal to abdicate his selfhood.

No less apparently authentic is the lyrical description of the spring morning to which Lucius awakes after his vision (11.7). This sense of rebirth, of the newness of everything, can also be paralleled in conversion narratives, but is not exclusive to them. It can be brought about by a sudden reprieve – from sentence of death by execution or cancer, for instance – or by anything which takes one right out of oneself, such as being in love:

It was not the first time they had seen trees, blue sky, green grass, not the first time they had heard running water and the wind blowing through the leaves; but certainly they had never yet admired it all as though nature had only just come into existence, or only begun to be beautiful since the gratification of their desires.[25]

It can be convincingly expressed by any writer with experience of life who has the gift of identifying with the emotions of his characters. This was what Dickens, who was an accomplished actor and less like a miser than any man who ever lived, did with Scrooge:

Running to the window, he opened it, and put out his head. No fog, no mist; clear, bright, jovial, stirring, cold; cold, piping for the blood to dance to; Golden sunlight; Heavenly sky; sweet fresh air; merry bells. Oh, glorious! Glorious![26]

No writer has ever more faithfully obeyed Horace's precept:

> Before you can move me to tears,
> you must grieve yourself.[27]

His is an extreme, but not an uncommon instance. The reader who has been moved by the poignancy of Wordsworth's 'Solitary Reaper' may be disconcerted to discover that the poet's source for the plaintive song of the Highland lass was not his own experience but a book.[28] That does not rob the poem of its value, but it is a salutary warning against drawing biographical inferences from imaginative literature.

Most of the Latin books that have come down to us were written by men who had been through the mill of an educational system which was grounded in the study and practice of classical rhetoric. This was essentially the art of persuasion, its aim plausibility. For a writer trained from childhood in its techniques it was not necessary actually to have been vouchsafed a vision of Isis or undergone initiation into her cult to be able to describe such things vividly and convincingly.[29] Since we chance to know that Lucius in *The Golden Ass* is not an original literary creation but a character taken over from the *Onos*, and that his adventures up to the moment of his purported conversion largely reproduce those of the Greek model, we might well suspect that the sequel too has been borrowed – perhaps with ulterior motives – from some lost narrative of a purported mystic experience. It therefore comes as something of a shock when at the very end of the novel it is authenticated by the sudden re-emergence of the author who had made so fleeting an appearance in the Prologue and then faded inconspicuously into the fictional narrator. Indeed he not only resurfaces but as good as names himself.

8

That the author of *The Golden Ass* was one Apuleius of the North African city of Madaura we know both from the manuscripts of his book and from the testimony of, among others, St Augustine. It is indeed Augustine who is our authority for the title under which it is best known, *The Golden Ass*, which he expressly states (*City of God*, 18. 18) was that given it by Apuleius himself. In the manuscripts it is called *Metamorphoses*, 'Transformations', on the face of it a more obviously appropriate title. The Prologue's announcement of it as a tale of changes of shape and vicissitudes of fortune points up its affinity to Ovid's great poem of the same name, which also depicts a world in which 'no event or character . . . can be trusted to remain what it may first seem to be'.[30] Apuleius clearly knew his Ovid, as can be seen, to take one particularly striking example, in his portrayal of Psyche's agonized indecision over whether to kill her husband (5.21 and note). It has never on the other hand been convincingly explained in what sense Lucius-as-ass is 'golden'; the Latin word should connote worth or splendour,[31] not qualities which can plausibly be attributed to him. To Isis the ass, identified in her cult with the malign Seth-Typhon, her enemy and the murderer of her husband Osiris, was a hateful beast (11.6); and Lucius' behaviour in that guise does nothing to redeem its reputation or his own character. The mischievous suggestion of Paula James that Apuleius' (if it was his) alternative title for his book was not *Asinus Aureus* but *Asinus Auritus*, 'the ass with ears', the listening or attentive ass,[32] is perilously attractive. That would be in the best vein of Apuleian irony, the ambiguity of *auritus* underlining the contrast between the efficiency of Lucius' ears as receptors (9.15) and his consistent inability to profit from what they tell him (1.1 and note).

To return to the author himself. After his brief and shadowy appearance in the Prologue, he becomes more or less invisible, apart from the joking apology for the language of Apollo's oracle (above, §4) and occasional arch reminders of the literary quality of what the reader is enjoying (2.12, 6.25, 6.29, 8.1 and notes), until the dream of the significantly named Asinius. To him it is revealed by Osiris himself that the candidate for the last and most important of his series of initiations is 'a man from Madaura' (11.27). This offhand identification of Lucius with his creator has rattled scholars; some have even emended Apuleius' text to eliminate it. Are we in fact obliged to take it seriously? Writers sometimes do this sort of thing just for fun. Evelyn Waugh's novel *The Ordeal of Gilbert Pinfold* ends with 'Pinfold' sitting down to record his adventures, and beginning by transcribing the title page and the first chapter-heading of the book that the reader has just come to the end of, minus in this case the name of the real author. This is a technically elegant device, a witty acknowledgement of what Waugh's friends at least were well aware of, that the book was based on his own experiences. In the case of *The Golden Ass* it is arguable that the author's sudden appearance represents a variation on the common literary device of the so-called *sphragis* or seal, an allusive registration of authorship incorporated in the text of the book itself.[33] In other words, is this perhaps simply an arch way of saying 'Apuleius wrote this book'? If so, he chose a way of doing so that was calculated, not merely to flutter the critical dovecotes centuries later, but to give his contemporary readers something to wonder about.

In identifying himself in this way Apuleius, as would not have been the case had he simply named himself, was deliberately drawing attention to his public persona. He was a notable figure in his province, the recipient of numerous civic honours and holder of an important priest-hood. His reputation rested on two pillars, his oratorical powers and his status as a Platonic philosopher. St Augustine calls him 'the famous Platonist'.[34] His native place was clearly proud of her distinguished son; there has survived the base of a statue put up there at public expense 'To the Platonic philosopher', which can hardly commemorate anybody but Apuleius.[35] Lucius is not a Platonic philosopher, but he boasts (1.2 and note) of his descent from Plutarch, who was a declared Platonist and who had written a work *On Isis and Osiris*, in which he set out to make philosophical sense of the gruesome Egyptian myth of the murder and dismemberment of Osiris by Typhon.[36] He had also written a treatise *On curiosity*,[37] very much to Lucius' address. Obviously the author of *The Golden Ass* cannot be identified *tout court* with its narrator,[38] but equally the ass and the Platonic philosopher cannot be considered to have nothing to do with each other. A strong argument to the contrary is the presence in the book of the story of Cupid and Psyche, its structural and thematic centrepiece.

9

Though often, for understandable reasons, detached and edited or translated separately, *Cupid and Psyche* is an organic and integral part of *The Golden Ass*. Structurally it is firmly anchored in the 'Charite-complex' (above, §5), the story being continued across the divisions between books 4–5 and 5–6, another technique characteristic of Ovid in the *Metamorphoses*.[39] Thematically the story of a, or rather the, human soul in quest of salvation through union with the divine is a parable for what is happening to Lucius even as he listens to it, though as with everything else he sees, hears, and suffers, it all goes in at one of his ass's ears and out at the other. It calls attention to itself as a unique feat of literary combination: a fairytale plot of a traditional type transformed into a universal allegory by the symbolic status of its protagonists, Love and the Soul, and presented in terms of a Platonizing duality.[40]

It is this last element that is important in the present context. In his contribution to the discussion in Plato's *Symposium* Pausanias had distinguished between two Aphrodites, Urania or Heavenly, and Pandemos or Vulgar, and two Eroses to correspond, their respective provinces being the love of souls and bodies (180d2–181b8). Apuleius was familiar with the passage, which he paraphrases in his *Apology* (ch. 12); and in *Cupid and Psyche* he displays Venus and Cupid in these dual Platonic guises contending for the human soul. The actual battle is carried on between Venus in her lower (II, Vulgaris = Aphrodite Pandemos) and Cupid in his higher guise (Amor I, Caelestis = Eros Uranios),[41] just as Venus in both guises, personified by Photis and Isis, contends for mastery over Lucius. The role of *Cupid and Psyche* in the economy of the novel as a philosophical commentary on the main narrative is central to an understanding of the book as a whole.

Contemporary awareness of Plato largely centred on the more popular and accessible dialogues. These included, in addition to the

Symposium, the *Phaedrus* and the *Phaedo*. Psyche's pursuit of Cupid and her fall to earth (5.24) recall the *Phaedrus*: 'When the soul is unable to follow God and fails to see, and through some misfortune grows heavy, being filled with forgetfulness and wickedness, it loses its wings[42] and falls to earth' (248c). In the *Phaedo* what is said about the need for the soul to purge itself of the defilements of bodily pleasure if it is to attain to eternal life with the gods (81a–c) is clearly relevant to both Psyche and Lucius; and the transformation which in the *Onos* appears to have no special significance takes on a new, metaphorical, dimension in *The Golden Ass* in the light of Socrates' suggestion that 'those who have thoughtlessly given themselves over to gluttony and violence and drunkenness are likely to be clothed in the shapes of asses and similar beasts' (81e).

We may also detect Plutarch behind the part played in the stories of both Psyche and Lucius by what the priest of Isis calls 'ill-starred curiosity', *curiositas improspera* (11.15). In his treatise on curiosity or importunate meddling Plutarch appeals to a standard philosophical distinction between proper objects of investigation, such as natural science, and things that are attractive merely because they are hidden (*De curiositate*, 5). Apuleius himself draws a similar distinction when rebutting accusations of sorcery in his *Apology* (29–41), and it is implicit in the contrast between the pursuits for which Lucius' family connections and educational advantages should have equipped him (1.2, 1.4 and notes) and his prurient obsession with the unclean secrets of witchcraft. Philosophy, as Plutarch had emphasized (*On Isis and Osiris*, 68), was the only true guide to the mysteries. These higher and lower forms of curiosity can also be seen as corresponding to the higher and lower forms of love that war for the souls of Psyche and Lucius.

IO

In the light of these various hints the attentive reader postulated in the Prologue can hardly fail to sense the lurking presence of the Platonic philosopher in *The Golden Ass*, and to suspect that Apuleius has taken a leaf out of the book of another Latin poet whom he evidently knew and admired, Lucretius. He, in a famous passage of the *De rerum natura*, twice repeated, had compared the poetry in which he had clothed the teachings of Epicurus to the honey smeared by the doctor on a cup of bitter medicine to induce children to drink it, an image which Apuleius could also have come across in Plato's *Laws* (*De rerum natura*, 1. 936–47, 4. 11–22; *Laws*, 659e). Thus the pleasure promised in the Prologue is a means to an end, the honey on the astringent cup of edification.

Apuleius' strategy, however, is more subtle than this suggests. The pleasure experienced by the irreflective reader of these amusing [43] stories is not, as in the case of Lucretius, morally neutral. It is implicitly on a par with that experienced by their narrator and with his slavish enjoyment of Photis. Plutarch taxes those of a prying disposition with shunning scientific research because 'there is nothing in it' and preferring 'histories' of which the staple is misfortune; and the catalogue of such 'histories' that follows is almost identical with the subjects of the inserted stories in *The Golden Ass* (*De curiositate*, 5). Our ideally alert and perceptive reader cannot, like Lucius, be a mere spectator of these events, but is, so to say, on his literary honour to participate in the book's dialectic and to make judgements of a moral order on what he reads. Whereas Lucius remains impervious throughout to the implications for himself of what is happening to him, even at one point going out of his way to remark that his experiences have left him no wiser (9.13 and note), and cannot be said to have earned his salvation by repentance, greater self-awareness, or (*pace* Nancy Shumate) intellectual enlightenment, the reader has no excuse, with the example of Lucius before him, for not perceiving that there is in all this some sort of moral, a lesson to be learned.

Nancy Shumate has argued eloquently that Lucius' 'conversion' is intellectually rather than morally motivated. It is difficult to extract this from the text. It is emotion – a combination of fear and disgust – rather than reason[44] that precipitates his flight from the world of confusion and disintegration into which his metamorphosis had plunged him to the vision of cosmic order embodied in the omnipotent and all-embracing godhead of Isis. The realization that she and she alone rules the destinies of mankind (11.1) is not arrived at by any process of ratiocination and has not been prepared for: it simply happens. The relationship of Fortune, Providence and Isis-as-Fortune/Providence remains as nebulous after the revelations of the priest as it was before (11.15 and note). For Lucius it is enough that he has found security. Nothing in the subsequent account of his devotions and initiations indicates the existence of an intellectual component in his religious experiences. The 'harbour of Tranquillity' into which he has been received (11.15) is a final resting-place, not a point of embarkation for a voyage of philosophical discovery. Moreover it must again be emphasized that Lucius has done nothing to earn his salvation, as the ignorant comments of the crowd ironically remind us (11.16 and note). A Platonic philosopher would surely have held that enlightenment had to be actively sought and worked for.

If *The Golden Ass* was seriously intended to edify, the conclusion to which the narrative of Lucius' experiences as a soul in quest of salvation ultimately comes is an unexpected one. That this indeed is what the book must be about is demonstrated by the presence in it of the story of Cupid and Psyche; its allegorical implications and its bearing on the story of Lucius himself clinch the matter. But did Apuleius, the famous 'Platonic philosopher', really mean to offer devotion to the cult of Isis and Osiris as the way to the highest good for a man? What would his contemporary admirers have made of that idea? Centuries later we find Macrobius expressing surprise that he had indulged himself in the composition of 'fictitious love-stories' (*Commentary on the Dream of Scipio*, 1. 2. 8). That, one would think, was nothing to the surprise that would have been felt by Apuleius' fellow citizens at the gloss that they were evidently expected to put on those stories. Were they, however, his intended audience?

The composition and publication of *The Golden Ass* is generally dated to the later period of his life, when he had returned from Rome and settled in Africa.[45] It is tempting to wonder whether he wrote it as a young man during his residence in Rome. Appeals to its style cut both ways: exuberance is no more a reliable sign of youth (Nabokov) than technical assurance is of maturity (Lucan, Macaulay). More cogent is the argument that this may seem more like the sort of book that would appeal to a metropolitan readership rather than to staider provincial tastes. The intrusive allusions, rather in the manner of Plautus, to matters specifically Roman and to legal quibbles (2.16, 4.18, 5.26, 5.29, 6.8,

6.22, 6.29, 9.10, 9.27, 10.29 and notes) may be thought to point in the same direction. One objection to this earlier dating is the presence in *The Golden Ass* of apparent references to the *Apology*.[46] About the circumstances in which this speech was delivered we are better informed. On his way home from Rome Apuleius was detained by illness at a place called Oea in Tripoli, where he married a wealthy widow, Pudentilla. This was at the instance of one of her sons, whom he had met in Rome, but other members of her family, who had an interest in the disposition of her fortune, prosecuted Apuleius on various charges, principally one of gaining Pudentilla's affections by magic. The *Apology*, a brilliantly witty and apparently effective rebuttal of these accusations, was delivered in about AD 160. That does not rule out the possibility that *The Golden Ass* was originally written at Rome to be read to selected audiences there, and that the passages containing the apparent allusions to the *Apology* were touched in later. There is, after all, nothing to show that the book was given to the world in Apuleius' lifetime. He might well not have wished his public image to be compromised by a youthful *jeu d'esprit* in which Platonism is harnessed to Oriental superstition.

That argument is weakened if in fact the tendency of the book is in the end to undermine rather than to proselytize. Lucius' uncritical raptures at his first initiation and his emotional parting from the Cenchrean Isis and her priest (11.24–5) are succeeded by surprise and a certain impatience on his part when he discovers that he is not as yet safely berthed in the harbour of Tranquillity. More initiations, and more expense, are needed before he can count himself really of the elect. It is natural to wonder if he is being taken for a ride, as at one point he himself suspects (11.29). It has been suggested that the original Greek *Metamorphoses* was a satire on credulity and superstition.[47] Is there an echo of this in Apuleius' adaptation? There is more than a hint of naivety in the satisfaction which Lucius takes in the resplendent get-up and the statuesque pose in which he is displayed to the congregation (11.24). However, it could be maintained that these ironies, if they were so intended, would have come across more sharply in Rome than in Madaura. In the eyes of educated Romans what sort of figure would a shaven-headed Isiac hierophant have cut in the Forum? Would Lucius' gleaming pate (11.10) have, as Winkler suggests, identified him in that setting as a buffoon? [48] Temples of Isis were scattered all over the Greek and Roman world, but that in Rome was particularly frequented by women and had a louche reputation (11.26 and note). Did Apuleius really mean his readers to feel that Lucius' final state is a truly enviable one? Or is he, when we take our leave of him, living in a fool's paradise? Is he as much of an ass as ever? And if so, how far down the garden path have we allowed ourselves to be led along with him by Apuleius' storytelling genius?

I I

The Golden Ass is a fictional romance. Papyrus discoveries have greatly enlarged our notions of the range and variety in subject-matter, treatment, and style of ancient Greek fiction. [49] Apuleius' book, viewed against this background, is not *sui generis*; it shares more of the characteristics of the genre – if this is not too precise a term for this diverse and fluid category of writing – than has been generally supposed. All narratives of separation, travel, and reunion of lovers look back to the *Odyssey*, as Lucius' ruminations in the mill acknowledge (9.13 and note), and as is even more explicitly and repeatedly signalled in Petronius' *Satyricon*. [50] Digressions and inserted narratives were a standard feature of epic as of prose romance. Pirates and bandits figure prominently in the novels; what is unusual about Apuleius' treatment of this theme is the comic disparity between the grim stronghold and warlike pretensions of his robber band and their often farcical incompetence in action. Is this a mild literary send-up? [51] Egypt had always fascinated the Greeks: the scene of Xenophon's *Ephesiaca*, Achilles Tatius' *Leucippe and Clitophon*, and Heliodorus' *Ethiopica* is set partially in Egypt, and a war between Persia and Egypt figures in Chariton's *Chaereas and Callirhoe*. The Egyptian element in *The Golden Ass* reflects this fascination and may have been incorporated by Apuleius for literary rather than autobiographical reasons. It may be that scholars have been too ready to take his evidence as to the details of Isiac cult at its face value and make insufficient allowance for his exuberant fancy (11.10, 16, 17, 30 and notes).

A pervasive theme in the Greek romances is the influence of Fortune. Fortune (Tyche) was widely worshipped in Greece, and her prominence in shaping the lives of the characters in the novels is often taken to reflect a general sense of insecurity in the life of ordinary people. In *The Golden Ass* this role is greatly enhanced. Fortune, not always distinguished from Providence, controls every turn of events.[52] She is not merely capricious, but actively malevolent, persecuting Lucius as Poseidon and Juno had persecuted the heroes of the *Odyssey* and *Aeneid*, and as Priapus had persecuted Encolpius in the *Satyricon*. Eventually her function in the scheme of things as anti-Isis, blind as opposed to (fore)seeing Fortune, is revealed in the priest's homily. Though the theological implications of this dichotomous or Manichaean conception of Fortune are never made clear (11.15 and note), here again Apuleius can be seen taking a theme from the common stock of romantic fiction and manipulating and exploiting it with some freedom for his own purposes. That what emerges from the process is not entirely clear or consistent – what for instance is the relationship of the Providence that watches over Psyche to that which rescues Lucius? – is something that by now we have perhaps come to expect.

If in the final analysis the reader is left wondering what *The Golden Ass* is really about, what exactly Apuleius is getting at, that may be just what its author intended. What he promises in the Prologue is enjoyment and wonder. The Latin word for 'wonder', *miror*, can connote bewilderment as well as admiration.[53] Like all great works of art, *The Golden Ass* stoutly resists simplification. In this it resembles that other great Latin narrative of changed fortunes, travel, heroic endurance, separation, union, and homecoming, Virgil's *Aeneid*. When we part company with Lucius he is enjoying himself, as we have been. Much of the pleasure of reading and rereading this great book is that of being kept guessing.

12

In another particular Apuleius turns out to have dealt faithfully with his readers. The promise of a literary *tour de force* conveyed in the image of the circus-rider, leaping from horse to horse in mid-gallop, is amply redeemed. *The Golden Ass* is a dazzling combination of parable, allegory, satire, robust humour, sex, violence, Grand Guignol, confession and buffoonery, a unique feat of creative fantasy. Its rich literary texture is matched by a linguistic exuberance and stylistic versatility that confronts the translator with a succession of thorny, sometimes insuperable, problems. How Apuleius himself handled the task of translation can be seen from comparison with the *Onos*.[54] He rarely renders the original word for word for long at a stretch, but subjects it to a process for which it is difficult to find a better term than souping up. Most of his innovations are by way of verbal amplification and the addition of picturesque detail, but the characterization is also enriched, and sometimes, as with Milo and Photis, radically revised. The general effect is to impart life and colour to a comparatively jejune original. This is typical of Roman treatment of Greek literary models, reminiscent for instance of what the comic dramatists, Plautus especially, did with their exemplars: what was called *uertere*, 'turning', something not adequately described by the word 'translation'.

Liberties of this sort are not for the translator nowadays, but it is interesting to note that one writer in modern times produced a 'version' of *The Golden Ass* which took more than Apuleian freedoms with the book. In 1708 one Charles Gildon, a well-known Grub Street figure of the time, published anonymously what he called *The New Metamorphosis; or, The Pleasant Transformation: being The Golden Ass of Lucius Apuleius of Medaura. Alter'd and Improv'd to the Modern Times and Manners* [55] – as indeed it had been with a vengeance. This purported to be a translation from the Italian of 'Carlo Monte Socio, Fellow of the Academy of the Humanities in Rome'; his account of the scandalous goings-on attributed to 'Nuns, Fryars, Jesuits', who are substituted for the dissolute priests of Atargatis, is no doubt not unconnected with the fact that Gildon himself had been educated for the Roman Catholic priesthood but had subsequently lapsed into deism. He made one ingenious and effective concession to plausibility by having the hero transformed into a lapdog rather than a donkey, and so freely admitted to the drawing-rooms and bedchambers of the society ladies whose licentious behaviour he so feelingly depicts.

Though more than once reprinted, Gildon's book has been little noticed. The version most familiar to educated Englishmen, which held the field until comparatively recently, is that of William Adlington, first published in 1566. Though the language inevitably sounds unfamiliar to those not brought up on the King James version of the Bible, it can still be read with pleasure; and in one respect both Adlington's and Gildon's versions have a useful lesson to teach. Any attempt to reproduce Apuleius' peculiar Latinity, its idiosyncratic mixture of colloquial, poetic, and archaizing vocabulary, which includes many words coined by Apuleius himself, its often wilfully contorted phraseology, and its elaborately balanced rhythmical structures – let alone to render it literally – would involve something like the creation of a new dialect of English. One feature of his writing, however, can be reproduced in modern English, and that is its fluency; and this is something that both Adlington and Gildon achieve and that has eluded some of their successors. Classical Latin writers – Cicero, Livy, even in his own way Tacitus – cultivated the periodic style, in which the utterance is built up from interdependent and interlocking clauses into a syntactical structure designed to postpone the full comprehension of the sense until the reader has reached the end of the sentence: a circular rather than a linear arrangement. Apuleius' sentence-structure is serial: the clauses do not as a rule interlock but succeed each other, and this, added to his habit of repeating and varying his expression for effect or emphasis, creates a flow and momentum in his prose analogous to the flow achieved by Ovid in the more strictly ordered medium of the epic hexameter. A student coming to him fresh from Cicero or Livy may well find his style disconcerting at first; but if one discounts its more rococo embellishments his is an easier and racier Latinity, with its roots reaching further back, a truly native style. The periodic sentence was a Greek importation and had to be painfully learned; some respectable writers, such as the Elder Pliny, never really got the hang of it. With Apuleius the reader is in contact with a late flowering of a tradition of free-flowing discourse that goes back to the very beginnings of Latin culture.

The present version, therefore, aims above all at doing justice to the movement of Apuleius' Latin in idiomatic contemporary English. It takes as its motto the words of Michael Grant: 'Simplicity . . . is the only hope . . . English *must* be readable, and readable *today*.'[56] This is in the tradition of Adlington, whose English is characterized in the anonymous Preface of the Abbey Classics edition of 1922 as 'simple, direct and fresh'. Occasionally, where Apuleius becomes, even for him, obtrusively mannered, some compromise with this principle must be allowed. If then here and there the English expression seems not altogether natural, it is likely to be because the expression of the Latin is so Apuleian that it would denature it altogether to reduce it to a blandly current idiom.

13

The widespread literary fame which Lucius promises himself, or rather his creator (2.12, 4.32, 6.25, 6.29 and notes), was in fact slow to materialize. Between the sixth and the thirteenth centuries *The Golden Ass* was largely lost to view, and it was as a magician that its author was celebrated. Augustine, in his discussion of the place of demons in the scheme of things (*City of God*, 8. 12–22), repeatedly cites Apuleius as prime witness of the Platonic position, and his uncertainty as to whether he had actually undergone metamorphosis (above, n. 38) evidently betokens acceptance of the fact that such things were possible. That would also have been true of many if not most of Apuleius' contemporaries. The picture that emerges from the *Apology* is that of a society where religion and magic perforce co-existed, however uneasily, and where people believed in and regulated their lives by both.[57] The very fact of the prosecution's being brought at all and the elaborate character of Apuleius' defence shows that these matters were taken seriously. Nor was this true only of Oea.[58] There was thus little or nothing in Lucius' narrative, with the possible exception of the dragon (8.21 and note), that even an educated reader would have necessarily found incredible.

It was at the Renaissance that Apuleius came into his own as a storyteller, when he was rediscovered by Boccaccio. Artistic exploitation of *The Golden Ass* speedily took off in a number of directions.[59] Its rich store of inserted tales was plundered by, among others, Boccaccio himself in the *Decameron*, Cervantes in *Don Quixote*, and Le Sage in *Gil Blas*. The ass-story lent itself readily to allegorical and satirical development. It is, however, unsurprisingly, through the tale of Cupid and Psyche that Apuleius' book has exerted its greatest influence. The story has been a perennial source of inspiration to poets, dramatists, composers for opera and ballet, and artists. That Shakespeare had read it in Adlington's translation appears from several plays, most notably *A Midsummer Night's Dream* and *Othello*.[60] Keats, Morris, and Bridges all fell under the spell. Perhaps, however, the peculiar charm of Apuleius' storytelling genius has been most tellingly communicated to English readers in the languorous prose of Walter Pater's recreation of the tale in *Marius the Epicurean*. These are only some, and by no means the last, of the multifarious transformations undergone by *The Golden Ass* during the six and a half centuries since it emerged from the long obscurity of the Dark and Middle Ages. It is this endless capacity for metamorphosis that truly identifies Apuleius as a magician.[61]

NOTES

1. H. E. Butler and A. S. Owen (eds.), *Apulei Apologia sive Pro se de magia* (Oxford, 1914), p. x, n. 4; Winkler, *Auctor & Actor*, p. 227; Grant, revision of Graves, p. xiv.
2. In the author's manuscript there would have been nothing by way of titling or numbering or paragraphing to set it off from what follows.
3. *OLD* s.vv. *intendo* 11, *intentus* 1a, 2a.
4. *lepido susurro*; on the recurrence of the word *lepidus* in the novel see 1.1 and note.
5. *OLD* s.v. *excolo* 2b, 3; the prefix *ex-* is intensive.
6. *Graecanicam*, not *Graecam*. Some detect a nuance, 'Greekish' or 'Greeklike'. It is hard to see the point, and more likely that this is one of many examples of the author's preference for the recherché to the familiar.
7. Here an interesting analogy suggests itself with Ovid in exile. Repeatedly in the *Tristia* he compares his tribulations to those of the epic heroes Ulysses and Aeneas, which as a poet he had shaped and manipulated. The resemblance may be fortuitous, but Ovid's influence is strongly felt in *The Golden Ass*: see Krabbe, *The Metamorphoses of Apuleius*, pp. 37–81, and below, nn. 9, 16, 17.

8. At 1.24. Similarly Psyche is not named until her story is well under way (4.30).

9. The manner in which the story straddles the divisions between books 4–5 and 5–6 and in which the divisions are used to mark important stages in the action and focus attention on the situation of the heroine is strongly reminiscent of Ovid's technique in the *Metamorphoses*. See above, n. 7.

10. He is *certus*, assured, confident, having certain knowledge: *OLD* s.v. 11, 12a.

11. They had been reinforced, or so it has been held, in a specifically Isiac way by the part played in Thelyphron's story by the Egyptian priest Zatchlas. If that was the author's intention, the message has been compromised by the association with necromancy (2.28 and note).

12. So the priest of Isis: 'Let the infidels behold, let them behold and know their error' (11.15).

13. Introduction to the Everyman edition (1910) of Henry Fielding, *Joseph Andrews*.

14. All of them more or less obscure. It is perhaps worth remarking that if *Met.* was by Lucian, it might have seemed a bold undertaking to translate and liberally embellish – some might say travesty – the work of a writer of his stature.

15. Some examples are given in the Notes, but it would be tedious and unprofitable to attempt to compile a complete catalogue. Some can be more or less plausibly explained away, but most must be ascribed to simple carelessness. The average reader is unlikely to be much worried by them, and they nowhere seriously impair the impact of the story. For examples of inconsistencies, loose ends and some sheer absurdities in nineteenth-century English fiction see J. Sutherland, *Is Heathcliff a Murderer?* (Oxford, 1996) and id., *Can Jane Eyre be Happy?* (Oxford, 1997).

16. J. B. Priestley, *Margin Released. A writer's reminiscences and reflections* (1963), p. 174. The same could be said, *mutatis mutandis*, of Ovid's *Metamorphoses*; see above, n. 7.

17. See Schlam, *The Metamorphoses of Apuleius*, pp. 34–6. Here too *The Golden Ass* recalls Ovid: the manner in which the stories at 9.14–31 are inset (see Appendix) recalls Ovid's 'Chinese-box' technique in, for instance, the Arethusa episode (*Metamorphoses*, 5. 337–678). See above, n. 7.

18. Ovid, *Amores*, 3. 12. 41–2, trans. Peter Green.

19. W. Nippel, *Public Order in Ancient Rome* (Cambridge, 1995), pp. 100–112.

20. As from his name it is to be inferred that Lucius is. The author of the *Onos* is more categorical: there both Lucius and his brother Gaius have the three names that identify them as Romanized Greeks (ch. 55).

21. *Satires*, 1. 147–9, trans. Peter Green.

22. That is, of being taken for a sorcerer. In one of the Apuleian additions to his original Lucius foresees and avoids this danger (3.29), from which he is finally secured by Isis (11.6 and note).

23. Shumate, *Crisis and Conversion*, p. 311, n. 19.

24. Gerald Brenan, *A Life of One's Own. Childhood and Youth* (Cambridge, 1979), pp. 77–8. Coleridge had a similar experience (R. Holmes, *Coleridge. Darker Reflections* (1998), p. 38).

25. Gustave Flaubert, *Madame Bovary*, Part 3, ch. 3, trans. Geoffrey Wall.

26. *A Christmas Carol*, Stave V.

27. *Art of Poetry*, 102–3, trans. Niall Rudd.

28. J. Beer, *Wordsworth and the Human Heart* (1978), pp. 134–5.

29. Shumate, *Crisis and Conversion*, pp. 327–8.

30. Tatum, *Apuleius and 'The Golden Ass'*, p. 21.

31. *OLD* s.v. *aureus* 5.

32. *OLD* s.v. *auritus* 1. See Paula James, 'Fool's gold . . . renaming the ass', *Groningen Colloquia on the Novel* 4 (Groningen, 1991), pp. 155–72. In the capital script in which the book would have been first written the two words could be easily confused.

33. So, at the end of the first book of his elegies, Propertius tells his readers where he comes from without actually naming himself (1. 22). Virgil's identification of himself at the end of the *Georgics* is more explicit (4. 559–66).

34. *Platonicus nobilis* (*City of God*, 8. 12).

35. Tatum, *Apuleius and 'The Golden Ass'*, pp. 105–8. For his philosophical writings see Walsh (1994), pp. xv–xvii.

36. D. A. Russell, *Plutarch* (1972), pp. 75–6, 82.

37. So usually described after the Latin title *De curiositate*, but 'meddlesomeness' is perhaps a more accurate rendering of the Greek *polypragmosyne*.

38. A question on which Augustine was evidently in two minds: did Apuleius record his experiences or make them up (*City of God*, 18. 18)?

39. See above, n. 9.

40. For a full analysis see Kenney, *Cupid and Psyche*, pp. 12–22.

41. For one of the odder metamorphoses in the book, Cupid's unexpected reversion at the end of the story to Amor II, see 6.22 and note. For a full analysis of the plot on these lines see Kenney, 'Psyche and her mysterious husband', in D. A. Russell (ed.), *Antonine Literature* (Oxford, 1990), pp. 175–98.

42. Here Apuleius can be seen adroitly fudging things. In art Psyche is winged; the butterfly, called in Greek *psyche*, is a common symbol for the soul. In Apuleius' fairytale she is a human princess; the momentarily Platonic Psyche-as-soul in a manner, by clinging on to Cupid, acquires wings which she loses by letting go of him.

43. On the recurrence of this term to describe the inserted tales see 1.1 and note.

44. The thoughts that pass through his mind at that moment (10.34) hardly amount to the revaluation of his activities detected by Shumate (*Crisis and Conversion*, p. 38).

45. There is little firm evidence: see Walsh, *The Roman Novel*, pp. 248–51.

46. See, for instance, 6.9 and note.

47. Perry, *The Ancient Romances*, pp. 211–35.

48. Winkler, *Auctor & Actor*, pp. 225–6.

49. Stephens and Winkler, *Ancient Greek Novels*, pp. 3–19.

50. Walsh, *The Roman Novel*, pp. 36–43.

51. The account of the robbers' carouse (4.8, 22) offers striking similarities with a fragment of Lollianus' *Phoenicica*. Unfortunately it cannot be shown who is borrowing from whom (Stephens and Winkler, *Ancient Greek Novels*, pp. 322–5).

52. As in Fielding's *Tom Jones*, where Fortune intervenes some twenty-odd times. Is there any other English novel where her role is so prominent?

53. *OLD* s.v. 1, 2.

54. About the relationship of the *Onos* as we have it to *Met.* scholars differ. It is here assumed that its author abridged rather than rewrote his original.

55. Two volumes, London, 1708, printed for S. Brisco and sold by J. Morphew. Reprinted, two volumes, London, 1821, for E. Wheatley. Other editions, in 1709 and 1724, are recorded by the *New Cambridge Bibliography of English Literature* (Cambridge, 1971), II, 1049.

56. Grant, revision of Graves, p. xvii.

57. J. H. W. G. Liebeschütz, *Continuity and Change in Roman Religion* (Oxford, 1979), pp. 217–20.

58. *OCD* s.v. magic; Liebeschütz, op. cit., pp. 126–39; A. A. Barb, 'The survival of magic arts', in A. Momigliano (ed.), *The Conflict between Paganism and Christianity in the Fourth Century* (Oxford, 1963), pp. 100–125.

59. See Elizabeth H. Haight, *Apuleius and His Influence* (New York, 1927), pp. 111–81.

60. Walsh (1994), pp. xlvi–xlvii.

61. Apuleius lived during the heyday of the period commonly called the Second Sophistic (see *OCD*, s.v.) when declamatory rhetoric exerted a dominating influence over education, literary culture and public life. Chairs of rhetoric were established by the emperors in major centres, and rhetorical skill was frequently an avenue to high civic or provincial office. Travelling lecturers, the so-called Sophists, could attract huge audiences to hear elaborate harangues on historical or popular philosophical and ethical topics. The Second Sophistic was an almost exclusively Greek phenomenon; Apuleius is its only clearly identifiable Latin representative (E. Bowie, *Cambridge Ancient History*, 2nd edn, vol. XI (2000), pp. 920–1). On his complementary personae as Platonic philosopher and sophist see Sandy, *Greek world*; Harrison, *Apuleius*; Kenney, 'In the mill . . .'.

Further Reading

The following list is severely selective and is restricted to works in English. The secondary literature on Apuleius and the ancient novel is large and constantly growing. Most of the books listed here contain bibliographies; those in the Groningen commentaries of Hijmans *et al.* are particularly ample.

TRANSLATIONS

Adlington, W., *The xi bookes of the Golden Asse, conteininge the Metamorphosie of Lucius Apuleius with the Mariage of Cupid and Psiches* (London, 1566 and frequently reprinted).

—— id., revised by S. Gaselee, Loeb Classical Library (New York and London, 1915).

Butler, H. E., *The Metamorphoses or Golden Ass of Apuleius of Madaura*, 2 vols. (Oxford, 1910). (Expurgated.)

Graves, R., *The Transformations of Lucius otherwise known as The Golden Ass by Lucius Apuleius* (Harmondsworth, 1950).

—— id., revised with a new Introduction by M. Grant (Harmondsworth, 1990).

Hanson, J. A. See below, A Note on the Text.

Walsh, P. G., *Apuleius. The Golden Ass* (Oxford, 1994; World's Classics, 1995).

For the *Onos* see the text and translation by M. D. Macleod in vol. VIII of the works of Lucian in the Loeb Classical Library (Cambridge, Mass. and London, 1967).

COMMENTARIES

Scobie, A., *Apuleius Metamorphoses (Asinus Aureus)* I. *A Commentary* (Meisenheim am Glam, 1975).

van der Paardt, R. T., *L. Apuleius Madaurensis. The Metamorphoses. A Commentary on Book III with Text & Introduction* (Amsterdam, 1971).

Hijmans, B. L., *et al.*, *Apuleius Madaurensis Metamorphoses. Book IV 1–27. Text, Introduction and Commentary* (Groningen, 1977).

—— *Books VI 25–32 and VII* (Groningen, 1981).

—— *Book VIII* (Groningen, 1985).

—— *Book IX* (Groningen, 1995).

Zimmerman, M., *Book X* (Groningen, 2000).

Gwyn Griffiths, J., *Apuleius of Madauros. The Isis-Book (Metamorphoses, Book XI)* (Leiden, 1975).

Purser, L. C., *The Story of Cupid and Psyche as related by Apuleius* [IV 28 – VI 24] (London, 1910; repr. New Rochelle, 1983).

Kenney, E. J., *Apuleius. Cupid and Psyche* [IV 28–VI 24], Cambridge Greek and Latin Classics (Cambridge, 1990).

BOOKS AND ARTICLES

Hägg, T., *The Novel in Antiquity* (Oxford, 1983).

Harrison, S. J. (ed.), *Oxford Readings in the Roman Novel* (Oxford, 1999).

—— *Apuleius. A Latin Sophist* (Oxford, 2000).

James, Paula, *Unity in Diversity. A study of Apuleius' 'Metamorphoses' with particular reference to the narrator's art of transformation and the metamorphosis motif in the tale of Cupid and Psyche* (Hildesheim–Zürich–New York, 1987).

Kahane, A., and Laird, A. (eds.), *A Companion to the Prologue of Apuleius' Metamorphoses* (Oxford, 2001).

Kenney, E. J., 'In the mill with slaves: Lucius looks back in gratitude', *Transactions of the American Philological Society* 133 (2003), pp. 159–92.

Krabbe, Judith K., *The Metamorphoses of Apuleius* (New York–Bern–Frankfurt am Main–Paris, 1989).

Perry, B. E., *The Ancient Romances. A literary-critical account of their origins* (Berkeley and Los Angeles, 1967).

Sandy, G. N., *The Greek World of Apuleius. Apuleius and the Second Sophistic* (Leiden–New York–Cologne, 1997).

Schlam, C. C., *Cupid and Psyche. Apuleius and the monuments* (University Park, Pa., 1976).

—— *The Metamorphoses of Apuleius. On making an ass of oneself* (London, 1992).

Shumate, Nancy, *Crisis and Conversion in Apuleius' 'Metamorphoses'* (Ann Arbor, Mich., 1996).

Stephens, Susan A., and Winkler, J. J., *Ancient Greek Novels: the Fragments* (Princeton, N.J., 1995).

Tatum, J., *Apuleius and 'The Golden Ass'* (Ithaca and London, 1979).

Walsh, P. G., *The Roman Novel. The 'Satyricon' of Petronius and the 'Metamorphoses' of Apuleius* (Cambridge, 1970).

Winkler, J. J., *Auctor & Actor. A narratological reading of Apuleius's 'Golden Ass'* (Berkeley–Los Angeles–London, 1985).

A Note on the Text

The text of *The Golden Ass* depends on a manuscript written at Monte Cassino in Italy in the eleventh century and now in the Biblioteca Mediceo-Laurentiana at Florence, Laurentianus 68. 2 (F). From it all other extant copies derive. Where its original readings have been defaced by wear and tear or correction, they can often be restored from another Florentine manuscript of the twelfth or thirteenth century, Laurentianus 29. 2 (φ), which was copied from F when it was more legible than it is now. As to how faithfully F transmits what Apuleius wrote, scholars are divided. Some, most notably the Groningen commentators, adopt a highly conservative approach; others, of whom the present translator is one, believe that correction is needed in a good many places. Fortunately it is not often that the sense is seriously in doubt, however editors may disagree about the form of the expression; and textual comment in the Notes has been kept to a minimum.

The most important critical editions are those of

van der Vliet, J., Bibliotheca Teubneriana (Leipzig, 1897).
Helm, R., 3rd edn. with supplement, Bibliotheca Teubneriana (Leipzig, 1992).
Robertson, D. S., 3 vols., Collection Budé (Paris, 1940–45). With French translation by P. Vallette.
Hanson, J. A., 2 vols., Loeb Classical Library (Cambridge, Mass. and London, 1989). With English translation.

The Groningen commentaries include a text which generally follows that of Helm, with occasional variations. They also incorporate in the commentary a paragraph-by-paragraph English translation.

This translation in the main follows the text of Robertson, but the readings of other editors and critics have been occasionally preferred. The book divisions are authorial. The chapter divisions given in the margin of the text, to which the notes are keyed, are editorial and modern, designed primarily to facilitate reference. The paragraphing is the translator's.

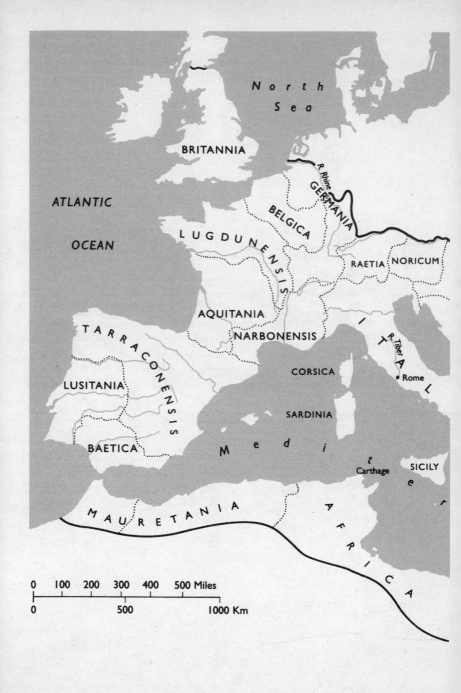

N

PANNONIA

DACIA

ILLYRICUM

Black Sea

R. Danube

MOESIA

THRACIA

MACEDONIA

BITHYNIA-PONTUS

GALATIA

EPIRUS

Aegean Sea

ASIA

CAPPADOCIA

CILICIA

PAMPHYLIA

Y

Athens

LYCIA

Antioch

R. Euphrates

ACHAEA

SYRIA

CYPRUS

r

CRETE

a   n   e   a   n

Sea

a

SYRIA-
PALAESTINA

Alexandria

ARABIA

CYRENAICA

EGYPT

R. Nile

Red Sea

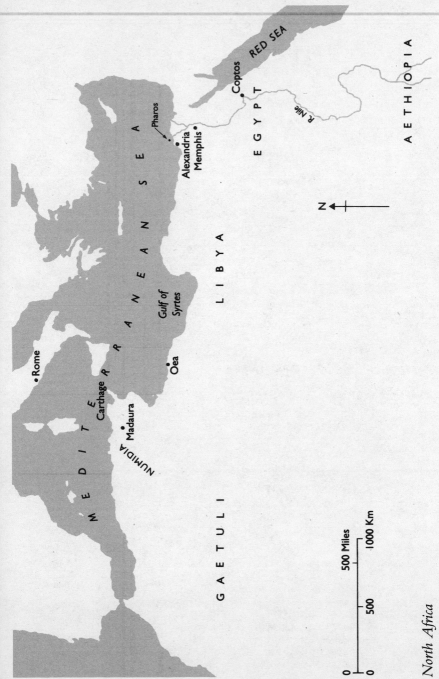

North Africa

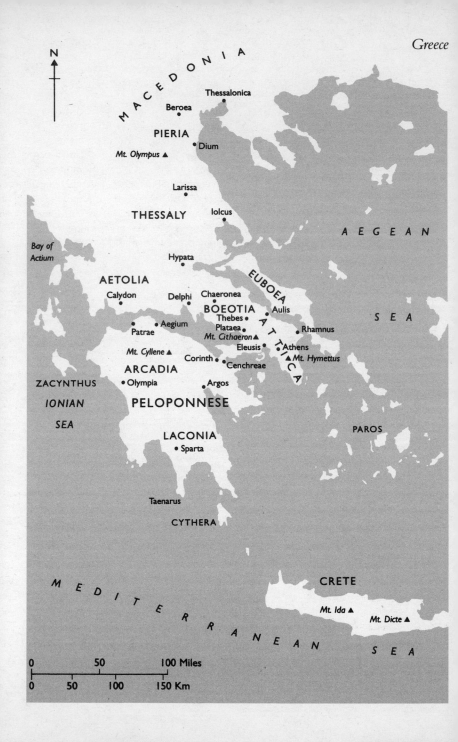

Greece

N

MACEDONIA

Thessalonica

Beroea

PIERIA

Dium

Mt. Olympus ▲

Larissa

THESSALY

Iolcus

AEGEAN

Bay of
Actium

Hypata

AETOLIA

SEA

EUBOEA

Calydon

Delphi

Chaeronea

BOEOTIA

Aulis

Thebes

Patrae

Aegium

Plataea

Rhamnus

Mt. Cithaeron ▲

Mt. Cyllene ▲

Eleusis

Athens

Corinth

Cenchreae

Mt. Hymettus ▲

ARCADIA

ZACYNTHUS

Olympia

Argos

PELOPONNESE

IONIAN

SEA

LACONIA

PAROS

Sparta

Taenarus

CYTHERA

CRETE

MEDITERRANEAN

Mt. Ida ▲

Mt. Dicte ▲

SEA

0   50   100 Miles

0   50   100   150 Km

ATTICA

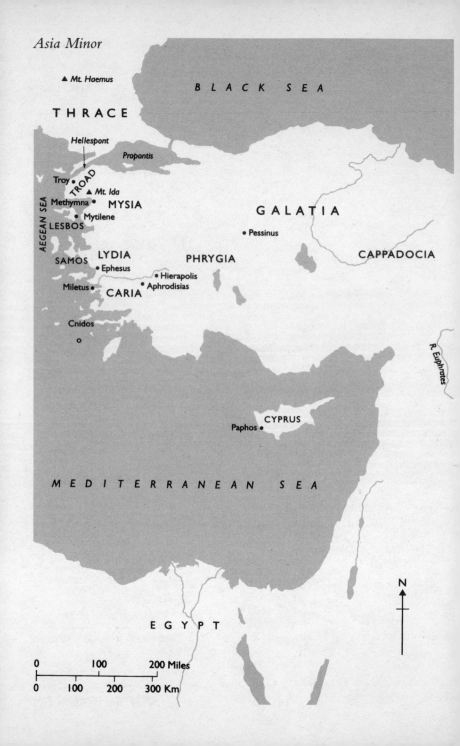

Asia Minor

Mt. Haemus

BLACK SEA

THRACE

Hellespont

Propontis

Troy

TROAD

Mt. Ida

Methymna

MYSIA

GALATIA

Mytilene

LESBOS

Pessinus

CAPPADOCIA

AEGEAN SEA

SAMOS

LYDIA

PHRYGIA

Ephesus

Hierapolis

Miletus

Aphrodisias

CARIA

Cnidos

R. Euphrates

CYPRUS

Paphos

MEDITERRANEAN SEA

N

0   100   200 Miles

0   100   200   300 Km

EGYPT

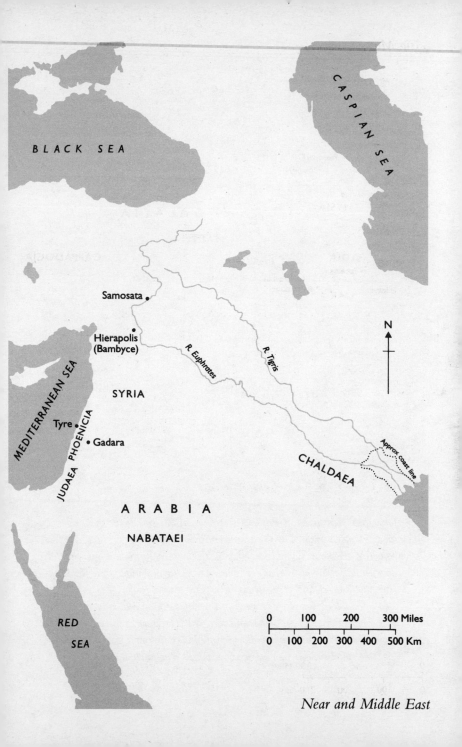

Near and Middle East

John Price (Latinized as Pricaeus) was born of Welsh parents in London in
1600. He was educated at Westminster School and Christ Church, Oxford,
though as a Roman Catholic he was ineligible to matriculate or graduate. He
spent much of his life abroad, living and working at various times in Paris,
Vienna, Florence and Pisa, where he was for a time Professor of Greek. He
died in about 1676 and was buried in the Augustinian monastery in Rome.
His commentaries on Apuleius and the New Testament gained him a high
reputation among his contemporaries; and his edition of The Golden Ass,
published at Gouda in 1650, is still a valuable resource.

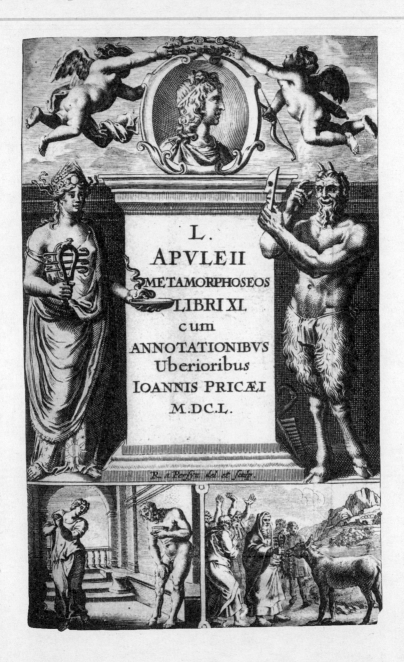

L.
APVLEII
METAMORPHOSEOS
LIBRI XI.
cum
ANNOTATIONIBVS
Uberioribus
IOANNIS PRICÆI
M.DC.L.

Contents

BOOK I

Prologue in which the author introduces himself – Lucius follows suit – on the way to Thessaly – Aristomenes' story – arrival at Hypata and reception by Milo – a puzzling experience in the market – hungry to bed

Now, what I propose in this Milesian discourse is to string together   1
for you a series of different stories and to charm your ears, kind
reader, with amusing gossip – always assuming that you are not too
proud to look at an Egyptian book written with the sharpness of a
pen from the Nile; and to make you marvel at a story of men's
shapes and fortunes changed into other forms and then restored all
over again. So I'll begin. But who is this? In brief: Attic Hymettus,
the Isthmus of Corinth, and Spartan Taenarus, fruitful lands immortalized in yet more fruitful books, these make up my ancient ancestry.
It was there that I served my earliest apprenticeship to the language
of Athens. Later, arriving in Rome a stranger to its culture, with no
teacher to show me the way, by my own painful efforts I attacked
and mastered the Latin language. That then is my excuse, if as an
unpractised speaker of the foreign idiom of the Roman courts I
should stumble and give offence. In fact this linguistic metamorphosis
suits the style of writing I have tackled here – the trick, you might
call it, of changing literary horses at the gallop. It is a Grecian story
that I am going to begin. Give me your ear, reader: you will enjoy
yourself.

I was on my way to Thessaly – for on my mother's side our family   2
goes back there, being proud to number among our ancestors the
distinguished philosopher Plutarch and his nephew Sextus – I was
on my way, I say, to Thessaly on particular business. I had negotiated
a succession of steep passes, muddy valleys, dewy pastures, and sticky

ploughlands, and like me, my horse, who was native-bred, a pure white animal, was getting pretty tired. Thinking I might shake off my own saddle-weariness by a little exercise, I dismounted, wiped my horse down, rubbed his forehead scientifically, caressed his ears, and took off his bridle; then I led him on at a gentle pace, to let him get rid of his fatigue through the natural restorative of a snack. And so, while he, with his head turned to the verges as he passed, was taking his breakfast on the hoof, I caught up with two fellow wayfarers who happened to have gone on a short way ahead. As I began to eavesdrop, one was roaring with laughter and saying: 'Do give over lying like that – I've never heard anything so utterly absurd.'

At that I, thirsting as always for novelty, struck in: 'No, please,' I said, 'let me in on this – not that I'm nosy, it's just that I'm the sort of person who likes to know everything, or at least as much as I can. And an agreeable and amusing yarn or two will lessen the steepness of this hill we're climbing.' 'Yes,' said the first speaker, 'these lies are just as true as it would be to say that because of magic rivers can suddenly reverse their flow, the sea be becalmed, the winds cease to blow, the sun stand still, the moon be milked of her dew, the stars uprooted, the daylight banished, the night prolonged.' Then I, emboldened, said: 'You, sir, who began this story, please don't be annoyed or too disgusted to tell us the rest'; and to the other man, 'But what you are stupidly refusing to listen to and stubbornly pooh-poohing may very well be a true report. Really, I think you are being ignorant and perverse when you account as a lie anything you've never heard of or aren't familiar with the sight of or just find too difficult for your understanding to grasp. If you look into these things a little more closely, you'll find out that they aren't only reliably attested but can easily happen. Look at me, yesterday evening: trying desperately to keep my end up at dinner, I rashly tried to cram down a piece of cheesecake that was too big, and the gooey stuff lodged in my throat and blocked my windpipe – I was very nearly a goner. Then again, when I was in Athens only the other day, in front of the Painted Porch, I saw with these two eyes a juggler swallow a sharp cavalry sabre, point first; and then the same man, encouraged by a small donation, lowered a hunting spear right down into his inside, lethal point first. And then, lo and behold, above the blade of the lance, where the shaft of the inverted weapon entered the man's throat and stood up over his head, there appeared a boy, pretty as a girl, who proceeded to wreathe himself round it in a bonelessly sensuous dance. We were all lost in amazement; you'd have thought it was Aesculapius' own rough-hewn staff, with his sacred serpent twining sinuously round it. But sir, please do go on with your story. I promise you I'll believe it even if our friend here won't, and at the first inn we come to I'll stand you lunch – there's your payment secured.'

'Very kind of you,' he said, 'but I'll start my story again in any case, thanks all the same. First however let me swear to you by this all-seeing divine Sun that what I'm going to tell you really happened; and if you get to the next town in Thessaly, you'll be left in no doubt; all this was done in public and everyone there is still talking about it. But to let you know who I am, and where I come from: my name is Aristomenes, from Aegium. Let me tell you how I get a living: I travel all over Thessaly and Aetolia and Boeotia in honey and cheese and suchlike innkeeper's staples. So, hearing that at Hypata – it's the most important place in Thessaly – there was some new and particularly tasty cheese on offer at a very reasonable price, I hurried off there to put in a bid for the lot. But as tends to happen, I got off on the wrong foot and was disappointed in my hope of making a killing: a wholesaler called Lupus had bought it all the day before.

'So, worn out by my useless hurry, I took myself off at sundown to the public baths; and who should I see there but my old friend Socrates. He was sitting on the ground, half wrapped in a tattered old coat, his face sickly yellow so that I hardly recognized him, miserably thin, looking just like one of those bits of Fortune's flotsam one sees begging in the streets. Seeing him looking like this, though as I say I knew him extremely well, it was with some hesitation that I went up to him. "Socrates, my dear fellow," I said, "what's up? Why are you looking like this? What have they done to you? Back home you've been mourned and given up for dead; and your children have been assigned guardians by the court. Your wife has given you a formal funeral; and now, disfigured by months of grieving and having wept herself nearly blind, she's being urged by her parents to cheer up the family misfortunes by getting happily married again. And here are you, looking like a ghost and putting us all to shame."

' "Aristomenes," he said, "you just don't understand the deceitful twists and turns of Fortune, her surprise attacks, her reversals of direction," and as he spoke he covered his face, which had become red with shame, with his rags and patches, leaving himself naked from navel to groin. I couldn't bear the pitiful sight of his distress, and tried to pull him to his feet. But he, keeping his head covered, cried: "Leave me alone, leave me, and let Fortune go on enjoying the spectacle of this trophy that she's set up." However, I got him to come with me, and taking off one of my tunics I dressed or at least covered him up with it, and took him off to the baths. I got him oil and towels and with much effort scrubbed off the horrible filth he was encrusted with; and then when he had been thoroughly put to rights (by which time I was worn out myself and was hard put to it to hold him up), I took him back to my inn, put him to bed to recover, gave him a good dinner and a relaxing glass or two of wine, and chatted to him to calm him down.

'He was just beginning to talk freely, to crack the odd joke, even to get mildly flippant and answer back, when suddenly, heaving an excruciating sigh from the depths of his chest and passionately slapping his forehead, he broke out: "Gods, what miserable luck! It was only because I went in search of a bit of pleasure, to see a gladiatorial show I'd heard a lot about, that I got into this dreadful mess. As you know, I'd gone to Macedonia on business. I'd been hard at it there for nine months, and having made a decent profit I was on my way home. Not far from Larissa, where I was planning to see the show on my way through, I was waylaid in a wild and watery glen by a gang of bandits – absolute monsters – and robbed of everything I had, though in the end I escaped with my life. Reduced to this desperate state, I took shelter at an inn kept by a woman called Meroe, not at all bad-looking for her age. I told her everything, why I'd been away so long, my anxiety to get home, and the lamentable story of the robbery. She welcomed me more than kindly, treating me first to a good dinner, free gratis and for nothing, and then to a share of her bed – she really was on heat. And that's how I came to grief: that first night with her was the start of a long and degrading association. Even the rags which the robbers had generously left me to cover myself with, even those I made over to her, along with the pittance I earned as a porter while I was still fit enough for the work. And that's how this worthy wife, so called, and the malevolence of Fortune between them have reduced me to what you saw just now."

' "Well, damn it," I said, "you deserve anything you get and   8
worse than that, for preferring the pleasure of fornicating with a leathery old hag to your home and children." But he put his finger to his lips and looked utterly horrified. "Shh, quiet," he said, looking round to see that we weren't overheard. "Don't talk like that about a woman with superhuman powers, or your rash tongue will get you into trouble." "Really?" I said. "What sort of woman is this mighty tavern-queen?" "A witch," he answered, "with supernatural powers; she can bring down the sky, raise up the earth, solidify springs, dissolve mountains, raise the dead, send the gods down below, blot out the stars, and illuminate Hell itself." "Come on," I said, "spare me the histrionics and let's have it in plain language." "Well," he said, "do you want to hear one or two of her exploits? There are lots I could tell you about. It's not only our own people that she can make fall madly in love with her, but the Indians, the Ethiopians – both lots – even the Antipodeans; that's nothing, the merest ABC of her art. But let me tell you what she did in full view of a crowd of eyewitnesses.

' "When one of her lovers was unfaithful to her, with a single   9
word she turned him into a beaver, because when they're afraid of being caught beavers escape their pursuers by biting off their balls – the idea being that something like that would happen to him. An innkeeper, who was a neighbour and therefore a trade rival, she changed into a frog; and now the poor old chap swims around in a barrel of his own wine and greets his old customers with a polite croak as he squats there in the lees. Another time she changed a lawyer who appeared against her in court into a ram, and it's as a

ram that he now pleads his cases. Again, the wife of another of her lovers she condemned to perpetual pregnancy for being witty at her expense; she shut up the woman's womb and halted the growth of the foetus, so that it's now eight years (we've all done the sum) that this unfortunate creature has been swollen with her burden, as if it was an elephant that she was going to produce.

10 ' "This sort of thing kept happening, and a lot of people suffered at her hands, so that public indignation grew and spread; and a meeting was held at which it was decided that on the following day she should receive drastic punishment by stoning to death. However, she thwarted this move by the strength of her spells – just like the famous Medea when, having obtained a single day's grace from Creon, she used it to burn up the old king's palace, his daughter, and himself, with the crown of fire. Just so Meroe sacrificed into a trench to the powers of darkness (she told me all this the other day when she was drunk), and shut up the whole population in their houses by silent supernatural force. For two whole days they couldn't undo their bolts or get their doors open or even break through their walls, until in the end they came to an agreement among themselves and all called out, swearing by what they held most sacred, that they would not lay a finger on her and that if anybody had other ideas they would come to her assistance. So she was appeased and let them all off, except for the man who had convened the public meeting. Him she whisked off at dead of night, with his whole house – walls, foundations, the ground it stood on – still shut up, a hundred miles away to another town which was situated on the top of a rocky and waterless mountain. And since the houses there were too closely packed to allow room for another one, she simply dumped it outside the town gates and decamped." '

11 ' "My dear Socrates," I said, "what you tell me is as ghastly as it's astonishing. You really have made me very uneasy – no, you've terrified me. It's not just a pinprick of anxiety but a positive spearthrust that you've inflicted – the fear that the old woman may invoke some supernatural aid as she's done before to eavesdrop on this conversation. So let's get to bed straight away, and when we've slept off our fatigue let's get as far as possible away from here before it's

light." Before I had finished offering this advice, my friend, who had been tried to the limit by so many wearing experiences and more wine than he was used to, was fast asleep and snoring noisily. So I closed the door and shot the bolts firmly, and also wedged my bed hard up against the hinges and lay down on it. At first my fear kept me awake for a time, but then about midnight I dropped off. Hardly had I done so when suddenly (you wouldn't think a whole gang of robbers could manage such an onslaught) the door was thrown open, or rather broken down and torn right off its hinges and sent crashing to the ground. My bed, which was only a cot, with a foot missing and riddled with worm, was overturned by this violent shock, and I was hurled out of it and rolled on to the floor with the bed upside down on top of me and hiding me.

'Then I discovered that some emotions naturally express them-   12
selves by their opposites. Just as one very often weeps tears of joy, so then, utterly terrified as I was, I couldn't help laughing at the idea of myself as a tortoise. Grovelling there in the dirt I was able from under the protection of my resourceful bed to get a sideways view of what was happening. I saw two elderly women, one carrying a lighted lamp, the other a sponge and a naked sword. So arrayed, they stood on either side of Socrates, who was still sound asleep. The one with the sword spoke first: "There he is, sister Panthia, my beloved Endymion, my Ganymede, who by night and day has played fast and loose with my tender youth, who scorns my love, and not content with calumniating me is trying to escape me. I take it I'm supposed to play abandoned Calypso to his wily Ulysses, left to mourn in perpetual solitude?" And then she pointed and indicated me to Panthia: "But here we have our friend Aristomenes the Counsellor, who is the author of this escape plan and now lies on the ground under that bed within a hair's-breadth of death, watching all this and thinking that the injuries he has done me will go unpunished. One day – what am I saying, now, this very moment – I'll make him sorry for his past impudence and his present curiosity."

'Hearing this I was in agony, drenched in an icy sweat and shaking   13
all over, so that the bed too was convulsed by my shudders and heaved up and down on top of me. Then said the amiable Panthia:

"Now, sister, shall we take this one first and tear him limb from limb like Bacchantes, or tie him down and castrate him?" But Meroe – for she it was, as I realized from what Socrates had told me – said: "No, let him survive to give a modest burial to the body of his poor friend," and twisting Socrates' head to one side she buried her sword up to the hilt in the left-hand side of his throat, catching the blood that spurted out in a leather bottle so neatly that not a drop was spilled. This I saw with my own eyes. Next dear Meroe, wanting I suppose to keep as closely as possible to the sacrificial forms, plunged her hand into the wound right down to his entrails, rummaged about, and pulled out my poor friend's heart. At this he let out through the wound in his throat, which the violent stroke of the sword had totally severed, an inarticulate whistling sound, and gave up the ghost. Then Panthia, blocking the gaping wound with her sponge, "Now, sponge," she said, "you were born in the sea – take care not to cross a river." With these words they left, but first they pulled the bed off me and squatted down and emptied their bladders over my face, leaving me soaked in their filthy piss.

14 'The moment they had gone the door reverted to normal: the hinges flew back into position, the bars returned to the doorposts, and the bolts shot back into the slot. As for me, I remained where I was, grovelling on the floor, fainting, naked, cold and drenched in piss, just like a new-born child – or rather half dead, a posthumous survivor of myself, an absolutely certain candidate for crucifixion. "What's going to happen to me," I said to myself, "when he's found in the morning with his throat cut? I can tell the truth, but who'll believe me? I can hear them now. 'Couldn't you at least have called for help if you couldn't cope with a woman – a big chap like you? A man murdered before your eyes, and not a peep out of you? And how is it that you weren't likewise made away with by these female desperadoes? Why should their cruelty have spared a witness who could inform against them? So, you escaped Death; now go back to him!'"

'While I was going over this in my mind again and again, the night wore on. The best plan then seemed to be to get clear surreptitiously before dawn and to take the road, though I had no

very clear idea where to go. So I shouldered my luggage and tried
to undo the bolts; but the upright and conscientious door, which
earlier had unbarred itself so readily, now only opened with much
reluctance and after many turnings of the key. Then, "Hey, porter,"   15
I called, "where are you? Open the front door. I want to be off
early." The porter was lying on the ground behind the door and
was still half asleep. "Have some sense," he said. "Don't you know
the roads are stiff with robbers, and you want to start out at this time
of night? You may have some crime on your conscience that makes
you eager to die, but I'm not such a fathead as to want to take your
place." "It's nearly light," I said, "and anyway, what can robbers
take away from a traveller who's got nothing? Don't be stupid: you
know that ten wrestlers can't strip a naked man." But he, drowsy
and half asleep, turned over in bed and muttered: "Anyway, how
do I know you haven't murdered your companion that you came in
with last night and aren't trying to save yourself by doing a bunk?"

'At that moment, I remember, I saw the earth opening and the
depths of Hell, and Cerberus hungering for me; and I realized that
it wasn't in pity that dear old Meroe had spared my life, but in a
spirit of sadism, saving me for the cross. So I went back to my room   16
to mull over the form my suicide was to take. Since the only lethal
weapon provided by Fortune was my bed, "Now, now, O bed," I
cried, "my dearest bed, thou who hast endured with me so many
sufferings, confidant and beholder of the night's happenings, the
only witness to my innocence that I can call against my accusers, do
you provide me as I hasten to the shades with the weapon that shall
save me." With these words I set about undoing the cord with
which it was strung and made one end of it fast to a beam which
jutted out under the window; the other end I knotted firmly into a
noose, and then climbing on the bed and mounting to my doom I
put my head into the halter. But when I kicked the support away,
so that the rope, tightened round my throat by my weight, should
cut off the function of my breathing – at that moment the rotten
old rope broke, and I fell from where I was standing on to Socrates,
who lay nearby, and rolled with him on to the floor. And precisely   17
at that very same moment the porter burst abruptly in, shouting:

"Where are you? You wanted to be off at dead of night, and now you're back in bed and snoring!" At this, aroused either by my fall or the porter's raucous bellowing, Socrates was on his feet first, remarking: "No wonder travellers hate all innkeepers! Look at this officious oaf, shoving in where he's not wanted – to see what he can steal, I expect – and waking me up with his noise when I was fast asleep and still tired out."

'I then got up too, happily revived by this unexpected stroke of luck. "There, O most faithful of porters," I said, "you see my companion and brother, the one that last night, when you were drunk, you accused me of murdering"; and as I spoke I embraced Socrates and kissed him. He was shocked by the smell of the foul fluid with which the witches had drenched me, and pushed me violently away, shouting "Get off me, you stink like the worst kind of urinal", and then proceeded to ask me facetiously why I smelled like that. Embarrassed and on the spur of the moment I cracked some stupid joke to divert his attention to another subject. Then, slapping him on the back, I said: "Come on, let's be off and enjoy an early start." So, shouldering my traps, I paid the bill, and we set out.

18   'When we had gone some way the sun rose; and now that it was fully light, I looked very closely at my friend's neck where I had seen the sword go in, and I said to myself: "You're crazy; you were dead drunk and had a horrible dream. There's Socrates whole, sound and unharmed. Where's the wound? Where's the sponge? And where's the fresh deep scar?" Aloud I said: "The doctors are quite right when they tell us that eating and drinking too much causes nightmares. Look at me; I had a drop too much yesterday evening, and I passed a night of such dreadful threatening dreams that I still can't believe I'm not spattered and defiled with human gore." He smiled and said: "It's not blood but piss you were drenched with. But to tell the truth, I too had a dream, that my throat was cut; I had a pain there, and I thought the heart was plucked out of me – and even now I feel faint, my knees are trembling and I can't walk properly. I think I need something to eat to put the life back in me." "Right," I answered, "I've got some breakfast all ready for

you," and taking off my knapsack I quickly gave him some bread
and cheese, adding, "let's sit down under that plane tree."

'This we did, and I too had a little something. He was eating   19
greedily, but as I watched him, I saw that his face was becoming
drawn and waxy pale, and his strength seemed to be ebbing away.
Indeed he was so altered by this deathly change of complexion that
I panicked, thinking of those Furies of last night; and the first piece
of bread I'd taken, not a very big one, lodged right in my throat
and refused either to go down or to come back up. What increased
my alarm was that there was almost nobody about. Who was going
to believe that one of a pair of companions had been done in without
foul play on the part of the other? Meanwhile Socrates, having made
short work of the food, became desperately thirsty, as well he might,
having wolfed down the best part of a first-rate cheese. Not far from
the plane tree there flowed a gentle stream, its current so slow that
it looked like a placid pool, all silver and glass. "There," I said,
"quench your thirst in that limpid spring." He got up, and finding
a place that sloped down to the water, he knelt and leaned over
eagerly to drink. He had hardly touched the surface with his lips
when the wound in his throat gaped wide open to the bottom and
the sponge shot out, followed by a little blood. His lifeless body
nearly pitched headlong into the water, but I managed to get hold
of one foot and drag him laboriously up the bank. There, after
mourning him as best I could in the circumstances, I covered my
unfortunate friend with the sandy soil to rest there for ever by the
river. Then, panic-stricken and in fear of my life, I made my escape
through remote and pathless wildernesses; and like a man with
murder on his conscience I left country and home to embrace
voluntary exile. And now I have remarried and live in Aetolia.'

That was Aristomenes' story. His companion, who from the start   20
had remained stubbornly incredulous and would have no truck with
what he told us, broke out: 'Of all the fairytales that were ever
invented, of all the lies that were ever told, that takes the biscuit';
and turning to me, 'But you,' he said, 'to judge from your dress and
appearance you're an educated man – do you go along with this
stuff?' 'Well,' I said, 'my opinion is that nothing is impossible and

that we mortals get whatever the Fates have decided for us. You, I, everybody, we all meet with many amazing and unprecedented experiences, which aren't believed when they're told to somebody who lacks first-hand knowledge of them. But I do, I assure you, believe our friend here, and I'm most grateful to him for diverting us with such a charming and delightful story. Here I've got to the end of this long and rugged road without effort and haven't been bored. I believe my horse too thinks you've done him a favour, for without tiring him I see I've reached the city gates transported not on his back but, you might say, by my ears.'

21   That was the end both of our conversation and of our companion-ship, since they now turned off to the left towards a nearby farm, while I went into the first inn I saw and questioned the old woman who kept it. 'Is this town Hypata?' I asked. She nodded. 'Do you know somebody called Milo – one of your foremost citizens?' She laughed and said: 'Yes, you could call him foremost all right – he lives right outside the city wall.' 'Joking apart, mother,' I said, 'tell me, please, who he is and where he lives.' 'Do you see those windows at the end there,' she replied, 'that look outwards towards the city, and on the other side a door giving at the back on to the neighbouring alleyway? That's his house. He's enormously rich, with money to burn, but he's a public disgrace, the lowest kind of miser, and lives in total squalor. He's a usurer on the grand scale and only accepts gold and silver as pledges; he shuts himself up in that tiny house and broods over the corroded coins that are his ruling passion. He has a wife to share his miserable existence, but his whole household consists of one slave-girl, and he always dresses like a beggar.'

This made me laugh. 'It's a really good turn my friend Demeas did me when I set out on my travels,' I said, 'giving me an introduction to a man like that. At least I needn't fear annoyance from kitchen
22   smokes and smells!' So saying I walked on and came to the door of the house, which I found firmly bolted. I proceeded to bang on it and shout, and at last a girl appeared. 'Now,' she said, 'after all that energetic knocking, what security are you offering for a loan? You must be aware that the only pledges we accept here are gold and silver.' 'God forbid,' I said; 'what I want to know is whether your

master is at home.' 'Yes, he is,' said she, 'but why do you want to know?' 'I've got a letter for him from Demeas of Corinth.' 'Stay where you are,' she said, 'and I'll tell him,' and bolting the door again she disappeared. Presently she reappeared and unbolted it, saying: 'He says, come in.'

In I went, and found him reclining on a very small couch and just beginning dinner, with his wife sitting at his feet. By them stood a table with nothing on it, and indicating this, 'Welcome to our guest,' said he. 'Thank you,' I said, and gave him Demeas' letter, which he read quickly. 'I'm most grateful to my friend Demeas,' he said, 'for sending me so distinguished a guest,' and making his wife get up he invited me to sit down in her place. When I modestly hesitated, he pulled me down by the tunic, saying: 'Sit here. We are so afraid of burglars that we can't provide couches or proper furniture.' I did so, and he went on: 'I should have guessed rightly that you were of good family from your gentlemanly appearance and your – if I may say so – virginal modesty, even if my friend Demeas hadn't told me so in his letter. So, please don't despise my humble shack. There's a bedroom just here where you'll be decently accommodated; enjoy your stay with us. By honouring our house with your presence you'll enhance its reputation, and you'll be following a glorious example by putting up with a humble lodging and so emulating the achievements of the hero Theseus after whom your father is named – he, you remember, didn't despise old Hecale's frugal hospitality. Photis,' he said, calling the maid, 'take our guest's luggage and stow it safely in his room, and then quickly get out of the store-cupboard some oil and towels for massage and drying, and anything else he needs, and show our guest the way to the nearest baths. He's had a long hard journey and must be worn out.'

Hearing this, and bearing in mind Milo's character and his mean-ness, I decided to get further into his good books. 'Thanks,' I said, 'but I don't need any of those things, which I always take with me on my travels; and I can easily ask the way to the baths. It's my horse that is the important thing; he's carried me well. Here's some money, Photis; please get him some hay and barley.' That done, and my things stowed in my room, I set off for the baths on my own; but

23

24

wanting first to see about something for our supper, I made for the provision market. Seeing some fine fish offered for sale I asked the price, which was a hundred sesterces; I demurred, and got them for eighty. I was just leaving when I met Pytheas, a fellow student at Athens. Recognizing me with delight after such a long time he rushed at me and embraced and kissed me affectionately. 'My dear Lucius,' he said, 'it's ages since we last saw each other, not indeed since we left Clytius' class. But what are you doing here so far from home?' 'I'll tell you tomorrow,' I said. 'But what's all this? My congratulations – for I see you with attendants and fasces and everything about you that befits a magistrate.' 'I'm an aedile,' he said. 'I regulate prices; if you want to do any shopping here, I'll take care of it.' I declined the offer, as I had provided myself amply with fish for supper. But Pytheas, looking at my basket and shaking up the fish to get a better sight of them, asked: 'What did you give for this rubbish?' 'I had a job,' I said, 'to get the fishmonger to take eighty sesterces.'

25   When I said this, he immediately seized me by the arm and took me back again to the market. 'Who did you buy this muck from?' he asked. I showed him an old man sitting in a corner, and he began to upbraid him sharply in his inspectorial capacity. 'So,' he said, 'this is the way you impose on my friends and visitors in general, putting ridiculous prices on your rubbishy fish and reducing our town, the pride of Thessaly, to a barren wilderness by making food so dear. But you're not getting away with it: I'll show you how roguery is going to be checked under my regime,' and emptying my basket on the ground he ordered his clerk to tread on my fish and trample them to pulp. Then, pleased with this display of severity, my friend Pytheas sent me on my way with the words: 'I think, Lucius, that that old man has been properly put in his place.' Astonished and completely bemused by all this, I took myself off to the baths, deprived of both my money and my supper by the energetic measures of my sagacious fellow student. Having had my bath, I came back to Milo's house and went to my room.

26   The maid Photis now appeared, saying: 'The master is asking for you.' Knowing Milo's parsimonious habits I made polite excuses,

saying that it was sleep rather than food I felt I needed to restore me after the wear and tear of my journey. This message produced Milo himself. Taking me by the arm he tried gently to make me accompany him; and when I hesitated and put up a mild resistance, he said: 'I won't leave the room unless you come with me,' backing his words with an oath. Yielding reluctantly to his persistence I was led to that couch of his and sat down. 'Now,' he asked, 'how is my friend Demeas? and his wife? and the children? and the servants?' I gave him all the details. Then he questioned me about the reasons for my journey. I told him all that. Then it was my home town, its leading men, the governor himself, that were the subjects of minute inquiries. Finally, realizing that, on top of the stresses and strains of my journey, the additional fatigue of this long conversation was making me nod off in the middle of my sentences and that I was so worn out that I was muttering disconnected words that made no sense, he at last let me go to bed. So, not before time, I escaped from this tiresome old man and the interrogation plus starvation that was his idea of entertainment; and weighed down, not with food but sleep, having dined solely on conversation, I went back to my room and surrendered myself to the repose that I was longing for.

BOOK 2

1   The moment the sun put the darkness to flight and ushered in a new day, I woke up and arose at once. Being in any case an all too eager student of the remarkable and miraculous, and remembering that I was now in the heart of Thessaly, renowned the whole world over as the cradle of magic arts and spells, and that it was in this very city that my friend Aristomenes' story had begun, I examined attentively everything I saw, on tenterhooks with keen anticipation. There was nothing I looked at in the city that I didn't believe to be other than what it was: I imagined that everything everywhere had been changed by some infernal spell into a different shape – I thought the very stones I stumbled against must be petrified human beings, I thought the birds I heard singing and the trees growing around the city walls had acquired their feathers and leaves in the same way, and I thought the fountains were liquefied human bodies. I expected statues and pictures to start walking, walls to speak, oxen and other cattle to utter prophecies, and oracles to issue suddenly from the very sky or from the bright sun.

2   So, spellbound and in a daze of tormented longing I went on prowling, though nowhere did I meet with the slightest trace of what I hoped to find. While wandering from house to house like some reveller out on the town, I found myself unexpectedly in the provision market. There I saw a woman passing by with a train of attendants, and hurried to overtake her. From her gold-mounted jewellery and the gold embroidery on her dress it was clear that she

was a person of some consequence. Walking with her was an old man; the moment he saw me, 'My God,' he cried, 'it's Lucius for sure,' and he embraced me and whispered in the woman's ear something I didn't catch. 'Now,' he said to me, 'won't you come and greet your foster-mother?' 'No, really,' I answered, 'I don't know the lady,' and I hung back blushing and shamefaced. But she looked at me and said: 'Yes, he's his sainted mother Salvia all over – it shows in his breeding and modesty. And his looks – it's uncanny, he couldn't be more like her: moderately tall, slim but muscular, nice complexion, a natural blond, simple hairstyle, eyes grey but alert and bright, really like an eagle's, a blooming countenance, a graceful but unaffected walk.' And she went on: 'It was I, Lucius, who brought you up with my own hands – naturally, being not only related to your mother but having shared a common upbringing. Both of us are descended from Plutarch, and we had the same wet-nurse and grew up together in the bond of sisterhood. The only difference between us is one of rank: she made a brilliant marriage, I a modest one. Yes, I'm Byrrhena: I expect you've often heard my name mentioned as that of one of those who brought you up. So you needn't hesitate to accept the hospitality of my house – or rather of your own, for yours it now is.' While she was speaking I had had time to recover from my confusion. 'My dear mother,' I said, 'I can't very well throw over my present host Milo, having no cause for complaint, but I'll do my best consistently with my obligation to him. Whenever I can find a reason for coming this way in future, I'll always stay with you.' Chatting like this we came after a short walk to Byrrhena's house.

There was a magnificent entrance-hall, with a column at each of its four corners supporting a statue of Victory. Each of these, wings outspread, appeared to hover without alighting on the unstable foothold of her rolling ball, which her dewy feet just brushed, not standing fixed but seemingly poised in flight. In the exact centre of the hall stood a Diana in Parian marble. It was a brilliant *tour de force* of sculpture: as one entered the room the goddess with flowing tunic seemed to be coming straight at one in her swift course, inspiring awe by her powerful godhead. To right and left she was flanked by

3

4

hounds, also of marble. Their look was menacing, their ears pricked, their nostrils flaring, their jaws ravening, and if any barking were heard nearby, you'd think it came from those stony throats. The crowning achievement of this accomplished sculptor's craftsmanship was that, while the hind feet of the dogs were braced firmly against the ground as they sprang forward, their front feet seemed to be running. Behind the goddess there arose a rock in the shape of a grotto, with moss and grass and leaves and branches, vines here and shrubs there, a whole plantation in stone. From inside the grotto the statue was reflected back in all its brilliance by the polished marble. Round the edge of the rock there hung grapes and other fruits so cunningly modelled that art had outdone nature in making them seem real. One would think that when at the time of the vintage the breath of autumn had ripened and coloured them, they could be picked and eaten; and when one stooped to look at the spring which gushed out at the goddess's feet and rippled away in a gentle stream, one would think the hanging clusters were not only real in every other way but were actually moving. From the middle of the foliage there peered out a figure of Actaeon in stone with his prurient gaze fixed on the goddess, the transformation into a stag already begun; one could see both him and his reflection in the spring as he waited for Diana to take her bath.

5   As I was examining every detail of the group with the utmost enjoyment, 'Everything you see,' said Byrrhena, 'is yours'; and so saying she took the others aside and told them to leave us. When they had gone she turned to me, saying: 'My dearest Lucius, I'm terribly worried about you – for I look on you as a son and want to see you securely provided for. Do, I implore you by Diana there, do be warned by me: watch out for the wicked wiles and criminal enticements of that woman Pamphile, the one that's married to Milo, him you call your host. Never lower your guard. They say she's a top-class witch, mistress of every kind of graveyard spell. By merely breathing on twigs or pebbles or any kind of small object she can plunge the light of the starry heavens above us into the depths of Tartarus and primeval chaos. The moment she sees a handsome young man, she becomes possessed by his charms and has

no eyes or thoughts for anything else. She lavishes endearments on him, moves in on his heart, and binds him in everlasting bonds of insatiable love. And anyone who won't cooperate or gets written off for not fancying her, she instantly turns into a rock or a sheep or some other animal, and some she simply eliminates. That's what I'm afraid of for you, and what I'm telling you to beware of. She's always on heat, and you with your youth and looks would be just what the doctor ordered.'

Byrrhena's words showed how worried she was for me. However, with my usual curiosity, directly I heard the magic word 'magic', so far from resolving to steer clear of Pamphile, I itched to enrol myself as her pupil and to pay handsomely for the privilege – in a word to take a running leap right into the abyss. So in a delirium of impatience I extracted myself from Byrrhena's embrace as if her hands had been manacles and bidding her a hasty goodbye I hurried off at speed back to Milo's. As I rushed along like a maniac, 'Now, Lucius,' I said to myself, 'watch your step and keep a cool head. Here's the chance you've dreamed of, what you've always wanted. You'll be able to enjoy wonderful stories to your heart's content. Never mind childish fears, get to grips with the thing bravely. Granted, you'd better keep clear of any amorous involvement with your hostess and religiously respect the virtuous Milo's marital couch, but Photis the maid – you can go all out to make a conquest of *her*. She's a pretty little thing, likes a joke, and is no fool. Why, when you went to bed last night, how sociably she took you to your room, how sweetly she helped you into bed, how lovingly she tucked you up and kissed your forehead! You could see from her face how reluctant she was to leave you; and she kept stopping to look back at you. It may be risky, but I'll have a go at Photis, and good luck to us!'

While I was arguing the matter out with myself I had arrived at Milo's door, and proceeded, as they say, to vote with my feet. I found neither Milo nor his wife at home, but only my dear Photis. She was getting dinner ready: pork rissoles, a succulent stew . . . and – I could smell it from outside – a splendidly savoury pâté. She was wearing a neat linen tunic, with a bright red waistband seductively

6

7

gathered up high under her breasts. Her pretty hands were engaged in stirring the pot with a brisk circular movement, to which her whole body kept time in a sinuous response, while her hips and supple spine swayed in a delightful undulating rhythm. I stood in amazement, my attention riveted, admiring the sight; and something else stood to attention as well. Finally I said: 'How prettily, darling Photis, you're stirring that pot, and what a jolly rearguard action! That's a delicious stew that you're cooking! It'd be a lucky chap with nothing more to wish for in this world that you allowed to dip his finger in there.' To which the witty little baggage answered: 'You stay away, right away, from my little hearth, or it'll be the worse for you. You've only to be touched by my tiniest spark, and you'll take fire and burn deep down inside you – and nobody will be able to put out the flames but me. I know all the best recipes, and I'm equally good at keeping things on the move in the kitchen and in bed.'

8   As she said this, she looked at me and laughed. But I lingered there to drink in every detail of her appearance. As to the rest of her, I've nothing to say: it's only a woman's head and her hair that I'm really interested in. It's what I like to feast my eyes on first in the street, and then enjoy in private indoors. There are good and positive reasons for this preference. The hair is the dominant part of the body: it's placed in the most obvious and conspicuous position and is the first thing we notice. The rest of the body achieves its effect through brightly coloured clothes, the hair through its natural sheen. In fact most women, when they want to show off their personal attractions, discard their clothes altogether and remove all covering, eager to display their beauty naked, and reckoning that rosy skin will please better than gold fabric. If on the other hand – though it's blasphemy even to mention it, and I devoutly hope that such a thing will never happen to make the point – if you were to despoil the head of even the most beautiful of women of its hair and rob her face of its natural adornment, though she had come down from heaven, though she had been born from the sea and reared among the waves, I say though she were Venus herself, escorted by her choir of all the Graces and the whole tribe of Cupids, wearing her cestus, fragrant with cinnamon and dripping with perfumes – if

she were bald, not even her Vulcan would love her. Then there is   9
the fascination of its colour and sheen: now vivid enough to outshine
the rays of the sun, now gently reflecting them; or varying its charm
as its colour varies and contrasts – sometimes bright gold shading
down into pale honey, sometimes raven-black with dark blue high-
lights like those on the necks of doves; or when, perfumed with
Arabian essences and delicately parted, it is gathered behind to give
back to the lover's gaze a more flattering reflection; or again when
it is so abundant that it is piled high on top of the head, or so long
that it flows right down the back. In a nutshell, hair is so important
that whatever adornments a woman may appear in – gold, jewels,
fine clothes – unless she's made the most of her hair, you can't call
her properly dressed. As for my dear Photis, it wasn't that she had
taken great pains with her hairstyle – it was its casualness that was
so fetching. Her luxuriant tresses were carelessly flung back, hanging
down her neck and over her shoulders; where they just touched the
upper edge of her tunic she had gently looped them up and gathered
the ends together into a knot on the top of her head.

I couldn't stand this exquisite agony of pleasure any longer, and   10
leaning over her I planted the most honey-sweet of kisses just where
her hair began its climb to the top. She turned her head, and looking
at me sideways with fluttering lashes, 'Steady on, youngster,' she
said, 'that's a bittersweet morsel you're sampling there. Watch out
that too much sweet honey doesn't bring on a chronic case of
acidity.' 'I'll risk it, sweetheart,' I said; 'just refresh me with a single
kiss, and I'm all ready to be spitted and roasted over that fire of
yours,' and so saying I hugged her tight and began to kiss her. By
now her passion was beginning to match and rival my own; her
mouth opened wide, and her perfumed breath and the ambrosial
thrust of her tongue as it met mine revealed her answering desire.
'This is killing me,' I said. 'I'm really done for unless you're going
to be kind to me.' Kissing me again, 'Keep calm,' she said, 'I feel
just the same, and I'm all yours, body and soul. Our pleasure shan't
be put off any longer; I'll come to your room at dusk. Now that's
enough; go and prepare yourself, for it's going to be a non-stop
battle all night long, with no holds barred.'

11   After a few more endearments of this kind we parted. Midday arrived, and there came from Byrrhena a welcoming present in the shape of a fat piglet, five pullets, and a flagon of vintage wine. 'Look,' I said, calling Photis, 'here's Bacchus come of his own accord as Venus' supporter and squire. We'll drink every drop of this tonight; it'll put paid to any shyness or backwardness on our part and tune our desires to concert pitch. When one embarks for Cythera the only provisions one needs for a wakeful voyage are plenty of oil in the lamp and wine in the cup.'

       The rest of the day was taken up with bath and dinner; for I had been invited to take my place at my friend Milo's elegant table and sample his delicate fare. Remembering Byrrhena's warnings I avoided his wife's gaze as much as I could, dropping my eyes before hers as if in fear of the bottomless pit. However, I kept encouraging myself by glancing over my shoulder at Photis, who was waiting on us. When evening began to fall, Pamphile looked at the lamp and said: 'We'll have a cloudburst tomorrow'; and when her husband asked her how she knew she just said that the lamp had predicted it. Milo laughed at this, saying: 'That's quite a prophetess that we keep here, this lamp which observes everything that happens in the heavens from her stand – or should I say her observatory?'

12   At this I struck in. 'That's just the ABC of this method of divination,' I said. 'In fact it's not surprising that this little flame, though it's produced by human agency, has divine foreknowledge of what that greater celestial fire is going to bring about in high heaven and is able to communicate it to us, being, so to speak, its offspring and sharing consciousness with it. Why, at this very moment there is a Chaldean staying in Corinth, where I come from, who's throwing the whole city into turmoil by his wonderful oracles, and publishing the secrets of Fate to all and sundry for cash down. He'll tell you the best day for making a lasting marriage or building a wall that won't fall down, the most suitable for business, the safest for a journey, the most appropriate for a sea voyage. When I asked him how this trip of mine would turn out he told me all sorts of different things, all equally marvellous: that I should win a brilliant reputation and become a legend, an incredible romance in several volumes.'

Milo smiled. 'What does this Chaldean of yours look like?' he 13 asked, 'and what's he called?' 'He's tall,' I said, 'and rather dark-complexioned. His name's Diophanes.' 'That's him,' said Milo, 'the very man. He came here too and uttered a great many prophecies to a great many people. He did quite well, indeed he made a very tidy thing out of it, but then he unfortunately came into collision with Fortune in her most perverse, or rather adverse, mood. He was issuing his predictions one day in the middle of a dense crowd of bystanders when a businessman called Cerdo came up wanting to know the best day for a journey. He got his answer, and had taken out his purse, produced his money and counted out a hundred denarii as the fee for the prophecy, when a fashionable young man came up quietly behind Diophanes and twitched his cloak. When he turned round he found himself embraced and affectionately kissed. He kissed the young man back and asked him to sit down beside him; and being taken completely aback by this sudden arrival forgot the business he was engaged in. "I've been expecting you," he began; "have you been here long?" "Only since yesterday evening," the other answered. "But tell me, my dear fellow, how your land and sea journey went after you had to leave Euboea in such a hurry."

'At this our worthy Chaldean Diophanes, still confused and not 14 master of himself, "It was frightful," he answered, "positively Ulyssean – I wouldn't have wished it on my worst enemy. The ship we were on was so battered by storms and winds from every quarter that she lost both her rudders and was driven on to the further shore, which she just made before sinking. We lost all our possessions and had to swim for our lives. Then everything that charitable strangers and kind friends had contributed was taken from us by a gang of robbers; and when my only brother Arignotus tried to resist their violence, he was murdered before my eyes." Before he had finished this lamentable story, Cerdo swept up the money he had intended for the fee and left abruptly. Only then did Diophanes come to his senses and realize what he had lost through his lack of forethought, seeing all us bystanders doubled up with laughter. However, master Lucius, let's hope that our Chaldean told you the truth for once, and the best of luck to you for your journey.'

15   While Milo continued to hold forth in this vein, I was inwardly groaning, horribly annoyed with myself for having gone out of my way to start this series of irrelevant anecdotes, and so wasting a good part of the evening and its delightful enjoyments. In the end I said to him bluntly: 'Well, Diophanes must take his chance. I only hope that what he plunders from the public he again bestows in equal shares on land and sea. As for me, I'm still dog-tired from yesterday, so if you'll excuse me, I'll go to bed early.' So, saying goodnight, I left them and went to my room, where I found everything most elegantly arranged for our supper. Beds had been made up on the ground for the slaves some way from the door, to keep them from overhearing the sounds of our lovemaking. By my bed was a table with all the nicest left-overs from dinner, good-sized cups already half full of wine only waiting to be diluted, and the flagon standing by opened and all ready to pour – just what was needed to prepare lovers for the duels to come.

16   I had only just got into bed when Photis, having seen her mistress settled for the night, appeared smiling, with a wreath of roses in her hair and a bunch of blooms tucked in her breast. She kissed me lovingly, garlanded me, and scattered blossoms over me; then she took a cup of wine and pouring warm water into it offered it to me. Before I had quite finished it she gently took it from me and drank what was left in a most bewitching manner, sipping in minute instalments and gazing at me as she did so. A second and a third cup passed back and forth between us, followed by several others, until at last I was well under the influence. Mind and body alike were throbbing with desire, and finally I couldn't control the impatience that was killing me. Lifting my tunic for a moment I showed Photis that my love could brook no more delay. 'Have pity on me,' I said, 'and come to my rescue – fast. That war that you declared without any diplomatic overtures will break out any minute now, and you can see I'm standing to arms and fully mobilized for it. Since I got cruel Cupid's first arrow right in the heart, my own bow has been strung so hard that I'm afraid it's overstrung and may break. But if you really want to please me, let your hair down when you come to bed so that it flows in waves all over us.'

Without more ado she quickly cleared away the table and whipped 17 off every stitch of clothing; then with her hair loose in delightful disarray she was prettily transformed before my eyes into Venus Anadyomene, shading her smooth femininity with her rosy fingers – more from a desire to provoke than to protect her modesty. 'Now fight,' she said, 'and fight stoutly; I shan't give ground or turn tail. Attack head on, if you call yourself a man; no quarter given; die in the breach. There'll be no discharge in this war.' Then climbing on the bed she let herself down slowly on top of me; and rising and falling at a brisk trot and sinuously rocking her supple body backwards and forwards she regaled me to repletion with the delights of Venus in the saddle, until exhausted and totally drained in body and soul alike we simultaneously collapsed, panting for breath, in each other's arms. In encounters of this kind we passed the whole night until dawn without a wink of sleep, from time to time resorting to the wine cup to reinvigorate ourselves, stimulate our desire and renew our pleasure. That was the pattern for many subsequent nights.

One day Byrrhena insisted that I should have dinner with her, 18 and though I made all sorts of excuses she would not take no for an answer. So I had to go to Photis and as it were take the auspices from her. She was reluctant to let me out of her sight, but kindly granted me a short furlough from our campaign of love. 'But look here,' she said, 'mind you get back early. There's a gang of young idiots of good family disturbing the public peace just now. You can see murdered men lying in the open street, and the provincial police are stationed too far away to save the city from these killings. You're well off and an obvious target, and as you're a stranger they won't be bothered about repercussions.' 'Don't worry, Photis dear,' I said. 'Apart from the fact that I'd have preferred my pleasures at home to dining out, I'll set your fears at rest by coming back early. And I shan't go alone either. My trusty sword will be strapped to my side, so I shall be carrying the wherewithal to protect my life.'

So equipped and forewarned I went out to dinner. I found a large 19 company there and, as you would expect in the house of such a great lady, the pick of local society. The sumptuous tables were of polished citron-wood and ivory, and the generous wine cups were all alike valuable in their different styles of beauty. Some were of glass skilfully decorated in relief, some of flawless crystal, some of shining silver or gleaming gold or amber hollowed out with wonderful art, and there were gems to drink from – you name it, it was there, possible or not. Great numbers of footmen in splendid liveries were deftly serving one ample course after another, while boy slaves, curly-haired and prettily dressed, kept on offering vintage wine in cups fashioned from whole gemstones. Now the lamps had been brought in, and the convivial talk reached a crescendo, with hearty laughter and witty quips and pleasantries flying back and forth. At this point Byrrhena asked me: 'Are you enjoying your stay here? My own belief is that when it comes to temples and public baths and buildings of that kind we needn't fear competition from any other city, and as for basic necessities we have all we want and more. The man of leisure can relax here, while the man of affairs will find all the bustle of Rome; and the visitor of limited means can enjoy rural seclusion. In fact, we're the pleasure-resort for the whole province.'

20 'Very true,' I said; 'and I don't think I've ever felt freer anywhere than I have here. But I really dread the dark and inescapable haunts of the magic arts. They say that even the dead aren't safe in their graves, but that their remains are gathered from tombs and funeral pyres, and pieces are snipped from corpses in order to destroy the living; and that at the very moment of the funeral preparations old hags of sorceresses will swoop down to snatch a body before its own people can bury it.' To this another guest added: 'Round here even the living aren't spared. Somebody we know had a similar experience which left him mutilated and totally disfigured.' At this the whole company burst into helpless laughter, and everybody's eyes turned to a man sitting in the corner. He was put out by this unwelcome attention and muttering indignantly got up to go. 'No, do stay for a bit, my dear Thelyphron,' said Byrrhena, 'and like the good fellow you are tell us your story again, so that my son Lucius here can enjoy your agreeable and amusing tale.' 'You, dear madam,' he answered, 'are always kind and considerate, but some people's rudeness is intolerable.' He was evidently upset, but when Byrrhena persisted

and pressed him, unwilling though he was, to tell his story as a personal favour to her, he eventually did as she asked.

So having piled the coverlets into a heap and reclining half upright 21 on one elbow, Thelyphron stretched out his right hand like a man making a formal speech, with the third and fourth fingers bent, the other two extended, and the thumb raised slightly as if in warning, and began. 'I had not yet come of age when I left Miletus to see the Olympic games. Then I wanted to visit this part of your famous province, and so after touring all over Thessaly I came in an evil hour to Larissa. My money was running low, and I was looking round the town in search of some remedy for my poverty, when I saw in the public square a tall old man. He was standing on a stone and loudly announcing that if anybody was willing to watch a corpse, he would negotiate a price. "What's this?" I asked a passer-by. "Are corpses here in the habit of running away?" "No, no," he said. "A mere boy and a stranger like you obviously can't be expected to realize that this is Thessaly you're in, where witches regularly nibble pieces off the faces of the dead to get supplies for their magic art."

' "But tell me, please," I said, "about this business of watching 22 over the dead." "First of all," he said, "you have to stay wide awake for the entire night; you mustn't close your eyes for a second but must keep them firmly fixed on the body. You mustn't let your attention wander or even steal a sidelong glance: these dreadful creatures, who can change themselves into anything, will take on the shape of any animal you like to name and creep up on you in stealth – it's no trouble to them to outwit the eyes even of the Sun or Justice herself. They can take on the forms of birds or dogs or mice or even flies. Then they lull the watchers to sleep with their infernal enchantments. There's no end to the tricks that these vile women contrive to work their wicked will. But the fee for this deadly job isn't as a rule more than five or six gold pieces. Oh, I nearly forgot: if the body isn't intact when it's handed over in the morning, whatever's been removed or mutilated has to be made good from the watcher's own person."

'Having taken this on board, I summoned up my courage and 23 went up to the crier. "You can stop shouting," I said. "Here's a watcher all prepared. Name the price." "You'll get a thousand sesterces," he said. "But look here, young fellow: this is the son of one of our chief citizens who's died, and you must guard his body faithfully against the evil Harpies." "Nonsense," I said, "don't give me that rubbish. You see before you a man of iron, who never sleeps, sharper-eyed than Lynceus or Argus, eyes all over him." I had hardly finished speaking when he took me straight off. The house to which he brought me had its front door closed, and he ushered me in through a small back door, then into a shuttered room where he showed me in the gloom a weeping woman in deep mourning. Standing by her, "Here's a man," he said, "who has engaged himself to guard your husband and is confident he can do the job." She parted the hair that hung down in front to reveal a face that was beautiful even in grief. Looking at me, she said: "Please, I beg you, do your duty with all possible alertness." "You need not worry," I said, "just so long as the fee is satisfactory."

24   'Agreement reached, she rose and took me into another room. There was the body draped in snow-white linen, and when seven witnesses had been brought in she uncovered it herself. After weeping over it for some time she invoked the good faith of those present and proceeded to call off meticulously every feature of the body while one of the witnesses carefully wrote down a formal inventory. "Here you are," she said. "Nose all there, eyes intact, ears entire, lips undamaged, chin in good shape. I ask you, fellow citizens, to note and attest this." The tablets with the list were then sealed and she made to leave the room. But I said: "Please, madam, will you give orders for me to be supplied with everything I'll need?" "What might that be?" she asked. "A large lamp," I said, "and enough oil to last until dawn, and warm water with flagons of wine and a cup, and a plate of left-overs from dinner." She shook her head. "You talk like a fool," she said, "asking for suppers and left-overs in a house of mourning where there hasn't even been a fire lit for days and days. Do you think you're here to enjoy yourself? You would do better to remember where you are and look sad and tearful." With these words she turned to a maid. "Myrrhine," she said, "make

haste and get a lamp and some oil, and then lock up the room and leave him to his watch."

'Left alone with the corpse for company I rubbed my eyes to arm them for their watch, and began to sing to encourage myself. Dusk came, and darkness fell, and time wore on until it was the dead of night. My fear was at its height when there suddenly glided in a weasel which stood in front of me and fixed me with a piercing stare. I was alarmed at seeing this tiny animal so bold. "Get out," I shouted, "you filthy beast, get back to your rat friends before I give you something to remember me by. Will you get out?" It turned and left the room, at which moment I was abruptly plunged into a bottomless abyss of sleep; the god of prophecy himself couldn't have told which of the two of us lying there was deader, so lifeless was I. Indeed I needed somebody to mount guard over me, since I might just as well have been elsewhere.

'The crowing of the crested company was singing truce to darkness when I at last woke up. With my heart in my mouth I rushed over to the body with the lamp, uncovered its face and checked off all the features: they were all there. Now the poor weeping widow, in great anxiety, came bursting in with yesterday's witnesses and fell on the body, covering it with kisses. Then after examining every detail by the light of the lamp she turned and called her steward Philodespotus. Having ordered him to pay over the fee immediately to their trusty watchman, which was done then and there, she added: "We are most grateful to you, young man; and what's more, for this faithful service we shall from now on count you as a particular friend." Delighted at this unexpected windfall and spellbound by the shining gold, which I was now jingling in my hand, "Madam," I said, "count me rather as one of your servants, and whenever you need my services, don't hesitate to command me." The words were scarcely out of my mouth when the whole household, cursing the evil omen, fell on me with every weapon they could lay their hands on. One punched me on the jaw, another thumped me across the shoulders, and a third jabbed me viciously in the ribs; they kicked me, they pulled out my hair, they tore my clothes. So, bloodied and ripped apart like another Pentheus or Orpheus, I was thrown out of the house.

27   'While I was getting my breath back in the street outside, I belatedly realized how thoughtless and ill-omened my words had been, and admitted to myself that I had got off more lightly than I deserved. At this point I saw that the final lamentations and last goodbyes had been uttered, and the corpse had now left the house. As was traditional for a member of an aristocratic family, it was being given a public funeral. The procession was passing through the city square when there appeared an old man in black, weeping and tearing his handsome white hair. Seizing the bier with both hands he cried loudly, his voice choked by sobs: "Citizens! I charge you, as you are true men and loyal subjects, to avenge a murdered fellow citizen and punish this wicked woman as she deserves for her horrible crime. She, and no one else, to please her lover and get her hands on the estate, has poisoned this unfortunate young man, my sister's son." These tearful complaints the old man loudly directed now to this individual and now to that. The crowd began to turn ugly, the probability of the thing leading them to believe his accusation. They called for fire, and started picking up stones and egging on the street-urchins to kill her. She burst into tears (which were obviously rehearsed), and by all that she held sacred called on the gods to witness that she denied this awful crime.

28   'Then the old man said: "Suppose we leave the proof of the truth to divine Providence. We have here in Zatchlas of Egypt a prophet of the first rank. He has already agreed with me a large fee to bring back the soul of the deceased from the Underworld for a short while and restore his body to life." So saying he led forward a young man dressed in a linen tunic and palm-leaf sandals with his head shaved bare. Repeatedly he kissed the man's hands and touched his knees in supplication. "Have pity, O Priest," he said, "have pity by the stars of heaven, by the infernal powers, by the natural elements, by the silences of night and the sanctuaries of Coptos, and by the risings of Nile and the secrets of Memphis and the sistrums of Pharos. Grant him a brief enjoyment of the sun and let a little light into those eyes which are closed for ever. We do not seek to resist Fate or to deny Earth what is rightfully hers; we beg only for a short spell of life so that we may find consolation in vengeance." The prophet,

propitiated, laid some sort of herb on the corpse's mouth and another on his breast. Then turning eastwards he silently invoked the majesty of the rising sun, arousing among the witnesses of this impressive performance excited expectations of a great miracle.

'I joined the crowd, and taking up a position on a tall stone just   29 behind the bier I watched the whole scene curiously. The corpse's chest began to fill, its pulse to beat, its breath to come; it sat up and the young man spoke. "Why, why," he said, "have you called me back for these few moments to life and its obligations, when I have already drunk the water of Lethe and embarked on the marshes of the Styx? Leave me, I beg you, leave me to my rest." To these words of the corpse the prophet returned a sharp answer: "Come now, tell the people everything and clear up the mystery of your death. Don't you know that my incantations can call up Furies and that your weary body can still be tortured?" The man on the bier answered and with a deep groan addressed the people: "I died by the wicked arts of my new wife; doomed to drink her poisoned cup I surrendered my marriage bed to an adulterer before it had grown cold." At this the exemplary widow put on a bold front and began to bandy words with her husband in a blasphemous attempt to rebut his accusations. The people were swayed this way and that, some calling for this abominable woman to be buried alive along with her husband's body, others holding that the corpse was lying and should not be believed.

'However, the young man's next words put an end to their doubts.   30 With another deep groan he said: "I will give you the clearest proof that I speak nothing but the truth, and I will tell you something that nobody else could know or predict." Then he pointed at me. "There is the man," he said, "who guarded my body. He performed his duties with the utmost alertness, so that the hags who were waiting to plunder my corpse, though they changed themselves into all sorts of shapes to achieve their purpose, failed to outwit his vigilance. At last they wrapped a cloud of sleep round him, and while he was buried in deep oblivion they kept calling me by name, until my numbed limbs and chilled body made reluctant efforts to obey their magic summons. But at this point he heard his own name, which is the same as mine, and being in fact alive, though sleeping like the dead, got up without knowing what he was doing and like a lifeless ghost walked mechanically over to the door. Though it had been carefully bolted, there was a hole in it, and through that they cut off first his nose and then his ears; so he suffered the mutilation that was meant for me. Then, so as not to give the game away, they made shapes of his missing ears and nose in wax and fitted them exactly in place. And there he stands, poor devil, paid not for his work but for his disfigurement." Horrified at what I had heard, I started to feel my face. I took hold of my nose, and it came off; I tried my ears, and so did they. Everybody was pointing at me, turning round to look at me, and there was a roar of laughter. Bathed in a cold sweat I slunk away through the crowd, and since then I've not been able to face returning home to be mocked, looking like this. So I've grown my hair long to hide my missing ears, and my shameful nose I keep decently covered with this linen pad.'

31   Directly Thelyphron had finished his story the guests again broke into drunken guffaws. While they were calling for the traditional toast to the god of Laughter, Byrrhena turned to me. 'Tomorrow,' she said, 'we have a festival which is as old as the city and unique to us, when we propitiate the god of Laughter with happy and joyful ritual. That you're here will make it even more agreeable. It would be nice if you could provide some witty diversion in honour of the god that would enhance our celebration of his great power.' 'Right,' I said, 'I'll do as you ask. I'd love to devise some suitably lavish adornment for this great god.' Then, reminded by my servant that night was coming on, and having by now had more than enough to drink, I got up and with a brief good-night to Byrrhena began to make my way unsteadily home.

32   But no sooner were we in the street than the torch on which we were relying was blown out by a gust of wind, leaving us hardly able to see our way in the sudden darkness and stubbing our toes on the stones in our fatigue as we continued on our homeward course, holding on to each other as we went. We were nearly there when suddenly there appeared three strapping fellows who hurled

themselves violently at our front door. Our arrival, so far from deterring them, made them redouble their attacks in competition with each other. Both of us, I in particular, naturally took it that they were robbers of the most savage description, and I at once drew from under my cloak the sword I had brought with me for just such an emergency. Without wasting time I charged into the thick of them, and taking on each in turn as he confronted me I buried it in him to the hilt, until at length, riddled with many gaping wounds, they expired at my feet. When the battle was over, Photis, who had been woken up by the noise, opened the door, and panting and sweating I dragged myself into the house, where, as exhausted as if I had slaughtered Geryon himself rather than three robbers, I fell into bed and passed out.

BOOK 3

*Tried for murder – all a joke which he does not appreciate – Photis
explains – watches Pamphile change herself into an owl and tries to
follow suit – is turned into an ass instead – inhospitable reception
in the stable – frustrated in attempt to break the spell – carried off
by robbers*

1   Rosy-fingered Dawn was just launching her crimson-caparisoned
team heavenwards when I started up from my peaceful sleep to find
that night had given place to day. My mind was in turmoil as I
recollected my exploits of the night before. Squatting on the bed
with my feet drawn up and my hands clasped on my knees I dissolved
into a flood of tears. I imagined the square, the court, the verdict,
the executioner. 'Where shall I find a jury mild and lenient enough
to acquit me, covered in gore from a triple murder and stained with
the blood of all these citizens? So this was the triumphant journey
so confidently predicted by Diophanes the Chaldean!'

I was going over these thoughts again and again and bewailing
my wretched luck, when there was a banging on the front door and
2   much shouting outside. Immediately it was opened, and in they
rushed, filling the whole house with magistrates and their attendants
and a motley crowd of other people. At an order from the magistrates
two of their attendants immediately arrested me – naturally I didn't
resist – and began to take me off. We were hardly outside the door
when the whole town turned out to follow us in a dense throng. I
was trudging along despondently with my head bowed downwards
to the ground – to hell, rather – but what I saw out of the corner
of my eye totally astonished me. In all that huge crowd of people
that surged around me there was nobody who wasn't in fits of
laughter. At length, when we had passed through every street and
I had been led in procession round every corner of the city, like one

of those victims that are paraded from place to place before being
sacrificed to expiate some threatening portent, we came to the
square, and I found myself at the bar of the court. The magistrates
had taken their places up on the bench, and the clerk of the court
was proclaiming silence, when suddenly there was a general demand
for this important trial to be adjourned to the theatre – everybody
shouting that this huge mob was dangerous and that people would
be crushed in it. At once the whole lot of them rushed off and in
no time at all had completely filled the auditorium. People were
packed into the passageways like sardines and were all over the roof;
some were clinging to columns or hanging on to statues; some could
be half glimpsed peering through windows or the coffering of the
ceiling. Nobody was paying the slightest attention to his safety;
everybody was madly eager to see. The officers of the court led me
like some sort of sacrificial victim out across the stage and placed
me in the middle of the orchestra.

Now once more the stentorian voice of the clerk was heard calling
on the prosecutor. An elderly man came forward; but first, to time
his speech, a jar was filled with water; this had holes like a filter,
through which the water ran off drop by drop. He then addressed
the people: 'Worshipful citizens, this is a very important case. It
concerns the peace of our whole community and will constitute a
weighty precedent. It is therefore the solemn duty of each and every
one of you to see to it, for the honour of the city, that this wicked
killer does not escape punishment for the butchery, the series of
bloody murders, that he has committed. I would not have you think
that I am actuated by private hostility or personal anger. I am the
commander of the night watch, and to this day I believe no one has
been able to find fault with my alertness and attention to duty. Let
me then put you in possession of the facts and tell you exactly what
happened last night. It was past midnight, and I was making my
rounds from house to house in the city, paying careful attention to
every detail, when I saw this bloodthirsty young fellow with drawn
sword, dealing death and destruction all around him. Already three
– yes, three – victims of his savagery were breathing their last,
weltering in gore, at his feet. Overcome, as well he might be, by

41

the guilt of his terrible crime, he at once took to his heels and under the cover of darkness slipped into a house where he hid for the rest of the night. But in the morning, thanks be to divine Providence, which never suffers the wrongdoer to escape justice, before he could evade me by some secret byway I cornered him and have had him brought before this august and solemn tribunal. He stands before you, a criminal polluted by repeated murders, caught red-handed, a foreigner. Be firm therefore and condemn this interloper for a crime which even if committed by a fellow citizen you would punish with severity.'

4   With these words my stern accuser ended his brutal indictment. The clerk then told me, if I had anything to say in reply, to begin. At first I could only weep, not so much because of the prosecutor's harshness as because of the reproaches of my own conscience. At last, however, some heaven-sent impulse emboldened me to answer: 'I am only too well aware how difficult it is, when the bodies of three citizens are lying there for all to see, for a man accused of their murder, even though he tells the truth and freely admits that he did it, to persuade this great assembly of his innocence. But if in your kindness you will grant me a short hearing, I shall have no trouble in proving that it is not my fault that I stand here in peril of my life, but that it is because of the unforeseen consequences of an outburst of justifiable indignation that I am subjected to this false and odious accusation.

5   'I was coming back rather late from dinner, a little drunk, I admit – that charge I will not deny – when at the front door of my lodging – I am stopping with your fellow citizen, the worthy Milo – I saw a number of ferocious brigands trying to effect an entry. They were competing with each other to force the front door by tearing it off its hinges, and as they wrenched violently at the bolts, which were firmly shot, they were already debating among themselves how to dispose of the occupants. One of them, the largest and the most violent, was encouraging the others thus: "Come on, lads, to the attack while they're asleep, with manly courage and lively force. Banish all hesitation, all cowardice from your hearts; let slaughter with drawn sword stalk the house. If anybody's asleep, cut

his throat where he lies; if he tries to resist, strike to kill. We'll escape alive only if nobody escapes us." I admit, gentlemen, that, thinking to do my duty as a good citizen and being in great apprehension for my hosts and myself, armed with the sword that I had with me for just such an emergency, I set about routing these desperate villains and putting them to flight. But, savages and brutes that they were, though they saw me sword in hand, so far from making off they boldly stood their ground.

'The battle-lines were drawn up. First their commander and standard-bearer charged me with all his strength, and grabbing me by the hair with both hands and bending me backwards was going to brain me with a stone; but while he was shouting for somebody to give him one, I ran him through with certain aim and left him for dead. Then the second, who was clinging to my legs like a limpet, I accounted for by a nicely judged thrust between the shoulders; and the third, as he ran headlong at me, I transfixed through the chest. So as defender of the peace and protector of my host's house and of the common safety I thought that, so far from being punished, I would be publicly commended. For I have never before had even the most trivial brush with the law; I have always been highly respected in my own city and reckoned an unblemished character the greatest of all blessings. I am at a loss to understand why I am now arraigned like this as a criminal for the just vengeance which I was impelled to take on these abandoned ruffians. Can anybody show that they were personal enemies of mine, or indeed that I had ever set eyes on them before? Or if greed for gain might plausibly have induced me to commit so heinous a crime, where are the profits from it? Produce them – if you can.' 6

I ended my plea by again bursting into tears and stretching my hands out in supplication, invoking the people's pity and everything they held most dear, imploring now this group, now that in my wretchedness. Then, when I thought their sympathies had been aroused and their pity stirred by my tears, I called the eyes of the Sun and of Justice to witness, and was just committing myself and my fate to divine Providence, when I happened to look up and found that everybody in sight was helpless with laughter, and that 7 my excellent host and second father Milo was absolutely doubled up. Seeing this I said to myself: 'So much for good faith! So much for conscience! Here am I, having killed to save my host and on trial for my life; and he, so far from taking my part and comforting me, actually mocks me in my extremity.'

8   At this point a woman ran out from the audience. Weeping, clad in black, she was carrying a small child in her arms; and she was followed by an old woman swathed in dirty rags and like her in tears. Both were waving olive branches. They embraced the bier where the bodies of the dead men lay covered and set up a howl of mourning and lamentation. 'As you are creatures of compassion,' they cried, 'as you are fellow human beings, pity these young men so shamefully done to death, and grant us, widowed and bereaved, the consolation of vengeance. Whatever you do, assist this unfortunate child, left an orphan on life's threshold, and atone for this affront to your laws and public order with this brigand's life.'

There then arose the senior magistrate and addressed the people thus: 'The crime itself, which must be severely punished, even the perpetrator cannot deny. However, one other matter still concerns us: to discover who else was implicated in this monstrous deed. We cannot be expected to believe that a single individual killed those three strong men. So the truth must be extracted from him by torture. The slave who was with him has made off and cannot be found: we have no choice but to put him to the question and force him to identify his accomplices, so that all fear of this dreadful gang can be utterly rooted out.'

9   Thereupon they began to carry in, Greek-style, fire, the wheel, whips of all kinds. This increased, nay doubled, my misery: I was not even to be allowed to die in one piece. But the old woman whose tears had created so much excitement now spoke up again. 'First, noble citizens,' she said, 'before you crucify this brigand who murdered these unfortunate children of mine, allow the bodies of the slain to be revealed, so that as you contemplate their youth and beauty your just indignation may be further inflamed, and the ferocity of your revenge proportioned to the enormity of the crime.' Her words were greeted with applause, and the magistrate then ordered

me to uncover the bodies myself, as they lay on the bier, with my own hand. For a long time I resisted and refused to give a repeat performance of yesterday's deed by this new display of it. However, the officers, on the orders of the magistrates, would take no denial; and in the end they forced my hand from where it hung beside me and made me stretch it out to its own ruination over the bodies. At last, having no choice, I gave in and reluctantly drew back the pall to reveal the corpses. Gods, what a sight! What a miracle! What a sudden alteration in my fortunes! One moment I was already an item of Proserpine's property, one of the household of Orcus, the next the whole aspect of things was reversed and I stood dumb-founded. Words fail me when I try to give an adequate account of what I now saw before me. For those 'bodies' of the slaughtered men were three inflated wineskins gashed open in various places, and, as I recalled my nocturnal battle, the gashes were exactly where I had wounded the robbers.

Hitherto some had been managing to hold in their laughter; now 10 it broke out and took the whole crowd by storm. Some were hooting wildly with glee, others were clasping their stomachs in silent agony. All of them were in an ecstasy of joy, and kept turning to look at me as they made their way out of the theatre. All this time, ever since taking hold of the pall, I had stood like one of the statues or columns in the theatre as if congealed to stone. It was only when Milo came up to me that I returned to life; though I tried to shake him off, bursting into a fresh flood of tears and convulsive sobs, he gently made me take his arm and, choosing unfrequented streets and byways, brought me back to his house. I was still in a state of shock, and though he did his best to comfort me with miscellaneous chit-chat, nothing he could say or do could alleviate my feeling of outrage at the indignity I had suffered, so deeply had it sunk into my heart.

But now the magistrates entered in state and laid themselves out 11 to appease me. 'Master Lucius,' they said, 'we are well aware of both your rank and your ancestry. Your illustrious family is famous throughout Thessaly. These mortifying experiences were not designed as an insult. Banish this sadness from your heart and forget your distress of mind. This diversion, which we ceremoniously stage every year as a public tribute to the kindly god of Laughter, always relies on some fresh stroke of invention for its success. You, as both author and actor of his rites, will from now on wherever you go enjoy his favour and loving companionship; he will never let you suffer grief in your heart but will always make glad your countenance in serenity and grace. For this service the city has unanimously conferred on you its highest honours: it has enrolled you among its patrons and has voted you a statue in bronze.' My reply was brief: 'To this most illustrious of all the cities of Thessaly I return for these great honours appropriate thanks; but as for statues and images, those I ask you to reserve for my elders and betters.'

12   With these modest words and a smile which I summoned up in an attempt to look cheerful, I took a polite leave of the magistrates. Now a slave entered in a hurry. 'A reminder from your aunt Byrrhena,' he said. 'You agreed yesterday to dine with her, and it's almost time.' Dismayed and horrified at the mere thought of her house, I answered: 'Tell her that I wish I could oblige her, but I can't break my word to my host. Milo has made me swear by the god who presides over today's festival to dine with him tonight, and he's with me now and won't let me out of his sight. I promise her it's only a postponement.' I hadn't finished speaking before Milo took me firmly by the arm and, ordering the bathing-gear to follow, led me off to the nearby baths. I avoided people's eyes and shrank from the laughter of the passers-by — laughter for which I was responsible — and walked by his side doing my best to escape notice. How I bathed, how I dried myself, how I got home again, shame prevents me from remembering; all those stares and nods and pointing fingers had reduced me to a state of mental collapse.

13   So, having quickly disposed of Milo's meagre supper, I pleaded a severe headache brought on by continual weeping, and no difficulty was made about letting me go to bed. I threw myself down and was gloomily recalling every detail of what had happened, when at last Photis appeared, having seen her mistress settled for the night. This was a very different Photis, not smiling and saucy but with wrinkled forehead and a downcast expression. At last, slowly and timidly, she

spoke: 'It was me, I've got to confess it; I brought all this trouble on you'; and so saying she took out a strap from her dress and gave it to me. 'Take it,' she said, 'take it, and avenge yourself on a traitress; and don't stop at beating me – no punishment would be too severe. But please, don't think it was my idea to devise this ordeal for you – God forbid that you should suffer the least anxiety because of me! If any misfortune threatens you, I'll shed my life's blood to avert it. It was through sheer bad luck on my part that what I was made to do for quite another reason resulted in your humiliation.'

This revived my habitual curiosity, and eager to get to the bottom   14
of the matter I said: 'As for this most wicked and audacious of straps which you meant me to beat you with, it will perish cut to ribbons at my hands before it touches your soft creamy skin. But tell me truthfully: what was it you did that Fortune perversely turned to my undoing? For I swear by your head that I love so much that nothing and nobody, not even yourself, will persuade me that you ever meant me any harm. And if no harm is intended there can be no blame, whatever accident or mischance may do.' With these words I pressed my lips to my dear Photis' half-closed eyes, and with thirsty kisses drank my fill as they melted and fluttered and brimmed over with yearning desire.

This cheered her up. 'First,' she said, 'let me shut the door firmly,   15
for if I'm overheard indiscreetly revealing these secrets I shall be held guilty of a great crime.' When she had shot the bolts and firmly secured the latch, she came back to me and putting both arms round my neck she began in a low and almost inaudible voice. 'I'm scared,' she said, 'and frankly terrified to disclose what this house conceals and to lay bare my mistress's secrets. But I know I can rely on your character and training: you are a man of noble birth and lofty intellect and have been initiated in several cults, so you well understand when silence is a sacred duty. Whatever secrets therefore I commit to the sanctuary of your pious heart, I beg you to enclose and guard them in that precinct, and repay the frankness of my story by never, never divulging it. In the whole world only I know these things, and it is only because of the love that binds me to you that I reveal them. Now you shall learn what this house really is, now you shall learn

my mistress's wonderful secret powers: through them the dead obey her, the stars change course, the gods do her bidding, the elements are her slaves. But she never resorts more eagerly to her art than when some handsome young man has caught her eye – something that often happens to her.

16 'Just now she is dying for love of a very good-looking young Boeotian, and she is furiously bringing all the tricks and devices of her art to bear on him. Only last night I heard her with my own two ears threatening the Sun himself with foggy gloom and everlasting darkness because he had been too slow in setting and giving way to night for her to be able to practise her enchantments. She had happened to catch sight of this young man yesterday at the barber's, while she was on her way back from the baths, and she told me to glean some of his hair surreptitiously from where it had fallen on the floor from the scissors. I was collecting it as ordered when the barber caught me in the act. We are already notorious all over the city as witches, so he at once pounced on me, shouting and threatening: "You scum, *will* you stop stealing the young gentlemen's hair? You know it's a crime, and if you don't lay off, I'll have you up before the magistrates – I mean it." And adding action to words, he reached right into my bosom to search me and angrily pulled out the hair I'd hidden there. This upset me terribly; knowing what my mistress is like and how when she hasn't got her way in something like this she's lost her temper and beaten me black and blue, I was thinking of running away; then I remembered you and gave that idea up.

17 'I was coming away disconsolate at having to go home empty-handed, when I noticed a man shearing three goatskin bags. They were hanging up, tightly tied and inflated, and the hair was lying on the ground. It was fair, just like that of the young Boeotian; so I carried some of it off and gave it to my mistress without telling her where it really came from. Then, at nightfall, before you came back from dinner, Pamphile, who was now quite beside herself, climbed up to her eyrie. This is on a wooden roof at the back of the house, open to the winds and having views in every direction, particularly towards the east. This is her secret hide-out, admirably

suited to her magical practices. First she set out all the usual apparatus of her infernal laboratory: every kind of strong-smelling drug, metal plaques inscribed with mysterious characters, the remains of birds of ill omen, and a whole array of different parts of dead and buried bodies – here noses and fingers, there nails from gibbets with flesh sticking to them, elsewhere a store of blood from men who have died a violent death, and skulls snatched half eaten from the jaws of wild beasts. Next she intoned a spell over some still quivering entrails 18 and made offerings of various fluids: spring water, cow's milk, mountain honey, and finally honey and wine mixed. Then she knotted and plaited the goat-hair together and threw it with many different perfumes on to the live coals to burn. Immediately, through the irresistible force of her magic art and the hidden power of the deities that she controls, the bodies whose hairs were crackling in the flame took on human life: they felt and heard and walked, and came here, drawn by the reek of their burning hair. It was they, instead of the young man from Boeotia, who were attacking the door in their eagerness to get in. And it was at that moment that you came on the scene drunk, and deceived by the blind darkness of night drew your sword and sprang to arms like another Ajax; but he only attacked and massacred a flock of sheep – you were much braver and slew three blown-up goatskins. You laid low your enemies without shedding a drop of blood, so I now embrace not a homicide but an utricide.'

This pleasantry of Photis' made me laugh, and I took up the joke. 19 'In that case,' I said, 'I can count this as the first of my own heroic exploits, on the model of the Labours of Hercules – for laying low three wineskins is surely equivalent to dealing with three-bodied Geryon or three-headed Cerberus. But I'm happy and willing to forgive you for what you did and what I suffered in consequence – on one condition. Will you do as I earnestly ask you, and show me your mistress when she is actually practising her supernatural arts? I want to see her when she invokes the gods, particularly when she changes shape; for I have a passionate longing to see magic done with my own eyes. You yourself, I'm sure, aren't by any means a novice or amateur in these matters. I know that very well; for though

49

up to now I've always despised the idea of affairs even with women of my own class, you, with those sparkling eyes and cherry lips and shining hair and open-mouthed kisses and sweet-smelling breasts, have absolutely made a slave and chattel of me – and I love it. Now indeed I don't miss my home or want to go back there; a night with you is worth the lot.'

20   'I'd love to do as you ask, Lucius,' Photis answered; 'but she's suspicious by nature and she always shuts herself up in absolute solitude when she performs these secret rituals. But to meet your wishes I'll disregard my own safety, and I'll be on the lookout for a suitable opportunity to do just what you want. But, as I said before, this is deadly serious, and you *must* be religiously discreet about it.' During these whispered exchanges our desire for each other had inflamed our minds and bodies alike. Tearing off our clothes we hurled ourselves stark naked into a Bacchic frenzy of love; and when I was worn out, Photis, by way of encore, generously and unprompted, offered herself to me like a boy. Finally, when our eyes were drooping from lack of sleep, oblivion came upon us and held us fast until it was broad day.

21   We had passed a few more nights of pleasure in this style, when Photis came to me one day in a great state of excitement to tell me that her mistress, having got nowhere in her love-affair by other means, was going that night to feather herself as a bird and fly off to her beloved in that shape, and to warn me to prepare myself, taking due precautions, to watch this great event. So shortly after nightfall, noiselessly and on tiptoe, she took me to the upper room and told me to watch through a crack in the door. This is what I saw. First Pamphile completely stripped herself; then she opened a chest and took out a number of small boxes. From one of these she removed the lid and scooped out some ointment, which she rubbed between her hands for a long time before smearing herself with it all over from head to foot. Then there was a long muttered address to the lamp during which she shook her arms with a fluttering motion. As they gently flapped up and down there appeared on them a soft fluff, then a growth of strong feathers; her nose hardened into a hooked beak, her feet contracted into talons – and Pamphile

BOOK 3

was an owl. Hooting mournfully she took off and landed once or twice to try her wings; then she launched herself in full flight out of the house and away high into the sky.

So Pamphile used her magic arts deliberately to transform herself; 22 whereas I, unenchanted, was so transfixed with amazement simply by this extraordinary scene that I seemed to be anything rather than Lucius. I was completely out of my mind, unhinged with astonishment, not knowing if I was awake or dreaming. For ages I kept rubbing my eyes to see if I was really awake; finally I came to my senses and took Photis by the hand. Putting it to my eyes, 'Please,' I said, 'while we have the opportunity, I implore you, my darling, by those breasts of yours, allow me to enjoy this great and unique proof of your love: give me a little of that ointment. Bind me as your slave for ever by a boon that I can never repay, and make me able to stand beside my Venus as a winged Cupid.' 'Oh, crafty!' she said, 'my lover tells me to make a rod for my own back. Even as you are, I'm hard put to it to keep the local wolf-pack off you; once you're a bird you'll disappear and I'll never see you again.'

'No,' I said, 'heaven preserve me from a crime like that. Though 23 I soared aloft on eagle's wings and roamed through the whole sky as Jove's faithful messenger and proud esquire, I'd leave those exalted honours behind and return without fail to my little nest. I swear by the knot with which you have bound your hair and my heart that Photis is the only girl for me. And then – I've just thought of it – if I'm magicked into that kind of bird, I shall have to give all houses a wide berth. A fine lover for a woman to enjoy an owl would be! Remember that, if such night-birds do get into a house, we see people rush to catch them and nail them to the door to make them expiate by their torments the destruction which their ill-omened flight portends to the family. But I nearly forgot to ask: what shall I have to do or say to shed my wings and return to being Lucius again?' 'So far as that goes, you've nothing to worry about,' she said. 'My mistress has shown me exactly how to restore to human shape anybody who is transformed in this way – not because she is especially fond of me, but so that when she returns home I can administer the antidote. But it's a strange thing that the herbs which produce this

51

great effect are so humble and ordinary: you soak a sprig of dill and some laurel leaves in spring-water, which you then bathe in and drink.'

24   She repeated this recipe several times, then very apprehensively she slipped into the room and took the box out of the chest. I seized it and kissed it, praying that it would grant me good luck on the wing; then I tore off my clothes, and plunging my hands into it scooped out a generous portion of the ointment and rubbed it all over myself; then I flapped my arms up and down in imitation of a bird. But no down or feathers appeared; instead my hair became coarse and shaggy, my soft skin hardened into hide, my fingers and toes lost their separate identity and coalesced into hooves, and from the end of my spine there protruded a long tail. My face became enormous and my mouth widened; my nostrils dilated and my lips hung down; and my ears became monstrously long and hairy. The only redeeming feature of this catastrophic transformation was that my natural endowment had grown too – but how could I embrace

25   Photis like this? In this hapless state I looked myself over and saw that I was now no bird, but an ass; and when I wanted to complain about what Photis had done, I couldn't speak or point like a human being. All I could do was to let my mouth hang open and my eyes fill with tears and look at her sideways in silent reproach. Seeing me like this, Photis hit herself frantically in the face, exclaiming: 'Oh God, that's torn it. I was in such a hurry and so confused that I mistook the box. Never mind, there's an easy way to put things right and change you back. All you need to do is to eat some roses and in a moment the ass will vanish and you'll be back as you were – my Lucius. If only I'd made us some garlands last night as usual, then you needn't have had to put up with this even for as long as one night. But directly it's light I'll rush the remedy to you.'

26   And so she carried on. I meanwhile, though I was now the complete ass and what had been Lucius was a beast of burden, still felt and thought like a man. I wondered long and hard whether I ought to set about this vile and infamous creature with my hooves and teeth and batter her to death. However, I thought better of this rash plan when I remembered that her death would also spell the death of my prospects of rescue. So, lowering and shaking my head,

and swallowing my temporary humiliation, I bowed to my harsh fate and took my place by the side of my own horse, who had carried me so well; and there in the stable I also found another ass belonging to my former host Milo. I imagined that if there were some sort of unspoken natural bond among brute beasts, that horse of mine would have recognized and pitied me and given me the red-carpet treatment as his guest. So much, however, for the gods of hospitality and good faith! That exemplary steed of mine and the ass immediately put their heads together and agreed to do for me. I suppose they were afraid for their own rations, for hardly had they seen me coming towards their manger when down went their ears and they set on me furiously with violent kicks, driving me away from the barley which only last night I had served out with my own hands to this ungrateful servant of mine.

Finding myself received in this way I left them to it and retreated 27
into a corner of the stable. While I was thinking about the behaviour of these colleagues of mine and rehearsing the punishment I would hand out to my faithless horse when the roses had come to my aid and I was Lucius once more, I noticed, halfway up the central pillar which held up the stable roof, an image of Epona sitting in a shrine – and it had been lovingly adorned with garlands of fresh roses! Perceiving my salvation, all eager and hopeful I reared up with a great effort as far as my front feet would reach, and stretching out my neck and pushing out my lips I strained every muscle to get at them. But luck was not on my side. My slave, who had the job of looking after the horse, suddenly saw what I was doing and jumped up indignantly. 'How long, for God's sake,' he shouted, 'are we going to put up with this miserable brute? First it was the other animals' food, now it's the very images of the gods that he's after. But I'll smash the sacrilegious devil, I'll cripple him.' He started looking round for a weapon and found a bundle of wood that happened to be lying there. Sorting out a leafy branch that was larger than all the others he proceeded to give me a fearful thrashing, only leaving off when there was a sudden uproar outside and a violent banging at the door; and as the whole neighbourhood echoed to a cry of 'Thieves!', he fled in terror.

28   Suddenly the doors burst open and there rushed in a gang of robbers, filling the house and surrounding every part of it with cordons of armed men, while others deployed themselves to resist the rescuers who came running from all sides. They were equipped with swords and torches, which lighted up the night; steel and flame gleamed like the rising sun. In the middle of the house there was a storeroom, strongly bolted and barred and crammed with all Milo's treasures. This they attacked and broke into with violent blows of their axes. Having made several openings they brought out all the contents, which they quickly tied up in bundles and shared out among themselves. There was more there than they could carry, but they were not checkmated by this superfluity of riches; they hauled us two asses and my horse out of the stable, loaded us to the limit with the heavier bundles, and drove us from the ransacked house with threats and blows. Leaving one of their number behind to report on any investigation of the crime, they beat us on over untrodden mountain passes at a steady trot.

29   By this time, what with my heavy load and the steep climb up the mountain and the length of the journey, I was practically expiring. At this point, rather late in the day, I had the bright idea of invoking my civil rights and freeing myself from all my troubles by appealing to the sacred name of the Emperor. So when, it being now broad daylight, we were passing through a largeish town with a busy market and a crowd all round us, I tried to call on the august name of Caesar in my native Greek. I did indeed produce a clear and convincing 'O', but the name 'Caesar' itself I couldn't manage. My discordant bray was not appreciated by the robbers, who laid into my wretched hide from all sides until there wasn't enough of it left to make a sieve. But great Jupiter did unexpectedly save me from one fatal mistake. We had passed a number of farms and cottages when I saw a delightful garden where among other attractive plants there were blooming roses fresh with morning dew. Open-mouthed and joyful, with eager hopes of deliverance, I made up to them; but just as I was reaching out with slavering lips I had second and wiser thoughts. If the ass disappeared to reveal me as Lucius, I should certainly meet my death at the hands of the robbers, either on suspicion of being

a wizard or as a possible informer if they were ever brought to justice. So, yielding to necessity, I turned away from the roses and resigning myself to my present situation I behaved as an ass should and munched my bit instead.

BOOK 4

The robbers' stronghold – stories of their recent exploits – arrival of the kidnapped girl Charite – the robbers' housekeeper tells her the story of Cupid and Psyche to comfort her – the story begun

1   At about midday, when it was beginning to get hot under the blazing sun, we stopped at a village with some elderly people who were clearly on good terms with the bandits. Even an ass could see this from their instant recognition and exchange of greetings and long conversations, and from the fact that the robbers presented them with some things they took off my back, and were evidently telling them in a confidential whisper that they were the fruits of brigandage. Then they unloaded us and the other animals and turned us into a nearby field to graze. The prospect of sharing a meal with the other ass and my horse was not attractive, especially as I was still unused to dining off grass. However, just behind the stable I saw a kitchen-garden, and this, as I was now perishing with hunger, I boldly invaded. Having stuffed myself with vegetables, raw as they were, I invoked the whole company of heaven and began to prospect the surrounding area to see if I could find roses in bloom anywhere in the neighbouring gardens. There was nobody else about, so I was pretty confident that if I could sneak away and eat the necessary remedy while hidden in the undergrowth, I could quit my stooping four-footed posture and stand up straight again as a human being without any witnesses.

2   Then while I was tossing about on this sea of thought, I saw a little way off a shady glen in a wood, and there, among all the different plants and luxuriant greenery, was the gleam of bright red roses. This grove I thought – for my mind was not wholly that of

an ass – must belong to Venus and the Graces, seeing the royal splendour of that festive flower glowing there in its dark recesses. So, invoking the benign and propitious god of Success, I took off for the place with such a turn of speed that I felt more like a racehorse than an ass. But all my nimble and heroic efforts were powerless to outrun the perverse malignity of my Fortune. For when I got there it was not roses I saw, delicate and fresh, dripping with divine dew and nectar, sprung from happy briars with blessed thorns, nor was there a glen anywhere in sight, only a river-bank edged with a dense belt of trees. These trees have luxuriant foliage like the laurel and produce long cup-shaped flowers, pale red in colour; in spite of their total lack of smell the countrypeople, knowing no better, call them laurel-roses. To all animals they are deadly poison.

Finding myself trapped in this way by Fate, I madly resolved to 3 renounce my hopes of salvation and take this 'rose'-poison of my own free will. But while I was hesitantly moving to pluck them, a young man, who was presumably the gardener whose vegetables I had plundered, had discovered the damage and came running at me in a fury with a big stick. He grabbed me and showered blows on me, so that my life would have been in danger if I had not eventually had the wit to come to my own assistance. Raising my haunches I let fly at him again and again with my rear hooves and then made my getaway, leaving him lying badly battered on the adjoining slope. But now there appeared over the hilltop a woman, evidently his wife; seeing him stretched out there half dead she rushed down to him wailing and weeping. Her pitiful outcry was likely to be my undoing then and there, for all the villagers, alarmed by her cries, whistled up their dogs and sicked them on from every quarter to tear me apart in their rage. At that moment I was sure I faced death, seeing this pack of huge hounds, capable of taking on bears or lions, bearing furiously down on me. Faced with this situation I gave up my plan of escape and galloped back to our stable. However, the villagers, having with some difficulty restrained their dogs, seized me and tied me to a ring with a stout rope; and would undoubtedly have finished me off with the beating which they proceeded to inflict, had not my belly, stuffed as it was with raw vegetables and so in a highly liquid state, contracted under the pain of the blows and shot out a jet of dung at them. Showered with this noisome fluid and repelled by the stench, my tormentors were driven off, leaving me and my battered behind to ourselves.

4   Soon after this, as evening came on, the robbers led us out of the stable and loaded us, me especially, more heavily than ever. We were well into the next stage of our journey when I came to a decision. I was exhausted with marching, sinking under the weight of my load, worn out by beating, and my sore hooves were making me limp and stumble. We had arrived at a little gently gliding river, and I thought this offered me the opportunity I needed: I would deliberately let my legs go and collapse, resolutely determined not to get up and go on however hard they beat me, prepared indeed to die under their blows or even their sword-thrusts. I reckoned that in my weak and enfeebled state I was entitled to a discharge on medical grounds; surely the robbers would not want to hang around, but would be so eager to press on with their escape that they would divide my load between the other animals and then, as a more severe punishment than any they could devise, leave me a prey to the wolves and vultures.

5   This admirable plan, however, was thwarted by a piece of shocking bad luck. The other ass, as if guessing and anticipating my design, suddenly feigned exhaustion, and collapsing under his load lay as if dead. Though they beat and goaded him and tried every way of getting him back on his feet, hauling him by the tail or the ears or the legs, he made no attempt to rise. At last, becoming weary of such a hopeless business, they put their heads together and decided not to delay their escape by dancing attendance any longer on an ass that was as good as dead or petrified. Dividing his load between me and the horse they drew their swords and cut all his hamstrings, then hauled him a little way off the road and threw him still breathing off the edge of the cliff into the valley below. With the fate of my unfortunate comrade before my eyes I then and there decided to abandon all tricks and deceits and to present myself to my masters in the role of a model ass. For I had overheard them telling each other that our next stopping-place was not far off and that this would

bring our journey to a peaceful end, since it was their permanent
headquarters. So, having climbed a gentle slope, we arrived at our
destination, where our loads were taken off and stowed inside, and
free at last from my burden I tried to shake off my weariness with
a roll in the dust in lieu of a bath.

The subject and the occasion itself demand that I here set out a   6
description of the locality and the cave that was the robbers' abode.
This will be an opportunity to put my literary talent to the proof,
and also to enable you to judge accurately whether my mind and
perceptions were those of an ass. There stood a mountain, wild and
rugged, covered with dense woods and towering to a peak. Its steep
sides, encircled by sharp and inaccessible crags, were traversed by
deep ravines, full of gullies and choked with thorny vegetation;
facing as they did every way they provided a natural defence. From
the summit there gushed out an abundant spring which flowed
down the slope in a cascade of silvery ripples; then, spreading out
into many different branches, it filled the ravines with standing
pools, so enclosing the whole area with a sort of landlocked sea or
slow-moving river. Above the cave, on the lower slopes of the
mountain, arose a high tower. By way of a wall, a stout palisade of
closely woven hurdles, such as are used for sheep-pens, ran all round
it, leaving a narrow entrance in front. A real bandits' reception-room
it was, believe you me. There was nothing else there but a small
hut roughly thatched with reed where, as I later discovered, a
sentry-group of robbers chosen by lot mounted guard each night.

One by one the robbers doubled themselves up and crept into   7
the cave, leaving us securely tied up just outside the entrance. An
old woman, bent with age, who seemed to be in sole charge of the
welfare and comfort of all these young men, now appeared, and was
instantly the target of violent abuse. 'All right,' they shouted, 'you
undertaker's leavings, you disgrace to the human race, you reject of
hell, are you going to sit there twiddling your thumbs and amusing
yourself? What about some late-night refreshment to put heart into
us after all our toils and dangers? All you ever do night and day is
pour down neat wine without stopping for breath into that insatiable
belly of yours.' Shaking with fear the old woman answered in a piping

voice: 'But, gentlemen, my most valiant and faithful protectors, look what I've got waiting for you. There's quantities of savoury stew, done to a turn, all the bread you can eat, and lashings of wine poured out into the cups, which I've polished up specially; and the hot water's all ready as usual for a bath the moment you want it.'

She had hardly finished speaking before they all stripped off and stood naked; after reviving themselves in the warmth of a blazing fire, they washed thoroughly in the hot water and rubbed themselves down with oil. Then they took their places at a dinner-table heaped

8   high with good things. They had scarcely done so when there arrived a much larger group of men, also robbers as anybody could see, since like the others they carried in a mass of booty – gold and silver coin and plate, and gold-embroidered silks. After likewise bathing and refreshing themselves, they joined their comrades at table, and some, chosen by lot, served the meal. As they ate and drank, it was every man for himself: they put away meat in mounds, bread in heaps, and wine non-stop by the gallon. Shouts and jests, talking and singing, abuse and badinage, were the order of the day – it was the Lapiths and Centaurs all over again.

In the middle of all this, one of them, the burliest of the lot, began to orate. 'Here's to us!' he proclaimed. 'We gallantly stormed the house of Milo of Hypata, we've a heap of booty won by our courage, and on top of that we've got back to base without losing a man – and, if it comes to that, with eight more feet on the strength. As for the rest of you, the Boeotian towns contingent, you've come back with heavy casualties and without your brave leader Lamachus, though I'd rate his life as more valuable than this stuff you've brought. What did for him, however it happened, was that he was too brave for his own good. But he was a hero, who will be held in remembrance and honour along with the great kings and generals of legend; whereas you, model brigands that you are, just go sneaking furtively round bath-houses and old women's hovels, ignominiously filching bits of rubbish for your flea-market.'

9   The challenge was immediately taken up by one of the second group. 'You know perfectly well,' he answered, 'that large houses are much easier targets. That's because, even though there are servants

all over a large house, every one is more concerned to look after himself than to safeguard his master's possessions. Simple people who live on their own, if they have any property, large or small, keep it dark, hide it away, and guard it fiercely, defending it with their lives. What happened to us will bear out what I'm saying. Directly we arrived at seven-gated Thebes we carried out the first step of our professional drill, a careful reconnaissance of the wealth of the locals. We found out that there was an enormously rich banker called Chryseros who took great pains to conceal his opulence for fear of being landed with the expense of public office. He lived on his own in seclusion, making do with a small but well-secured little house, sleeping in dirt and rags on bags of gold. So we decided to attack him first, scouting the idea of serious resistance from a lone individual and expecting to carry off all his wealth without exerting ourselves.

'That very night, as soon as it was dark, we mustered in front of the house. We decided not to try to slip the bolts or force the door, let alone break it down, since the noise might rouse the neighbourhood, when we should be done for. Then it was that our noble leader Lamachus, confident in his tried and tested courage, stealthily inserted his hand into the keyhole, intending to wrench the bar loose by force. But meanwhile, if you please, that blot on the human race Chryseros had been awake and taking it all in, and now, slowly creeping up with noiseless footsteps in total silence, he suddenly with one mighty blow fastened our leader's hand to the panel of the door by a huge nail. Then, leaving him there fatally crucified, he climbed to the roof of his hovel and shouted at the top of his voice to summon the neighbours; calling each one by name he gave out that his house had suddenly caught fire, reminding them that this involved the safety of them all. So everybody, frightened by the danger next door, came running in alarm to help. 10

'Now we found ourselves faced with two equally painful altern-atives, to let ourselves be captured or to desert our comrade. On the spur of the moment we hit on a drastic solution: with one carefully directed blow we cut our leader's arm right off at the elbow joint, and leaving the rest of it there we tied up the wound with a 11 thick bandage so that there should be no trail of blood to show which way we went, and hurriedly made off with what remained of Lamachus. We desperately wanted to do our duty by him, but we were hurried into headlong flight by the menacing roar of the crowd and fear of the danger that threatened us, while he could neither keep up with us nor be safely left behind. That hero, lofty of soul and pre-eminent in courage, repeatedly begged and prayed and tearfully adjured us, by the right hand of Mars, by our oath of loyalty, to save a faithful comrade from both torture and capture. How could a brave brigand outlive the loss of his hand, which was his only means of plunder and murder? He would count himself supremely lucky to die willingly by a comrade's hand. But when nothing he could say would induce any of us to commit this self-elected parricide, he drew his sword with his other hand, kissed it lingeringly, and with a mighty thrust drove it straight into his heart. Then we, having paid tribute to our great-hearted leader's valour, wrapped what remained of him carefully in a linen sheet and entrusted it to the sea to hide. And so now our Lamachus is at rest with a whole element as his tomb.

12   'He then ended his life in a manner worthy of his manly virtues. Alcimus, however, could not persuade cruel Fortune to favour his cunning enterprise. He had broken into an old woman's hovel while she was asleep and gone upstairs into her bedroom; but instead of disposing of her then and there by throttling her as he should have done, he chose to throw out her things item by item through the window, which was a largeish one, for us to carry off – at least that was the idea. Having done a thorough job of heaving everything else out, he decided even to include the bed where the old girl was lying asleep. So he tipped her out of it and pulled off the bedclothes, which he was just going to send down after the rest, when the old bitch fell at his feet and pleaded with him: "Look, my son, why are you making a present of a poor old woman's miserable ragged bits and pieces to my rich neighbours? It's their house that this window overlooks." Hearing this, Alcimus was taken in by her cunning ruse and believed every word she said. Of course he was alarmed by the thought that not only what he had already thrown out but also what

he had been going to throw out before he realized his mistake might be finding its way, not to his comrades, but into somebody else's house. So he craned out of the window to have a good look round, particularly to try to assess the wealth of this next-door house that the old woman talked of. This was an enterprising but imprudent move; while he was in this precarious position, with no eyes for anything but what he was looking at, the evil old hag gave him a sudden and unexpected push; feeble as it was, it was enough to send him hurtling down head first. This was from a considerable height, and also he fell on a large stone which lay underneath. His rib-cage was shattered and split open, and he vomited up torrents of blood from deep inside him; he did not suffer long, but died after telling us what had happened. We buried him as we had Lamachus, a worthy attendant on his leader.

'Discouraged by this double bereavement we now abandoned our Theban campaign and went on up to Plataea, the nearest town. There we found everybody talking about someone called Demochares and the gladiatorial show he was going to put on. He was a man of noble birth, enormously rich and correspondingly generous, who was in the habit of providing popular entertainments of a splendour that matched his fortune. It would take more wit and eloquence than I am master of to do justice to each and every aspect of all his various preparations. There were gladiators renowned for their fighting prowess, hunters of proven speed and agility, and desperate criminals with nothing to lose who were being fattened up to fatten the beasts in their turn. There was an elaborate timber structure of several stories like a movable house, and brightly decorated enclosures for the wild-beast show. The number and variety of the animals beggared description, for Demochares had gone to endless trouble to import exotic species to serve as tombs for the condemned. On top of the rest of the outfit for this splendid show he had pretty well used up everything he possessed in procuring a large number of huge bears. Some of these had been caught locally, some bought for vast sums, and some were contributed by the competitive generosity of different friends; all of them he was feeding and looking after with no expense spared.

14   'However, these fine and lavish preparations to entertain the public did not escape the baleful glance of Envy. The bears, exhausted by their prolonged captivity, wilting in the summer heat, and enfeebled by lack of exercise, were attacked by a sudden infection to which nearly every one of them succumbed. On pretty well every street you could see the stranded corpses of these beasts lying half dead. The common people, whose life of squalid poverty forbade them to be fastidious in matters of diet and who had perforce to stay their shrunken stomachs with whatever free food they could find, however repellent, naturally fell on this feast which lay there for the taking. Seeing this, Eubulus here and I hit on an ingenious plan. Choosing a particularly large specimen, we carried off one of the bears to our hideout as if to prepare it for eating. There we skinned it neatly, taking special care to preserve the claws, and leaving the animal's head intact down to the neck-line; we scraped down the whole skin thoroughly, sprinkled it with fine ash, and laid it in the sun to dry. While the moisture was being drawn out of it by the blazing heat, we meanwhile had a fine feed on the meat and issued orders for the coming operation. It was decided that one of us, not just the strongest, but also the bravest, and who above all must be a volunteer, should dress in the bear's skin, and in that guise get himself introduced into Demochares' house. Then, at the right moment, at dead of night, it would be easy for him to open the door and let us in.

15   'Excited by this ingenious scheme many of our valiant brotherhood volunteered for the assignment. Of these Thrasyleon was chosen by popular acclaim to brave the dangers of this perilous stratagem; and, the skin being now pliant and soft to handle, he got into it with a cheerful expression. Then with minute stitches we sewed together the edges of the skin, covering over the seam, which in fact was scarcely noticeable, with the thick hair which surrounded it. We got Thrasyleon to push his head up through the top end of the animal's gullet where the neck had been hollowed out, and made small holes near the nostrils and eyes for him to see and hear through. Then we took our brave comrade, now every inch a bear, to a cage which we had picked up cheap, and into this he immediately marched with strong and steadfast step.

'These preliminaries taken care of, we addressed ourselves to the rest of our masquerade. We had got hold of the name of a Thracian 16 called Nicanor, who was an intimate friend of Demochares, and concocted a letter which purported to come from him, saying that he had dedicated the first fruits of his hunting to embellish his old friend's games. Late in the evening, taking advantage of the darkness, we presented Demochares with the caged Thrasyleon and the spurious letter. Lost in admiration of the beast's size and delighted by his friend's timely generosity, he at once ordered ten gold pieces to be paid from his coffers to us, the bearers of these (as he thought) joyful tidings. People are naturally attracted by new and unexpected sights, so great crowds flocked to admire the beast; while Thrasyleon cleverly discouraged too close an inspection by frequent threatening charges at the bars. The whole town joined in celebrating the good fortune and happiness of Demochares, who after the wholesale loss of his animals had somehow managed with this fresh supply to outface Fortune.

'He now ordered the bear to be transferred immediately with all due care to his park in the country. Here, however, I intervened. "This bear," I said, "is tired out from the hot sun and the long 17 journey. I would advise you, sir, not to introduce it into the company of a lot of other animals – who, I'm told, aren't in very good health. Wouldn't it be better to look around for some open and well-ventilated place in your house, if possible next to a pond, where it's cool? As I'm sure you know, this type of animal always makes its home in woods and damp caves and by pleasant springs." Demochares was alarmed by my warning, and remembering how many animals he had previously lost he agreed without more ado, and readily allowed us to choose a place for the cage. "And what's more," I said, "we are quite happy to mount guard by the cage all night. The bear is worn out with heat and harassment, and we'll do a more careful job of feeding and watering it at the proper time and in the way it's used to." "No, thanks," he answered, "we don't need any help from you. Most of my people have had plenty of practice in feeding bears."

'After this we took our leave. As we emerged from the city-gate 18 we noticed a large tomb standing at some distance from the road in a retired and unfrequented spot. We found there a number of mouldering and half-closed coffins, the dwelling-places of men long turned to dust and ashes, and some of these we opened up as hiding-places for the booty we were expecting. In accordance with professional practice, we waited for the moon to set, the time when sleep, mounting its first and most vigorous offensive, attacks and overpowers the minds of men. Then, when the time came, our party armed itself and mustered outside Demochares' front door to keep our appointment with plunder. Thrasyleon was equally punctual in picking the exact time of night for banditry. Creeping out of his cage he lost no time in dispatching with his sword every one of the attendants who were sleeping nearby. Then he dealt similarly with the doorkeeper, and possessing himself of the man's key he opened the doors for us. In a moment we were inside and had taken complete possession of the house, and he was showing us the strongroom, where he had been quick to note a quantity of silver plate being put away the evening before. We at once broke it open by a concerted charge, and I told off the rest of the party to take as much gold or silver as they could carry and entrust it quickly to the incorruptible safekeeping of the dead, and then to come back at the double for another load. I meanwhile would act in the general interest by taking up a position near the front door and keeping a careful lookout in all directions while they were away – for I thought that the sight of the bear careering around the house would be enough to deter any of the household we might happen to wake up. Anybody, however strong and brave, encountering such a huge beast, especially at dead of night, would certainly take to his heels, lock the door of his room in a panic, and stay there.

19   'All this sound and careful planning, however, was thwarted by Ill Success. While I was on tenterhooks waiting for my comrades to return, a slave, woken up I suppose by the noise – no doubt divine influence was at work – quietly emerged and saw the bear running about all over the house. Without making a sound he withdrew and managed to pass on what he had seen to the entire household. Within seconds the whole place was filled with hordes of slaves.

The darkness vanished in a blaze of light from torches, lamps, tapers, candles, and everything else you can think of. Every man jack of them emerged with a weapon of some kind; each one equipped with a cudgel or a spear or even a drawn sword, they blocked off all the entrances. At the same time they were sicking on their hunting-dogs – long-eared shaggy brutes – to bring the beast down. As the uproar grew I began to beat a gradual retreat, but as I was 20 hiding behind the door I had a fine view of the wonderful show that Thrasyleon was putting up against the dogs. Though he knew his last hour had come, he remained true to himself, his comrades, and the courage which never left him, fighting back with the jaws of Cerberus yawning before him. Indeed, as long as the breath was in his body he kept up the role for which he had volunteered: with various bearlike postures and movements he would now retreat, now stand at bay, until finally he managed to get clear of the house. However, even in the open street he could not escape, for all the dogs from the neighbourhood – a large and ferocious pack – appeared in a body to join forces with the hunting-dogs, who had likewise followed hot on his heels. It was a grim and pitiful spectacle to see our friend Thrasyleon surrounded and beset by these packs of ravening dogs and torn apart by innumerable bites.

'Finally I couldn't bear this painful sight any longer, and worming my way into the milling crowd I tried to assist my comrade discreetly in the only way possible by dissuading the leaders of the hunt. "This is an outrage!" I shouted. "This is a magnificent animal, and a valuable one, that we're destroying." However, my artful intervention did 21 not help my unfortunate friend, for there now ran out of the house a tall strong fellow who without a moment's hesitation thrust a spear right into the bear's vitals. Another immediately followed suit, and then several more mastered their fears and competed with each other to come to close quarters and plunge in their swords. As for Thrasyleon, the pride and glory of our band, his great spirit, ever worthy to be held in honour, was finally taken by storm, but there was no surrender. True to his oath he let no human cry or scream escape him, but horribly mauled and grievously wounded as he was he went on bellowing and growling like a beast, and endured his

inevitable doom with noble fortitude. And so his life he surrendered
to destiny, but his glory he kept for himself. However, so great was
the terror and awe that he had inspired in the mob that it was dawn
– broad day, indeed – before anybody dared even to touch the beast,
motionless as it was. Finally in fear and trembling a butcher, more
daring than the rest, slit open the beast's belly and stripped our hero
of his bear's skin. Thus Thrasyleon was lost to us, but in his glory
he will live on. The rest of us hurriedly packed up the bundles which
the faithful dead had been guarding for us and left the territory of
Plataea by forced marches. On our way we pondered in our minds
this fact: it is no wonder that Good Faith is nowhere to be found
in this life, for she has gone to live among the spirits of the dead in
disgust at human perfidy. And so, every man worn out with our
heavy loads and the rough road, and mourning the loss of three
comrades, we have brought back the booty you see.'

22   At the end of this story they pledged the memory of their dead
comrades in arms in neat wine drunk from gold cups; then they
sang some hymns to Mars to propitiate him, and went to sleep for
a while. To us the old woman doled out quantities of fresh barley
without stint. My horse thought this generous spread, which he had
all to himself, a real Salian banquet. As for me, I had only ever eaten
barley finely milled and in the form of porridge, so I investigated
the corner where the surplus bread was stored, and there I gave my
jaws, which had become enfeebled and cobwebbed from long fasting,
a good work-out. But then late at night the robbers woke up and
took the field again; variously equipped, some armed with swords,
some got up as ghosts, they marched off at a smart pace. As for me,
not even the onset of sleep could check my steady and steadfast
munching. When I was Lucius, I could leave the table content with
one or two rolls; now, enslaved to my bottomless belly, I was already
on my third basketful. I was still intent on my task when broad day
found me at it.

23   In the end, however, I was induced by my asinine sense of fitness
to tear myself reluctantly away and slake my thirst at a nearby stream.
Just then the robbers reappeared in an unusual state of excitement
and agitation. They were carrying nothing whatever in the way of

loot, not so much as a rag or bone; having turned out every man on the strength, armed to the teeth, all they had brought back was one young girl. You had only to look at her to see that she was of high birth, one of the provincial nobility, as her dress indicated – and extremely desirable, even to an ass like me. They brought her into the cave, sobbing and tearing her hair and clothes, and tried to calm her distress with soothing words. 'You needn't be alarmed,' they told her, 'either about your life or your honour. It's only the pressure of poverty that has driven us to this calling. Just be patient while we realize our profit – it won't be very long. Your parents are enormously rich, and however miserly they may be, they'll soon come up with a proper ransom for their own flesh and blood.'

They went on with this sort of soft soap for some time, but it did 24 nothing to assuage her grief. She simply put her head between her hands and sobbed and sobbed. They then called the old woman in and told her to sit by the girl and comfort her as best she could with soothing chit-chat while they went about their usual business. But nothing the old woman could say would divert the girl from her grief: she bewailed her fate with even more piercing cries and her whole body shook with her sobs – I too was forced to weep in sympathy. 'Haven't I a right to be miserable?' she cried. 'Torn away from my beautiful home, my host of attendants, my dear servants, my honoured parents, made the booty and chattel of a calamitous robbery, imprisoned like a slave in this rocky dungeon, this torture-chamber, despoiled of all the luxuries to which I was born and bred, in peril of my life, among all these robbers and this horrible gang of cutthroats – how can I stop weeping or even go on living?'

She continued lamenting like this until, sick at heart, hoarse with crying, and completely worn out, she let her eyelids droop and dozed off. But her eyes had hardly closed when she suddenly started 25 up from sleep like a madwoman and fell on herself even more violently, belabouring her breast with fierce blows and punching that lovely face of hers. The old woman pressed her to explain this fresh outbreak of grief; but all she would say, with an even deeper sigh, was: 'No, no, this is the end; I'm finished now, completely done for – goodbye now to all hope of rescue. A noose or a sword or a clifftop, that's the only way left for me.' This irritated the old woman, and looking at her crossly she asked her what in God's name she was crying for and why when she had just got off nicely to sleep she should all of a sudden start up these overdone wailings again. 'I know what you're thinking,' she said; 'you're planning to do the lads out of the handsome profit they expect from your ransom. If you keep this up, I'll see to it myself, for all your tears – and they don't cut much ice with robbers – that you're burned alive.'

26   The girl was frightened by this and kissed the old woman's hands. 'Have mercy on me, mother,' she said, 'and of your kindness and pity help me a little in my desperate plight. For, full of years as you are, I can't believe, when I look at your venerable white hairs, that compassion has altogether withered away in you. Now, listen to my story; it's a real tragedy. Imagine a handsome young man, the leader of his age-group. The city has unanimously elected him a Son of the People; he's also my cousin, just three years older than me. We were brought up together as children, and we grew up as inseparable companions in the same house, even sharing a room and a bed. We were pledged to each other by chaste affection on both sides, and we had for a long time been engaged to be married. Our parents had given their consent, he was named in the marriage-contract as my husband, and surrounded by a crowd of friends and relations who had come to honour the occasion he was sacrificing in the temples and shrines of the city. The whole house, a bower of laurel and ablaze with torchlight, was resounding to the marriage-hymn. My unhappy mother was embracing me and arraying me in my bridal finery, and with many loving kisses and many an anxious prayer was already looking forward to grandchildren – when at that moment there was a sudden invasion of armed men, a scene of savage warfare, the glittering menace of naked blades. They did not set themselves to kill or plunder, but burst straight into our room in a tightly packed mass. None of our servants fought back or put up the least resistance, and they snatched me, half dead with pitiful fright and overcome by cruel terror, from my mother's arms. And

that is how my marriage, like those of Attis and Protesilaus, was broken up and brought to nothing. But now my wretchedness has 27 been renewed and redoubled by a dreadful nightmare. I thought I had been rudely snatched from my home, my room, my bridal chamber, and my bed, and was lost in the wilderness calling the name of my unfortunate husband; and he, just as he was when torn from my arms, perfumed and garlanded, was following in my tracks while I fled from him on feet over which I had no control. As he was loudly lamenting the rape of his beautiful wife and calling on the people to help him, one of the robbers, enraged by this troublesome pursuit, seized a large stone from the ground and with it killed my unhappy young husband. It was because I was terrified by this ghastly vision that I woke up in a sudden panic from my ill-omened sleep.'

The old woman was sighing in sympathy with the girl's tears. 'Cheer up, little lady,' she answered, 'and don't be frightened by an empty dream – it doesn't mean anything. Everybody says that daytime dreams are untrue; and what's more important, night-time dreams generally foretell the opposite of what actually happens. So weeping or being beaten, or sometimes even being murdered, is a promise of money and profit, whereas smiling or stuffing yourself with sweetmeats or meeting a lover is a sign that grief or illness and all sorts of other misfortunes are in store. But come, now let me take your mind off your troubles: here's a pretty fairytale, an old woman's story' – and with that she began

The Story of Cupid and Psyche

There was once a city with a king and queen who had three beautiful 28 daughters. The two eldest were very fair to see, but not so beautiful that human praise could not do them justice. The loveliness of the youngest, however, was so perfect that human speech was too poor to describe or even praise it satisfactorily. Indeed huge numbers of both citizens and foreigners, drawn together in eager crowds by the fame of such an extraordinary sight, were struck dumb with admiration of her unequalled beauty; and putting right thumb and forefinger to their lips they would offer outright religious worship to her as the goddess Venus. Meanwhile the news had spread through the nearby cities and adjoining regions that the goddess born of the blue depths of the sea and fostered by its foaming waves had made public the grace of her godhead by mingling with mortal men; or at least that, from a new fertilization by drops from heaven, not sea but earth had grown another Venus in the flower of her virginity.

29 And so this belief exceeded all bounds and gained ground day by day, ranging first through the neighbouring islands, then, as the report made its way further afield, through much of the mainland and most of the provinces. Now crowds of people came flocking by long journeys and deep-sea voyages to view this wonder of the age. No one visited Paphos or Cnidos or even Cythera to see the goddess herself; her rites were abandoned, her temples disfigured, her couches trampled, her worship neglected; her statues were ungarlanded, her altars shamefully cold and empty of offerings. It was the girl to whom prayers were addressed, and in human shape that the power of the mighty goddess was placated. When she appeared each morning it was the name of Venus, who was far away, that was propitiated with sacrifices and offerings; and as she walked the streets the people crowded to adore her with garlands and flowers.

This outrageous transference of divine honours to the worship of a mortal girl kindled violent anger in the true Venus, and unable to contain her indignation, tossing her head and protesting in deep

30 bitterness, she thus soliloquized: 'So much for me, the ancient mother of nature, primeval origin of the elements, Venus nurturer of the whole world: I must go halves with a mortal girl in the honour due to my godhead, and my name, established in heaven, is profaned by earthly dirt! It seems that I am to be worshipped in common and that I must put up with the obscurity of being adored by deputy, publicly represented by a girl – a being who is doomed to die! Much good it did me that the shepherd whose impartial fairness was approved by great Jove preferred me for my unrivalled beauty to those great goddesses! But she will rue the day, whoever she is,

when she usurped my honours. I'll see to it that she regrets this beauty of hers to which she has no right.'

So saying, she summoned that winged son of hers, that most reckless of creatures, whose wicked behaviour flies in the face of public morals, who armed with torch and arrows roams at night through houses where he has no business, ruining marriages on every hand, committing heinous crimes with impunity, and never doing such a thing as a good deed. Irresponsible as he already was by nature, she aroused him yet more by her words; and taking him to the city and showing him Psyche – this was the girl's name – she 31 laid before him the whole story of this rival beauty. Groaning and crying out in indignation, 'By the bonds of a mother's love,' she said, 'I implore you, by the sweet wounds of your arrows, by the honeyed burns made by your torch, avenge your mother – avenge her to the full. Punish mercilessly that arrogant beauty, and do this one thing willingly for me – it's all I ask. Let this girl be seized with a burning passion for the lowest of mankind, some creature cursed by Fortune in rank, in estate, in condition, someone so degraded that in all the world he can find no wretchedness to equal his own.'

With these words, she kissed her son with long kisses, open-mouthed and closely pressed, and then returned to the nearest point of the seashore. And as she set her rosy feet on the surface of the moving waves, all at once the face of the deep sea became bright and calm. Scarcely had she formed the wish when immediately, as if she had previously ordered it, her marine entourage was prompt to appear. There came the daughters of Nereus singing in harmony, Portunus with his thick sea-green beard, Salacia, the folds of her robe heavy with fish, and little Palaemon astride his dolphin. On all sides squadrons of Tritons cavorted over the sea. One softly sounded his loud horn, a second with a silken veil kept off the heat of her enemy the Sun, a third held his mistress's mirror before her face, and others yoked in pairs swam beneath her car. Such was the retinue that escorted Venus in her progress to Ocean.

Psyche meanwhile, for all her striking beauty, had no joy of it. 32 Everyone feasted their eyes on her, everyone praised her, but no one, king, prince, or even commoner, came as a suitor to ask her in marriage. Though all admired her divine loveliness, they did so merely as one admires a statue finished to perfection. Long ago her two elder sisters, whose unremarkable looks had enjoyed no such widespread fame, had been betrothed to royal suitors and achieved rich marriages; Psyche stayed at home an unmarried virgin mourning her abandoned and lonely state, sick in body and mind, hating this beauty of hers which had enchanted the whole world. In the end the unhappy girl's father, sorrowfully suspecting that the gods were offended and fearing their anger, consulted the most ancient oracle of Apollo at Miletus, and implored the great god with prayers and sacrifices to grant marriage and a husband to his slighted daughter. But Apollo, though Greek and Ionian, in consideration for the writer of a Milesian tale, replied in Latin:

33
          On mountain peak, O King, expose the maid
            For funeral wedlock ritually arrayed.
          No human son-in-law (hope not) is thine,
            But something cruel and fierce and serpentine;
          That plagues the world as, borne aloft on wings,
            With fire and steel it persecutes all things;
          That Jove himself, he whom the gods revere,
            That Styx's darkling stream regards with fear.

The king had once accounted himself happy; now, on hearing the utterance of the sacred prophecy, he returned home reluctant and downcast, to explain this inauspicious reply, and what they had to do, to his wife. There followed several days of mourning, of weeping, of lamentation. Eventually the ghastly fulfilment of the terrible oracle was upon them. The gear for the poor girl's funereal bridal was prepared; the flame of the torches died down in black smoke and ash; the sound of the marriage-pipe was changed to the plaintive Lydian mode; the joyful marriage-hymn ended in lugubrious wailings; and the bride wiped away her tears with her own bridal veil. The whole city joined in lamenting the sad plight of the afflicted family, and in sympathy with the general grief all public business was immediately suspended.

34   However, the bidding of heaven had to be obeyed, and the

unfortunate Psyche was required to undergo the punishment
ordained for her. Accordingly, amid the utmost sorrow, the ceremonies of her funereal marriage were duly performed, and escorted
by the entire populace Psyche was led forth, a living corpse, and in
tears joined in, not her wedding procession, but her own funeral.
While her parents, grief-stricken and stunned by this great calamity,
hesitated to complete the dreadful deed, their daughter herself
encouraged them: 'Why do you torture your unhappy old age with
prolonged weeping? Why do you weary your spirit – my spirit
rather – with constant cries of woe? Why do you disfigure with
useless tears the faces which I revere? Why by tearing your eyes do
you tear mine? Why do you pull out your white hairs? Why do you
beat your breasts, those breasts which to me are holy? These, it
seems, are the glorious rewards for you of my incomparable beauty.
Only now is it given to you to understand that it is wicked Envy
that has dealt you this deadly blow. Then, when nations and peoples
were paying us divine honours, when with one voice they were
hailing me as a new Venus, that was when you should have grieved,
when you should have wept, when you should have mourned me
as already lost. Now I too understand, now I see that it is by the
name of Venus alone that I am destroyed. Take me and leave me
on the rock to which destiny has assigned me. I cannot wait to enter
on this happy marriage, and to see that noble bridegroom of mine.
Why should I postpone, why should I shirk my meeting with him
who is born for the ruin of the whole world?'

After this speech the girl fell silent, and with firm step she joined 35
the escorting procession. They came to the prescribed crag on the
steep mountain, and on the topmost summit they set the girl and
there they all abandoned her; leaving there too the wedding torches
with which they had lighted their path, extinguished by their tears,
with bowed heads they took their way homeward. Psyche's unhappy
parents, totally prostrated by this great calamity, hid themselves away
in the darkness of their shuttered palace and abandoned themselves
to perpetual night. Her, however, fearful and trembling and
lamenting her fate there on the summit of the rock, the gentle breeze
of softly breathing Zephyr, blowing the edges of her dress this way

and that and filling its folds, imperceptibly lifted up; and carrying her on his tranquil breath smoothly down the slope of the lofty crag he gently let her sink and laid her to rest on the flowery turf in the bosom of the valley that lay below.

BOOK 5

The story of Cupid and Psyche continued

In this soft grassy spot Psyche lay pleasantly reclining on her bed of   1
dewy turf and, her great disquiet of mind soothed, fell sweetly asleep.
Presently, refreshed by a good rest, she rose with her mind at ease.
What she now saw was a park planted with big tall trees and a spring
of crystal-clear water. In the very centre of the garden, by the outflow
of the spring, a palace had been built, not by human hands but by
a divine craftsman. Directly you entered you knew that you were
looking at the pleasure-house of some god – so splendid and delightful
it was. For the coffering of the ceiling was of citron-wood and ivory
artfully carved, and the columns supporting it were of gold; all the
walls were covered in embossed silver, with wild beasts and other
animals confronting the visitor on entering. Truly, whoever had so
skilfully imparted animal life to all that silver was a miracle-worker
or a demigod or indeed a god! Furthermore, the very floors were
divided up into different kinds of pictures in mosaic of precious
stones: twice indeed and more than twice marvellously happy those
who walk on gems and jewellery! As far and wide as the house
extended, every part of it was likewise of inestimable price. All the
walls, which were built of solid blocks of gold, shone with their
own brilliance, so that the house furnished its own daylight, sun or
no sun; such was the radiance of the rooms, the colonnades, the
very doors. The rest of the furnishings matched the magnificence
of the building, so that it would seem fair to say that great Jove had
built himself a heavenly palace to dwell among mortals.

2   Drawn on by the delights of this place, Psyche approached and, becoming a little bolder, crossed the threshold; then, allured by her joy in the beautiful spectacle, she examined all the details. On the far side of the palace she discovered lofty storehouses crammed with rich treasure; there is nothing that was not there. But in addition to the wonder that such wealth could exist, what was most astonishing was that this vast treasure of the entire world was not secured by a single lock, bolt, or guard. As she gazed at all this with much pleasure there came to her a disembodied voice: 'Mistress, you need not be amazed at this great wealth. All of it is yours. Enter then your bedchamber, sleep off your fatigue, and go to your bath when you are minded. We whose voices you hear are your attendants who will diligently wait on you; and when you have refreshed yourself

3   a royal banquet will not be slow to appear for you.' Psyche recognized her happy estate as sent by divine Providence, and obeying the instructions of the bodiless voice she dispelled her weariness first with sleep and then with a bath. There immediately appeared before her a semicircular seat; seeing the table laid she understood that this provision was for her entertainment and gladly took her place. Instantly course after course of wine like nectar and of different kinds of food was placed before her, with no servant to be seen but everything wafted as it were on the wind. She could see no one but merely heard the words that were uttered, and her waiting maids were nothing but voices to her. When the rich feast was over, there entered an invisible singer, and another performed on a lyre, itself invisible. This was succeeded by singing in concert, and though not a soul was to be seen, there was evidently a whole choir present.

4   These pleasures ended, at the prompting of dusk Psyche went to bed. Night was well advanced when she heard a gentle sound. Then, all alone as she was and fearing for her virginity, Psyche quailed and trembled, dreading, more than any possible harm, the unknown. Now there entered her unknown husband; he had mounted the bed, made her his wife, and departed in haste before sunrise. At once the voices that were in waiting in the room ministered to the new bride's slain virginity. Things went on in this way for some little time; and, as is usually the case, the novelty of her situation

78

became pleasurable to her by force of habit, while the sound of the unseen voice solaced her solitude.

Meanwhile her parents were pining away with ceaseless grief and sorrow; and as the news spread her elder sisters learned the whole story. Immediately, sad and downcast, they left home and competed with each other in their haste to see and talk to their parents. That night her husband spoke to Psyche – for though she could not see him, her hands and ears told her that he was there – as follows: 'Sweetest Psyche, my dear wife, Fortune in yet more cruel guise threatens you with mortal danger: I charge you to be most earnestly on your guard against it. Your sisters, believing you to be dead, are now in their grief following you to the mountain-top and will soon be there. If you should hear their lamentations, do not answer or even look that way, or you will bring about heavy grief for me and for yourself sheer destruction.' She agreed and promised to do her husband's bidding, but as soon as he and the night had vanished together, the unhappy girl spent the whole day crying and mourning, constantly repeating that now she was utterly destroyed: locked up in this rich prison and deprived of intercourse or speech with human beings, she could not bring comfort to her sisters in their sorrow or even set eyes on them. Unrevived by bath or food or any other refreshment and weeping inconsolably she retired to rest.

It was no more than a moment before her husband, earlier than usual, came to bed and found her still in tears. Taking her in his arms he remonstrated with her: 'Is this what you promised, my Psyche? I am your husband: what am I now supposed to expect from you? What am I supposed to hope? All day, all night, even in your husband's arms, you persist in tormenting yourself. Do then as you wish and obey the ruinous demands of your heart. Only be mindful of my stern warning when – too late – you begin to be sorry.' Then with entreaties and threats of suicide she forced her husband to agree to her wishes: to see her sisters, to appease their grief, to talk with them. So he yielded to the prayers of his new bride, and moreover allowed her to present them with whatever she liked in the way of gold or jewels, again and again, however, repeating his terrifying warnings: she must never be induced by the evil advice of her sisters to discover what her husband looked like, or allow impious curiosity to hurl her down to destruction from the heights on which Fortune had placed her, and so for ever deprive her of his embraces. Psyche thanked her husband and, happier now in her mind, 'Indeed,' she said, 'I will die a hundred deaths before I let myself be robbed of this most delightful marriage with you. For I love and adore you to distraction, whoever you are, as I love my own life; Cupid himself cannot compare with you. But this too I beg you to grant me: order your servant Zephyr to bring my sisters to me as he brought me here' – and planting seductive kisses, uttering caressing words, and entwining him in her enclosing arms, she added to her endearments 'My darling, my husband, sweet soul of your Psyche.' He unwillingly gave way under the powerful influence of her murmured words of love, and promised to do all she asked; and then, as dawn was now near, he vanished from his wife's arms.

7   The sisters inquired the way to the rock where Psyche had been left and hurriedly made off to it, where they started to cry their eyes out and beat their breasts, so that the rocky crags re-echoed their ceaseless wailings. They went on calling their unhappy sister by name, until the piercing noise of their shrieks carried down the mountainside and brought Psyche running out of the palace in distraction, crying: 'Why are you killing yourselves with miserable lamentation for no reason? I whom you are mourning, I am here. Cease your sad outcry, dry now your cheeks so long wet with tears; for now you can embrace her for whom you were grieving.' Then she summoned Zephyr and reminded him of her husband's order. On the instant he obeyed her command and on his most gentle breeze at once brought them to her unharmed. Then they gave themselves over to the enjoyment of embraces and eager kisses; and coaxed by their joy the tears which they had restrained now broke out again. 'But now,' said Psyche, 'enter in happiness my house and
8   home and with your sister restore your tormented souls.' With these words she showed them the great riches of the golden palace and let them listen to the retinue of slave-voices, and refreshed them sumptuously with a luxurious bath and the supernatural splendours of her table. They, having enjoyed to the full this profusion of divine

riches, now began deep in their hearts to cherish envy. Thus one of them persisted with minute inquiries, asking who was the master of this heavenly household and who or what was Psyche's husband. Psyche, however, scrupulously respected her husband's orders and did not allow herself to forget them; she improvised a story that he was a handsome young man whose beard had only just begun to grow and that he spent most of his time farming or hunting in the mountains. Then, fearing that if the conversation went on too long some slip would give away her secret thoughts, she loaded them with gold plate and jewellery, immediately summoned Zephyr, and handed them over to him for their return journey.

No sooner said than done. The worthy sisters on their return 9 home were now inflamed by the poison of their growing envy, and began to exchange vociferous complaints. So then the first started: 'You see the blindness, the cruelty and injustice of Fortune! – content, it would seem, that sisters of the same parents should fare so differently. Here are we, the elder sisters, handed over to foreign husbands as slaves, banished from our home, our own country, to live the life of exiles far from our parents, while she, the youngest, the offspring of a late birth from a worn-out womb, enjoys huge wealth and a god for husband. Why, she doesn't even know how to make proper use of all these blessings. You saw, sister, all the priceless necklaces, the resplendent stuffs, the sparkling gems, the gold everywhere underfoot. If this husband of hers is as handsome as she says, she is the happiest woman alive. Perhaps, though, as he learns to know her and his love is strengthened, her god-husband will make her a goddess too. Yes, yes, that's it: that explains her behaviour and her attitude. She's already looking to heaven and fancying herself a goddess, this woman who has voices for slaves and lords it over the winds themselves. And I, God help me, am fobbed off with a husband older than my father, bald as a pumpkin and puny as a child, who keeps the whole house shut up with bolts and bars.'

Her sister took up the refrain: 'And I have to put up with a 10 husband bent double with rheumatism and so hardly ever able to give me what a woman wants. I'm always having to massage his twisted, stone-hard fingers, spoiling these delicate hands of mine with stinking compresses and filthy bandages and loathsome plasters – so that it's not a dutiful wife I look like but an overworked sick-nurse. You must decide for yourself, sister, how patiently – or rather slavishly, for I shall say frankly what I think – you can bear this; as for me, I can no longer stand the sight of such good fortune befalling one so unworthy of it. Do you remember the pride, the arrogance, with which she treated us? How her boasting, her shameless showing off, revealed her puffed-up heart? With what bad grace she tossed us a few scraps of her vast wealth and then without more ado, tiring of our company, ordered us to be thrust – blown – whistled away? As I'm a woman, as sure as I stand here, I'll hurl her down to ruin from her great riches. And if you too, as you have every right to do, have taken offence at her contemptuous treatment of us, let us put our heads together to devise strong measures. Let us not show these presents to our parents or to anybody else, and let us pretend not to know even whether she is alive or dead. It's enough that we've seen what we wish we hadn't, without spreading this happy news of her to them and to the rest of the world. You aren't really rich if nobody knows that you are. She is going to find out that she has elder sisters, not servants. Now let us return to our husbands and go back to our homes – poor but decent – and then when we've thought things over seriously let us equip ourselves with an even firmer resolve to punish her insolence.'

11   The two evil women thought well of this wicked plan, and having hidden all their precious gifts, they tore their hair and clawed their cheeks (no more than they deserved), renewing their pretence of mourning. In this way they inflamed their parents' grief all over again; and then, taking a hasty leave of them, they made off to their homes swollen with mad rage, to devise their wicked – their murderous – plot against their innocent sister. Meanwhile Psyche's mysterious husband once more warned her as they talked together that night: 'Don't you see the danger that threatens you? Fortune is now engaging your outposts, and if you do not stand very firmly on your guard she will soon be grappling with you hand to hand. These treacherous she-wolves are doing their best to lay a horrible

trap for you; their one aim is to persuade you to try to know my face – but if you do see it, as I have constantly told you, you will not see it. So then if those vile witches come, as I know they will, armed with their deadly designs, you must not even talk to them; but if because of your natural lack of guile and tenderness of heart you are unequal to that, at least you must refuse to listen to or answer any questions about your husband. For before long we are going to increase our family; your womb, until now a child's, is carrying a child for us in its turn – who, if you hide our secret in silence, will be divine, but if you divulge it, he will be mortal.' Hearing this, Psyche, blooming with happiness, clapped her hands at the consoling thought of a divine child, exulting in the glory of this pledge that was to come and rejoicing in the dignity of being called a mother. Anxiously she counted the growing tale of days and months as they passed, and as she learned to bear her unfamiliar burden she marvelled that from a moment's pain there should come so fair an increase of her rich womb.

But now those plagues, foulest Furies, breathing viperine poison and pressing on in their devilish haste, had started their voyage; and once more her transitory husband warned Psyche: 'The day of reckoning and the last chance are here. Your own sex, your own flesh and blood, are the enemy, arrayed in arms against you; they have marched out and drawn up their line, and sounded the trumpet-call; with drawn sword your abominable sisters are making for your throat. What disasters press upon us, sweetest Psyche! Have pity on yourself and on us both; remember your duty and control yourself, save your home, your husband, and this little son of ours from the catastrophe that threatens us. You cannot call those wicked women sisters any longer; in their murderous hatred they have spurned the ties of blood. Do not look at them, do not listen to them, when like the Sirens aloft on their crag they make the rocks ring with their deadly voices.'

As she replied, Psyche's voice was muffled by sobs and tears: 'More than once, I know, you have put my loyalty and discretion to the proof, but none the less now you shall approve my strength of mind. Only once more order our Zephyr to do his duty, and

83

instead of your own sacred face that is denied me let me at least behold my sisters. By those fragrant locks that hang so abundantly, by those soft smooth cheeks so like mine, by that breast warm with hidden heat, as I hope to see your face at least in this little one: be swayed by the dutiful prayers of an anxious suppliant, allow me to enjoy my sisters' embrace, and restore and delight the soul of your devoted Psyche. As to your face, I ask nothing more; even the darkness of night does not blind me; I have you as my light.' Enchanted by her words and her soft embrace, her husband dried her tears with his hair, promised to do as she asked, and then left at once just as day was dawning.

14   The two sisters, sworn accomplices, without even visiting their parents, disembarked and made their way at breakneck speed straight to the well-known rock, where, without waiting for their conveying wind to appear, they launched themselves with reckless daring into the void. However, Zephyr, heeding though reluctantly his royal master's commands, received them in the embrace of his gentle breeze and brought them to the ground. Without losing a second they immediately marched into the palace in close order, and embracing their victim these women who belied the name of sister, hiding their rich store of treachery under smiling faces, began to fawn on her: 'Psyche, not little Psyche any longer, so you too are a mother! Only fancy what a blessing for us you are carrying in your little pocket! Think of the joy and gladness for our whole house! Imagine what pleasure we shall take in raising this marvellous child! If he is, as he ought to be, as fair as his parents, it will be a real Cupid that will be born.'

15   With such pretended affection did they little by little make their way into their sister's heart. Then and there she sat them down to recover from the fatigues of their journey, provided warm baths for their refreshment, and then at table entertained them splendidly with all those wonderful rich eatables and savoury delicacies of hers. She gave an order, and the lyre played; another, and there was pipe-music; another, and the choir sang. All these invisible musicians soothed with their sweet strains the hearts of the listeners. Not that the malice of the wicked sisters was softened or quieted even by the honeyed

sweetness of the music; directing their conversation towards the trap their guile had staked out they craftily began to ask Psyche about her husband, his family, his class, his occupation. She, silly girl that she was, forgetting what she had said before, concocted a new story and told them that her husband was a prosperous merchant from the neighbouring province, a middle-aged man with a few white hairs here and there. However, she did not dwell on this for more than a moment or two, but again returned them to their aerial transport loaded with rich gifts.

No sooner were they on their way back, carried aloft by Zephyr's calm breath, than they began to hold forth to each other: 'Well, sister, what is one to say about that silly baggage's fantastic lies? Last time it was a youth with a fluffy beard, now it's a middle-aged man with white hair. Who is this who in a matter of days has been suddenly transformed into an old man? Take it from me, sister, either the little bitch is telling a pack of lies or she doesn't know what her husband looks like. Whichever it is, she must be relieved of those riches of hers without more ado. If she doesn't know his shape, obviously it is a god she has married and it's a god her pregnancy will bring us. All I can say is, if she's called – God forbid – the mother of a divine child, I'll hang myself and be done with it. Meanwhile then let us go back to our parents, and we'll patch together the most colourable fabrication we can to support what we've agreed on.'

On fire with this idea they merely greeted their parents in passing; and having spent a disturbed and wakeful night, in the morning they flew to the rock. Under the protection as usual of the wind they swooped down in a fury, and rubbing their eyelids to bring on the tears they craftily accosted the girl: 'There you sit, happy and blessed in your very ignorance of your misfortune and careless of your danger, while we can't sleep for watching over your welfare, and are suffering acute torments in your distress. For we know for a fact, and you know we share all your troubles and misfortunes, so we cannot hide it from you, that it is an immense serpent, writhing its knotted coils, its bloody jaws dripping deadly poison, its maw gaping deep, if only you knew it, that sleeps with you each night. Remember now the Pythian oracle, which gave out that you were fated to wed a wild beast. Many peasants and hunters of the region and many of your neighbours have seen him coming back from feeding and bathing in the waters of the nearby river. They all say that it won't be for long that he will go on fattening you so obligingly, but that as soon as the fullness of your womb brings your pregnancy to maturity and you are that much more rich and enjoyable a prize, he will eat you up. Well, there it is; it's you who must decide whether to take the advice of your sisters who are worried for your life, and escape death by coming to live in safety with us, or be entombed in the entrails of a savage monster. However, if a country life and musical solitude, and the loathsome and dangerous intimacy of clandestine love, and the embraces of a venomous serpent, are what appeals to you, at all events your loving sisters will have done their duty.'

Then poor Psyche, simple and childish creature that she was, was seized by fear at these grim words. Beside herself, she totally forgot all her husband's warnings and her own promises, and hurled herself headlong into an abyss of calamity. Trembling, her face bloodless and ghastly, she scarcely managed after several attempts to whisper from half-opened lips: 'Dearest sisters, you never fail in your loving duty, as is right and proper, and I do not believe that those who have told you these things are lying. For I have never seen my husband's face and I have no idea where he comes from; only at night, obeying his voice, do I submit to this husband of unknown condition – one who altogether shuns the light; and when you say that he must be some sort of wild beast, I can only agree with you. For he constantly terrifies me with warnings not to try to look at him, and threatens me with a fearful fate if I am curious about his appearance. So if you can offer some way of escape to your sister in her peril, support her now: for if you desert me at this point, all the benefits of your earlier concern will be lost.'

The gates were now thrown open, and these wicked women stormed Psyche's defenceless heart; they ceased sapping and mining, drew the swords of their treachery, and attacked the panic-stricken thoughts of the simple-minded girl. First one began: 'Since the ties of blood forbid us to consider danger when your safety is at stake, let us show you the only way that can save you, one that we have long planned. Take a very sharp blade and give it an additional edge by stropping it gently on your palm, then surreptitiously hide it on your side of the bed; get ready a lamp and fill it with oil, then when it is burning brightly put it under cover of a jar of some kind, keeping all these preparations absolutely secret; and then, when he comes, leaving his furrowed trail behind him, and mounts the bed as usual, as he lies outstretched and, enfolded in his first heavy sleep, begins to breathe deeply, slip out of bed and with bare feet taking tiny steps one by one on tiptoe, free the lamp from its prison of blind darkness; and consulting the light as to the best moment for your glorious deed, with that two-edged weapon, boldly, first raising high your right hand, with powerful stroke, there where the deadly serpent's head and neck are joined – cut them apart. Our help will not be wanting; the instant you have secured yourself by his death, we shall be anxiously awaiting the moment to fly to you; then we will take all these riches back along with you and make a desirable marriage for you, human being to human being.'

Their sister had been on fire; these words kindled her heart to a 21 fierce flame. They immediately left her, fearing acutely to be found anywhere near such a crime. Carried back as usual on the wings of the wind and deposited on the rock, they at once made themselves scarce, embarked, and sailed away. But Psyche, alone now except for the savage Furies who harried her, was tossed to and fro in her anguish like the waves of the sea. Though she had taken her decision and made up her mind, now that she came to put her hand to the deed she began to waver, unsure of her resolve, torn by the conflicting emotions of her terrible situation. Now she was eager, now she would put it off; now she dared, now she drew back; now she was in despair, now in a rage; and, in a word, in one and the same body she loathed the monster and loved the husband. However, when evening ushered in the night, she hurried to prepare for her dreadful deed. Night came, and with it her husband, who, having first engaged on the field of love, fell into a deep sleep.

Then Psyche, though naturally weak in body, rallied her strength 22 with cruel Fate reinforcing it, produced the lamp, seized the blade, and took on a man's courage. But as soon as the light was brought out and the secret of their bed became plain, what she saw was of all wild beasts the most soft and sweet of monsters, none other than Cupid himself, the fair god fairly lying asleep. At the sight the flame of the lamp was gladdened and flared up, and her blade began to repent its blasphemous edge. Psyche, unnerved by the wonderful vision, was no longer mistress of herself: feeble, pale, trembling and powerless, she crouched down and tried to hide the steel by burying it in her own bosom; and she would certainly have done it, had not the steel in fear of such a crime slipped and flown out of her rash hands. Now, overcome and utterly lost as she was, yet as she gazed and gazed on the beauty of the god's face, her spirits returned. She saw a rich head of golden hair dripping with ambrosia, a milk-white neck, and rosy cheeks over which there strayed coils of hair becomingly arranged, some hanging in front, some behind, shining with such extreme brilliance that the lamplight itself flickered uncertainly. On the shoulders of the flying god there sparkled wings, dewy-white with glistening sheen, and though they were at rest the soft delicate down at their edges quivered and rippled in incessant play. The rest of the god's body was smooth and shining and such as Venus need not be ashamed of in her son. At the foot of the bed lay a bow, a quiver, and arrows, the gracious weapons of the great god.

23 Curious as ever, Psyche could not restrain herself from examining and handling and admiring her husband's weapons. She took one of the arrows out of the quiver and tried the point by pricking her thumb; but as her hands were still trembling she used too much force, so that the point went right in and tiny drops of blood bedewed her skin. Thus without realizing it Psyche through her own act fell in love with Love. Then ever more on fire with desire for Desire she hung over him gazing in distraction and devoured him with quick sensuous kisses, fearing all the time that he might wake up. Carried away by joy and sick with love, her heart was in turmoil; but meanwhile that wretched lamp, either through base treachery, or in jealous malice, or because it longed itself to touch such beauty and as it were to kiss it, disgorged from its spout a drop

of hot oil on to the right shoulder of the god. What! Rash and reckless lamp, lowly instrument of love, to burn the lord of universal fire himself, when it must have been a lover who first invented the lamp so that he could enjoy his desires for even longer at night! The god, thus burned, leapt up, and seeing his confidence betrayed and sullied, flew off from the loving embrace of his unhappy wife without uttering a word.

But as he rose Psyche just managed to seize his right leg with 24 both hands, a pitiful passenger in his lofty flight; trailing attendance through the clouds she clung on underneath, but finally in her exhaustion fell to the ground. Her divine lover did not abandon her as she lay there, but alighting in a nearby cypress he spoke to her from its lofty top with deep emotion: 'Simple-minded Psyche, forgetting the instructions of my mother Venus, who ordered that you should be bound by desire for the lowest of wretches and enslaved to a degrading marriage, I myself flew to you instead as your lover. But this I did, I know, recklessly; I, the famous archer, wounded myself with my own weapons and made you my wife – so that, it seems, you might look on me as a monster and cut off this head which carries these eyes that love you. This is what I again and again advised you to be always on your guard against; this is what I repeatedly warned of in my care for you. But those worthy counsellors of yours shall speedily pay the price of their pernicious teaching; your punishment shall merely be that I shall leave you.' And with these last words he launched himself aloft on his wings.

Psyche, as she lay and watched her husband's flight for as long as 25 she could see him, grieved and lamented bitterly. But when with sweeping wings he had soared away and she had altogether lost sight of him in the distance, she threw herself headlong off the bank of a nearby stream. But the gentle river, in respect it would seem for the god who is wont to scorch even water, and fearing for himself, immediately bore her up unharmed on his current and landed her on his grassy bank. It happened that the country god Pan was sitting there with the mountain nymph Echo in his arms, teaching her to repeat all kinds of song. By the bank his kids browsed and frolicked at large, cropping the greenery of the river. The goat-god, aware no matter how of her plight, called the lovesick and suffering Psyche to him kindly and caressed her with soothing words: 'Pretty child, I may be a rustic and a herdsman, but age and experience have taught me a great deal. If I guess aright – and this indeed is what learned men style divination – from these tottering and uncertain steps of yours, and from your deathly pallor, and from your continual sighing, and from your swimming eyes, you are desperately in love. Listen to me then, and do not try to destroy yourself again by jumping off heights or by any other kind of unnatural death. Stop weeping and lay aside your grief; rather adore in prayer Cupid, greatest of gods, and strive to earn his favour, young wanton and pleasure-loving that he is, through tender service.'

26   These were the words of the herdsman-god. Psyche made no reply, but having worshipped his saving power went on her way. But when she had wandered far and wide with toilsome steps, as day waned she came without realizing it by a certain path to the city where the husband of one of her sisters was king. On discovering this, Psyche had herself announced to her sister. She was ushered in, and after they had exchanged greetings and embraces she was asked why she had come. Psyche replied: 'You remember the advice you both gave me, how you persuaded me to kill with two-edged blade the monster who slept with me under the false name of husband, before he swallowed me up, poor wretch, in his greedy maw. I agreed; but as soon as with the conniving light I set eyes on his face, I saw a wonderful, a divine spectacle, the son of Venus himself, I mean Cupid, deeply and peacefully asleep. But as I was thrilling to the glorious sight, overwhelmed with pleasure but in anguish because I was powerless to enjoy it, by the unhappiest of chances the lamp spilt a drop of boiling oil on to his shoulder. Aroused instantly from sleep by the pain, and seeing me armed with steel and flame, "For this foul crime," he said, "leave my bed this instant and take your chattels with you. I shall wed your sister" – and he named you – "in due form." And immediately he ordered Zephyr to waft me outside the boundaries of his palace.'

27   Before Psyche had finished speaking, her sister, stung by frantic lust and malignant jealousy, concocted on the spot a story to deceive

her husband, to the effect that she had had news of her parents' death, and immediately took ship and hurried to the well-known rock. There, though the wind was blowing from quite a different quarter, yet besotted with blind hope she cried: 'Receive me, Cupid, a wife worthy of you, and you, Zephyr, bear up your mistress', and with a mighty leap threw herself over. But not even in death did she reach the place she sought: for as she fell from one rocky crag to another she was torn limb from limb, and she died providing a banquet of her mangled flesh, as she so richly deserved, for the birds of prey and wild beasts. The second vengeance soon followed. For Psyche again in her wanderings arrived at another city, where her second sister likewise lived. She too was no less readily taken in by her sister's ruse, and eager to supplant her in an unhallowed marriage she hurried off to the rock and fell to a similar death.

Meanwhile, as Psyche was scouring the earth, bent on her search 28 for Cupid, he lay groaning with the pain of the burn in his mother's chamber. At this point a tern, that pure white bird which skims over the sea-waves in its flight, plunged down swiftly to the very bottom of the sea. There sure enough was Venus bathing and swimming; and perching by her the bird told her that her son had been burned and lay suffering from the sharp pain of his wound and in peril of his life. Now throughout the whole world the good name of all Venus' family was besmirched by all kinds of slanderous reports. People were saying: 'He has withdrawn to whoring in the mountains, she to swimming in the sea; and so there is no pleasure anywhere, no grace, no charm, everything is rough, savage, uncouth. There are no more marriages, no more mutual friendships, no children's love, nothing but endless squalor and repellent, distasteful, and sordid couplings.' Such were the slanders this garrulous and meddlesome bird whispered in Venus' ear to damage her son's honour. Venus was utterly furious and exclaimed: 'So then, this worthy son of mine has a mistress? You're the only servant I have that I can trust: out with it, the name of this creature who has debauched a simple childish boy – is it one of the tribe of the Nymphs, or one of the number of the Hours, or one of the choir of the Muses, or one of my attendant Graces?' The voluble bird answered promptly: 'I do not know, my lady; but I think it's a girl called Psyche, if I remember rightly, whom he loves to distraction.' Venus, outraged, cried out loud: 'Psyche is it, my rival in beauty, the usurper of my name, whom he loves? Really? I suppose my lord took me for a go-between to introduce him to the girl?'

29   Proclaiming her wrongs in this way she hurriedly left the sea and went at once to her golden bedchamber, where she found her ailing son as she had been told. Hardly had she passed through the door when she started to shout at him: 'Fine goings-on, these, a credit to our family and your character for virtue! First you ride roughshod over your mother's – no, your sovereign's – orders, by not tormenting my enemy with a base amour; then you, a mere child, actually receive her in your vicious adolescent embraces, so that I have to have my enemy as my daughter-in-law. I suppose you think, you odious good-for-nothing lecher, that you're the only one fit to breed and that I'm now too old to conceive? Let me tell you, I'll bear another son much better than you – better still, to make you feel the insult more, I'll adopt one of my household slaves and give *him* those wings and torch, and bow and arrows too, and all that gear of mine, which I didn't give you to be used like this – for there

30   was no allowance for this outfit from your father's estate. But you were badly brought up from a baby, quarrelsome, always insolently hitting your elders. Your own mother, me I say, you expose and abuse every day, battering me all the time, despising me, I suppose, as an unprotected female – and you're not afraid of that mighty warrior your stepfather. Naturally enough, seeing that you're in the habit of providing him with girls, to torment me with his infidelities. But I'll see to it that you're sorry for these games and find out that this marriage of yours has a sour and bitter taste. But now, being mocked like this, what am I to do? Where am I to turn? How am I to control this reptile? Shall I seek assistance from Sobriety, when I have so often offended her through this creature's wantonness? No, I won't, I won't, have any dealings with such an uncouth and unkempt female. But then the consolation of revenge isn't to be scorned, whatever its source. Her aid and hers alone is what I must enlist, to administer severe correction to this layabout, to undo his

quiver, blunt his arrows, unstring his bow, put out his torch, and coerce him with some sharper corporal medicine. I'll believe that his insolence to me has been fully atoned for only when she has shaved off the locks to which I have so often imparted a golden sheen by my caressing hands, and cut off the wings which I have groomed with nectar from my own breasts.'

With these words she rushed violently out in a fury of truly Venerean anger. The first persons she met were Ceres and Juno, who seeing her face all swollen with rage, asked her why she was frowning so grimly and spoiling the shining beauty of her eyes. To which she answered: 'You've come just at the right moment to satisfy the desire with which my heart is burning. Please, I beg you, do your utmost to find that runaway fly-by-night Psyche for me, for you two must be well aware of the scandal of my house and of what my son – not that he deserves the name – has been doing.' They, knowing perfectly well what had happened, tried to soothe Venus' violent rage: 'Madam, what has your son done that's so dreadful that you are determined to thwart his pleasures and even want to destroy the one he loves? Is it really a crime, for heaven's sake, to have been so ready to give the glad eye to a nice girl? Don't you realize that he is a young man? You must have forgotten how old he is now. Perhaps because he carries his years so prettily, he always seems a boy to you? Are you, a mother and a woman of sense, to be forever inquiring into all his diversions, checking his little escapades, and showing up his love-affairs? Aren't you condemning in your fair son your own arts and pleasures? Gods and men alike will find it intolerable that you spread desire broadcast throughout the world, while you impose a bitter constraint on love in your own family and deny it admission to your own public academy of gallantry.' In this way, fearful of his arrows, did they flatter Cupid in his absence with their ingratiating defence of his cause. But Venus took it ill that her grievances should be treated so lightly, and cutting them short made off quickly in the other direction, back towards the sea.

31

BOOK 6

*The story of Cupid and Psyche concluded — Lucius is lamed and
condemned to death by the robbers — makes a break for freedom
with Charite on his back — recaptured — Charite condemned to
death with him*

1   Psyche meanwhile was wandering far and wide, searching day and
night for her husband, and the sicker she was at heart, the more
eager she was, if she could not mollify him by wifely endearments,
at least to appease his anger by beseeching him as a slave. Seeing a
temple on the top of a steep hill, 'Perhaps,' said she, 'my lord lives
there'; at once she made for it, her pace, which had flagged in her
unbroken fatigues, now quickened by hope and desire. Having
stoutly climbed the lofty slopes she approached the shrine. There
she saw ears of corn, some heaped up, some woven into garlands,
together with ears of barley. There were also sickles and every kind
of harvesting gear, all lying anyhow in neglect and confusion and
looking, as happens in summer, as if they had just been dropped
from the workers' hands. All these things Psyche carefully sorted
and separated, each in its proper place, and arranged as they ought
to be, thinking evidently that she should not neglect the shrines or
worship of any god, but should implore the goodwill and pity of
them all.

2   She was diligently and busily engaged on this task when bountiful
Ceres found her, and with a deep sigh said: 'So, poor Psyche! There
is Venus in her rage dogging your footsteps with painstaking inquiries
through the whole world, singling you out for dire punishment,
and demanding revenge with the whole power of her godhead; and
here are you taking charge of my shrine and thinking of anything
rather than your own safety.' Psyche fell down before her, and

bedewing her feet with a flood of tears, her hair trailing on the ground, she implored the goddess's favour in an elaborate prayer: 'I beseech you, by this your fructifying hand, by the fertile rites of harvest, by the inviolate secrets of the caskets, by the winged chariot of your dragon-servants, by the furrows of the Sicilian fields, by the car that snatches and the earth that catches, by your daughter Proserpine's descent to her lightless wedding and her return to bright discovery, and all else that the sanctuary of Attic Eleusis conceals in silence: support the pitiful spirit of your suppliant Psyche. Allow me to hide for only a very few days among these heaps of corn, until the great goddess's fierce anger is soothed by the passing of time or at least until my strength is recruited from the fatigues of long suffering by an interval of rest.' Ceres answered: 'Your tearful prayers 3 indeed move me and make me wish to help you; but I cannot offend my kinswoman, who is a dear friend of long standing and a thoroughly good sort. So you must leave this place at once, and think yourself lucky that you are not my prisoner.'

Disappointed and rebuffed, the prey of a double sadness, Psyche was retracing her steps, when in the half-light of a wooded valley which lay before her she saw a temple built with cunning art. Not wishing to neglect any prospect, however doubtful, of better hopes, but willing to implore the favour of any and every god, she drew near to the holy entrance. There she saw precious offerings and cloths lettered in gold affixed to trees and to the doorposts, attesting the name of the goddess to whom they were dedicated in gratitude for her aid. Then, kneeling and embracing the yet warm altar, she wiped away her tears and prayed: 'Sister and consort of great Jove, 4 whether you are at home in your ancient shrine on Samos, which alone glories in having seen your birth, heard your first cries, and nourished your infancy; or whether you dwell in your rich abode in lofty Carthage, which worships you as a virgin riding the heavens on a lion; or whether by the banks of Inachus, who hails you now as bride of the Thunderer and queen of goddesses, you rule over the famous citadel of Argos; you who are worshipped by the whole East as Zygia and whom all the West calls Lucina: be in my desperate need Juno who Saves, and save me, worn out by the great sufferings

I have gone through, from the danger that hangs over me. Have I not been told that it is you who are wont to come uncalled to the aid of pregnant women when they are in peril?' As she supplicated thus, Juno immediately manifested herself in all the awesome dignity of her godhead, and replied: 'Believe me, I should like to grant your prayers. But I cannot for shame oppose myself to the wishes of my daughter-in-law Venus, whom I have always loved as my own child. Then too I am prevented by the laws which forbid me to receive another person's runaway slaves against their master's wishes.'

5 Psyche was completely disheartened by this second shipwreck that Fortune had contrived for her, and with no prospect of finding her winged husband she gave up all hope of salvation. So she took counsel with herself: 'Now what other aid can I try, or bring to bear on my distresses, seeing that not even the goddesses' influence can help me, though they would like to? Trapped in this net, where can I turn? What shelter is there, what dark hiding-place, where I can escape the unavoidable eyes of great Venus? No, this is the end: I must summon up a man's spirit, boldly renounce my empty remnants of hope, give myself up to my mistress of my own free will, and appease her violence by submission, late though it will be. And perhaps he whom I have sought so long may be found there in his mother's house.' So, prepared for submission with all its dangers, indeed for certain destruction, she thought over how she should begin the prayer she would utter.

6 Venus, however, had given up earthbound expedients in her search, and set off for heaven. She ordered to be prepared the car that Vulcan the goldsmith god had lovingly perfected with cunning workmanship and given her as a betrothal present – a work of art that made its impression by what his refining tools had pared away, valuable through the very loss of gold. Of the many doves quartered round their mistress's chamber there came forth four all white; stepping joyfully and twisting their coloured necks around they submitted to the jewelled yoke, then with their mistress on board they gaily took the air. The car was attended by a retinue of sportive sparrows frolicking around with their noisy chatter, and of other sweet-voiced birds who, singing in honey-toned strains, harmoni-

ously proclaimed the advent of the goddess. The clouds parted, heaven opened for his daughter, and highest Aether joyfully welcomed the goddess; great Venus' tuneful entourage has no fear of ambushes from eagles or rapacious hawks.

She immediately headed for Jove's royal citadel and haughtily 7 demanded an essential loan – the services of Mercury, the loud-voiced god. Jove nodded his dark brow, and she in triumph left heaven then and there with Mercury, to whom she earnestly spoke: 'Arcadian brother, you know well that your sister Venus has never done anything without Mercury's assistance, and you must be aware too of how long it is that I have been trying in vain to find my skulking handmaid. All we can do now is for you as herald to make public proclamation of a reward for her discovery. Do my bidding then at once, and describe clearly the signs by which she can be recognized, so that if anybody is charged with illegally concealing her, he cannot defend himself with a plea of ignorance'; and with these words she gave him a paper with Psyche's name and the other details. That done, she returned straight home.

Mercury duly obeyed her. Passing far and wide among the peoples 8 he carried out his assignment and made proclamation as ordered: 'If any man can recapture or show the hiding-place of a king's runaway daughter, the slave of Venus, by name Psyche, let him report to Mercury the crier behind the South turning-point of the Circus, and by way of reward for his information he shall receive from Venus herself seven sweet kisses and an extra one deeply honeyed with the sweetness of her thrusting tongue.' This proclamation of Mercury's and the desire for such a reward aroused eager competition all over the world. Its effect on Psyche was to put an end to all her hesitation. As she neared her mistress's door she was met by one of Venus' household named Habit, who on seeing her cried out at the top of her voice: 'At last, you worthless slut, you've begun to realize you have a mistress? Or will you with your usual impudence pretend you don't know how much trouble we've had looking for you? A good thing you've fallen into *my* hands; you're held in the grip of Orcus, and you can be sure you won't have to wait long for the punishment of your disobedience.' So saying, she laid violent hands 9 on Psyche's hair and dragged her inside unresisting. As soon as Venus saw her brought in and presented to her, she laughed shrilly, as people do in a rage; and shaking her head and scratching her right ear, 'So,' she said, 'you have finally condescended to pay your respects to your mother-in-law? Or is it your husband you've come to visit, who lies under threat of death from the wound you've dealt him? But don't worry, I will receive you as a good daughter-in-law deserves.' Then, 'Where are my handmaids Care and Sorrow?' she asked. They were called in, and Psyche was handed over to them to be tormented. In obedience to their mistress's orders they whipped the wretched girl and afflicted her with every other kind of torture, and then brought her back to face the goddess. Venus, laughing again, exclaimed: 'Look at her, trying to arouse my pity through the allurement of her swollen belly, whose glorious offspring is to make me, thank you very much, a happy grandmother. What joy, to be called grandmother in the flower of my age and to hear the son of a vile slave styled Venus' grandson! But why am I talking about sons? This isn't a marriage between equals, and what's more it took place in the country, without witnesses, and without his father's consent, and can't be held to be legitimate. So it will be born a bastard, if indeed I allow you to bear it at all.'

10   With these words, she flew at Psyche, ripped her clothes to shreds, tore her hair, boxed her ears, and beat her unmercifully. Then she took wheat and barley and millet and poppy-seed and chick-peas and lentils and beans, mixed them thoroughly all together in a single heap, and told Psyche: 'Now, since it seems to me that, ugly slave that you are, you can earn the favours of your lovers only by diligent drudgery, I'm now going to put your merit to the test myself. Sort out this random heap of seeds, and let me see the work completed this evening, with each kind of grain properly arranged and separated.' And leaving her with the enormous heap of grains, Venus went off to a wedding-dinner. Psyche did not attempt to touch the disordered and unmanageable mass, but stood in silent stupefaction, stunned by this monstrous command. Then there appeared an ant, one of those miniature farmers; grasping the size of the problem, pitying the plight of the great god's bedfellow and execrating her

mother-in-law's cruelty, it rushed round eagerly to summon and convene the whole assembly of the local ants. 'Have pity,' it cried, 'nimble children of Earth the all-mother, have pity and run with all speed to the aid of the sweet girl-wife of Love in her peril.' In wave after wave the six-footed tribes poured in to the rescue, and working at top speed they sorted out the whole heap grain by grain, separated and distributed the seed by kinds, and vanished swiftly from view.

At nightfall Venus returned from the banquet flushed with wine, 11 fragrant with perfume, and garlanded all over with brilliant roses. When she saw the wonderful exactness with which the task had been performed, 'Worthless wretch!' she exclaimed, 'this is not your doing or the work of your hands, but his whose fancy you have taken – so much the worse indeed for you, and for him'; and throwing Psyche a crust of coarse bread she took herself to bed. Meanwhile Cupid was under strict guard, in solitary confinement in one room at the back of the palace, partly to stop him from aggravating his wound through his impetuous passion, partly to stop him from seeing his beloved. So then the two lovers, though under the same roof, were kept apart and endured a melancholy night. As soon as Dawn took horse, Venus called Psyche and said: 'You see that wood which stretches along the banks of the river which washes it in passing, and the bushes at its edge which look down on the nearby spring? Sheep that shine with fleece of real gold wander and graze there unguarded. Of that precious wool see that you get a tuft by hook or by crook and bring it to me directly.'

Psyche set out willingly, not because she expected to fulfil her 12 task, but meaning to find a respite from her sufferings by throwing herself from a rock into the river. But then from the river a green reed, source of sweet music, divinely inspired by the gentle whisper of the soft breeze, thus prophesied: 'Psyche, tried by much suffering, do not pollute my holy waters by your pitiable death. This is not the moment to approach these fearsome sheep, while they are taking in heat from the blazing sun and are maddened by fierce rage; their horns are sharp and their foreheads hard as stone, and they often attack and kill men with their poisonous bites. Rather, until the midday heat of the sun abates and the flock is quietened by the soothing breeze off the river, you can hide under that tall plane which drinks the current together with me. Then, when their rage is calmed and their attention is relaxed, shake the branches of the nearby trees, and you will find the golden wool which sticks everywhere in their entwined stems.'

13   So this open-hearted reed in its humanity showed the unfortunate Psyche the way to safety. She paid due heed to its salutary advice and acted accordingly: she did everything she was told and had no trouble in helping herself to a heaped-up armful of the golden softness to bring back to Venus. Not that, from her mistress at least, the successful outcome of her second trial earned her any approval. Venus bent her brows and with an acid smile said: 'I am not deceived: this exploit too is that lecher's. Now, however, I shall really exert myself to find out whether you have a truly stout heart and a good head on your shoulders. You see the top of the steep mountain that looms over that lofty crag, from which there flows down the dark waters of a black spring, to be received in a basin of the neighbouring valley, and then to water the marshes of Styx and feed the hoarse streams of Cocytus? There, just where the spring gushes out on the very summit, draw off its ice-cold water and bring it to me instantly in this jar.' So saying she gave her an urn hollowed out from crystal, adding yet direr threats.

14   Psyche eagerly quickened her pace towards the mountain-top, expecting to find at least an end of her wretched existence there. But as soon as she approached the summit that Venus had shown her, she saw the deadly difficulty of her enormous task. There stood a rock, huge and lofty, too rough and treacherous to climb; from jaws of stone in its midst it poured out its grim stream, which first gushed from a sloping cleft, then plunged steeply to be hidden in the narrow channel of the path it had carved out for itself, and so to fall by secret ways into the neighbouring valley. To left and right she saw emerging from the rocky hollows fierce serpents with long necks outstretched, their eyes enslaved to unwinking vigilance, forever on the watch and incessantly wakeful. And now the very water defended itself in speech, crying out repeatedly 'Be off!' and 'What are you doing? Look out!' and 'What are you about? Take

care!' and 'Fly!' and 'You'll die!' Psyche was turned to stone by the sheer impossibility of her task, and though her body was present her senses left her: overwhelmed completely by the weight of dangers she was powerless to cope with, she could not even weep, the last consolation.

But the suffering of this innocent soul did not escape the august 15 eyes of Providence. For the regal bird of almighty Jove, the ravisher eagle, suddenly appeared with outspread wings, and remembering his former service, how prompted by Cupid he had stolen the Phrygian cupbearer for Jupiter, brought timely aid. In honour of the god's power, and seeing his wife's distress, he left Jove's pathways in the heights, and gliding down before the girl he addressed her: 'Do you, naive as you are and inexperienced in such things, hope to be able to steal a single drop of this most holy and no less terrible spring, or even touch it? You must have heard that this water of Styx is feared by the gods themselves, even Jupiter, and that the oaths which mortals swear by the power of the gods, the gods swear by the majesty of Styx. Give me that urn' – and seizing and holding it he took off, and poising himself on his mighty hovering wings he steered to left and right between the raging jaws and flickering three-forked tongues of the dragons, to draw off the waters, though they resisted and warned him to retreat while he could do so in safety – he pretending meanwhile that he had been ordered to fetch it by Venus and that he was in her service; and thus it was a little easier for him to approach.

Psyche joyfully received the full urn and took it back at once to 16 Venus. Even then, however, she could not satisfy the wishes of the cruel goddess. Threatening her with yet worse outrages, she addressed Psyche with a deadly smile: 'I really think you must be some sort of great and profoundly accomplished witch to have carried out so promptly orders like these of mine. But you still have to do me this service, my dear. Take this casket' (giving it to her) 'and be off with you to the Underworld and the ghostly abode of Orcus himself. Present it to Proserpine and say: "Venus begs that you send her a little of your beauty, enough at least for one short day. For the supply that she had, she has quite used up and exhausted in looking after her ailing son." Come back in good time, for I must make myself up from it before going to the theatre of the gods.'

17   Then indeed Psyche knew that her last hour had come and that all disguise was at an end, and that she was being openly sent to instant destruction. So much was clear, seeing that she was being made to go on her own two feet to Tartarus and the shades. Without delay she made for a certain lofty tower, meaning to throw herself off it: for in that way she thought she could most directly and economically go down to the Underworld. But the tower suddenly broke into speech: 'Why, poor child, do you want to destroy yourself by a death-leap? Why needlessly give up at this last ordeal? Once your soul is separated from your body, then indeed you will go straight to the pit of Tartarus, but there will be no coming back for

18   you. Listen to me. Not far from here is Sparta, a famous city of Greece. Near to it, hidden in a trackless countryside, you must find Taenarus. There you'll see the breathing-hole of Dis, and through its gaping portals the forbidden road; once you have passed the threshold and entrusted yourself to it, you will fare by a direct track to the very palace of Orcus. But you must not go through that darkness empty-handed as you are; you must carry in your hands cakes of barley meal soaked in wine and honey, and in your mouth two coins. When you have gone a good way along the infernal road you will meet a lame donkey loaded with wood and with a lame driver; he will ask you to hand him some sticks fallen from the load, but you must say nothing and pass by in silence. Directly after that you will come to the river of death. Its harbourmaster is Charon, who ferries wayfarers to the other bank in his boat of skins only on payment of the fee which he immediately demands. So it seems that avarice lives even among the dead, and a great god like Charon, Dis's Collector, does nothing for nothing. A poor man on his deathbed must make sure of his journey-money, and if he hasn't got the coppers to hand, he won't be allowed to expire. To this unkempt old man you must give one of your coins as his fare, making him take it himself from your mouth. Then, while you are crossing the sluggish stream, an old dead man swimming over will raise his decaying hands to ask you to haul him aboard; but you

must not be swayed by pity, which is forbidden to you. When you   19
are across and have gone a little way, some old women weavers will
ask you to lend a hand for a moment to set up their loom; but here
too you must not become involved. For all these and many other
ruses will be inspired by Venus to make you drop one of your cakes.
Don't think the loss of a paltry barley cake a light thing: if you lose
one you will thereby lose the light of the sun. For a huge dog with
three enormous heads, a monstrous and fearsome brute, barking
thunderously and with empty menace at the dead, whom he can no
longer harm, is on perpetual guard before the threshold and dark
halls of Proserpine, and watches over the empty house of Dis. Him
you can muzzle by letting him have one of your cakes; passing him
easily by you will come directly to Proserpine, who will receive you
kindly and courteously, urging you to take a soft seat and join her
in a rich repast. But you must sit on the ground and ask for some
coarse bread; when you have eaten it you can tell her why you have
come, and then taking what you are given you can return. Buy off
the fierce dog with your other cake, and then giving the greedy
ferryman the coin you have kept you will cross the river and retrace
your earlier path until you regain the light of heaven above. But
this prohibition above all I bid you observe: do not open or look
into the box that you bear or pry at all into its hidden store of divine
beauty.'

So this far-sighted tower accomplished its prophetic task. Psyche   20
without delay made for Taenarus, where she duly equipped herself
with coins and cakes and made the descent to the Underworld.
Passing in silence the lame donkey-driver, paying her fare to the
ferryman, ignoring the plea of the dead swimmer, rejecting the crafty
entreaties of the weavers, and appeasing the fearsome rage of the
dog with her cake, she arrived at Proserpine's palace. She declined
her hostess's offer of a soft seat and rich food, and sitting on the
ground before her feet, content with a piece of coarse bread, she
reported Venus' commission. The box was immediately taken away
to be filled and closed up in private, and given back to Psyche.
By the device of the second cake she muzzled the dog's barking,
and giving the ferryman her second coin she returned from the

Underworld much more briskly than she had come. Having regained and worshipped the bright light of day, though in a hurry to complete her mission, she madly succumbed to her reckless curiosity. 'What a fool I am,' said she, 'to be carrying divine beauty and not to help myself even to a tiny bit of it, so as perhaps to please my beautiful lover.' So saying she opened the box. But she found nothing whatever in it, no beauty, but only an infernal sleep, a sleep truly Stygian, which when the lid was taken off and it was let out at once took possession of her and diffused itself in a black cloud of oblivion throughout her whole body, so that overcome by it she collapsed on the spot where she stood in the pathway, and lay motionless, a mere sleeping corpse.

But Cupid's wound had now healed and, his strength returned, he could no longer bear to be parted for so long from Psyche. He escaped from the high window of the room in which he was confined; and, with his wings restored by his long rest, he flew off at great speed to the side of his Psyche. Carefully wiping off the sleep and replacing it where it had been in the box, he roused her with a harmless prick from one of his arrows. 'There, poor wretch,' he said, 'you see how yet again curiosity has been your undoing. But meanwhile you must complete the mission assigned you by my mother with all diligence; the rest I will see to.' So saying, her lover nimbly took flight, while Psyche quickly took back Proserpine's gift to Venus.

Meanwhile Cupid, eaten up with love, looking ill, and dreading his mother's new-found austerity, became himself again. On swift wings he made his way to the very summit of heaven and pleaded his cause as a suppliant with great Jupiter. Jupiter took Cupid's face in his hand, pulled it to his own, and kissed him, saying: 'In spite of the fact, dear boy, that you have never paid me the respect decreed me by the gods in council, but have constantly shot and wounded this breast of mine by which the behaviour of the elements and the movements of the heavenly bodies are regulated, defiling it repeatedly with lustful adventures on earth, compromising my reputation and character by low intrigues in defiance of the laws, the Lex Julia included, and of public morals, changing my majestic features into the base shapes of snakes, of fire, of wild animals, of birds and of farmyard beasts – yet in spite of all, remembering my clemency and that you grew up in my care, I will do what you ask. But you must take care to guard against your rivals; and if there is now any pre-eminently lovely girl on earth, you are bound to pay me back with her for this good turn.'

So saying, he ordered Mercury to summon all the gods immedi- 23
ately to assembly, proclaiming that any absentees from this heavenly meeting would be liable to a fine of ten thousand sesterces. This threat at once filled the divine theatre; and Jupiter, towering on his lofty throne, announced his decision. 'Conscript deities enrolled in the register of the Muses, you undoubtedly know this young man well, and how I have reared him with my own hands. I have decided that the hot-blooded impulses of his first youth must somehow be bridled; his name has been besmirched long enough in common report by adultery and all kinds of licentious behaviour. We must take away all opportunity for this and confine his youthful excess in the bonds of marriage. He has chosen a girl and had her virginity: let him have and hold her, and embracing Psyche for ever enjoy his beloved.' Then turning to Venus, 'Daughter,' he said, 'do not be downcast or fear for your great lineage or social standing because of this marriage with a mortal. I shall arrange for it to be not unequal but legitimate and in accordance with the civil law.' Then he ordered Psyche to be brought by Mercury and introduced into heaven. Handing her a cup of ambrosia, 'Take this, Psyche,' he said, 'and be immortal. Never shall Cupid quit the tie that binds you, but this marriage shall be perpetual for you both.'

No sooner said than done: a lavish wedding-feast appeared. In 24
the place of honour reclined Psyche's husband, with his wife in his arms, and likewise Jupiter with his Juno, and then the other gods in order of precedence. Cups of nectar were served to Jove by his own cupbearer, the shepherd lad, and to the others by Liber; Vulcan cooked the dinner; the Seasons made everything colourful with roses and other flowers; the Graces sprinkled perfumes; the Muses discoursed tuneful music. Then Apollo sang to the lyre, and Venus, fitting her steps to the sweet music, danced in all her beauty, having

arranged a production in which the Muses were chorus and played the tibia, while a Satyr and a little Pan sang to the shepherd's pipe.

Thus was Psyche married to Cupid with all proper ceremony, and when her time came there was born to them a daughter, whom we call Pleasure.

25 That then was the tale told by the drunken garrulous old woman to the captive girl. I meanwhile was standing close by, vexed that I lacked the means of writing down such a pretty story. At this point the robbers returned loaded with plunder, having evidently been involved in some serious fighting. However, I gathered that some of the more enterprising of them were in a hurry to go back and retrieve the rest of their booty from where they had hidden it in some cave or other, leaving the wounded behind to look after their injuries. So they wolfed down some supper, and then brought me and my horse out to go with them and collect the stuff, urging us on our way with a rain of blows. The road was long, hilly, and winding, and it was evening when we finally came, exhausted, to the cave, where, without allowing us the least breathing-space, they loaded us heavily and drove us back at full speed. They were in such a hurry and beat me on so savagely that I stumbled over a stone by the roadside and fell. This provoked further beating, but enfeebled as I now was and lame on both sides, they had the utmost difficulty

26 in getting me on my feet again. 'How long,' said one of them, 'are we going to go on wasting fodder on this clapped-out ass? Now he's lame into the bargain.' 'Yes,' said another, 'it's an ill-omened beast. Ever since we got him we've had no gains worth mentioning, only wounds and the loss of our bravest comrades.' 'As far as I'm concerned,' said another, 'he'll deliver these bundles whether he likes it or not, and then I'll pitch him over a cliff for the vultures to enjoy.'

While these paragons of humanity were still arguing about how to dispose of me, we had arrived back home – for fear had lent wings to my hooves. Our loads were quickly taken off; and then, with no regard for the welfare of their animals or the question of my death, they pressed into service the wounded who had previously been left behind, to go with them and bring back the rest of the plunder, being, as they said, fed up with our slowness. Meanwhile I was the prey of desperate anxiety as I thought about the death that threatened me. 'Come on, Lucius,' I said to myself, 'why stand about waiting for the end? Death – and a horrible one – is what these brigands have decided is in store for you. It won't be any trouble to carry out the sentence: there are those ravines over there bristling with jagged rocks – they'll pierce you through and tear you apart before you reach the bottom. That wonderful magic of yours has equipped you with an ass's shape and an ass's hard life, but not his thick skin; yours is as thin as a leech's. So, why not play the man at last and save your life while you can? This is your last chance to escape, while the robbers are out of the way. You surely aren't afraid of a guard that consists of an old woman with one foot in the grave? Lame though you are, you can finish her off with one kick. But where in the world are you to flee to, and who will take you in? A silly question, a really asinine one: any passer-by will be glad to carry off a mount to carry him on his way.'

And with a vigorous pull I broke my halter and took off at a   27
gallop. I didn't however succeed in eluding the kite-like vision of that crafty old hag. Seeing me free, with a boldness that belied her age and sex she grabbed my halter and tried as hard as she could to wrench my head round and bring me back. Remembering the robbers' atrocious intentions, I had no compunction about lashing out at her with my hind hooves and dashing her to the ground. But even sprawled on the ground she hung on doggedly and trailed along behind me in my flight for quite a distance, at the same time screaming loudly for help from some stronger hand. Her shouting and weeping had no effect, as there was nobody there who could help her, except for the captive girl. Alarmed by the outcry, she ran out and beheld a truly memorable scene: a Dirce in the shape of an old woman, fastened not to a bull but to an ass. With a man's resolution she brought off a superbly daring exploit: tearing the bridle from the old woman's hands she slowed me down in my flight with soothing noises, vaulted nimbly on my back, and then urged me once more into a gallop.

28   My own desire to escape and my eagerness to rescue the girl, not forgetting the occasional touches of the whip with which she encouraged me, all combined to send me flying along with thundering hooves at racehorse speed. As we went, I was trying to whinny endearments to her, and every now and then, while pretending to scratch my back, I would turn my head to nuzzle her pretty feet. She meanwhile, sighing deeply and looking anxiously up to heaven, was praying: 'You gods above, assist me in my desperate peril, and you, cruel Fortune, let there now be an end to your savagery: I have surely suffered and sorrowed enough to appease you. As for you, protector of my life and liberty, if you bring me home and restore me unharmed to my parents and my handsome bridegroom, you shall have all the thanks, all the honours, all the food, that are mine to bestow. The first thing I shall do is to comb this mane of yours nicely and adorn it with my girlish jewellery; then I'll curl your fringe and plait it becomingly; then I'll give your tail, which is rough and matted for want of washing, a thorough grooming; and in a caparison glittering with a myriad gold studs like the stars in heaven you shall process in triumph amid the rejoicings of the people. Every day I shall bring you nuts and other delicacies

29   in a fold of my silk gown, and feed you, my deliverer, myself. But fine food and endless leisure and utter material well-being will not be all: glory and honour shall also be yours, for I shall signalize the memory of today's happy events and the intervention of divine Providence by a testimony that will outlive us. In the hall of my house I shall dedicate a picture of this flight of ours. People will come to see it, and the artless story of "The Princess who escaped from Captivity on the back of an Ass" will be told around the world and immortalized in the pages of the learned. You too will join the catalogue of the Wonders of Old, and your true example will lead us to believe that Phrixus really did make his crossing on the ram, that Arion rode the dolphin, and that Europa perched on the bull. And if it was in fact Jupiter who bellowed in the guise of the bull, well, perhaps there lurks in this ass of mine the shape of a man or the form of a god.'

    While the girl was going on in this vein, her prayers repeatedly intermingled with sighs, we had come to a crossroads. She was hauling on my bridle in a determined effort to make me go to the right, because that was her way home. I knew that this was also the road that the robbers had taken to recover the rest of their plunder, and stoutly resisted, protesting silently in my mind: 'Unhappy girl, what are you doing, for God's sake? Do you want to go straight to perdition? Why make *me* take you there? It's not just you, it's me you're going to do for.' And while we were pulling in opposite ways like this, like neighbours at law with each other over boundaries – though in this case it was apportionment of the road rather than the ownership of land that was in dispute – the robbers appeared loaded with their spoils and caught us fair and square, having seen us already from some way off by the light of the moon.

They greeted us with mocking laughter, and one of them hailed us: 'Whither away? What's this hasty moonlight flit? Aren't you afraid of ghosts and bogies at this time of night? You must have been in a great hurry, dutiful daughter that you are, to see your parents! Better let us protect your solitary state and show you the shortest way back home.' And suiting the action to the word he seized my bridle and wrenched my head around, not sparing me the usual beating from the knotty stick he carried. Now that I was being forced to return to imminent death, I remembered my sore hooves and began to limp with drooping head. 'So!' said the man who had tugged me round, 'you're stumbling and limping again, are you? Those feeble feet of yours can gallop, but they can't walk – only a moment ago you were outflying Pegasus.' While my amiable friend, with whacks from his stick, was joking in this way with me, we had come to the outer defences of their stronghold. There what should we find but the old woman hanging by the neck from a branch of a tall cypress tree. They simply took her down and threw her as she was, noose and all, over the cliff; then they fettered the girl and fell like starving animals on the supper which the old woman, diligent even in death, had left ready for them.

While they were voraciously dispatching everything in sight they started to deliberate about our punishment and their revenge. As usual in such an unruly crowd there was lively disagreement. One wanted the girl to be burned alive, another said she should be thrown to the beasts, a third thought she should be crucified, and a fourth was all for torturing her to death; the one point on which they were unanimous was that die she must. Then, when the hubbub had died down, one quietly took up the running. 'It is repugnant,' he said, 'both to our principles as professionals and our humanity as individuals, not to mention my own ideas of moderation, to allow you to punish this crime more savagely than it merits. Rather than invoking the beasts or the cross or fire or torture, or even giving her a quick death, if you will be guided by me you will grant the girl her life – but in the form that she deserves. You won't, I'm sure, have forgotten what you've already decided to do with that bone-idle ass that does nothing but eat; deceitful too, shamming lame and aiding and abetting the girl's escape. My proposal therefore is that tomorrow we slaughter him, remove his insides, and sew the girl up in his belly naked – since he prefers her company to ours – with just her head showing and the rest of her hugged tight in his bestial embrace. Then we'll leave this dainty dish of stuffed donkey on some rocky crag to cook in the heat of the sun. In that way both of them will undergo all the punishments to which you have so justly sentenced them. The ass will die as he richly deserves; the girl will be torn by beasts when the worms gnaw her, she will be roasted when the blazing sun scorches the ass's belly, and she will be gibbeted when the dogs and vultures drag out her entrails. And think of all her other sufferings and torments: to dwell alive in the belly of a dead animal, to suffocate in an intolerable stench, to waste away and die of prolonged fasting, and not even to have her hands free to compass her own death.'

He had hardly finished before the robbers carried his motion by acclamation without troubling to vote. As for me, listening to this with every inch of my long ears, I could do nothing but mourn for the corpse that I would be next morning.

32

BOOK 7

Haemus appears and takes command — revealed as Charite's lover
Tlepolemus in disguise — she is rescued and the robbers
exterminated — she makes much of Lucius — he is sent out to grass
— yoked to the mill — attacked by the stallions — persecuted by a
cruel boy — threatened with castration — blamed for the boy's death

The darkness was just giving way to daylight and the sun's shining   1
chariot was just beginning to brighten the world when another
robber appeared on the scene — at least so he must have been from
the greetings that passed. He sat down at the entrance to the cave,
and when he had got his breath back he made the following report
to his colleagues:

'So far as the business of plundering Milo's house is concerned,
we can dismiss our worries and relax. After you had bravely cleared
the place out and returned to camp, I mingled with the crowd of
townspeople, pretending to share their anger and indignation, so as
to discover and report back to you, as you had ordered, what was
going to be decided about investigating the affair and how far the
search for the perpetrators was to be taken. The whole lot of them
were agreed that the obvious culprit was some man called Lucius.
This was not mere guesswork, the evidence was plain: within the
last few days he had passed himself off to Milo as a respectable
character by a forged letter of introduction, and had so successfully
won his confidence that he was received into his house as a guest
and treated as an intimate friend. In the course of a few days he had
wormed his way into the affections of Milo's maid by pretending
to fall in love with her. That enabled him to carry out a thorough
inspection of the lock on the front door and to reconnoitre the part
of the house where all the family property was stored. As a conclusive   2
proof that he was the villain of the piece it was pointed out that he

had disappeared that night at the very moment of the robbery and had not been seen since. To assist his escape and to enable him to foil his pursuers and hole up at a safe distance, he had the means at hand in the shape of the white horse that he had brought with him to aid his getaway. They had found his slave still in the house and had of course arrested him and imprisoned him on the order of the magistrates, expecting him to provide evidence of his master's nefarious plans. However, when next day he had been put to all kinds of tortures, though he nearly died in the process, he made no admission of any kind. Nevertheless several messengers had been dispatched to Lucius' home town to find him and bring him to justice.'

Listening to this story and comparing Lucius as he had been and his former happy condition with the woes of the wretched ass that he now was, I groaned within myself. The learned men of old, I reflected, knew what they were talking about when they envisaged and portrayed Fortune as totally blind. It is invariably on the wicked and undeserving, I thought, that she bestows her favours; her choices are never grounded on reason, indeed she goes out of her way to frequent the company of those she ought to avoid like the plague if she could see. And the worst of it is that she distributes reputation so capriciously, indeed downright perversely: the evildoer glories in the character of a man of virtue, while the innocent is branded as a criminal. Here was I, cruelly attacked and transformed by her into the shape of a beast, and one of the lowest sort at that, reduced to a condition which might inspire grief and pity in my worst enemy, accused of robbing a dear friend and host – indeed parricide would be a more accurate name for it than robbery. And I was not in a position to defend myself or to utter a single word of denial. However, I thought that if I stayed silent when such a heinous charge was brought against me in my presence, it might seem that I assented to it because I had a guilty conscience. This I could not endure, and I tried at least to call out 'No, I didn't do it!' The 'No' I did utter again and again at the top of my voice, but the rest I couldn't manage; try as I might to round out the vigorous vibration of my hanging lips, I couldn't get beyond the first word and just went on braying

'No, no'. But what is the point of stringing out complaints against the perversity of Fortune? She even had no compunction about allowing me to become the fellow slave and yokemate of the horse who had formerly been my servant and mount.

Harassed by such thoughts as these, I was suddenly struck by a more pressing anxiety, when I recollected the robbers' decision to sacrifice me to Charite's ghost; and I kept looking down at my belly and imagining myself already pregnant with the wretched girl. Meanwhile the fellow who had just reported this false indictment against me produced a thousand gold pieces that he had hidden by sewing them into his clothing, which he said he had taken off various wayfarers, and by way of demonstrating his honesty paid them into the common treasury. Then he began to ask earnestly after the fate of his comrades. On learning that several of them, the bravest indeed, had been lost in various ways on active service, he proposed that they should give the roads a spell of peace for a time and declare a truce in their campaigning in order to concentrate on recruiting, so as to restore their forces to full strength and fighting efficiency by a new intake of manpower. The reluctant could be terrified into enlisting, the willing would be attracted by the prospect of loot, and there would be many who would be happy to renounce a down-trodden and slavish existence for a life of almost princely power. He himself had just met a man who was tall, young, heftily built, muscular and vigorous, and after some urging had persuaded him to turn to more profitable employment powers which had for too long been idle and torpid, to make the most of the boon of good health while he could, and to use those strong hands of his for raking in riches rather than holding them out for charity.

This was unanimously carried, and they agreed to enrol this man, as he seemed to have the right qualifications, and to beat up for more recruits to bring the company up to strength. His proposer went out and shortly returned bringing with him a young man of immense size, just as he had promised; nobody else there could hold a candle to him, for he was not only massively built but taller by a head than anybody present – this though his beard was only just beginning to sprout. He was dressed in a motley collection of rags, precariously stitched together, which only half covered him, so that his midriff with its thick layer of muscle could be seen peeping through.

That was how he looked as he stood there. 'Votaries of mighty Mars and fellow soldiers, as I may already call you,' he said, 'I salute you. Receive me as readily as I come to you, a man of dash and daring, one who would rather take hard blows on his body than hard cash in his hand, one who defies the death that others dread. Don't think me a beggar or an outcast, or judge my worth from these rags. I was captain of a valiant company and I have laid waste all Macedonia; I am the famous bandit Haemus of Thrace, whose name is feared throughout the Empire. My father Theron was an equally renowned robber; I was nourished on human blood and brought up in the ranks of our band to be the heir and rival of my father's prowess. But I lost every one of my brave comrades and all my riches in a matter of moments. In an evil hour I had attacked as he passed by an Imperial commissioner (he had been a two-hundred-thousand man but had been dismissed in disgrace) – but I had better make things clear by starting at the beginning.

'This man had held a number of offices at court, in which he had won distinction, and he was held in high regard by the Emperor himself. On false charges cunningly trumped up by certain individuals he was sent into exile, the victim of cruel Envy. However, his wife Plotina, a woman of altogether exceptional loyalty and chastity, who had given him ten children, rejecting in disdain the pleasures and luxuries of the city, went with him in his flight and shared his ruin. She cut her hair, dressed herself in men's clothes, and stowed in her girdle her most valuable jewellery and some gold money; then moving undismayed among armed guards and drawn swords she shared all her husband's dangers, watching over his life with sleepless vigilance and enduring countless hardships with the fortitude of a man.

'After undergoing many trials along the way and braving the terrors of the sea, they were making for Zacynthus, which had been assigned by the decree of destiny as their temporary residence. They had put in near Actium just when we, having come down from

Macedonia, were operating in those parts, and had taken refuge from the sea in a little inn near where they had landed. Late that night we fell on the place and made a clean sweep of the contents, but it was only by the skin of our teeth that we escaped. The moment Plotina heard the first sounds of our entry, she rushed into the outer room and filled the whole place with cries of alarm, calling on the soldiers and servants by name and summoning the whole blessed neighbourhood to the rescue. It was only because of the general panic, each man skulking to save his own skin, that we were able to get away unscathed.

'But this most noble lady, for so I must call her, this paragon of loyalty, lost no time in using the influence her exemplary behaviour had won her: she successfully petitioned the Emperor's divinity for an immediate pardon for her husband and condign punishment for his assailants. That was that: the Emperor willed that Haemus the robber's company should cease to exist, and cease to exist it did. Such is the power of a great prince's mere wish. Our entire band was hunted down, cut to pieces, and exterminated by detachments of soldiers; I alone just managed to escape from the very jaws of Orcus, which I did as follows. I put on a woman's dress, brightly coloured and hanging in loose folds, covered my head with a gauze turban, and slipped on my feet a pair of those thin white shoes that women wear. So disguised as a member of the weaker sex and riding an ass loaded with barley I made my getaway through the enemy ranks. They allowed free passage to what they thought was a mere donkey-woman – and indeed at that time my complexion was still that of a boy and my cheeks were smooth and hairless. 8

'Since then I have been true to my father's renown and my own prowess. Surrounded as I was by hostile swords, I felt somewhat nervous; but in solitary raids on farmhouses and villages under the cover of my disguise I have scraped together a little journey-money' – and with that he opened his rags and poured out a couple of thousand gold pieces. 'There,' he said, 'is my contribution – my dowry if you like; I freely offer it to your company, and along with it myself, if you will agree, as your trusty commander, one who will very soon transform this house of stone into a house of gold.'

9   Without a moment's hesitation the robbers unanimously voted to confer the leadership on him, and produced a rather more elegant robe for him to put on in place of the rags which had turned out to be so rich. So transformed he embraced every man individually; then he took the seat of honour at the table and was formally installed with great feasting and carousing. In the course of conversation he heard about Charite's escape, how I had carried her, and the horrible death they planned for us. He asked where she was and was taken to see her. At the sight of her loaded with chains he came back wrinkling his nose in disapproval. 'It would be stupid and rash of me,' he said, 'to veto your decision, but I shall not be able to face the accusations of my conscience if I don't tell you what I really think. First of all, please believe me when I say that it is for your interests that I am concerned; and after all, if you don't like my proposition, you can always revert to your original plan. My own view is that robbers, at least those who know their business, should count nothing more important than their own profit, not even revenge, which has a habit of rebounding on its author. If you dispose of this girl inside the ass, you will have achieved nothing except to give vent to your resentment. What I would suggest is that we take her to some city or other and sell her there. A pretty young girl like that will fetch a good price. It so happens that I have a number of friends who are pimps, and one or other of them, I've no doubt, can well afford to pay a hefty sum for her, one in keeping with her high birth. She will then be consigned to a brothel (and she won't be allowed to escape a second time), and you will have your revenge into the bargain, and a hugely satisfactory one, when she is serving her sentence there. That I honestly hold to be the most expedient course; but the decision and the conduct of your affairs must rest with you.'

10   In this manner did our Treasury Pleader, this admirable protector of both girl and ass, present our case. The others, however, debated for a long time, putting my heart to the torture by their protracted discussions; indeed I all but expired in my agony. Finally they agreed to the newcomer's proposal, and at once released the girl from her fetters. As soon as she saw Haemus and heard what they were saying

about pimps and brothels, she became elated and began laughing
merrily. That, I felt, justified me in condemning the entire female
sex, when I saw this girl who had pretended to be in love with her
betrothed and to be pining for a chaste marriage, now suddenly
delighted by the mention of a filthy sordid brothel. At that moment
the whole race of women and their morals hung in the balance,
with an ass holding the scales.

However, the young man now went on: 'Should we not,' he
asked, 'at once propitiate Mars the Comrade in Arms, before we set
out to sell the girl and find recruits? But so far as I can see we haven't
any animals for sacrifice or even enough wine to drink, let alone a
surplus. Choose ten men to go with me; they will be all I shall need
to attack the nearest village and bring back a real Salian banquet for
you.' He then set out, while the rest of them built up a huge fire
and made an altar to Mars from green turf.

The foraging party soon returned carrying skins full of wine and   11
driving before them a herd of animals. From these they chose a large
he-goat, old and hairy, to sacrifice to Mars, Helper and Comrade.
They then prepared a sumptuous supper. The new arrival spoke up
again. 'You must look to me,' he said, 'to give you a vigorous lead,
not only in your expeditions and plunderings but also in your
pleasures'; and he set to work energetically, attending to every detail
with extraordinary efficiency. He swept the floor, laid the table,
cooked, arranged the various dishes, served them dextrously, and
above all plied every man with bumper after bumper until they were
all awash. Meanwhile, on the pretext of fetching and carrying fresh
supplies, he was constantly at the girl's side, smilingly offering her
filched titbits and sips of wine from his own cup. She for her part
eagerly accepted these attentions, and when he several times offered
to kiss her she kissed him back with ardour. This emphatically
displeased me. 'So, young lady,' I said to myself, 'you've forgotten
your marriage and the lover whom you love, and you prefer this
stranger, this bloodstained assassin, to that new husband, whoever
he is, to whom your parents wed you? Doesn't your conscience
prick you, or are you happy to trample true love under foot and
play the whore here among spears and swords? Suppose the other

robbers notice what's happening? It'll be back again to death by donkey for you, and you'll take me to perdition along with you. It's somebody else's hide you're gambling with.'

12   However, while I was silently rehearsing these slanderous charges in high indignation, I became aware from some words that passed between them – ambiguous but clear enough to an intelligent ass – that this was not in fact Haemus the notorious robber but her husband Tlepolemus. For as they went on talking, ignoring me as if I were really dead, he raised his voice a little. 'Cheer up, sweetest Charite,' he said. 'Very soon these enemies will be *your* prisoners', and drunk as they already were and full to overflowing, he reapplied himself even more insistently to thrusting wine on them, now serving it neat and slightly mulled. He himself didn't touch a drop. I really couldn't help suspecting that he was adding some soporific drug to their cups, for finally the whole lot of them, every man jack, lay overcome with wine as if dead. Then it was the easiest thing in the world for him to tie them all up and completely immobilize them; after which he mounted the girl on my back and set off for home.

13   On our arrival the whole city turned out to see this longed-for sight. There were parents, relatives, dependants, children, servants, all with happiness in their faces and joy in their hearts. There was to be seen a crowd of both sexes and all ages escorting this novel and never-to-be-forgotten spectacle, a virgin riding in triumph on an ass. I myself played my part manfully in the rejoicing, and not to seem out of place or out of harmony with the proceedings, I pricked up my ears, inflated my nostrils, and brayed vigorously – or indeed a better word would be thunderously. Charite was taken straight to her room, where her parents made much of her, while Tlepolemus took me and a large number of other pack-animals and townspeople back again at a great pace. I was by no means unwilling to go, for my usual curiosity was whetted by my desire to see the robbers taken prisoner. We found them still immobilized, more by the wine than by their bonds. All their plunder was unearthed and carried outside; and the gold and silver and the rest of the loot was loaded on to us. Some of the robbers, tied up as they were, they dragged to the edge

of a nearby ravine and threw over; the others they dispatched with their own swords and left them where they lay.

Delighted with our vengeance we returned joyfully to the city. The treasure was consigned to public safekeeping, and Tlepolemus was restored to the legitimate possession of his bride. The new wife at once proclaimed me her saviour and took generous care of me; on her wedding day she ordered my manger to be filled to overflowing with barley, and had enough hay served out to me to feed a Bactrian camel. You can imagine how horribly I cursed Photis for having turned me into an ass and not a dog, when I saw the whole canine population gorged and bloated with the leavings and filched morsels of that lavish marriage-feast. The unique night and her first experience of love came and went, and the new bride never stopped talking to her parents and husband of her thankfulness to me, until they promised to invest me with supreme honours. Finally a group of solid citizens was convened to decide on the most suitable way of rewarding me. One of them suggested that I should be kept in the house to lead a life of leisure, fed richly on choice barley and beans and vetch. However, another was concerned for my liberty, and his opinion carried the day: he proposed that I should be allowed to run loose in the fields to take my pleasure with the horses, so that I could mount the mares and from these superior matings produce many mules for my masters to rear.

Accordingly the head stableman was summoned, and after a long recommendation I was handed over to him to be taken off. I was indeed happy and carefree as I trotted ahead of him: I could, I thought, now say goodbye to carrying baggage and other burdens, and having gained my freedom I should be sure when spring came and the fields were in bloom to find roses somehow or other. And then another thought struck me: if all these thanks and honours had been bestowed on me when I was an ass, how much more lavishly should I be feted and rewarded when I regained my human shape! However, once that herdsman had got me well away from the city, there were no comforts awaiting me; I wasn't even set free. His wife, an odious grasping creature, yoked me to a rotary mill, and by repeatedly beating me with a leafy branch she proceeded to get

14

15

bread for herself and her family at the expense of my hide. Moreover, she was not satisfied with overtasking me like this merely for her own needs; she hired out my circumambulations to the neighbours to grind their grain for them as well. To make matters worse, I wasn't allowed even the usual ration of food for these hard labours. My barley, crushed and ground by the selfsame mill that I was turning, she sold to the farmers round about; I, for a whole day of hard work fastened to that machine, was not fed until the evening, and then what she served out to me was just the husks, unsifted and full of dirt and grit.

16   Ground down as I was by these troubles, cruel Fortune then delivered me over to fresh torments – to enable me, I suppose, to boast of glory earned for deeds of valour at home and abroad. Rather late in the day the worthy herdsman finally recollected his masters' orders and turned me loose among the horses. Free at last, ass that I was, I rejoiced and kicked up my heels; and parading around with dainty steps I began to choose out the mares that I thought would make the best concubines. However, these agreeable prospects ended in disaster. It was the breeding season, and the stallions had for weeks been thoroughly fattened up and fed to bursting. Formidable at the best of times and stronger than any ass, they regarded me in the light of a threat, and to prevent what they saw as an adulterous debasement of the breed, and setting the divine law of hospitality at naught, they fell on me in a fury of hatred. One reared his great chest in the air, and with his head and crest towering above me battered me with his front hooves; another turned his rump on me, bulging with muscles, and attacked me with his heels; a third, whinnying spitefully, threatened me with ears laid back, and baring his gleaming teeth like so many hatchets nipped me all over. It was just like the story I had once read of the king of Thrace who consigned unfortunate strangers to his wild horses to rend and devour; that powerful tyrant was so sparing of his barley that he assuaged the hunger of his voracious stud by largesse of human flesh.

17   Finding myself similarly attacked and savaged by all these horses, I began hankering for my old round in the mill. However, Fortune's appetite for tormenting me was unappeased, and she now visited

me with a fresh plague. I was told off to carry wood down from the mountain, and the boy who was put in charge of me was without question the most objectionable specimen of boyhood there ever was. Not only did I exhaust myself climbing the steep slopes of the mountain and wear out my hooves traversing its sharp-edged rocks; I was so incessantly thrashed by blow after blow from his stick that the pain of the cuts penetrated the marrow of my bones. By perpetually aiming his blows at one particular place on my right flank he split the skin and opened up a gaping sore – a pit, a crevasse; and still went on beating the wound until it ran with blood. He piled such a weight of faggots on my back that you'd have thought it a load for an elephant rather than an ass. And whenever the load became unbalanced and slipped sideways, instead of relieving me by removing some faggots from the heavier side and so taking off some of the pressure, as he should have done, or at least evening up the load by transferring them to the other side, his remedy for the imbalance was to pile stones on top. As if these tribulations were 18 not enough, the size of my load still did not satisfy him; huge though it was, when we had to cross the stream which ran alongside the road, to save his boots from a wetting he would jump up and perch on my back – a trivial addition, I suppose he thought, to my enormous burden. The river bank was muddy and slippery, and from time to time I would overbalance under my load and go down in the mire. A good driver would have lent a hand, would have held me up by the bridle or hauled me up by the tail, or at least taken off some of my vast load until I could get to my feet again. Not he: so far from offering to help me in my exhaustion, he would beat every inch of me with his great stick, starting at my head and not forgetting my ears, until his blows acted as a kind of medical treatment to get me up again.

Yet another torture did he devise for me. He made up a bunch of thorns with formidably sharp and poisonous prickles and fastened it to my tail to hang there and torment me, so that as I walked it would swing about and hurt me cruelly with its deadly spikes. So 19 either way I was in trouble. If I put on speed to escape his savage blows, the thorns pricked me harder than ever; and if I slowed down for a moment to ease the pain, I was thrashed into a gallop once more. This detestable boy seemed to have no other object in life but to finish me off one way or another, and indeed he more than once threatened and swore to do just that. Then something happened to goad his abominable malice to fresh lengths. One day he was behaving so outrageously that my patience gave way and I let fly at him with a vigorous kick. This was what he then planned to do to me. He loaded me with a large bundle of tow which he roped tightly to my back, and then drove me on to the road. He then helped himself to a burning coal from the first farm he came to and pushed it into the middle of my load. In a moment the loose mass had ignited and burst into flame, enveloping me in its lethal heat with no apparent hope of escaping from the fatal menace or of saving my

20 life; a fire like that allows no delay or time to think things over. In this calamity Fortune for once smiled on me; no doubt she was saving me for future dangers, but now at least she delivered me from instant and certain death. Catching sight of a muddy pool of water from yesterday's rain by the roadside, without stopping to think I plunged into it head over ears. Then, when the flames were finally extinguished, I emerged, relieved of my load and delivered from destruction. But that dreadful boy had the effrontery to blame his vile deed on me, telling all his fellow herdsmen that I had stumbled on purpose when passing the neighbour's stove and had deliberately set myself on fire, adding with a laugh, 'So how long are we going to go on wasting fodder on this incendiary ass?'

Only a few days later he played an even worse trick on me. Having sold the wood I was carrying at a nearby cottage he was leading me back unloaded when he started to proclaim that he could no longer cope with my wicked ways and that he had had enough of such a thankless task. This was the style of the complaint that he had

21 concocted: 'Look at this ass – lazy, idle, too asinine to be true. On top of all the other shocking things he's done, now he's getting me into fresh trouble and danger. Every time he sees a passer-by, whether it's a pretty woman, a young girl, or a handsome boy, in a second he's sent his load flying, and often his saddle as well, and makes a mad rush at them – a lover like this in search of a human mate!

Slavering with desire, he hurls them to the ground as he attempts to indulge his unlawful pleasures and unspeakable lusts, urging them to bestial unions while Venus looks away in horror. He even distorts his shameless mouth into a parody of a kiss as he butts and bites his victims. These goings-on are likely to involve us in serious lawsuits and quarrels, and probably criminal prosecutions as well. Only just now, catching sight of a respectable young woman, he threw off his load of wood and scattered it all over the place, went for her in a frenzy and had her down in the mud, did our merry philanderer, and then and there in full view of everybody did his level best to mount her. It was only because some passers-by were alarmed by her screams and rushed to the rescue that she was freed and pulled out from right under his hooves; otherwise the unhappy woman would have been trampled and torn apart – an agonizing end for her and the prospect of the death penalty as her legacy to us.'

These lies he interspersed with all sorts of other stories, all the more galling to me because I had to stay modestly silent. They aroused in the herdsmen a violent determination to do for me. 'Let's make a sacrifice of this public husband,' said one, 'this adulterer to the community; that's what his monstrous marriages deserve. Come on, young fellow,' he added, 'cut his throat here and now, throw his guts to the dogs, and keep the meat for the workforce's dinner. We'll sprinkle his skin with ash and dry it to take back to our masters; we can easily pretend that he was killed by a wolf.'

Without more ado my delinquent accuser constituted himself executioner of the herdsmen's sentence, and gleefully mocking my misfortunes and still resenting my kick – how I regretted that it hadn't been more effective! – started to whet a sword. But one of the rustics in the crowd intervened. 'It would be a shame,' he said, 'to kill such a fine ass and lose his labour and valuable services by passing this sentence on his amatory excesses. If we castrate him, that will put paid to his lovemaking for good and relieve you of all fear of danger, and he'll be much the stouter and stronger for it. I've known not merely many idle asses but lots of very unruly horses with an excessive sexual drive which made them wild and unmanageable, but after this operation they at once became tame and docile, quite suitable as pack-animals and submissive to any other kind of work. So, unless you strongly disagree, give me a day or two – I've got to be at the next market meanwhile – to fetch the instruments I need for the operation from home and come straight back to you; then I'll whip this nasty brute of a lover's thighs open and take out his manhood, and you'll find him as meek and mild as an old bell-wether.'

24   By this decision I was snatched from the hands of Orcus, but only to be reserved for a fate almost worse. I began to lament and mourn myself as dead – for that was what I should be without my latter end. So I started to look round for ways of destroying myself, by a hunger-strike or jumping off a cliff – I'd still be dead, but at least I'd be dead in one piece. I was still undecided about my choice of ending when the next morning that assassin of a boy once more led me up the mountain by the usual route. He tied me to a branch that hung down from a huge ilex, while he climbed a little way up above the path with a hatchet to cut the wood he had to fetch. At that moment there emerged from a nearby cave the huge towering head of a deadly she-bear. The instant I saw her I panicked; terrified by this sudden apparition I reared back with the whole weight of my body on my hind legs and my head high in the air, snapped my tether, and took off at top speed. Headlong and hell for leather downhill I went, hurling myself bodily through the air with my feet hardly touching the earth, until I reached the level ground below; all I wanted was to escape that monster of a bear and that even worse monster of a boy.

25   At this point a passer-by, seeing me straying ownerless, grabbed hold of me, jumped on my back, and beating me with the stick he carried rode off with me along an unfamiliar side road. I was more than willing to cooperate in any course that would save me from the butchery of my virility; and the blows did not much bother me, used as I was to regular beatings. However, Fortune, determined as ever to persecute me, in her lamentable readiness to thwart my lucky escape now laid a fresh trap for me. My herdsmen had been scouring the countryside in search of a lost heifer, and now they happened to run into us and at once recognized me and seized my bridle in

an attempt to take possession of me. My rider, however, boldly and stoutly resisted them, calling men and gods to witness and shouting: 'What's the meaning of this? Why this violence? Why are you attacking me?' 'Oh,' said they, 'so *we're* treating *you* uncivilly, when you've stolen our ass and are making off with him? It would be more to the point to confess where you've hidden the boy who was in charge of him – obviously you've murdered him.' And with that they pulled him to the ground and beat and thumped him with fists and feet, while he swore that he'd seen no driver; he'd merely come across an ass that was wandering about loose and caught it for the sake of the reward, fully intending to restore it to the owner. 'If only the ass himself,' he said, '(and I wish I'd never set eyes on him) could speak and bear witness to my innocence: you'd be sorry for mistreating me like this.'

These protestations got him nowhere. Those vexatious herdsmen took him into custody and brought him to the wooded mountain-side which was the boy's usual beat. He was nowhere to be seen, 26 only fragments of a body, torn limb from limb and scattered all over the hillside. I knew perfectly well that it was the teeth of that she-bear that had done this, and I should certainly have told them what I knew had I had the power of speech. As it was, all I could do was silently to congratulate myself on my belated revenge. The boy's body was in pieces all over the place, but in the end with some difficulty they found it all and reassembled it, and then buried it on the spot. My Bellerophon they declared clearly guilty of theft and bloody murder, tied him up, and took him to their village for the night, meaning, they said, to bring him before the magistrates early next day to pay the penalty for his crime. Meanwhile the boy's parents were mourning him with tears and lamentations, when the farmer turned up true to his promise and proposed to operate on me. 'Well,' said one of the herdsmen, 'our loss today was nothing to do with him; but tomorrow we can if we feel like it relieve this pestilent ass not just of his genitals but of his head. You won't lack for helpers.'

So it happened that my doom was postponed to the morning, 27 and I thanked my friend for granting me at any rate one day's stay of execution by his death. However, I wasn't left in peace to congratulate myself for very long; the boy's mother burst into my stable, lamenting her son's untimely death with floods of tears. Dressed in black, ash on her head, tearing her grey hair with both hands, she wailed and protested endlessly, violently thumping and battering her breast. 'Look at him,' she screamed, 'lying there in his stall without a care in the world, indulging his gluttony and stuffing his insatiable bottomless belly – eat, eat, eat, with no pity for me in my affliction, no thought of his dead master's horrible fate. Yes, he scorns and despises my feeble old age and thinks he'll get away with this monstrous crime and come off scot free. Of course he takes it for granted that he's not guilty; your really desperate villains always defy conscience and expect to get away with it. In God's name, you miserable animal, if you could speak for a moment or two, how could you persuade even a complete idiot that you weren't to blame for this atrocity? You could have defended the poor child with your hooves, you could have protected him with your teeth. Often and often you'd lashed out at him with your heels – no trouble; why weren't you as eager to rescue him from death? You could at least have carried him off on your back and snatched him from the bloody clutches of that savage robber. How could you make off alone and desert and leave in the lurch your fellow slave, your master, your comrade, your good shepherd? Don't you know that anybody who refuses to help those in danger of death is guilty of antisocial behaviour and is liable to punishment on that score? But you aren't going to exult over my misfortunes much longer, murderer. I'll make you realize that nature lends strength to misery and grief.'

28   So saying, she pulled off her breastband and tied up my feet as tightly as she could with it, so that I should have no way of retaliating; then she seized the pole which was used to hold the stable door shut, and only stopped beating me with it when her strength gave out and the pole fell from her hands under its own weight. Then, complaining that her arms had tired so quickly, she rushed to the fire and took out a glowing brand, which she thrust right into my groin; whereat I resorted to the only defence that was left to me and ejected a stream of liquid filth which befouled her face and eyes. So,

by blindness and stench, my doom was finally averted; otherwise, like another Meleager, an ass would have perished by the firebrand of an insane Althaea.

BOOK 8

Tragic deaths of Charite and Tlepolemus — their slaves decamp in panic with the animals — misadventures on the way — Lucius sold to the priests of Atargatis — their scandalous activities — another death sentence

1 That night at cockcrow a young man arrived from the city who looked to me like a slave of Charite's, the girl who had suffered along with me at the hands of the robbers. He brought strange and dreadful news: she was dead and her whole house destroyed. He told his tale sitting by the fire with all his fellow slaves clustered around him: 'Grooms, shepherds, cowherds: our mistress Charite is no more; the poor child has perished by the cruellest of fates, but when she went down to the realm of ghosts it was not alone. But so that you may know the whole story, let me tell you everything that happened from the beginning; it deserves to be written down and shaped into a formal narrative by some scholar on whom Fortune has conferred the gift of writing.

'There lived in the city next to ours a young man of very distinguished family, a prominent figure on that account and very wealthy, but a confirmed debauchee, gourmandizing, whoring and drinking all day. This life-style had led him into bad company, and he was in league with gangs of robbers, and his hands were stained with human blood. Thrasyllus was his name, and he lived 2 up to his reputation. When Charite came of marriageable age, he was one of her principal suitors, and he put everything he knew into his wooing. However, though he outranked all his noble competitors and tried to win over her parents by rich gifts, they objected to his character, and he had to suffer the humiliation of being turned down. And even after my masters' daughter had been

128

wedded to the excellent Tlepolemus, Thrasyllus, still obviously
nursing the love that had been brought so low and brooding resent-
fully on the marriage that had been denied him, never ceased to
watch for the chance of a bloody revenge. Finally he hit on a
convenient opportunity of being on the spot, and made his preparations for the crime that he had been planning for so long. On the
day when Charite had been rescued from the deadly swords of the
robbers by her astute and valiant husband, he drew attention to
himself by his exuberant behaviour as he mingled with the crowd
who had come to offer their congratulations, expressing his delight
at seeing the newly-married couple safely rescued, and at the prospect
of children to come. In honour of his distinguished family, he
was received into our house as one of the principal guests and
treacherously masqueraded as a faithful friend while all the time
dissembling his wicked purpose. He constantly frequented their
society and was often invited to dine and drink with the family; so
he had become by degrees ever more dear to them and had gradually
and insensibly plunged into a deep abyss of desire. What else was to
be expected? The first warmth of cruel Love, while his flame is still
small, is delightful; but when it is fed by habit it flares up and
consumes us in its uncontrollable blaze.

'Thrasyllus was for a long time perplexed. He could discover no   3
opportunity for a secret meeting and saw that the possible openings
for an adulterous intrigue were being increasingly blocked off: the
couple's new and growing affection constituted a bond that had
become unbreakable, and even if, which was inconceivable, the girl
were willing, she was too closely guarded for any attempt at seduction
to be practicable. Nevertheless it was this impossible goal to which
his destructive passion drove him on, as if it were possible. What at
first he had thought difficult, now, as his love daily grew in strength,
seemed easy to accomplish. See, all of you, mark, learn, and inwardly
digest, the lengths to which the frenzy of desire can drive a man.

'A day came when Tlepolemus took Thrasyllus with him to hunt   4
wild beasts, if roe deer may be so described; for Charite would not
let her husband go after anything with teeth or horns. They had
come to a thickly wooded hill where the dense foliage hid the quarry

from their sight, and sent in the hounds, specially bred for scenting, to flush the deer from where they lay couched. At once, faithful to their careful training, the dogs divided up and covered all the approaches; at first there was only the odd whimper, then on a sudden signal they gave tongue and filled the wood with their wild and discordant barking. But it was not a roe deer or a panic-stricken fallow deer or a hind, meekest of all animals, that started up, but a wild boar, a fearsome animal – nothing like it had ever been seen before. Its muscles bulged under its tough hide, its coat was thick and rough, the bristles stood erect along its hairy spine; it foamed at the mouth as it loudly whetted its tusks, its eyes glared blazing menace, and the savage onrush of its ravening jaws was like a thunderbolt. Such of the more daring hounds as closed with it, it mangled and killed with sideways thrusts of its tusks, then it trampled down the nets which had slowed its first charge, and took off.

5   'The rest of us were all panic-stricken, being used to hunting only harmless animals and having no means of offence or defence, and hid ourselves in the undergrowth or behind the trees for protection. Thrasyllus, however, saw this as an opportunity to carry out his treacherous plan, and appealed artfully to Tlepolemus: "Why are we standing here in amazement and groundless panic like these grovelling slaves or timorous women? Are we going to let this choice prize slip from our grasp? Quick! Let's mount and go after him! Here, you take a boar-spear and I'll take a lance." The next moment they had leapt on to their horses and were off in hot pursuit. The boar, following its fighting instincts, turned to bay, hot with savage rage, and stood eyeing them, undecided which to charge and gore first. Tlepolemus took the lead and hurled his spear at the beast's back. Thrasyllus ignored the boar and with a thrust from his lance hamstrung Tlepolemus' horse. Unable to help itself, it collapsed and lay wallowing in its blood, throwing its master to the ground. In a moment the maddened boar was on him as he lay, repeatedly savaging first his clothes, then Tlepolemus himself as he tried to rise. So far from his good friend's feeling any remorse for his wicked exploit, his cruelty was not appeased by the sight of his victim in this mortal danger. That by no means satisfied him; as Tlepolemus,

in his desperation at the boar's attacks, was trying unavailingly to protect his lacerated legs and calling piteously for help, Thrasyllus speared him in the right thigh, reckoning confidently that a spear-thrust would be indistinguishable from the wounds inflicted by the boar. Then he likewise adroitly dispatched the boar itself.

'So young Tlepolemus was dead, and we all came out of hiding. 6 Sadly his household gathered at the spot; Thrasyllus, though delighted to have achieved his purpose and to see his enemy laid low, dissembled his joy, put on a mournful expression, and feigned grief. Lovingly embracing the corpse that was of his own making, with scrupulous hypocrisy he performed all the observances of mourning – only the tears would not come. So he produced an imitation of our real grief, fastening the blame for his own crime on the boar.

'The evil deed was scarcely done before Fame spread the report of it abroad. It found its way first to the house of Tlepolemus, where it fell on the ears of his ill-starred bride like a thunderbolt: beside herself at the news, the worst she was ever to hear, she launched out madly, like a Bacchante, on a wild course through the crowded city streets and the countryside around, proclaiming her husband's fate with frenzied shrieks. Groups of mourning citizens assembled, and all who met her followed her, sharing her grief; the city was emptied of its people, so eager were they to see. And now her husband's corpse appeared; fainting she threw herself on it and very nearly gave up to him then and there the life she had vowed to him. However, she was with much ado torn away by her attendants and reluctantly stayed alive, while the body was carried in solemn procession and escorted to its resting-place by the entire population.

'Thrasyllus meanwhile threw off all restraint. He cried and 7 lamented, and shed the tears – no doubt of joy – that he had not been able to command in his first demonstration of grief. Truth herself might have been hoodwinked by the profusion of his endear-ments: this was the friend he had grown up with, his comrade – in his mourning invocations he even added the name of brother. He was constantly with Charite, restraining her from beating her breast, calming her grief, quieting her lamentations, blunting the pangs of bereavement with soothing words, and consoling her by citing a string of examples to show that nobody is immune from misfortune. But all these kindnesses and this pretended friendship were merely an excuse to caress the girl, and his perverse attempts to please her only fed his odious love. However, directly the funeral rites had been performed, Charite was at once eager to join her husband in the world below, and tried every way she knew, especially the gentle and peaceful one which requires no weapons but resembles tranquil sleep. So the poor girl starved and neglected herself, hiding away in darkness and squalor and bidding farewell to the light of day. But Thrasyllus, partly by his own continued persistence, and partly working through other friends and relatives, not least her parents, forced her in the end, when she was deathly pale, filthy, and on the verge of collapse, to revive herself with a bath and food. Being the dutiful daughter that she was, she submitted, though unwillingly, to the demands of filial piety, and went about the business of life as they bade her, looking not exactly cheerful but somewhat less disturbed. Deep down inside, however, in the inmost core of her being, she was eating her heart out with grief and sorrow. All her days and nights were passed in mourning her loss; she had images of the dead man made as the god Liber, which she worshipped with divine honours, giving herself wholly over to this service – a consolation that was itself a torment.

8 'But Thrasyllus, always hasty and as rash as his name, could not wait for her to weep away her grief, for her distraction and frenzy to subside, and for her sorrow to exhaust itself by its very excess. While she was still lamenting her husband, still rending her clothes, still tearing her hair, he had the hardihood to propose marriage to her, and the imprudence to reveal the inmost secrets of his heart and his unspeakable treachery. Charite recoiled in loathing from these hideous disclosures; like one struck by a thunderclap or a meteor or Jupiter's lightning she collapsed bodily in a dead faint. After a short while she gradually came to, crying out repeatedly like a wounded animal; and now that she saw through the wicked Thrasyllus' plot, she put off her eager suitor to give herself time to perfect a plan. Meanwhile the ghost of the foully murdered Tlepolemus, his face bloodstained, pale and disfigured, appeared to

his wife as she lay chastely asleep. "Wife," he said, "I call you by the name which only I have a right to use, if any memory of me still remains in your heart. But if my untimely death has caused you to forget the ties of our love, marry whom you will and be happier than I could make you; only do not accept Thrasyllus' impious hand. Have nothing to do with him, shun his bed and board. Fly from the bloodstained hand of my assassin; do not enter into marriage with a murderer. The wounds from which you washed the blood with your tears are not those of the boar's tusks; it was Thrasyllus' spear that took me from you" – and he told her the rest, revealing the whole enactment of the crime.

'For a time Charite slept on, with her face pressed into the pillow and the tears streaming down her face, just as when she had first dropped off in her grief. Then, starting up in torment from her unrestful rest, she broke into fresh lamentations and prolonged wailing, tearing her nightdress and beating her shapely arms with savage blows. She told nobody of her dream but kept the information of the crime entirely to herself, resolving secretly to punish the wicked murderer and to put an end to her own life of suffering. Now once more the odious Thrasyllus, still recklessly pursuing his pleasure, appeared to thrust his proposal of marriage on her deaf ears. This time she rebuffed his approach gently, responding to his pressing endearments and humble solicitations with a remarkably clever piece of acting. "Until now," she said, "the fair face of your brother and my dearest husband has lingered before my eyes; I still sense the balmy fragrance of his heavenly body, and beautiful Tlepolemus still lives in my heart. Your most considerate course, therefore, will be to grant an unhappy woman the period of mourning that is necessary and customary, and to wait until a year is up. That will safeguard my honour and also your own interests and safety; by marrying too soon we might stir up my husband's vengeful ghost to destroy you in his just resentment."

'So far from being sobered down by her words or comforted by this temporizing promise, Thrasyllus persisted in pressing his shameless blandishments on her, going on and on until finally Charite pretended to yield. "But one thing, Thrasyllus," she said, "I must earnestly ask, and you cannot refuse me: for the time being, until the rest of the year has passed, our lovers' meetings must be a secret known only to ourselves and to nobody else in our families." Thrasyllus, outmanoeuvred, assented to her crafty proposal, willingly agreeing to keep their lovemaking secret. Forgetting everything else in his single-minded eagerness to possess her, he could not wait for night and the cover of darkness. "Now listen," said Charite. "Cover yourself completely in your cloak and bring nobody with you. Come to my door at nightfall without making a sound, and whistle just once, then wait for my nurse – you know her – who will be waiting just inside the door for you to arrive. She will open up and let you in, then she will bring you to my room, and there will be no lamp to share our secret."

11   'Thrasyllus was pleased with the arrangements for his fatal wedding. He suspected nothing, but on edge with anticipation complained only that the day was so long and evening so slow in coming. When the sun finally gave place to night, he appeared dressed in accordance with Charite's instructions, and entrapped by the nurse's watchful craft entered the bedroom in eager hope. Then, following her mistress's orders, the old woman slyly produced wine cups and a jar of wine mixed with a narcotic drug. Cajoled by her he thirstily drank off cup after cup, suspecting nothing, while she explained that her mistress was delayed by having to sit up with her father, who was ill. So it was easy for her to lay him to rest; then, as he lay sprawled there exposed to whatever anyone might do to him, she summoned Charite, who flew at the murderer, raging with manlike spirit and deadly intent. Standing over him, "Look at you," she said,

12   "there you lie – my husband's loyal comrade, the noble hunter, my dear betrothed. This is the hand that shed my blood, this the breast which contrived those treacherous schemes for my ruin, these the eyes in which I have found an unholy favour – eyes that already anticipate the coming punishment as they begin to experience the darkness that awaits them. Sleep well! Sweet dreams! It is not the sword, not cold steel, that I shall take to you; perish the thought that in the manner of your death you should be my husband's equal. You will live, but your eyes will die, and only asleep shall you see.

I shall have seen to it that your enemy's death seems more fortunate to you than your life. This is your fate: you will never again see the light, you will need an attendant to lead you, you will not have Charite, no happy marriage will be yours. You will neither rest in the peace of death nor enjoy the pleasures of life, but you will be a ghost wandering uncertainly between hell and heaven. You will forever search in vain for the hand that put out your eyes, and your worst misfortune of all will be that you will never know whom to blame. With your eyes' blood I shall pour a libation at the tomb of my Tlepolemus, and your sight shall be an offering to appease his sainted shade. But why this delay? Why grant you a respite from the torment that you deserve, while you perhaps are dreaming of my fatal embraces? Quit now the darkness of sleep and awaken to another darkness, that of your punishment. Raise your empty eyes, know your doom, understand your calamity, reckon up your sufferings. This is how you have found favour with a chaste woman, this is how the marriage-torches have lighted your bridal chamber. Your matrons of honour shall be the avenging Furies, and blindness your best man, and the prick of conscience will haunt you to eternity."

'So she prophesied; then, taking a hairpin from her head, she plunged it deep into both eyes, leaving him totally blinded. While this as yet uncomprehended pain was shaking him out of his drunken sleep, she seized the naked sword that Tlepolemus had always worn and rushed off through the city, setting her frenzied course straight for her husband's tomb, obviously intent on some dreadful deed. We, indeed the whole population, all left our houses and followed her as fast as we could, urging each other to wrest the sword from her maddened grasp. But Charite stood by Tlepolemus' coffin and kept us all off with her gleaming blade. Then, seeing us all weeping profusely and lamenting, "No tears!" she cried. "They have no place here. No grieving! Grief has nothing to do with what I have accomplished. I have taken vengeance on my husband's bloodstained assassin, I have punished the murdering ruffian who destroyed my marriage. Now it is time for me to seek with this sword the way down to my Tlepolemus." And then, having related everything that her husband had told her in her dream and the ruse

13

14

with which she had ensnared Thrasyllus, she ran herself through under the right breast and collapsed; lying in a pool of her own blood she muttered some incoherent words and breathed out her manly spirit. Her attendants quickly washed the unhappy Charite's body with great care and restored her to her husband to lie with him in the same tomb as his wife for ever. Thrasyllus, when he had heard everything that had happened, thinking immediate extinction an inadequate punishment and knowing that even death by the noose could not match the heinousness of his crime, went of his own accord to the tomb. Crying repeatedly "You angry ghosts, here is a willing victim for you", he shut the doors tightly behind him, resolved to put an end by starvation to a life on which he himself had passed sentence of execution.'

15   That was his story, told with many deep sighs and tears. His rustic audience were profoundly moved by it, and in their heartfelt grief at their masters' domestic calamities and their fear of what a change of ownership might bring about, they decided to decamp. The head stableman, he to whose care I had been consigned with such pressing recommendations, loaded on to me and the other pack-animals everything of value that he had stored in his house, and left his home taking it all with him. We were carrying children, women, fowls, cage-birds, kids, puppies – anything that might have slowed down our flight because it was weak on its own feet was conveyed on ours. The weight of my load, huge as it was, did not trouble me: I was too glad to get away from that awful fellow who was proposing to castrate me.

After negotiating a steep pass over a wooded mountainside and traversing a wide and remote plain, we came as evening was closing in on us to a large and prosperous village. The inhabitants tried to discourage us from going on that night or indeed the next day, telling us that the whole countryside around was infested by great packs of wolves, beasts of monstrous size and savage ferocity that were accustomed to plundering at their pleasure. It had got to the point where, just like bandits, they lay in ambush at the roadside and set on travellers; mad with ravening hunger they actually took the neighbouring farmhouses by storm, and human beings now found themselves threatened with the same fate as their defenceless flocks. Why, all along the road we should have to take there were lying half-eaten human bodies and whitening bones denuded of their flesh. This, they said, should be a warning to us. We should never relax our guard and take particular care not to travel until it was broad day and the sun was well up and shining brightly. In that way we should avoid their concealed ambushes, since the aggressive instincts of these fearsome beasts were blunted by daylight. Also we should not straggle on the march but move in a compact phalanx. With these precautions we ought to be able to negotiate the hazards safely.

However, our absconding leaders, damn them, were in too much 16 of a blind hurry and too fearful of possible pursuit to heed these salutary warnings. Not even waiting for daylight they loaded us up and drove us on our way while it was still dark. I got as nearly as I could into the middle of the crowd, since by unobtrusively ensconcing myself in among the mass of animals I reckoned I would protect my behind from the attacks of the wolves. Everybody was amazed to see the pace I set, outstripping even the horses. That, however, was a symptom of fear rather than zeal: I thought to myself that it was fear that made a flier out of the great Pegasus and that it made sense for him to be represented with wings, seeing that it was in terror of the jaws of the fire-breathing Chimaera that he went bounding aloft to heaven itself. Meanwhile the herdsmen who were leading us had armed themselves in warlike fashion. One carried a lance, one a hunting-spear, another a javelin; some had clubs, some stones, of which there was a plentiful supply along our rocky route, and some brandished sharpened stakes; most relied on flaming torches to keep off the wolves. We only needed a trumpeter to complete the military picture.

But though these fears turned out to be quite baseless, we now became involved in a much more serious predicament. The wolves, possibly deterred by the noise from our serried ranks or more probably by the blaze of light, or possibly because they were on the rampage elsewhere, did not attack us, and indeed did not put in an appearance. However, the workers on an estate which we happened 17 to be skirting, thinking from our numbers that we were bandits, in their anxious concern for their property were thrown into a state of panic, and set their dogs on us with hunting cries and a general hullabaloo. These were ferocious great animals, as savage as any wolf or bear, specially reared as guard-dogs. Fierce as they were by nature, they were now further enraged by the uproar made by their masters, and flew at us, attacking from all quarters, tearing at beasts and men alike, until at length their violence had left most of our company down on the ground. The sight was not so much memorable as miserable: this great pack of infuriated dogs, some seizing on those who tried to escape, some grappling with those who stood their ground, some standing over the fallen, rending and ranging through the length and breadth of our caravan. This was bad enough, but worse was to follow. From the rooftops and from a hill nearby the peasants began to hurl down at us a barrage of stones, so that we were hard put to it to know which danger to beware of more, the dogs at close quarters or the stones at long range. One of the latter indeed suddenly hit the woman who was riding me on the head. Her tears and cries of pain immediately brought her husband, the head groom, to her aid. He loudly invoked the gods, and as he wiped away her blood he protested at the top of his voice: 'What is this barbarity? Why attack and stone distressed travellers, human beings like yourselves? What plunder are you hoping for? What wrongs have you to avenge? You aren't wild animals or savages, denizens of caves or rocks, that you should take pleasure in shedding human blood.'

18

He had scarcely uttered these words when the rain of stones stopped, the fierce dogs were called off, and the tumult died down. Then one of the villagers called out from the top of a cypress: 'We're not brigands and we don't want to plunder you – we thought *you* were, and that was the danger we were trying to beat off. Now you can go on your way safely in peace.' That was all very well, but it was with heavy casualties all round that we set out again, some bruised by stones, some displaying bites – nobody had escaped injury. After we had gone some distance we came to a grove of tall trees and green grass, a pleasant spot, where our leaders decided to rest and recuperate for a time while they attended carefully to their various injuries. First they all collapsed and lay on the ground to recover from their fatigue; then they set about applying appropriate remedies to their wounds. One was washing off the blood with water from a nearby stream, another was putting a vinegar compress on his bruises, another was bandaging an open wound. So each man took thought for his own welfare.

Meanwhile an old man was watching us from the top of a 19
neighbouring hill, obviously a shepherd, for there were goats grazing around him. One of our men asked him whether he had any milk for sale, either fresh or in the form of new cheese. For a long time he merely shook his head. At last, 'Are you thinking,' he asked, 'of food or drink or any kind of refreshment *now*? Haven't you any idea where you've chosen to stop?' And so saying he rounded up his flock, turned about, and left the scene. His words and his disappearance greatly alarmed our herdsmen. Panic-stricken, they were anxiously asking each other what sort of a place this was and finding nobody to tell them, when there appeared on the road another old man, this one tall but bowed down by age, leaning heavily on a staff and wearily dragging his feet, and weeping profusely. When he saw us he burst out crying, and supplicating each man in turn he uttered the following appeal:

'I implore you by your Fortunes and your Guardian Spirits, if 20
you hope to reach my age in health and happiness, come to the aid of an old man in his bereavement, rescue my little boy from death and restore him to his white-haired grandfather. My grandson, my darling travelling-companion, was trying to catch a bird that was singing in the hedgerow, and fell into a yawning pit in the bottom of the thicket. Now he is in peril of his life; I know he is alive, for I can hear him crying and calling "Grandfather" over and over again, but as you see I am too feeble in body to be able to rescue him. But you are young and strong, and it will be no trouble to you to help a poor old man and to restore to me this child, the last of my line and all the family I have left.'

As he uttered this plea and tore his white hair, everybody pitied 21
him. Then one of them, braver and younger and stronger than the

rest, the only one who had come off unscathed from the recent battle, jumped up eagerly and asked where exactly the boy had fallen in. The old man pointed out a thicket not far away, and the volunteer went off briskly with him. After a while, when we animals had grazed and the men had seen to themselves and felt restored, they all began to pack up and get ready to move off. First of all they called the volunteer by name, with loud and repeated shouts; then alarmed by the prolonged delay they sent a messenger to find him and warn him that it was time to leave, and bring him back. Almost immediately the messenger reappeared, deathly pale and terrified, with dreadful news of his fellow servant. He had found him lying half-eaten, with a monstrous serpent crouched over him and devouring him, and of the poor old man not a sign anywhere. Hearing this and recollecting what the old shepherd had said, they realized that this indeed was the fierce denizen of the region that he had been threatening them with, and at once quitted the pestilential place and fled precipitately, urging us animals on with continual beating. So after a long stage at top speed we came to a village where we rested for the night. At this place there had been perpetrated a deed that was so memorable that I propose to put it on record.

It concerned a certain slave to whom his master had confided the whole management of his household and who was the steward of the large estate where we had stopped. He had as his consort another slave from the household, but he was madly in love with somebody else, a free woman who was not a member of the family. His wife was so enraged by his infidelity that she made a bonfire of all her husband's account-books and the entire contents of the barns and storehouses. Then, not thinking this enough of a revenge for the affront to her marriage-bed, she turned her fury against her own flesh and blood: passing a noose around her neck, with the same rope she tied to herself the little boy that she had had by her husband, and threw herself down a deep well, dragging the child down with her. Their master, greatly upset by her death, arrested the slave whose lust had been the cause of such a crime, had him stripped naked and smeared all over with honey and lashed tightly to a fig-tree. This had in its hollow trunk an ants' nest, swarming and seething with their multitudinous comings and goings. Directly they sensed the sweet honeyed scent of the man's body they battened on it with their tiny jaws, nibbling endlessly away in their thousands until after many days of torture they had devoured him completely, entrails and all, leaving his bones bare; only his gleaming white skeleton, stripped of flesh, was left fastened to the fatal tree.

Leaving its inhabitants in deep mourning we quitted this abomin- 23 able place and set out again across the plain. At evening we arrived tired out at a certain large and famous city. Here the herdsmen decided to take up permanent residence; they thought it a secure refuge from even the most determined pursuit, and, an added attraction, provisions were good and plentiful. They allowed three days for feeding us animals up, so as to be more saleable, and then they took us to market. The auctioneer called out the price of each animal in a loud voice, and the horses and the other asses were knocked down to prosperous buyers; I alone was left, contemptuously passed over by nearly everybody. In the end I became tired of being handled by people trying to calculate my age from my teeth, and when one of them started scraping my gums with his filthy fingers, I clamped my jaws on his dirty stinking hand good and hard. After that none of the bystanders would venture to make an offer for such a savage animal. So the auctioneer, at the top of his voice and to the detriment of his vocal chords, started to make fun of me and my unfortunate condition. 'How long,' he shouted, 'have I got to waste my time trying to sell this clapped-out old hack? Look at him: his hooves are so worn he can hardly stand, he's deformed by ill-treatment, he's as vicious as he's idle, he's nothing but a sieve on four legs. All right: I'll make a present of him to anybody who doesn't mind wasting fodder.'

With jokes of this kind the auctioneer kept the crowd in fits of 24 laughter. But now my cruel Fortune, whom, though I fled never so far afield, I had not been able to escape or appease by all that I had suffered, once again turned her blind eyes on me and, wonderful to relate, produced a buyer who could not have suited my unhappy circumstances more perfectly. Let me describe him: he was a real old queen, bald apart from a few grizzled ringlets, one of your street-corner scum, one of those who carry the Syrian Goddess around our towns to the sound of cymbals and castanets and make her beg for her living. He was keen to buy me and asked the auctioneer where I came from. He pronounced me to be a genuine Cappadocian and quite a strong little beast. Then he asked my age; the auctioneer answered humorously: 'Well, an astrologer who cast his horoscope said he was in his fifth year, but the beast himself could tell you better from his tax return. I know I'd be liable to the penalties of the Cornelian law if I sold you a Roman citizen as a slave, but here's a good and deserving servant who can be of use to you both at home and abroad. Won't you buy him?' But my tiresome purchaser persisted with one question after another, wanting particularly to know if he could warrant me tractable. 'Why,' said the man, 'this here isn't a donkey, it's an old bell-wether: he's placid, will do anything you want, he doesn't bite or kick — you'd think it was a well-behaved man dwelling in an ass's skin. You can easily find out — put your face between his thighs, and you'll soon discover the extent of his patience.'

These witticisms at the old guzzler's expense were not lost on him, and putting on a great show of indignation he retorted: 'You zombie, you stuffed dummy, damn you and your auctioneer's blether, may the almighty mother of all, she of Syria, and holy Sabadius and Bellona and the Idaean Mother and queen Venus with her Adonis strike you blind for the coarse buffoonery I've had to take from you. You bloody fool, do you think I can entrust the goddess to an unruly beast who might suddenly upset the divine image and throw it off, leaving its unfortunate guardian to run about with her hair all over the place looking for a doctor for her goddess lying on the ground?' When I heard this I wondered if I shouldn't suddenly start bucking as if possessed, so that seeing me in a savage temper he would break off the negotiation. However, he was so anxious to buy me that he paid the price down on the nail and nipped that idea in the bud. My master, I suppose, was so pleased to see the last of me that he readily took seventeen denarii for me, and handed me over with a bit of rope for bridle to Philebus, that being my new owner's name.

Taking delivery of this new member of the family he led me off   26
home, where as soon as he got indoors he called out: 'Look, girls,
at the pretty little slave I've bought and brought home for you.' But
these 'girls' were a troupe of queens, who at once appeared jumping
for joy and squealing untunefully in mincing effeminate tones, in
the belief that it really was a human slave that had been brought to
serve them. When they saw that this was not a case of a hind
substituting for a maiden but an ass taking the place of a man, they
began to sneer and mock their chief, saying that this wasn't a servant
he'd brought but a husband for himself. 'And listen,' they said.
'You're not to gobble up this nice little nestling all on your own –
we're your lovey-doveys too, and you must let us have a share
sometimes.' Exchanging badinage of this sort they tied me up next
to the manger. They also had in the house a beefy young man, an
accomplished piper, whom they had bought in the market from the
proceeds of their street collections. Out of doors he tagged along
playing his instrument when they carried the goddess around, at
home he was toyboy in ordinary to the whole establishment. As
soon as he saw me joining the household, without waiting for orders
he served me out a generous ration of food and welcomed me
joyfully. 'At last,' he said, 'here's somebody to spell me in my
loathsome duties. Long life to you! May you please our masters and
bring relief to my exhausted loins!' When I heard this I began to
picture to myself the ordeals that lay ahead of me.

Next day they all put on tunics of various hues and 'beautified'   27
themselves by smearing coloured gunge on their faces and applying
eye-shadow. Then they set forth, dressed in turbans and robes, some
saffron-coloured, some of linen and some of gauze; some had white
tunics embroidered with a pattern of purple stripes and girded at the
waist; and on their feet were yellow slippers. The goddess, draped
in silk, they placed on my back, and baring their arms to the shoulder
and brandishing huge swords and axes, they capered about with
ecstatic cries, while the sound of the pipes goaded their dancing to
frenzy. After calling at a number of small houses they arrived at a
rich man's country estate. The moment they entered the gates there
was bedlam; they rushed about like fanatics, howling discordantly,

twisting their necks sinuously back and forth with lowered heads, and letting their long hair fly around in circles, sometimes attacking their own flesh with their teeth, and finally gashing their arms with the weapons they carried. In the middle of all this, one of them was inspired to fresh excesses of frenzy; he began to gasp and draw deep laboured breaths, feigning madness like one divinely possessed – as if the presence of a god sickened and enfeebled men instead of making them better!

28   Anyway, let me tell you how heavenly Providence rewarded him. Holding forth like some prophet he embarked on a cock-and-bull story about some sacrilegious act he accused himself of having committed, and condemned himself to undergo the just punishment for his crime at his own hands. So, seizing a whip such as these effeminates always carry about with them, its lashes made of twisted wool ending in long tassels thickly studded with sheep's knuckle-bones, he laid into himself with these knotted thongs, standing the pain of the blows with extraordinary hardihood. What with the sword-cuts and the flogging, the ground was awash with the contaminated blood of these creatures. All this worried me a good deal: seeing all these wounds and gore all over the place I was afraid that, just as some men drink asses' milk, this foreign goddess might conceive an appetite for asses' blood. Finally, however, exhausted or sated with lacerating themselves, they gave over the carnage, and started to stow away in the roomy folds of their robes the coppers, indeed the silver money, that people crowded round to bestow on them – and not only money but jars of wine and milk and cheeses and a quantity of corn and wheat; and some presented the bearer of the goddess with barley. They greedily raked in all this stuff, crammed it into the sacks that they had ready for these acquisitions, and loaded it on my back, so that I was carrying a double load, a walking barn and temple combined.

29   In this way they roved about plundering the whole countryside. In one village they enjoyed a particularly lavish haul and decided to celebrate with a banquet. As the price for a fake oracle they got a fat ram from one of the farmers, which they said was to be sacrificed to appease the hungry goddess. Having made all the arrangements

for dinner they went off to the baths, whence having bathed they brought back with them to share their dinner a robust young peasant, finely equipped in loin and groin. Dinner was hardly begun and they had scarcely started on the hors-d'œuvre when the filthy scum became inflamed by their unspeakable lusts to outrageous lengths of unnatural depravity. The young man was stripped and laid on his back, and crowding round him they made repeated demands on his services with their loathsome mouths. Finally I couldn't stand the sight and tried to shout 'Romans, to the rescue!'; but the other letters and syllables failed me and all that came out was an 'O' – a good loud one, creditable to an ass, but the timing was unfortunate. It so happened that some young men from the next village were looking for an ass that had been stolen that night and were conducting a thorough search of all the lodging-houses. Hearing me braying inside and believing that their quarry was hidden away there, they burst in unexpectedly in a body to reclaim their property then and there, and caught our friends red-handed at their vile obscenities. They immediately called all the neighbours to witness this shocking scene, ironically praising the priests for their spotless virtue.

Demoralized by this scandal, news of which soon spread and naturally got them loathed and detested by one and all, they packed up everything and left the place surreptitiously at about midnight. By sunrise they had covered a good many miles, and by the time it was broad day they found themselves in a remote and desolate area. There they stopped and held a long discussion, as a result of which they prepared to kill me. They removed the goddess from my back and placed her on the ground, stripped me of all my accoutrements, and tied me to an oak-tree; then with that whip with its bone-studded thongs they scourged me almost to death. One of them threatened to hamstring me with his axe for having (he said) made a shameful conquest of his unblemished honour; but the rest of them, thinking not so much of my welfare as of the goddess lying there on the ground, voted for sparing my life. So they loaded me up again, and threatening me with the flat of their swords, they arrived at a certain important city. There one of the principal citizens, an extremely devout and godfearing man, came running out to meet us, roused by the clash of cymbals and the beating of tambourines and the seductive strains of the Phrygian music; being under a vow to welcome and receive the goddess, he allowed us to camp in the precincts of his large house and laid himself out to propitiate her godhead with pious worship and rich sacrifices.

31   It was in this place, I remember, that I had the narrowest of all my escapes from death. It happened that one of the tenants had been hunting and sent his master the fat haunch of a fine stag as his share of the kill. This was carelessly left hanging up within reach near the kitchen door, where one of the dogs, itself a hunter, got at it unnoticed and hastily made off in triumph with his booty without anybody spotting him. When the cook discovered his loss he cursed himself for his carelessness and wept many unavailing tears; then when his master started to ask when dinner would be ready, he said goodbye to his little son, took a rope, and was preparing to hang himself. When his faithful wife grasped her husband's desperate intention, she tore the fatal noose out of his hands. 'Are you out of your mind?' she demanded. 'Has this calamity unnerved you so much that you can't see the remedy that divine Providence is offering out of the blue? If this misfortune hasn't left you too dizzy to see sense, snap out of it and listen to me. Take this ass that's just arrived to somewhere out of the way and slit his throat. You can cut off a haunch to match the one we've lost, and if you cook it skilfully and season it well with savoury herbs you can serve it to the master instead of the venison.' The brute approved this plan to save his life at the expense of mine, damn him, and loudly praising his consort's ingenuity he began to sharpen his knives for the intended butchery.

BOOK 9

*A lucky escape – the story of the lover and the jar – the priests
arrested for theft – Lucius sold to a miller – in the mill again – the
miller's evil wife – more stories of adultery – death of the miller –
sold to a market-gardener – the story of a house destroyed –
commandeered by the military*

While my infamous executioner was thus arming his ungodly hands ⟨1⟩
against me, I did not waste time in protracted thought: the danger
was too acute and immediate to allow of indecision, and I resolved
to escape from the butchery that threatened me by flight. Without
more ado I wrenched myself free of my tether and took off at full
gallop, covering my retreat by a vigorous rearguard action with my
hind hooves, and passing at speed through the connecting colonnade
I catapulted myself into the dining-room where the master of the
house was holding a sacrificial feast with the priests. My headlong
entry sent everything flying, plates, dishes, tables, torches, the lot.
Our host was greatly put out by this unsightly havoc and my
inopportune intrusion, and handed me over to an attendant with
strict orders to shut me up safely somewhere where I wouldn't
disturb their peaceful gathering with any more such skittishness.
Protected by this clever plan of mine and wrested from the butcher's
clutches, I was quite happy to be locked up in prison safe and sound.

But it's a dead certainty that nothing can go right for any human
being if Fortune sets her face against him, and no decision, however
prudent, no counter-measures, however cunning, can upset or
change what divine Providence has decreed and ordained. In my
case the very scheme which I thought had saved my bacon for the
time being now gave rise to a new and alarming peril, sheer destruction indeed, from another quarter. For as the guests were quietly ⟨2⟩
conversing there now suddenly burst into the dining-room a slave,

his face convulsed with terror, who reported to his master that a rabid bitch had just rushed violently in at the back door and had in a frenzy attacked the pack of hounds; then she had invaded the stable next door and similarly savaged many of the animals there, and finally the staff themselves had not escaped. Myrtilus the muleteer and Hephaestio the cook and Hypnophilus the groom of the chambers and Apollonius the doctor and a number of others had all been bitten in different places while trying to drive her away. It was, he said, clear that many of the animals had been infected by her poisonous bites and must likewise be rabid.

This news greatly alarmed everybody, and believing that I too had taken the infection and was mad they grabbed whatever weapons came to hand, and exhorting each other to combine against the common peril – though they were the ones who were really mad – they came after me. They would certainly have hacked me limb from limb with their lances and spears and even hatchets which the servants hurried to supply, had I not grasped the danger of this whirlwind assault and at once rushed into the room where the priests were lodged. They immediately shut and bolted the door after me and mounted guard outside, preserving themselves from contact with me and leaving me to succumb to the devouring and inexorable madness of the fatal infection. Thus, free at last, I embraced the solitude granted me by Fortune, and lying down on a proper bed I slept the first human sleep I had enjoyed for many a long day.

3   It was broad daylight when I got up; I was in excellent form, my weariness dispelled by the softness of my bed. I could hear the people who had been on watch outside all night wondering how I was. 'Do you think the poor beast is still raging mad?' 'No, it's more likely that the poison has increased in violence and that he's dead.' They decided to settle the difference of opinion by having a look, and peeping through a crack they found me standing there quietly, sane and composed. Then they ventured to open the door wider to see if I were now quite docile. However, one of them, whom I must regard as a saviour sent to me from heaven, explained to the others how to prove whether I was sane or not. It was to offer me a bucketful of fresh water to drink: if I drank it eagerly and

without any sign of fear as usual, they could be sure I was sane and wholly free of the infection. If on the other hand I backed away and panicked at the sight or touch of water it would be clear that the madness persisted. This was the standard test, recorded in the ancient authorities.

They agreed, and quickly fetched a large pail of sparkling water   4
from the nearest fountain, which they offered me, though still with some hesitation. I, however, far from hanging back, came forward to meet them, stretched out my neck thirstily, plunged my head right into that literally life-saving water, and drank up every drop of it. Then I quietly let them pat me and fondle my ears and lead me by the bridle and test me in any other way they liked, until I had proved to everybody's satisfaction that, contrary to their insane assumption, I was completely docile. And that was how I escaped from my double danger. The next day I was loaded up again with the goddess and her attributes and led out to the sound of the castanets and cymbals on my beggar's progress. After visiting a number of cottages and hamlets we came to a village built in the ruins of what the inhabitants told us had once been a flourishing city. There we put up at the first inn we came to, where we heard an amusing story of how a poor man was cuckolded, which I should like you to hear too.

This man was extremely poor; he made his living by hiring himself   5
out as a day-labourer at very low wages. He had a wife, as poor as himself, but notorious for her outrageously immoral behaviour. One day, directly he had left early for the job he had in hand, there quietly slipped into the house her dashing blade of a lover. While they were busily engaged with each other, no holds barred, and not expecting visitors, the husband, quite unaware of the situation, and not suspecting anything of the kind, unexpectedly came back. Finding the door closed and locked he commended his wife's virtue, and knocked, whistling to identify himself. The cunning baggage, who was past mistress in goings-on of this kind, disentangled her lover from her tight embraces and quietly ensconced him in an empty storage-jar which stood half hidden in a corner. Then she opened the door, and before her husband was well inside she greeted

him acidly. 'So,' said she, 'I'm to watch you strolling about idly, doing nothing and with your hands in your pockets instead of going to work as usual and seeing about getting us something to live on and buy food with? Here am I wearing my fingers to the bone night and day with spinning wool, just to keep a light burning in our hovel! Don't I wish I was Daphne next door, rolling about in bed with her lovers and already tight by breakfast-time!'

6   Her husband was put out. 'What's all that for?' he asked. 'The boss has got to be in court, so he's given us the day off; but I *have* done something about today's dinner. You know that jar that never has anything in it and takes up space uselessly – doing nothing in fact but get in our way? I've just sold it to a man for six denarii, and he's coming to pay up and collect his property. So how about some action and lending me a hand for a minute to rout it out and hand it over?' The crafty minx was quite equal to this and shrieked with laughter. 'Some husband I've got! Some bargainer! He's disposed of it for six, and I, a mere woman, I've already sold it for seven without even leaving the house!' Her husband was delighted by the increased price. 'Where is this chap who's made such a good offer?' he asked. 'He's inside it, stupid,' she answered, 'giving it a good going-over to see if it's sound.'

7   Her lover did not miss his cue. Emerging at once, 'If you want me to be frank, ma'am,' he said, 'this jar of yours is pretty antique, and there are yawning cracks all over it'; and turning to the husband as if he had no idea who he was, 'Come on, chum, whoever you are, get cracking and fetch me a light, so I can scrape away all the inside dirt and see if the thing's fit to use – money doesn't grow on trees, you know.' Her admirable husband, sharp fellow, suspected nothing, and at once lighted a lamp. 'Come out, old man,' he said. 'Sit down and make yourself comfortable, and let me get it cleaned out properly for you.' So saying, he stripped and taking the lamp in with him started to scrape the encrusted deposits off the rotten old jar. Meanwhile her smart young gallant made the man's wife lean face downwards across the jar, and without turning a hair gave her too a good going-over. She lowered her head into the jar and enjoyed herself at her husband's expense like the clever whore she

was, pointing at this place or that or yet another one that needed scouring, until both jobs were finished. Then the unfortunate artisan took his seven denarii and was made to carry the jar himself to the adulterer's house.

Having stayed in this place for a few days, fattened by public charity and stuffed with the ample proceeds of their prophesying, these most chaste of priests devised a new way of making money. They composed one all-purpose oracle and used it to bamboozle the crowds of people who came to consult them about all sorts of things. This was how it went:

> The yokèd oxen drive the furrow now,
> So that one day luxuriant crops shall grow.

Then if somebody consulted them, say, about getting married, they would answer that it was obvious: the couple should yoke themselves in wedlock and raise a crop of children. If somebody asked about buying an estate, there it was in so many words, oxen and yokes and flourishing crops. If somebody was worried about undertaking a journey and sought divine guidance, the answer was that the tamest beasts in the world were harnessed and ready to start and that the luxuriant crops meant profit. If somebody was going on military service or on an expedition against bandits and wanted to know whether their enterprise would succeed, they declared that victory was absolutely guaranteed by the oracle: the necks of the enemy would bow beneath the yoke and there would be a rich and fruitful yield in the shape of plunder.

By this crafty method of divination they raked in a good deal of money. However, under the ceaseless flow of questions they began to run short of answers, and set off on their travels again. This road was much worse than any we had journeyed over yet, potholed and rutted, sometimes leading through standing pools, sometimes slimy and slippery with mud. I lost count of the number of times I stumbled and fell; I knocked myself about so much that when we finally reached level ground I was almost too tired to go on. At that moment we were suddenly overtaken by a troop of armed horsemen; reining in their horses with difficulty from their wild gallop, they fell on

8

9

Philebus and his colleagues and seized them by the scruff of the neck, accusing them of sacrilege and worse and pummelling them with their fists as they spoke. Then they fettered them all and began to harangue them insistently, pressing them to 'produce the gold cup. Come on,' they said, 'produce it, produce the proceeds of your crime. You filched it from the innermost sanctum of the Mother of the Gods while you pretended to perform your secret ceremonies – and then as if you could escape the punishment of so heinous a crime by a moonlight flit, you left the town before daybreak.' And suiting the action to the word one of them laid hold of me, and rummaging in the very bosom of the goddess whom I carried found the gold cup and displayed it to everybody. However, it would have taken more than this revelation of their iniquity to abash or dismay such lost souls as these. They simply laughed and affected to make a joke of it. 'See how wrong and unjust you can get!' they said. 'As usual, it's the innocent who are accused and put at risk! All because of one little goblet which the Mother of the Gods presented to her Syrian sister-goddess as a memento of her stay, respectable priests are to be treated like criminals on a capital charge!'

All this nonsense and a lot more like it got them nowhere; the villagers took them back and confined them in chains in the local Clink. The cup and the image which I was carrying they consecrated and deposited in the temple treasury. The next day they brought me out and put me up for sale once again, and I was knocked down to a miller from a neighbouring village for seven sesterces more than Philebus had paid for me. He immediately loaded me heavily with some corn that he had just bought and led me by a steep path, strewn with stones and stumps of all kinds, to his mill.

11   In this place a large number of animals were employed in turning round and round mills of various sizes. It was not only by day but all night long that they kept the machinery in perpetual motion and burned, so to speak, the midnight oil to produce their nightly quota of flour. I, however, was treated as a distinguished guest by my new master, I suppose because he thought that if I were immediately initiated into this slavery I should cut up rough. So he gave me my first day off, and my manger was abundantly supplied with food.

This life of leisure and happy repletion lasted for just that one day. Early next morning I was harnessed to what seemed to be the largest of the mills, blindfolded, and immediately forced round the circular track, restricted by the revolving motion, and so walking back and forth and always retracing my footsteps, wandering but never deviating in my wanderings. However, acute and sensible as ever, I declined to submit tamely to this apprenticeship. Though, when I was a man among men, I had often seen this sort of machinery in operation, I now pretended to have no experience or knowledge of such work and stood stock still in feigned bewilderment. I thought, you see, that I would be considered unsuited to this kind of employment and absolutely useless at it, and be set to some lighter work or even be left to feed in idleness. My cleverness got me nowhere – far from it, for several of them at once armed themselves with sticks and standing in a circle – being blindfolded I had no idea what was happening – at a given signal they all shouted and laid into me. I was so startled by the commotion that I totally jettisoned all my plans, and scientifically throwing my weight into the collar I broke into a brisk trot. This abrupt change of policy occasioned general merriment.

The day was nearly over and I was pretty well worn out when they undid my harness, released me from my attachment to the mill, and tethered me to my manger. But, fatigued as I was and desperately needing to restore my strength – I was indeed nearly dying of hunger – yet my natural curiosity possessed me, and neglecting my plentiful supply of food I became totally absorbed in studying, with a kind of pleasure, the routine of this unpleasant establishment. As to the human contingent – what a crew! – their whole bodies picked out with livid weals, their whip-scarred backs shaded rather than covered by their tattered rags, some with only a scanty loin-cloth by way of covering, and all of them showing through the rents in what clothes they had. There were branded foreheads, half-shaven heads, and fettered ankles; their faces were sallow, their eyes so bleared by the smoky heat of the furnaces that they were half blind; and like boxers, who sprinkle themselves with dust before fighting, they were dirty white all over with a floury powder.

12

13   When I turn to my fellow inmates in the stable, words almost fail me. What an array of old mules and clapped-out nags of horses! Their heads down in the trough, they were gobbling up great quantities of chaff; there they stood, with suppurating sores on their sagging necks, their nostrils dilated with perpetual coughing, their chests galled by the continual rubbing of their harness, their ribs laid bare by countless beatings, their hooves monstrously enlarged by their endless circlings, and their coats dirty and rough and mangy from starvation.

Seeing this lamentable household I feared a similar fate for myself, and remembering Lucius as he was in happier days and with the end now finally staring me in the face, I let my head hang down and abandoned myself to grief. The only comfort I had in this wretched existence was the entertainment furnished by my inborn curiosity, since everybody behaved and spoke with complete freedom in front of me, paying no attention to my presence. Very rightly did the divine originator of ancient Greek poetry, when he wished to define a consummately wise man, sing of one who attained supreme virtue by visiting many cities and acquainting himself with many peoples. Speaking for myself, I am devoutly grateful to the ass that I once was, for it was he, when I was concealed under his hide and was buffeted by so many tribulations, who rendered me, no wiser, I must admit, but very widely informed.

14   Now, let me present to you an exceptionally good story, a prettily polished production. The miller who had bought me was himself an honest and thoroughly decent man, but the wife who had fallen to his lot was a dreadful woman, the worst of her sex, and made his bed and board such a misery to him that even I silently groaned at what he had to put up with. Not a single vice was wanting in this abominable woman's make-up; her heart was like a slimy cesspit in which every kind of moral turpitude had collected. She was hard-hearted, perverse, man-mad, drunken, and stubborn to the last degree. Tight-fisted in the squalid pursuit of gain, lavish in spending on debauchery, she had no use for loyalty and was a sworn enemy to chastity. Worse still, she had rejected and spurned the heavenly gods, and in place of true religion she had falsely and blasphemously

set up a deity of her own whom she proclaimed as the One and Only God; and having bamboozled the world in general and her husband in particular by meaningless rituals of her own invention, she was able to give herself over to a day-long course of drinking and prostitution.

That then was his wife, and she persecuted me with extraordinary 15 venom. Before dawn, while she was still in bed, she would call for the new ass to be harnessed to the mill; and as soon as she was up and about she would come and stand there and order them to thrash me as hard as they could while she watched. When it was time for dinner and the other animals were released, she would not let me be taken to the manger until much later. This cruel treatment whetted my natural curiosity about her behaviour. I was aware that there was a young man who regularly visited her bedroom, and I very much wanted to see his face, if my eyes ever got a moment's freedom from their blindfold – for my resourcefulness would have been entirely adequate to uncover, somehow or other, this detestable woman's delinquencies. There was an old crone, her accomplice in her debauchery and the go-between in her affairs, who was in her company all day and every day. The two of them would breakfast together, and then over their neat wine they would conspire to plan their next campaign, devising tortuous schemes and treacherous plots for the undoing of her unfortunate husband. Though I was still very angry with Photis for her mistake in making me an ass instead of a bird, I had this one consolation in my woeful deformity, that the long ears with which I was equipped enabled me to follow everything that was happening even at a considerable distance.

One day then this old woman's voice came hesitantly to my ears. 16 'Madam,' she said, 'of course it's your affair entirely; it was you who acquired, without consulting me, this slug, this poltroon of a lover, who supinely dreads the frown of that tiresome and obnoxious husband of yours and, his passion enfeebled and slackened by fear, hurts you by his failure to respond to your willing embraces. What a contrast to Philesitherus! *He*'s young, handsome, generous and vigorous, a stalwart match for any husband's useless precautions. He deserves, if any man does, to enjoy the favours of every wife, he deserves a crown of gold if only for the masterly scheme he recently devised against a jealous husband. Let me tell you about it, and you'll see how different lovers can be. You know Barbarus, one of our town councillors – the people call him the Scorpion because he's so sharp in his ways. He had a wife of good family and great beauty whom he kept locked up at home under extraordinarily strict guard.' Here the miller's wife struck in: 'Of course, I know her well; Arete was at school with me.' 'Then,' said the old woman, 'I suppose you know the whole story of her and Philesitherus?' 'Not at all,' she answered, 'but I'm dying to hear it. Please, mother, tell me everything just as it happened.' At once the garrulous old gossip began: 'Barbarus, having to be away from home and wishing to protect his beloved wife's chastity with the utmost care, gave secret instructions to a slave called Myrmex whom he knew to be completely trustworthy, and assigned to him the entire responsibility for looking after his mistress. He threatened him with perpetual imprisonment and a slow death by starvation if he allowed anybody whatever to so much as touch her in passing; and he confirmed his threat with an oath by all the gods. And so, leaving the terrified Myrmex in close attendance on his wife, Barbarus departed with his mind quite at ease.

'Worried sick, Myrmex absolutely refused to let his mistress leave the house, declining to be parted from her even when she was busy with her woolwork. When in the evening she had to go out to the baths, he attached himself firmly to her, holding on to the hem of her robe; and in this way with admirable keenness he faithfully fulfilled the assignment with which he was entrusted. But the noble dame's beauty did not escape the watchful eye of the susceptible Philesitherus. The fame of her virtue and the excessive strictness with which she was guarded were enough in themselves to provoke and inflame his desire: ready to do or die in the attempt he mustered all his forces to take the citadel by storm. Knowing full well that men's loyalty is a frail thing, that no obstacle is proof against money, and that gold will force open even gates of steel, he contrived to get Myrmex on his own, revealed his love, and begged and prayed him to relieve his torments. His mind, he said, was firmly made up: if he did not achieve his desire soon, he would kill himself without more ado. Not, he added, that Myrmex had anything to be afraid of: the thing was easy – he could slip into the house alone at evening safely concealed and protected by the darkness, and leave again in a matter of moments. To these and similar persuasions he added finally a powerful lever, calculated to uproot and overturn the slave's rock-like determination: holding out his hand he showed him thirty bright new gold pieces, twenty for the girl and ten, in the goodness of his heart, for Myrmex himself.

'Myrmex was horrified at this outrageous proposal and rushed away stopping his ears. But he was haunted by the fiery vision of that gleaming gold, and though he made haste to remove himself from the scene and made off home at speed, he still kept on seeing the beautiful sheen of the coins, and could think of nothing else but that rich booty. For many hours the unfortunate man, tormented and distracted, was vacillating, his purpose driven this way and that like a wave-tossed boat: loyalty on the one hand, gain on the other, torture on that side, pleasure on this. Finally gold overcame his fear of death; and so far from his lust for that lovely money abating with the passing of time, the plague took over and preoccupied his nights: though his master's threats kept him at home, the gold was beckoning him outside. In the end he swallowed his scruples, and without more ado took the message to his mistress. She, fickle like all women, acted in character and agreed to sell her honour for the accursed metal. Myrmex, overjoyed, flew off to accomplish the downfall of his loyalty, lusting not merely to possess but actually to hold the money that he had seen and that was to be his undoing. Happy and excited, he announced to Philesitherus that, thanks entirely to his Herculean efforts, what he so much longed for was accomplished, and in the same breath demanded the agreed reward. Then Myrmex' hand grasped gold coins – a hand hitherto unconversant even with copper. 19

'So at dead of night he brought the adventurous lover, alone and with his head well muffled, to the house and ushered him into his mistress's bedroom. The two of them lost no time in making an offering of their embraces to Love the Raw Recruit, and, stripped 20

for action, were just beginning their first campaign under Venus'
banner, when quite unexpectedly, having stolen a march under
cover of night, her husband suddenly presented himself at the door
of the house. He knocked, he shouted, he banged on the door with
a stone, and as every moment's delay heightened his suspicions
he began to threaten Myrmex with dire punishment. He, totally
confused by this unforeseen calamity and not knowing what to do
in his distraught state, made the only excuse he could think of, that
the door-key had been so carefully hidden that he could not find it
in the dark. Meanwhile Philesitherus, hearing the noise, quickly
huddled on his tunic, but in his hurry to leave the room ran out
barefoot. Then Myrmex finally unlocked and opened the door and
let his master in, still invoking the gods; and while he made straight
for the bedroom, Philesitherus was quietly and quickly let out. With
him clear of the threshold, Myrmex locked up the house and went
back to bed with nothing (so he thought) to worry about.

21   'But when day came and Barbarus got up, he saw under the bed
a pair of sandals that he did not recognize, the ones that Philesitherus
had worn on his visit, and immediately guessed what had been going
on. However, he said nothing of his anguished suspicions either to
his wife or to any of the household, but quietly picked up the sandals
and hid them in his clothes. Then, merely ordering his fellow slaves
to tie Myrmex up and bring him to the public square, he rapidly
made his own way there, stifling his repeated groans, certain that the
evidence of the sandals would enable him to uncover the adulterer's
tracks without any difficulty. But as the angry Barbarus was coming
down the street, all scowls and frowns, with Myrmex behind him
loaded with chains – though he had not been caught red-handed,
he was demoralized by his guilty conscience and was trying ineffec-
tually to arouse pity by frantic weeping and wailing – at that moment
Philesitherus met them on his way to an appointment elsewhere
about quite a different matter. Though startled by this unexpected
sight he was not dismayed. He immediately realized the mistake he
had made in his hurried departure and acutely guessed what must
have happened; summoning up his habitual assurance, he pushed
aside the escorting slaves and fell on Myrmex shouting at the top of

his voice and pretending to pummel his face unmercifully. "Thief!
Perjurer!" he bawled. "May your master here, may all the gods in
heaven, that you had the nerve to call as witnesses to your oath,
damn you to hell! It *was* you who stole my slippers yesterday in the
baths! By God, you deserve to keep those chains on you until you've
worn them out – you really ought to be in the dark behind bars."
The enterprising lover's timely ruse took Barbarus in and indeed
left him quite happy and credulous as before. On his return home
he called Myrmex, gave him the slippers, and without more ado
forgave him completely, urging him to restore them to their owner
that he had stolen them from.'

At this point in the old woman's chatter the wife interrupted: 22
'Lucky her, free to enjoy so steadfast a friend! What a contrast to
me, landed with a lover who trembles at the sound of the mill or
the sight of that mangy ass there.' The old woman answered: 'Leave
it to me: I'll talk him over and put heart into him, and I'll go bail
for his appearance – you'll find him a really sprightly lover.' With
that she left the room, promising to return that evening. Meanwhile
this chaste wife set to and prepared a regular Salian banquet, decanting
rare wines and garnishing freshly cooked ragouts with preserved
delicacies. Having set the table thus lavishly she awaited the arrival
of her paramour as of some god. (Luckily it happened that her
husband was dining out that evening with one of his neighbours, a
fuller.) It was now nightfall, and I had at last been unharnessed and
left to relax and refresh myself. However, I was congratulating myself
less on being freed from my labours than on the fact that, my eyes
being now uncovered, I had an uninterrupted view of all this
woman's carryings-on. Now the sun had sunk beneath the waves
of Ocean and was lighting the subterranean regions of the world,
when the evil old crone reappeared with the dashing adulterer in
tow. He was no more than a lad, fresh-complexioned and smooth-
chinned, himself still an adulterer's delight. The wife welcomed him
with a shower of kisses and invited him to sit down to dinner.

However, the young man had scarcely sipped his first cup of wine   23
and nibbled the hors-d'œuvre when the husband arrived back long
before he was expected. The virtuous wife, consigning him to

perdition and wishing he would break both legs, hastily hid her lover, panic-stricken and white with fear, under a wooden trough used for husking grain, which happened to be near at hand. Then, passing off her infamous behaviour with the cunning of her sex and feigning nonchalance, she asked her husband why he had left his good friend's dinner and come back so early. He answered despondently and with many a sigh: 'It was because I couldn't stand the shocking misconduct of that abandoned woman that I came away. Ye gods, how could a virtuous and well-conducted wife like that besmirch and disgrace herself so foully? I swear by holy Ceres over there that with women like that around I don't trust my eyes any more.' Her interest excited by her husband's words, his audacious wife was eager to hear all about it and kept on and on at him to tell the whole story from beginning to end. She persisted until he gave in and, unaware of what was going on under his own roof, proceeded to recount the misfortunes of another man's house.

24   'My friend the fuller's wife,' he said, 'was a woman, so it seemed, of unimpeachable chastity and shining reputation, presiding virtuously over her husband's house. She had, however, secretly fallen for a lover, and lost no opportunity of clandestine meetings with him. At the very moment that we arrived for dinner after our bath, she and the young man were making love. Alarmed by our unexpected appearance, she had a bright idea, and hid him under a wickerwork frame, a sort of wigwam on which cloth is draped to be bleached with sulphur fumes. Having ensconced him there, safely as she thought, she joined us at table without a care in the world. Meanwhile, however, the young man, choked and stifled by the pungent fumes of the sulphur, began to suffocate and – the usual effect of

25   this potent chemical – began to emit a series of loud sneezes. At first, when he heard these sneezes coming from his wife's direction, her husband thought they were hers and said the usual "bless you", but when this had happened several times he began to think that it was rather too much of a good thing, and finally guessed the true state of affairs. Pushing the table abruptly aside he whipped off the frame and revealed her lover, who was now almost at his last gasp. Burning with rage at this affront he called for a sword and was

hell-bent on accelerating the man's end by cutting his throat. However, I managed with some difficulty to restrain his fury, reckoning
that we should all be in danger as accessories, and pointing out that
his enemy would soon die in any case from the violent effects of
the sulphur without any help from us. He calmed down, not so
much because of anything I said as because of the hard facts of the
situation, the man being already half dead, and dragged him out and
left him in the neighbouring alley. Meanwhile I gave his wife some
discreet advice, and finally got her to leave the shop for a while and
get herself taken in by one of her women friends, to give her
husband's anger time to cool down. He was so red-hot and mad
with rage that he was clearly thinking of doing both himself and her
some fatal mischief. That was my friend's dinner-party, and that's
why I've left it and come back home in disgust.'

All the while the miller was telling his story, his brazen-faced wife   26
was heaping abuse on the fuller's wife, calling her faithless, shameless,
a disgrace to her .sex, who had held her virtue cheap, who had
trampled on the bond of the marriage-bed, who had dishonoured
her husband's house by turning it into a brothel, and had thrown
away the dignity of a wife by exchanging it for the name of whore.
Women like that, she added, deserved to be burned alive. She was,
however, uneasily aware of her own secret amour and her guilty
conscience, and wanting to release her lover from his uncomfortable
refuge as soon as possible, she repeatedly suggested to her husband
that it was high time for bed. But he had had his dinner cut short
and had come away practically starving, so he politely said he would
like something to eat. She at once produced supper, though with a
bad grace, having intended it for somebody else. As for me, I was
deeply upset to contemplate this abominable woman's misdeeds and
the way in which she was now brazening the thing out; and I thought
carefully how I might assist my master by uncovering and disclosing
her deceit, and how by knocking over the trough under which he
lay tortoise-like, I might display her lover to the eyes of the world.

While the thought of the indignity inflicted on my master was   27
tormenting me, Providence for once smiled on me. There was a
lame old man who was in charge of the stable, and as it was now

time for us to be watered he came to lead us all out together to the nearby pond. This gave me the perfect opportunity for the revenge on which I was set. As I was going by I saw the man's fingers sticking out from under the edge of the trough, which was rather too narrow for him; and treading sideways on them as hard as I could I ground them to pulp. Unable to bear the pain he yelled aloud and threw off the trough, and being thus restored to public view he uncovered this vile woman's charade. The miller, however, did not seem unduly put out by this affront to his honour. Regarding the pale and trembling boy with an expression of calm benevolence he spoke soothingly to him. 'Don't be afraid, my boy,' he said, 'I'm not going to be harsh with you. I'm no barbarian or brutish peasant; and I'm not going to follow the fuller's cruel example and suffocate you with the deadly fumes of sulphur. I certainly shan't invoke the severity of the law on adultery and demand the death sentence for such a pretty little lad as you. All I'm going to do is share you equally with my wife. I shan't sue for the division of family property but for its common enjoyment, so that without controversy or dispute the three of us agree together in one bed. I've always lived so harmoniously with my wife that, as the wise recommend, our views on everything have always coincided. However, equity forbids the wife to have more authority than the husband.'

28   With mocking blandishments of this sort he led the boy, who did not want to come but had no choice but to follow, to bed. His chaste wife he locked in another room; and then alone in bed with the boy he enjoyed a most gratifying revenge for the ruin of his marriage. As soon as it was light he called for two of his strongest slaves and had the boy hoisted aloft and tied up. Then he took a cane and thrashed him, saying: 'What business has a delicate little creature like you, a mere child, to be cheating your lovers of the enjoyment of your youthful beauty and to be chasing women – free women at that – and breaking up legal marriages and usurping the name of adulterer before you're of age?' After a lot more to the same effect, all to the accompaniment of a thorough beating, he threw the boy out of the house. So our valiant seducer made off very sorry for himself, having unexpectedly escaped with his life, but with that

white bottom of his a good deal the worse for wear after the experiences of both the night and the morning. The miller then followed suit with his wife, serving notice of divorce and throwing her too out of the house.

She, however, on top of her natural malevolence was infuriated 29
by this insult, richly though she deserved it, and took to her old ways again, resorting in her anger to the familiar arts of her sex. She took great pains to discover a certain old woman, past mistress of her profession, who it was believed could bring about anything by her curses and spells, and loading her with gifts she begged her earnestly to do one of two things: either to pacify her husband and reconcile him to her, or if that proved impossible, to send in a ghost or some evil spirit to put a violent end to his life. The witch, who could control the gods themselves, in her first offensive deployed only the light arms of her nefarious art, trying to soften the husband's grievously wounded feelings and revive his love. When that did not succeed as she had expected, she took umbrage at the infernal powers, and incited as much by their lack of cooperation as by the reward she had been promised, she mounted an attack on the unfortunate man's life, and raised the ghost of a woman who had died a violent death to destroy him.

But perhaps at this point the attentive reader will start to pick 30
holes in my story and take me up on it. 'How is it, you clever ass you,' they will say, 'that while you were confined in the mill you were able, as you say, to know what these women were doing in secret?' All right: let me tell you how a man of an inquiring turn of mind in the guise of a beast of burden found out the whole story of this plot against the miller's life. Round about midday a woman suddenly appeared at the mill got up as if she were on trial for her life, strangely disfigured and woebegone, barely covered in pitiful rags, barefoot, deathly pale and drawn, her grizzled hair dishevelled, dirty and sprinkled with ash, hanging down in front and hiding most of her face. This apparition gently laid hold of the miller and, as if wishing to talk to him in private, drew him into his room and shut the door. Nothing was then heard for a long time. Meanwhile the instalment of grain which the mill-hands had been grinding was

finished, and they needed to ask for more. The slaves stood by the door and called their master, asking for a fresh supply. When they got no response from him to their loud and repeated shouts, they began to knock hard on the door; finding it tightly barred they feared an accident or foul play, and by breaking and dislodging the hinges with a violent heave they finally gained an entry. They saw no sign of the woman anywhere, but there was their master hanging from a beam, strangled and lifeless. They released him from the noose and took him down, and with much weeping and lamentation washed the body and performed the last rites, then carried him to the grave followed by a long train of mourners.

31   The next day the miller's daughter, who was married and lived in a nearby village, arrived in mourning, tearing her disordered hair and beating her breast. She already knew the whole story, but not from any messenger; her father's ghost had appeared to her in a dream in pitiable guise, with the noose still around his neck, and had told her all about her stepmother's crimes, her adultery and witchcraft, and how the evil spirit had possessed him and carried him down to hell. For a long time she tortured herself with weeping, but finally, restrained by the friends who rallied round her, she allowed her grief to subside. When after the canonical nine days the ceremonies at the tomb had been duly performed, as heiress to the estate she put everything, slaves, plant and animals, up for auction. So Fortune, irresponsible as ever, through the unpredictable operation of a sale scattered the whole establishment to the four winds. As for me, I was bought by a poor market-gardener for fifty sesterces – an awful lot of money, as he said, but he hoped that with the two of us on the job he could eke out a living for himself.

32   At this point the subject demands that I expound the routine of my new service. Each morning my master would load me up with produce and take me to the nearest town, and having consigned his wares to the retailers he would ride home on my back. Then, while he slaved away at digging and watering and all his other chores, I meanwhile had nothing to do and could recuperate in peace and tranquillity. But the stars had now performed their ordained revolutions and the year had again come full circle; leaving behind autumn

and the pleasures of the vintage, it had now entered Capricorn with its winter frosts. What with the continual rain and the heavy dews at night, I was suffering agonies of cold, confined as I was to a stall that was open to the elements. My master was so poor that he could not afford bedding of any kind or even the scantiest of coverings for himself, let alone for me; he had to be content with what shelter his small thatched hut offered. On top of this, morning would find me standing barefoot in freezing mud and splinters of ice and dying of cold; and I couldn't even fill my belly with my usual food. Dinner was exactly the same for both my master and me, and meagre enough it was: nasty old lettuces that had bolted and gone bad; they had run to seed and looked like large brooms, and their juice was bitter and foul.

One night a proprietor from a nearby village who had lost his way in the dark, there being no moon, and had got soaked in a downpour, finding himself benighted and his horse tired out, stopped at our place. He received a friendly reception, the best our circumstances allowed, and though his entertainment was far from luxurious he at least got the rest he needed. Wishing to requite his host's kindness, he promised to give him some corn and olive oil and two jars of wine as well from his estate. The very next day my master, armed with a sack and two empty wineskins, mounted me bareback, and we set off on our journey, a matter of some seven miles. We arrived and found the farm as directed, where his amiable host at once sat my master down to an excellent dinner. While they were chatting over their wine there occurred a truly remarkable portent. One of the flock of fowls was running about the barnyard loudly clucking as a hen usually does before laying an egg. Seeing her, 'Faithful and fruitful servant!' said the master. 'You've never failed to supply us with our eggs every day, and I can see that you're proposing to give us a treat now. Here, boy,' he called, 'put the laying-basket in the usual corner.' The slave did as he was told, but the hen ignored her usual nesting-apartment and gave birth right at her master's feet – a premature birth, and a very worrying one: for it was no egg as we know it, but a perfectly formed pullet complete with wings, feet, eyes and voice which immediately began to follow its mother around.

34   On top of this there followed a much more sinister happening, which caused general consternation, as well it might. Right there, under the table, which still had the remains of dinner on it, a yawning gap appeared in the floor which spurted a veritable fountain of blood, the spray from which drenched the table in gore. Then, while everybody was rooted in astonishment and terror at this warning from heaven, a servant ran in from the cellar to announce that all the wine which had some time ago been racked off had become scalding hot and boiled over out of every cask as if it had a blazing fire underneath it. Meanwhile outside the house there had been seen a weasel dragging a dead snake along in its mouth; a small green frog had jumped out of the mouth of one of the sheepdogs; and the same dog had been attacked by a ram that was standing nearby and throttled with a single bite. The master and the entire household were petrified with fear and thrown into the depths of despair by all these events, at a loss to know what to do first and what next, what to do and what not to do, which and what sort of victims should be sacrificed in expiation to avert these threats from heaven.

35   While everyone was still numbed by apprehension and dread, a slave arrived bringing his master news of complete and utter disaster. He had three grown-up sons, well educated and irreproachably behaved, who were his pride and joy. They had for some time been friendly with a poor man who owned a small cottage. Bordering on this cottage was a large and prosperous estate owned by a powerful neighbour. This was a rich young man of noble family, who by trading on his proud ancestry had become an influential figure in city politics and got his own way in everything. This man declared war on his humble neighbour and harried his poor little domain, killing his animals, driving off his cattle, and trampling down his young crops. Having despoiled him of all his modest fortune, he determined to evict him from his land, and by cooking up a spurious lawsuit about boundaries he laid claim to his entire property. Un-assertive as he was, the farmer, stripped of everything by this rich man's greed, still wanted to keep at least his ancestral plot to be buried in, and in great fear and trembling had enlisted the aid of a number of friends to testify formally as to the boundaries. These

included the three brothers, who had come to give what help they could to their friend in his misfortune.

So far from being deterred or put out of countenance in the 36 slightest by such a crowd of citizens, this madman was no less violent in his language than in his acts of brigandage. When they tried to reason with him gently and pacify his hot temper with conciliatory words, he burst out with a solemn oath by his own life and the life of all those dear to him that he did not give a damn for all these mediators, and that as for this neighbour of his, his slaves were going to take him by the ears and send him packing then and there. This statement caused outrage in the minds of all who heard it. One of the brothers immediately and now without mincing his words answered that it was no use his relying on his wealth to carry off his threats and his tyrannical arrogance: under the free protection of the laws even poor men were secured against the insolence of the rich. Like oil on flames, like sulphur on a blaze, like a whip laid on a Fury, so these words fed the man's savagery. Enraged to outright madness, he shouted that all of them and the laws as well could go to hell; and ordered his dogs to be loosed and sicked on to attack and kill them. These were herdsmen's dogs from his estate, huge fierce brutes that were used to feeding on corpses left lying about the countryside and had been trained to savage passing wayfarers indiscriminately. At once, their fury kindled by the herdsmen's usual signal, they rushed at the people in a mad frenzy and fell on them with dreadful discordant baying, wounding, tearing, and lacerating them all over.

In the midst of this carnage and the jostling of the panic-stricken 37 crowd the youngest brother caught his foot on a stone and fell headlong to the ground, so providing the savage pack with an atrocious repast; finding him lying there a helpless prey, in a moment they were rending him limb from limb. His brothers heard his cries of agony, and ran in anguish to his assistance; wrapping their cloaks round their left hands they tried to defend him and drive off the dogs with a volley of stones. They were, however, powerless to frighten or beat off the savage beasts, and the unfortunate young man was torn in pieces and died adjuring them with his last breath to take vengeance for their younger brother's death on that rich villain. They, not so much in desperation as not caring whether they lived or died, rushed blazing with anger at the rich man and attacked him with a furious salvo of stones. But the bloodstained assassin, schooled in many an earlier outrage of the same kind, hurled his spear and transfixed one of them through the chest. But though killed outright, the young man did not fall to the ground, for the spear had been hurled so violently that it passed right through him and, sticking out behind for most of its length, lodged firmly in the ground, leaving his body balanced in mid-air. Then one of the slaves, a large hefty fellow, came to the aid of his cutthroat master and at long range aimed a stone at the third brother's right arm. The stone, however, unexpectedly missed and fell harmlessly after merely grazing his fingertips.

38   This happy accident offered the astute young man a faint hope of revenge. Pretending that his hand was disabled he addressed his cruel enemy: 'Very well: exult in the destruction of our whole house, glut your insatiable cruelty with the blood of three brothers, triumph gloriously over your humiliated fellow citizens – but remember this, that though you can strip poor men of their possessions and push your boundaries wider still and wider, you will always have a neighbour. As for this hand of mine, which should have cut off your head, through the injustice of fate it is bruised and useless.' Angry as he was already, these words maddened the ruffian; and sword in hand he rushed furiously at the hapless youth to dispatch him. But the man he had challenged was no less tough than he, and he met with a resistance that he had by no means expected. With a grip of iron the young man seized his right hand, and wielding his sword with all his strength with blow upon blow he expelled the rich villain's polluted soul from his body. Then, to escape the crowd of retainers who were coming at him, he cut his own throat on the spot with the blade that still dripped with his enemy's blood.

These were the events that the portents had foretold; this was what the unfortunate master had been warned of. With these calamities thick upon him, the old man could not utter a single word or even shed a silent tear. Seizing the knife with which he had just been helping his guests to cheese and other eatables, he followed the example of his unhappy son and plunged it repeatedly into his throat; then collapsing forwards on to the table he washed away the bloodstains from the portent in a fresh torrent of blood.

The gardener was left pitying the plight of this house, thus brought low in a matter of hours, but also sadly lamenting his own misfortune – tears as the price of his dinner and empty hands which he could only wring over and over again. There was nothing to do but mount me and go back the way we had come, but even that was not accomplished safely. A burly individual, apparently from his dress and behaviour a legionary soldier, accosted us and asked in overbearing and arrogant language where he was going with that unloaded ass? My master, still grieving and bemused, and in any case not understanding Latin, was passing on without answering. At this the soldier's natural insolence flared up, and angry at his silence, which he took as an insult, he knocked him off my back with a blow of the vine-staff which he carried. The gardener humbly answered that he didn't know the language and couldn't understand what he was saying. So in Greek the soldier asked: 'Where are you taking that ass?' The gardener said he was going to the next town. 'But I need his services,' said the soldier. 'He's wanted to carry my commander's gear from the fort over there with the rest of the baggage-animals': and with that he laid hold of my bridle and began to lead me away. The gardener, wiping off the blood that was flowing from the blow he had received to the head, begged him, calling him 'mate', to behave more civilly and kindly, reinforcing his pleas by invoking all his hopes of professional success. 'And in any case,' he added, 'it's a useless beast with a vicious disposition, and it's on its last legs with some horrible disease; it has just about enough life and breath in its body to carry the odd bundle of vegetables from my garden here without collapsing – it's certainly not fit to bear anything heavier.'

However, seeing that the soldier, so far from being mollified by any entreaties, was becoming exasperated and looked like doing him a mischief, seeing him indeed preparing to reverse his cudgel and brain him with the knob, the gardener resorted to desperate measures. Pretending that he was going to touch his knees to stir him to pity,

39

40

he crouched down low, then suddenly laying hold of both his feet he lifted him high in the air and threw him heavily to the ground; then at once he attacked him with his fists, his elbows, his teeth, and even with a stone snatched from the road, battering him all over, face, hands, and body. The soldier, once stretched on the ground, was powerless to fight back or defend himself, but kept on threatening that if he once got up he would cut him in little bits with his sword. That gave the gardener an idea: he drew the sword himself and threw it well away, then resumed his attack, beating him even more savagely. The soldier, prostrated and handicapped by his injuries, resorted to his only remaining hope of survival and shammed dead. Then the gardener took the sword, got on my back, and posted straight to town, where, without troubling even to call in at his garden, he went to a friend's house. He told him the whole story and begged for help in his peril, asking him to hide the two of us for a little while; two or three days' concealment would allow him to escape prosecution on a capital charge. The man was mindful of their old friendship and at once took him in. I had my feet tied together and was hoisted up a ladder into the loft; the gardener stayed downstairs in the shop, where he took refuge in a chest with the lid fastened down over him.

41 The soldier, however, as I learned later, did in the end recover consciousness, with all the symptoms of a severe hangover, and in great pain from his wounds and supporting himself with difficulty on his stick, made his way with uncertain steps to the town. He was too much ashamed of his violent behaviour and the poor show he had put up to say anything about the affair to the townspeople, but swallowed his resentment until he came across some fellow soldiers, to whom he confided the story of his disaster. It was decided that he should secrete himself in his quarters for a while – for quite apart from his personal humiliation he feared that the loss of his sword was a sacrilegious breach of his military oath – while his comrades, who had taken careful note of our particulars, should spare no pains to track us down and exact vengeance. They soon found a treacherous neighbour, who told them exactly where we were hidden. The soldiers summoned the magistrates with a yarn that they concocted

about a valuable silver cup belonging to their commander that they had lost on the road and how a certain gardener had found it and refused to give it up, and was now hiding in a friend's house. On hearing of the loss and the commander's name the magistrates appeared before the door of the house where we were and loudly called on our host to hand us over – 'we know they're in there', they shouted – if he wanted to save his own skin. He was not in the least frightened but was concerned only to safeguard the friend he had sworn to protect: he denied all knowledge of us and said he had not set eyes on the gardener for days. The soldiers maintained that he was hiding there in that very place, and swore it by the Emperor's genius. At last, as the man persisted in his stubborn denial, the magistrates decided to get at the truth by a search. The constables and other public officers were accordingly sent in with orders to investigate carefully every corner of the house, and they reported that not a soul, and certainly no ass, was to be found inside.

Then the dispute waxed hotter on both sides, the soldiers asserting 42 that they knew perfectly well that we were in there and repeatedly invoking the name of Caesar, while our host persisted in denying it, calling for his part the divine powers to witness. Hearing this noisy argument, curious as usual and, like an ass, brash and impatient, I angled my neck out of a little window, eager to see what the hubbub was all about. It happened that one of the soldiers at that moment caught a glimpse of my shadow and called his comrades to look. There was a great to-do, and some of them immediately climbed the ladder, grabbed me, and hauled me down like a prisoner. There was now no hesitation: every nook and cranny was minutely scrutinized, the chest was uncovered, and the wretched gardener was pulled out and arraigned before the magistrates. He was carried off to the town prison, it was assumed to certain execution; while there was much merriment and endless jokes on the subject of my peeping out. This was the origin of the common proverb about 'The peeping ass and his shadow'.

BOOK 10

*The story of the wicked stepmother – sold again – the pastrycook
and the chef – caught in the act – Lucius the almost human – the
noble mistress and the ignoble substitute – degraded to make a
Corinthian holiday – the Judgement of Paris – escape to Cenchreae*

1   What happened next day to my master the gardener I never found
out. Nobody objected when I was taken off by the soldier whose
outrageous violence had earned him such a sound thrashing to what
I took to be his quarters and loaded up with his personal gear. When
he led me out on to the road I was arrayed in full military panoply:
I was carrying a brilliantly polished helmet and a shield that was
visible for miles, plus a spear with a remarkably long point. These
arms were carefully set out and displayed on the top of the heap of
gear in proper campaigning style, not of course for genuine military
reasons but to put the fear of God into unfortunate wayfarers. We
came by a quite easy road through flat country to a small town,
where we put up, not at an inn, but at the house of one of the town
councillors. The soldier handed me over to one of the servants and
immediately went in accordance with his orders to report to his
commanding officer, who was in charge of a thousand men.

2   A few days later I remember that there was committed in that
place a particularly wicked and horrible crime: which I write down
so that you too can read about it. The master of the house had a
young son, to whom he had given so excellent an education that
he was all that a dutiful and modest boy ought to be, just such a son
as you, dear reader, would wish to have yourself. His mother had
died years before, and the husband had remarried and had another
son by his second wife, who was now in his thirteenth year. His
stepmother, who owed the powerful position she occupied in her

husband's home more to her looks than her morals, whether because
she was unchaste by nature or whether it was Fate that impelled her
to this ultimate infamy, cast lustful eyes on her stepson. And with
that, dear reader, you know that it's a tragedy, no mere tale, that
you're reading: from the sock we mount the buskin.

So long as the infant passion was still in the early stages of its
growth, the woman was easily able to resist Cupid's as yet feeble
power and control her blushes in silence. But when the frenzy blazed
up and took entire possession of her, when Love raged and seethed
unrestrained deep in her breast, then she yielded to the cruel god
and, pretending to feel ill, passed off the wound in her heart as bodily
indisposition. As everybody knows, the outward signs and symptoms
of sickness and lovesickness are identical: a sickly pallor, languid
eyes, no strength in the legs, sleepless nights, and sighs which grow
ever deeper as the torment is prolonged. One might have thought
that it was merely the heat of fever that made her toss and turn,
were it not that she also wept. 'Alas, th' unknowing minds of –
doctors!' What do you make of the case, gentlemen? The throbbing
pulse, the hectic flush, the laboured breathing, the constant tossing
from side to side in bed? For God's sake, isn't the diagnosis obvious
to anybody who's taken a course in the school of Venus, even if he
doesn't have a medical diploma, when you see somebody on fire
without a temperature?

So finally, unable to control the passion which shook her to the   3
core, she broke silence and sent for her son – though she would
have preferred, had it been possible, not to call him by that name,
which was a reminder of her shame. The boy instantly obeyed his
sick mother's command, and, as his duty to his father's wife and his
brother's mother demanded, came to her room wearing a worried
frown that was older than his years. For a long time in her distress
and torment she could not utter a word; aground, as it were, on the
shoals of indecision, every time anything occurred to her that fitted
the occasion, she would have second thoughts, and with her chastity
still poised in the balance she hesitated, not knowing how best to
begin. The boy, who as yet suspected nothing amiss, took the
initiative and respectfully asked what was the matter with her. They

were alone together: embracing the fatal opportunity she threw caution to the winds, and veiling her face in her robe and weeping bitterly she spoke to him briefly in a trembling voice: 'The cause and the source of my pain, but also the only remedy and cure for it – is you, you yourself. It is your eyes that have shot through mine to the depths of my heart and kindled a fierce blaze in my inmost being. Pity then her who is dying because of you, and do not be held back by scruples about duty to your father. You will be saving a wife for him who would otherwise die. It is his likeness that I see in you: no wonder I love you. We are alone, and have nothing to worry about; the opportunity is here – you cannot refuse. What nobody knows about to all intents and purposes hasn't happened.'

4   The young man was aghast at this bombshell, but though his first reaction to the idea of such a crime was one of horror, he thought it better to calm the situation by delaying tactics – diplomatic promises rather than an abrupt and outright refusal, which would only aggravate matters. So he heaped assurances on her, urging her insistently to cheer up and to concentrate on getting well again, and to wait until his father had to be away, when they would be free to enjoy themselves. Then as soon as he could he removed himself from his stepmother's loathed presence. Thinking that in this dire family crisis there was need of expert advice, he went straight to the wise and experienced old man who had been his tutor. After much deliberation it was decided that the best course was to escape the disastrous rage of Fortune by an immediate departure. The wife, however, could not endure any delay, however short, and inventing some pretext or other with amazing artfulness quickly managed to persuade her husband to hurry off to visit some outlying estates. With his departure, in a frenzy at the realization of her hopes, she immediately demanded that the boy fulfil his promise and gratify her lust. He, with one excuse after another, contrived to put off the abominable rendezvous, until she realized that all these contradictory messages meant that he was clearly not going to keep his promise. At this with lightning fickleness her wicked love was transformed to yet more wicked hate. She at once enlisted the aid of a villainous

slave, part of her dowry, a fellow to whom crime had become a way of life, and to him she confided her treacherous plans. It was decided that the best course was to murder the unfortunate young man. Accordingly this villain was sent to obtain a particularly deadly poison, and this was carefully mixed with wine and laid by for the destruction of her innocent stepson.

But while these vile creatures were considering when would be the best opportunity to administer the drink, it so happened that the younger boy, this dreadful woman's own son, came back home one day after his morning lessons, ate his lunch, and felt thirsty. Finding the cup of wine with the poison lurking in it, unaware of the danger, he drained it at a draught; and having drunk the death that had been prepared for his brother, he fell lifeless to the ground. His attendant, terrified by the boy's sudden seizure, set up a piercing outcry which brought his mother and the whole household on to the scene. As soon as it was realized that the poisoned drink was responsible for his death, everybody began to accuse everybody else of this fearful crime. However, that she-devil, that unique exemplar of step-motherly malignity, so far from being moved by her son's untimely death, or the guilt of murder, or the calamity to their house, or her husband's grief, or the distress of the funeral, was interested only in using the family disaster to further her revenge. She immediately sent a courier to find her husband and announce to him the ruin of his house; and when he returned, which he did at once, she put on a breathtakingly bold front and charged her stepson with the crime of poisoning her son. This was not totally untrue, in so far as the one boy had anticipated the death meant for the other; but she pretended that her stepson had made away with his younger brother because she had refused to yield to his criminal lust and resisted his attempt to rape her. Even these monstrous lies did not satisfy her: she added that he had also threatened her with his sword for denouncing his crime. The wretched father, reeling from the loss of two sons, was tossed to and fro on a stormy sea of suffering. His younger son he had to see buried before his eyes, and the elder must inevitably, it seemed, be condemned to death for incest and fratricide. On top of this, the wife whom he loved all too dearly was all the time, with her vocal pretence of heartfelt grief, inciting him to a relentless hatred of his own flesh and blood.

6   Scarcely was the funeral over and his son buried than the poor old man went straight from the pyre, his face still streaming with tears and his white hair torn and smeared with ash, to the market-place. There, weeping and pleading and embracing the knees of the town councillors, ignorant as he was of his wicked wife's treachery, he set himself, with all the passion at his command, to secure his remaining son's destruction. He was, he said, incestuous – he had violated his father's bed; a parricide – he had murdered his brother; an assassin – he had threatened to cut his stepmother's throat. His grief kindled such pity and anger, not only in the council but also in the townspeople, that they were all for dispensing with the tedious formality of a trial, the presentation of the evidence by the prosecution, and the carefully rehearsed twists and turns of the defence, clamouring for instant public vengeance on this public menace by stoning.

Meanwhile, however, the magistrates became alarmed at the possible consequences to themselves if these minor manifestations of anger were allowed to develop into riots and the total subversion of public order in the city. Some of them therefore reasoned with the councillors, while others calmed down the crowd, and got them to agree to hold a regular trial in the traditional manner and arrive at a verdict and sentence according to law after the allegations on both sides had been properly examined. That, they said, was surely preferable to condemning a man unheard, in the manner of a savage tribe or an irresponsible despot; in a time of peace and tranquillity that would set a shocking example and be a blot on the age.

7   This sensible advice carried the day, and the herald was at once ordered to convene the council. As soon as the members had taken their usual seats in order of precedence, the voice of the herald was again heard, and the accuser entered. Then the accused was summoned and appeared in his turn; and following Athenian legal practice as observed in the court of the Areopagus, the herald formally reminded the advocates that introductory speeches and appeals to pity were not allowed. All this I learned from overhearing various conversations. However, the exact words used by the prosecutor in

urging his case and the precise terms used by the defendant in rebuttal, the various speeches and exchanges, all that, not having been in court but tied up to my manger, I don't know and am in no position to report to you; what I did reliably learn, I will set down in this account.

Directly the speeches on both sides were over, it was agreed that the truth and credibility of the charges in such an important case must be established by reliable proofs, not on the basis of mere guesswork and suspicions; and that the first priority was to put on the stand the slave who was supposed to be the only person who knew what had really happened. That gallows-meat was not in the slightest degree perturbed either by the uncertain outcome of a trial such as this or the sight of the packed court, let alone the consciousness of his crime. He launched straight into his totally fictitious story, stoutly and repeatedly affirming the truth of what he was saying. The young man (so it ran), angry at being rebuffed by his stepmother, had enlisted his help; in revenge for that indignity he had told him off to murder her son; he had promised a large sum of money as the price of his silence; he had threatened him with death when he refused to cooperate; he had mixed the poison with his own hands and given it to him to administer to his brother; finally, suspecting that he was disobeying his orders and holding on to the cup of poison as evidence, he had poisoned the boy himself. All this the villain trotted out as plausibly as you please, with a show of nervousness; and that concluded the trial.

By now not a single councillor remained impartial; all were agreed   8
that the young man was clearly guilty of parricide and deserved to be sewn up in the sack. The unanimous votes, every one bearing the word 'Guilty', were about to be dropped into the bronze urn in accordance with immemorial custom – and once that was done, it was all up with the defendant; there was no going back, and his life was delivered into the hands of the executioner – when there arose a senior councillor, a man noted for his integrity and a highly respected doctor. He covered the mouth of the urn with his hand to prevent any votes being cast prematurely, and addressed the council as follows.

'It has been a great satisfaction to me, gentlemen, in the course of a long life, to have earned your esteem; and therefore I cannot allow the murder – for that is what it amounts to – of a man falsely accused, or allow you, who are sworn to reach a just verdict, to be led to perjure yourselves by the lies of a despicable slave. Speaking for myself, I cannot trample on the reverence I owe the gods or break faith with my conscience by giving an untrue verdict. So, learn from me the real facts of this case.

9   'This scoundrel came to me not long ago, anxious to purchase an instantaneous poison, for which he offered a hundred gold pieces. His story was that he needed it for a sick man who was in the lingering agony of an incurable illness and wanted desperately to be quit of a life that was mere torture. However, I saw through the scoundrel's patter and his clumsy explanations, and had no doubt that he was hatching some diabolical crime or other. So I gave him his potion all right; but with the possibility of a subsequent inquiry in mind I declined to take the money then and there. "Just in case," I said to him, "any of these coins turn out to be counterfeit or below standard, let them stay in the bag and seal it with your signet, and then later on we can get a banker and have him test them." He was persuaded and sealed up the money; and directly he was called as a witness I sent one of my staff post-haste to fetch it from my office and bring it to me – and, gentlemen, here it is, and I now show it to the court. Let him look at it and acknowledge his seal. How can the brother be taxed with the poison, when it was this fellow who procured it?'

10   At this the scoundrel was seized with panic: his natural complexion became deathly pale and a cold sweat broke out all over him; he shuffled his feet back and forth and scratched his head all over; and mouthing through half-closed lips he stuttered out a lot of nonsense – nobody could reasonably have believed him innocent. Then, however, his natural cunning reasserted itself, and he stoutly denied everything and persisted in calling the doctor a liar. He, quite apart from his juror's oath, seeing his private honour publicly impugned, pressed home his accusations against the scoundrel even more vehemently. Finally the magistrates ordered the public officers to examine

the villain's hands, on which they found an iron ring, which they compared with the seal on the bag; the comparison confirmed everybody's suspicions. The wheel and the rack, as usual in Greece, were immediately brought into action, but he held out against torture with extraordinary obstinacy, and neither flogging nor even the fire made him give in.

Finally the doctor spoke out: 'No, I will not allow it, I will not 11 allow you to punish this innocent young man and let this fellow escape the penalty for his crime and make a mockery of justice. I will give you a clear proof of the real state of affairs. When this rascal was so eager to buy a deadly poison, I thought it improper for one of my profession to provide anybody with the means of death. I had been taught that medicine had been invented to save life, not destroy it. However, I feared that if I declined to give it to him, I should merely be aiding and abetting his crime and do more harm than good by my refusal; he would acquire his deadly potion from somebody else or in the last resort carry out his abominable plan with a sword or some other weapon. So I gave him his "poison"; but it was a soporific draught of mandragora, a proven narcotic, as you know, which induces a sleep indistinguishable from death. You need not be surprised that this desperate villain, knowing that he must suffer the extreme penalty of the law as laid down by our ancestral custom, braves these tortures as light in comparison. But if what the boy drank was really the drink that I compounded, he is alive and sleeping peacefully, and soon he will shake off his torpor and return to the light of day. If, however, death has claimed him, we must look for the cause elsewhere.'

The old man's speech carried conviction, and not a moment was 12 lost in hastening to the tomb where the boy's body had been laid. The whole council, all the chief citizens, in fact the entire population, converged on the spot, in a fever of curiosity. It was the father himself who removed the lid of the coffin with his own hands; and at once the boy shook off his deathlike lethargy and sat up, risen from the dead. His father gathered him into his arms and embraced him, speechless for the moment with joy, and showed him to the people. Just as he was, still wrapped in his grave-clothes, the boy was carried back to the court. So finally the crimes of the wicked slave and the even wickeder stepmother were brought to light, and naked Truth came forward for all to see. The woman was sentenced to perpetual exile and the slave to crucifixion. All agreed that the good doctor should be allowed to keep the gold, as the price of that timely sleep. As for the old man, his famous, indeed fabulous, experience ended in a way worthy of divine Providence: in a matter of moments, seconds indeed, he was rescued from the prospect of total childlessness and suddenly found himself the father of two young sons.

13   As for me, I was once again launched on my fated voyage. The soldier who had bought me from no vendor and paid nothing for me received orders from his commanding officer to take a letter to the Emperor at Rome, and so sold me to two brothers for eleven denarii. These were the slaves of a rich master: one was a pastrycook, who produced bread and sweet cakes, the other a chef, who concocted savoury dishes seasoned with delicious sauces. They lived together and maintained a joint establishment; they had bought me to transport the large numbers of containers required for various purposes by their master, who travelled about a good deal. So I was admitted as a third member of this partnership, and never before or since did I find myself so well off. Every evening, after a luxurious dinner splendidly served, my masters would take home generous portions of the food. The chef brought back large helpings of pork, chicken, fish, and all sorts of ragouts; the pastrycook brought rolls, biscuits, cakes, fritters and pastries of all shapes and sizes, and various sweetmeats. Then when they locked up their quarters and went to the baths to refresh themselves, I would gorge myself on this heaven-sent banquet; for I was not such a fool or an actual ass as to reject this delicious food and make my dinner on rough spiky hay.

14   For some time my artful thievery went swimmingly; I was cautious and only stole a little from the plenty that was on offer, and they never thought of suspecting an ass of pilfering. But as I grew confident of avoiding detection I began to wolf down all the particularly choice bits and single out the most delicious sweetmeats to lick up, and that disturbed the brothers, who became extremely suspicious.

Though even then they did not connect me with the matter, they set out to try to discover who was responsible for this daily thieving. In the end they began to tax each other with this sordid plundering, and they redoubled their precautions, maintaining an even stricter supervision and counting and checking off every dish. At last one could no longer contain himself and spoke out: 'It really isn't fair what you're doing – it's no way for a man to behave – to make away with the choice bits every day and sell them so as to increase your own nest-egg on the sly, and then claim an equal share of what's left. If you're dissatisfied with our partnership, we can go on being brothers in everything else, but give up this sharing arrangement. I can see that this dispute about our losses is going to get out of hand and provoke a disastrous quarrel between us.' To this his brother replied: 'I admire your nerve, I really do. Every day you've been quietly filching all the choice morsels, and now you get in ahead of me with the very complaint that I've held back all this time, suffering in secret because I didn't want to be seen accusing my brother of this squalid thieving. But it's just as well to thrash it out between us and look for a solution together; if we go on bottling up our feelings one of us might end up doing an Eteocles.'

After more recriminations of this kind, each swore solemnly that he was innocent of any deceit or theft; and they agreed that what they had to do was discover by fair means or foul the thief who was responsible for their common loss. The ass, they reasoned, the only other occupant of the premises, could not be attracted by this kind of food, but nevertheless the best bits *were* disappearing every day, and it couldn't be the flies that were invading the place – they would have to be as big as the Harpies that used to carry off Phineus' dinner. Meanwhile, on this rich and lavish diet of human food I had rounded out and grown fat, my hide had become soft and supple, and my coat long and sleek. But my handsome appearance brought about shame and confusion for me. The brothers were struck by my increased bulk, and noticing that my daily ration of hay was untouched, they concentrated their attention on me. One evening they locked up the house at the usual time as if they were going to the baths, and then, looking through a small crack in the wall they

15

saw me tucking in to the array of eatables. They were no longer bothered about their loss, only lost in wonder at this unnatural gourmandise on the part of an ass; roaring with laughter they called their fellow slaves one by one until there was a whole crowd of them there, and showed them this unheard-of vagary of appetite in a brute beast of burden.

Their laughter was so loud and hearty that it came to their master's
16 ears as he was passing. He asked what they all found so comical; and when he was told he looked through the hole himself. He was highly amused and in fact laughed so much that he got a pain in his inside. He then had the door opened and came in to observe at close quarters. Seeing that Fortune was at last relenting to some degree and smiling on me, and reassured by the general hilarity, I was not in the least put out but went on eating at my ease. In the end the master was so pleased by this unusual spectacle that he ordered me to be brought into the house, indeed he conducted me into the dining-room himself, and had the table set out and laid with every kind of eatable and dish, all whole and intact. Though I was already pretty full, I wanted to play up to him and get into his good books, and so I fell to greedily on the assembled delicacies. They had taken great pains to work out what an ass would find most uncongenial, in order to see how domesticated I really was; so they served me meat seasoned with silphium, capons liberally peppered, and fish swimming in exotic sauces. All the while the whole company were in fits of laughter. Then said a wag who was present: 'Give our friend here some wine – neat.' The master took him up: 'Not such a bad idea of yours, you rascal,' he said. 'It's quite possible that our guest would like a cup of honey-wine with his dinner', and turning to a slave, 'You there, wash out that gold bowl carefully, mix and fill it, and offer it to my guest – and when you do so, tip him the wink that I've drunk his health.' The other guests were all agog. I was not in the slightest degree abashed, but quite at my ease and in convivial style I shaped the ends of my lips into a ladle and drank off the whole of this large bowl at a draught. This was greeted with
17 a shout as all present with one voice wished me good health. The master was highly delighted, and calling in the slaves who had bought

me ordered them to be given four times what they had paid; and he handed me over to his confidential freedman, a person of some substance, with orders to look after me well.

This man treated me with great humanity and kindness, and to ingratiate himself with his patron, he took great pains to entertain him with my clever tricks. First he taught me to recline at table on my elbow, then to wrestle and even to dance on my hind legs, and what was thought most extraordinary, to answer when spoken to, by nodding upwards for 'no' and downwards for 'yes'; and when I was thirsty to look at the wine-waiter and ask for drink by opening and shutting my eyes. I had no trouble in learning my lessons, for of course I could have done all these things without being shown. However, I was afraid that if I behaved untaught in too human a fashion, they would think this a sinister omen and kill me and consign me to the vultures to feast on as a monster and a prodigy. Meanwhile the news got around, and my master had become a public figure on account of my wonderful performances. Everybody had heard of him as the man who had an ass as boon companion, an ass that could wrestle and dance and understand human speech and express himself by nodding.

But first I should do what I ought to have done in the first place 18 and tell you now who my master was and where he was from. His name was Thiasus and he came from Corinth, the capital of the province of Achaea. As one would expect of a man of his birth and rank, he had passed through the different grades of office to the quinquennial magistracy; and to honour the occasion in a suitably brilliant manner and by way of displaying his munificence to the full he had undertaken to provide a three-day gladiatorial show. So eager indeed was he for popularity that he had been as far afield as Thessaly to procure wild beasts and celebrated gladiators, and now that he had acquired and arranged all he needed he was preparing to return to Corinth. His luxurious carriages and splendid covered and uncovered wagons were left to trail along ignominiously at the rear of the procession, as were his Thessalian horses and Gaulish ponies and the rest of his expensive bloodstock. It was I whom he bestrode – I, tricked out in golden ornaments and richly dyed saddle-cloths and purple housings and silver reins and embroidered girths and sweetly chiming bells – all the time addressing me in terms of affectionate endearment and declaring that what pleased him most of all was that in me he had both a companion and a conveyance.

19   When, after a journey partly on land and partly by sea, we reached Corinth, great crowds of citizens turned out, not so much, it seemed, in honour of Thiasus as because they were dying to have a look at me. In fact I had become so famous in those parts also that my keeper did extremely well out of me. Seeing the numbers of those who could not contain their eagerness to watch my performances, he barred the doors and only let them in one at a time, and the tips that he took every day added up to a tidy sum.

There was in that select company a certain noble and wealthy lady who like everybody else paid to see me and was delighted by all my various antics. Gradually her continued admiration of me changed to an extraordinary passion for me. For this unnatural lust the only remedy she could devise was to play Pasiphae, this time with an ass for lover. Her whole heart thus set on enjoying my embraces, she finally offered my keeper a large fee for one night with me. He, not in the least worried about whether the affair would turn out agreeably for me, but only happy at the prospect of profit for himself, agreed.

20   So having dined we left the master's table and found the lady in my apartment, where she had been waiting for some time. Ye gods, what splendid preparations she had made! Four eunuchs busied themselves in making a bed for us on the ground with a heap of pillows puffed up airily with the finest down, over which they carefully draped a coverlet embroidered with gold and dyed with Tyrian purple; and on top of all they scattered an ample supply of smaller pillows, dainty affairs such as those on which elegant ladies are accustomed to rest their heads. Then, without delaying their mistress's pleasure by lingering any longer, they withdrew and shut the door, leaving the room brilliantly lit by candles whose flames illuminated the darkness for us.

21   Now the lady removed every stitch of clothing, even the band

confining her beautiful breasts, and standing by one of the lamps she anointed herself with quantities of balsam from a pewter vessel, which she also rubbed generously over me, paying special attention to my nostrils. Next she kissed me lovingly, not the sort of kisses that pass current in the brothel, those of whores eager to extract money or clients as eager to withhold it; hers were the real thing and heartfelt, as were her endearments – 'I love you', 'I want you', 'You're the only one I love', 'I can't live without you', and all the other things women say to excite men and prove how much they care for them. Then she took hold of my halter and got me to lie down in the way I had learned. That was a simple matter: what I had to do presented itself to me as neither novel nor difficult, especially when after all this time I was about to go to bed with so beautiful and so willing a mistress. Moreover I had drunk copiously of the wine, which was extremely fine, and the sweet ointment had also aroused my desire.

No, what worried me a great deal as I thought about it was this 22 – how was I, with my four clumsy legs, to mount this exquisite lady? How could I embrace her soft white body, all milk and honey, with my horny hooves? How could I kiss those delicate red lips, fragrant as ambrosia, with my great ugly mouth and its teeth like a row of rocks? And how – and this was what really troubled me – though *I* was on fire to get started, every inch of me – how was *she* going to cope with my immense organ? I was already mourning for myself: thrown to the beasts as an item in my master's games for splitting a patrician lady in two! Meanwhile she went on murmuring endearments and kissing me repeatedly and moaning tenderly and fluttering her eyelids seductively, and then finally, 'I have you,' she cried, 'I have you, my dove, my sparrow', and with that she showed how empty and foolish my worries and fears had been. For holding me tightly embraced she welcomed me in – all of me, and I mean all. Every time I pulled myself back in an effort to go easy on her, she would thrust violently forward in her frenzy, and grasping my back would cling to me even more closely. I really believed that I might prove inadequate to satisfy her desires; and I could quite see how the mother of the Minotaur had found so much pleasure with a lowing lover. After a sleepless and laborious night she left me while it was still dark to avoid detection, having first agreed to pay the same price for another night.

23   My keeper was more than happy to allow her to enjoy me as often as she wanted, partly because he was making a very good thing out of it, and partly because here was a way of providing his master with a fresh spectacle. He therefore lost no time in letting him into the secret of our erotic performances. The master rewarded his freedman liberally and decided to make a public exhibition of me. Since, however, my noble 'wife' was ineligible because of her rank, and nobody else could be found to take her place at any price, he brought in a degraded creature whom the governor had condemned to the beasts to prostitute her virtue with me in front of the people – this, he reckoned, was sure to pack the theatre. I found out why she had been condemned; the story was as follows.

Her husband's father, having to be away on a journey, left instructions with his wife, her mother-in-law, who was pregnant, that if the child turned out to be a member of the weaker sex, it should be put to death at birth. While he was away a girl was born; but mother-love was too strong for her, and disobeying her husband's orders she entrusted the child to neighbours to bring up. On his return she told him that it was a daughter and had been duly put to death. Meanwhile the girl grew up to be of marriageable age, but as she could not be given a dowry suitable to her rank without her father's knowledge, the wife did the only thing she could and revealed the secret to her son. There was also the fear, which worried her greatly, that by some mischance he might be carried away by the warmth of a young man's feelings and become involved with the girl, neither of them realizing that they were brother and sister. The young man, a model son and brother, behaved with scrupulous and dutiful respect towards both his mother and his sister. He consigned these family secrets to the safekeeping of religious silence, and passed off what he proceeded to do as an act of mere common decency, fulfilling his duty to his kin by taking his sister under his protection and receiving her into his house simply as a girl from the neighbourhood who had no family or parents to protect her. His next move was to marry her to a close friend to whom he was deeply attached, giving her a generous dowry from his own resources.

Admirable and entirely innocent as these arrangements were, they 24 could not escape the deadly malevolence of Fortune, and at her prompting there came to the young man's house cruel Jealousy. At once his wife, the woman condemned to the beasts because of this business, began first to suspect the girl as a rival who would supplant her in her husband's bed, then to hate her, and finally to lay a cruel and murderous trap for her. This was what she devised.

She surreptitiously possessed herself of her husband's ring and went to one of his country houses. From there she sent a slave who was as loyal to her as he was disloyal to Loyalty herself, with a message to the girl that the young man was at the place and wanted her to join him, adding that she was to come quite alone and as quickly as she could. In case the girl should hesitate about coming, she gave him the stolen ring to show her as authenticating the message. In obedience to her brother's orders (as she but nobody else knew him to be) and the sight of the ring, the girl at once did exactly as she was told and came unaccompanied as fast as she could. But directly the horrible trap closed on her and she was enmeshed in the snare, this admirable wife, goaded to inhuman frenzy by lustful fury, had her husband's sister stripped naked and flogged her to within an inch of her life; then, though the girl kept crying out, what was the truth, that there was no reason for her to be angry, that there had been no adultery, that he was her brother, her brother – the woman called her a liar who had made all this up, and thrusting a white-hot firebrand between her thighs put her to a most cruel death.

At the news of the girl's grievous death her brother and husband 25 came in haste and buried her with much mourning and lamentation. The brother could not come to terms with his sister's death, so pitiful and so little deserved; shaken to the core by grief and possessed by destructive passions, in his anger and melancholy he burned with a raging fever, so that he himself was clearly in need of medical help. His wife – though she had long ago forfeited her right to that name along with her honour – consulted a doctor, a notorious rascal with many victorious battles and many notable trophies of his prowess to his credit. She offered him fifty thousand sesterces if he would sell her an instant poison, thus enabling her to purchase her husband's death. This was agreed; what he made up purported to be a famous specific, one scholars call the Lifegiver, for calming internal disorders and eliminating bile. Instead what was administered was rather a Lifetaker. So, with the family and a number of friends and relatives all gathered around, the doctor carefully mixed the draught and was about to offer it to the sick man.

26   At this point, however, the shameless woman, thinking at once to eliminate her accomplice and save the money she had promised, laid hold of the cup before them all. 'Dear doctor,' she said, 'you shall not give this medicine to my dearest husband until you yourself have drunk a good half of it. How do I know that there isn't a deadly poison lurking in it? I know that a sensible professional man like yourself won't be offended by this expression of a devoted wife's care for her husband's health and the duty she must feel towards him.' Such an unexpected and outrageous ploy by this monstrous creature took the doctor totally by surprise. All his ideas deserted him, and there was no time for him to reflect; so at once, before any sign of agitation or hesitation could betray his guilty conscience, he took a deep draught of the medicine. Thus reassured, the young man took the cup from him and emptied it. His business done, the doctor was impatient to get home at top speed, in a hurry to cancel the deadly effect of the poison he had swallowed with an antidote. The audacious woman, however, would not be deflected from the wicked course on which she had embarked and forbade him to stir from her side, 'until,' she said, 'the medicine has been digested and we see its effects.' In the end, however, she allowed him to wear her down by his repeated pleas and entreaties and was reluctantly prevailed on to let him go. But all this time the hidden plague had been raging throughout his vitals and had penetrated to his very marrow; desperately ill and already sunk deep in a deathly torpor he barely got himself home. There he just managed to tell his wife the whole story and charge her at least to demand the agreed price for two deaths, not one, before in a violent paroxysm this ornament to his profession gave up the ghost.

The young man had maintained his grip on life no longer than   27
the doctor, but expired in the same manner amid the feigned tears
and pretended lamentations of his wife. After his funeral and the
interval of a few days in which the last respects are paid to the dead,
the doctor's widow appeared to claim payment for the two deaths.
The woman, true to herself, dissembling her evil purposes under a
show of good faith, answered her pleasantly with a whole series of
promises, and undertook to pay the stipulated price directly – all she
asked was a little more of the potion to finish off what she had
begun. In short, the widow fell into her wicked trap and readily
agreed, immediately fetching the entire stock of the poison and
handing it over to the woman. She, being now furnished with ample
materials for criminality, proceeded to stretch her bloodstained hands
far and wide.

She had a small daughter by her murdered husband. This child   28
was by law her father's heir, a fact that the woman bitterly resented;
avid to take the whole of her daughter's inheritance she planned to
take her life as well. Knowing that a mother stood to inherit from
a child prematurely deceased, she showed herself just such a parent
as she had been a wife. At a dinner specially arranged for the occasion
she poisoned at one stroke both the doctor's widow and her own
daughter. The little girl's weak chest and delicate stomach succumbed
at once to the deadly poison; the widow, feeling the noxious effects of
the abominable draught spreading through her lungs like a hurricane,
began to suspect the truth. Then, as she started to suffocate, she
knew for certain, and made her way at speed to the house of the
governor of the province, where with loud cries she invoked his
protection, causing a noisy crowd to gather. On hearing of the
dreadful crimes that she had come to reveal, the governor at once
let her in and listened to her story. She told it all from the beginning
of the cruel wife's atrocities; and then she fainted, overcome by a
sudden vertigo, and tightly closing her half-open lips and grinding
her teeth she let out a prolonged groan and fell dead at the governor's
feet. An experienced administrator who did not let the grass grow
under his feet, he lost no time in dealing with this fiendish poisoner's
long series of crimes. He at once had the woman's personal attendants

arrested and got the truth out of them under torture. The woman herself he sentenced to be thrown to the beasts – a better fate than she deserved, but nobody could devise a more suitable punishment for her.

29   This then was the woman with whom I was to be publicly joined in holy matrimony. It was with feelings of deep distress and painful anticipation that I looked forward to the day of the games. More than once I was minded to do away with myself rather than be defiled by contact with this wicked woman and be put to shame and disgraced by being made a public spectacle. However, lacking as I did hands and fingers, I could find no way with my stubby rounded hooves of drawing a sword. My one consolation and ray of hope – slender enough – in my desperate plight was that spring had come once more. Everywhere there was colour: flowers were in bud, the meadows were putting on their bright summer garments, and roses were just beginning to break out of their thorny coverings and diffuse their fragrant scent – the roses which could make me once again the Lucius I had been.

Now the day of the games had arrived, and I was led to the theatre in ceremonial procession, escorted by crowds of people. While the show was being formally inaugurated by a troupe of professional dancers, I was left for a while outside the gate, where I had the pleasure of cropping the lush grass which was growing in the entrance. At the same time, as the gates were left open, I was able to feast my eyes on the very pretty sight inside.

First I saw boys and girls in the very flower of their youth, handsome and beautifully dressed, expressive in their movements, who were grouping themselves to perform a pyrrhic dance in Greek style. In the graceful mazes of their ballet they now danced in a circle, now joined hands in a straight line, now formed a hollow square, now divided into semi-choruses. Then a trumpet-call signalled an end to their complicated manoeuvres and symmetrical interweavings, the curtain was raised and the screens folded back to reveal the stage.

30   There was a hill of wood in the shape of that famous mount Ida sung by the poet Homer. It was a lofty structure, planted with shrubs

and living trees, and on its summit the architect had contrived a spring from which a stream flowed down. Some goats were browsing on the grass; and a young man got up as the Phrygian shepherd Paris in a handsome tunic, draped in a mantle of oriental style, with a golden tiara on his head, was playing herdsman. To him there entered an extremely pretty boy, naked except for a cloak such as teenage boys wear over his left shoulder. From his blond hair, a striking sight, there projected a matching pair of little golden wings; the wand he carried identified him as Mercury. He danced forward and extended to the actor who represented Paris an apple plated with gold which he was carrying in his right hand, while with a nod he conveyed Jupiter's orders; then he gracefully retired and left the stage. Next there appeared a handsome girl representing Juno, with a shining diadem on her head and carrying a sceptre. She was followed by another girl, who could only be Minerva; she wore on her head a gleaming helmet with a wreath of olive round it and held aloft a shield and brandished a spear, just as she appears in battle.

After them there entered a third girl, the loveliest of the three, 31 proclaimed as Venus by her ravishing ambrosial complexion, Venus as she was when still a virgin. She was completely naked, showing off her beauty in all its perfection, except for a wisp of thin silk that covered her pretty secrets. This little bit of material, however, the prurient wind in its amorous play now wafted aside to reveal the blossom of her youth and now skittishly flattened against her to cling closely and outline every detail of her voluptuous figure. The white colour of the goddess's skin, symbolizing her descent from heaven, contrasted with the blue of her dress, recalling her connection with the sea.

Each of the girls enacting the goddesses had a supporting escort. Juno was attended by actors impersonating Castor and Pollux, wearing egg-shaped helmets with a star for crest. This actress with restrained and natural gestures performed a dignified piece of miming, moving to an accompaniment of airs on the Ionian pipe, in which she promised to confer on the shepherd, if he adjudged the prize of beauty to her, dominion over Asia. The girl whose warlike get-up had made a Minerva of her was flanked by two boys, the armed attendants of the goddess of battles, Terror and Fear, leaping about with naked swords. Behind them a Dorian piper sounded a martial strain, alternating bass notes with strident trumpet-like tones to stimulate their brisk and vigorous dancing. This goddess, tossing her head and glaring threateningly, with rapid and complicated gestures indicated vividly to Paris that if he awarded her the victory in the beauty contest, he would with her aid be a great warrior with a glorious roll of battle-honours.

32   But now Venus, to immense applause from the audience, took centre stage. Surrounded by a throng of happy little boys, she stood sweetly smiling, an enchanting sight. These chubby children with their milk-white skin were for all the world like real Cupids just flown in from the sky or the ocean. Their little wings and their little bows and arrows and the rest of their costume made the resemblance perfect; and as if their mistress was on her way to a wedding-breakfast they lighted her footsteps with flaming torches. Next there entered a crowd of pretty unmarried girls, on this side the gracefullest of Graces, on that the loveliest of Hours, strewing garlands and flowers in honour of their goddess and in the intricacies of their artful dance essaying to delight the queen of heaven with all the rich bounty of the spring. Now the pipes breathed sweet Lydian harmonies; and while these were seducing the hearts of the spectators, Venus, even more seductive, began to dance. Advancing with slow and deliberate steps, her supple figure gently swaying and her head moving slightly in time to the music, she responded to the languishing melody of the pipes with elegant gestures. Now her eyes fluttered provocatively, now they flashed sharp menaces, and at times she danced only with them. As soon as she appeared before the judge it was plain from the movement of her hands that she was promising that, if she were preferred to the other goddesses, she would give Paris a wife of pre-eminent loveliness matching her own. At this the Phrygian youth readily handed the girl the golden apple he was holding as the token of her victory.

33   Now, you sweepings of humanity, you beasts of the bar, you gowned vultures, do you wonder that nowadays all judges and juries put their verdicts up for sale, when in the very dawn of time, in a

suit between gods and men, the course of justice was perverted by corruption and subornation? When a judge chosen by the wisdom of great Jupiter, a rustic shepherd-boy, sold the first judicial decision in history to gratify his lust and destroyed his whole race into the bargain? Yes, and there was that later case between the two famous Greek generals, when the wise and learned Palamedes was falsely accused of treason and condemned to death and Ulysses was preferred to Ajax, greatest and most valiant of warriors. And what about that verdict that was returned by the Athenians, those acute lawgivers with their encyclopedic learning? An old man of godlike understanding, whom the Delphic oracle had pronounced the wisest of all human beings, ensnared by the malignant envy of a vile faction on the charge of corrupting the young, whom he had always curbed and restrained, was put to death by the deadly juice of a poisonous weed, leaving his fellow countrymen bearing the stigma of perpetual shame – when now, all those years later, distinguished philosophers embrace his doctrines as holy writ and in their devoted pursuit of happiness swear by his name. But I have allowed myself to be carried away by my indignation, and my readers may be objecting – 'Do we now have to put up with an ass playing the philosopher?' So I will come back to where I digressed in my story.

The Judgement of Paris being over, Juno and Minerva left the stage, looking glum and angry and expressing by their gestures their indignation at losing; while Venus, happy and smiling, manifested her delight in a dance with the whole troupe. Then at the top of the mountain there burst forth from a hidden jet a shower of wine mixed with saffron, which rose high in the air and then drifted down over the browsing goats and drenched them in its sweet-smelling spray, so that beautified by this variegation they changed from their usual white colour to saffron yellow. Then the wooden mountain was swallowed up and disappeared into the ground, leaving the whole theatre perfumed with the sweet fragrance.

Now, in response to the demands of the crowd, a soldier came out and along the street to fetch the woman who, as I said, had for her series of crimes been condemned to the beasts and was to partner me in these brilliant nuptials of ours. Already what was to be our

34

marital bed was being lovingly made up, an affair of polished Indian tortoiseshell, heaped high with cushions stuffed with down and bright with silken coverlets. Apart from the shame of having to do this act in public, and apart from the pollution of contact with this loathsome and detestable woman, I was in acute and grievous fear for my life. For I thought: there we should be, locked together in a loving embrace, and whatever animal was let loose to devour the woman was hardly likely to be so discriminating or well trained or so firmly in control of its appetites as to tear to pieces the woman at my side and spare me as the uncondemned and innocent party.

35   It was therefore no longer my honour but my life about which I was concerned. My master was fully occupied in seeing that the bed was properly set up, and the slaves were all either engaged in looking after the animals or lost in admiring enjoyment of the spectacle. That left me free to come to a decision. Nobody thought that much of a watch need be kept on so docile an ass; so I began to move step by step towards the nearest door, then once outside I took off at my fastest gallop and kept it up for six whole miles, until I arrived at Cenchreae. This town belongs to the famous colony of Corinth and lies beside the Aegean sea, on the Saronic gulf. It is a very safe harbour for shipping and has a large population. I steered clear of the crowds and found a secluded spot on the shore; and there in a soft sandy hollow near the breaking waves I stretched out and rested my weary limbs. By now the sun's chariot had covered the last leg of its course, and surrendering myself to the evening hush I was overcome by sweet sleep.

BOOK II

Vision on the seashore — appeal to Isis — the goddess appears and promises rescue — her festival — Lucius himself again — devotes himself to the goddess's service — initiated — goes to Rome — two further initiations — promised a distinguished future as an advocate and admitted to office in an ancient priestly college by Osiris himself — happy at last

It was not yet midnight when I awoke with a sudden start to see the full moon just rising from the sea-waves and shining with unusual brilliance. Now, in the silent secrecy of night, was my opportunity. Knowing that this greatest of goddesses was supremely powerful; that all human life was ruled by her Providence; that not only all animals, both tame and wild, but even lifeless things were animated by the divine power of her light and might; that as she waxed and waned, so in sympathy and obedience every creature on earth or in the heavens or in the sea was increased or diminished; and seeing that Fate was now seemingly satiated with my long tale of suffering and was offering me a hope, however late in the day, of rescue: I decided to beg for mercy from the awesome manifestation of the goddess that I now beheld. At once, shaking off my sluggish repose, I jumped up happily and briskly, and eager to purify myself I plunged into the sea. Seven times I immersed my head, since that is the number which the godlike Pythagoras has told us is most appropriate in religious rituals, and then weeping I uttered my silent prayer to the all-powerful goddess.

'Queen of heaven, whether you are Ceres, nurturing mother and creatrix of crops, who in your joy at finding your daughter again set aside the ancient acorn, fodder for wild beasts, and taught man the use of civilized food, and now fructify the ploughlands of Eleusis; or whether you are Venus Urania, who in the first beginnings of the world by giving birth to Love brought together the opposite sexes and so with never-ending regeneration perpetuated the human race, and now are worshipped in the sanctuary of sea-girt Paphos; or whether you are Phoebus' sister, who by relieving women in labour with your soothing remedies have raised up many peoples, and now are venerated in your shrine at Ephesus; or whether you are Proserpine of the fearful night-howling and triple countenance, you who hold back the attacks of ghosts and control the gates of hell, who pass at will among the sacred groves and are propitiated with many different rites; you who brighten cities everywhere with your female light and nourish the fertile seeds with your moist warmth and dispense according to the motions of the Sun an ever-changing radiance; by whatever name, in whatever manner, in whatever guise it is permitted to call on you: do you now at last help me in this extremity of tribulation, do you rebuild the wreck of my fortunes, do you grant peace and respite from the cruel misfortunes that I have endured: let there be an end of toils, an end of perils. Banish this loathsome animal shape, return me to the sight of my friends and family, restore Lucius to himself; or if I have offended some power that still pursues me with its savagery and will not be appeased, then at last let me die if I may not live.'

3   Such were the prayers that I poured forth, accompanied with pitiful lamentations; then sleep once more enveloped my fainting senses and overcame me in the same resting-place as before. I had scarcely closed my eyes when out of the sea there emerged the head of the goddess, turning on me that face revered even by the gods; then her radiant likeness seemed by degrees to take shape in its entirety and stand, shaking off the brine, before my eyes. Let me try to convey to you too the wonderful sight that she presented, that is if the poverty of human language will afford me the means of doing so or the goddess herself will furnish me with a superabundance of expressive eloquence.

First her hair: long, abundant, and gently curling, it fell caressingly in spreading waves over her divine neck and shoulders. Her head was crowned with a diadem variegated with many different flowers; in its centre, above her forehead, a disc like a mirror or rather an image of the moon shone with a white radiance. This was flanked on either side by a viper rising sinuously erect; and over all was a wreath of ears of corn. Her dress was of all colours, woven of the finest linen, now brilliant white, now saffron yellow, now a flaming rose-red. But what above all made me stare and stare again was her mantle. This was jet-black and shone with a dark resplendence; it passed right round her, under her right arm and up to her left shoulder, where it was bunched and hung down in a series of many folds to the tasselled fringes of its gracefully waving hem. Along its embroidered border and all over its surface shone a scattered pattern of stars, and in the middle of them the full moon radiated flames of fire. Around the circumference of this splendid garment there ran one continuous garland all made up of flowers and fruits. Quite different were the symbols that she held. In her right hand was a bronze sistrum, a narrow strip of metal curved back on itself like a sword-belt and pierced by a number of thin rods, which when shaken in triple time gave off a rattling sound. From her left hand hung a gold pitcher, the upper part of its handle in the form of a rampant asp with head held aloft and neck puffed out. Her ambrosial feet were shod with sandals woven from palm-leaves, the sign of victory. In this awesome shape the goddess, wafting over me all the blessed perfumes of Arabia, deigned to answer me in her own voice.

'I come, Lucius, moved by your entreaties: I, mother of the universe, mistress of all the elements, first-born of the ages, highest of the gods, queen of the shades, first of those who dwell in heaven, representing in one shape all gods and goddesses. My will controls the shining heights of heaven, the health-giving sea-winds, and the mournful silences of hell; the entire world worships my single godhead in a thousand shapes, with divers rites, and under many a different name. The Phrygians, first-born of mankind, call me the Pessinuntian Mother of the gods; the native Athenians the Cecropian Minerva; the island-dwelling Cypriots Paphian Venus; the archer Cretans Dictynnan Diana; the triple-tongued Sicilians Stygian Proserpine; the ancient Eleusinians Actaean Ceres; some call me Juno, some Bellona, others Hecate, others Rhamnusia; but both races of Ethiopians, those on whom the rising and those on whom the setting sun shines, and the Egyptians who excel in ancient learning, honour

4

5

me with the worship which is truly mine and call me by my true name: Queen Isis. I am here in pity for your misfortunes, I am here with favour and goodwill. Cease now your weeping, put an end to your lamentation, banish your grief: now by my Providence the day of your release is dawning. Attend therefore with your whole mind to the orders I give you.

'The day which will be born of this night has been consecrated to me by immemorial religious usage. It is the day on which the tempests of winter have abated and the stormy sea-waves have subsided, when the ocean is again navigable and my priests sacrifice a brand-new ship as the first-offering of the season's trade. It is this ceremony that you must await without anxiety and without unholy thoughts. My priest has been warned by me; he will be carrying in his right hand as part of his processional equipment a sistrum wreathed with a garland of roses. You must not hesitate, but make your way briskly through the crowd and join the procession, relying on my goodwill. Approach the priest and, as if kissing his hand, gently take a bite of the roses, and in a moment you will divest yourself of the hide of this vile beast that has always been so hateful to me. Do not fear that anything I tell you to do will be difficult. At the very moment that I am appearing to you, I am also present to my priest while he sleeps, telling him what must be done next. At my orders the serried ranks of the crowd will give you passage, and amid the joyful ceremonies and festive spectacles no one will be repelled by that ugly appearance you wear or put a sinister construction on your sudden change of shape and make spiteful accusations against you.

'But this you must remember well and keep forever stored up in your inmost heart: the remaining course of your life right up until your last breath is now solemnly promised to me. It is only just that you should make over all the rest of your time on earth to her by whose beneficence you will be made human again. And you will live happily, you will live gloriously under my protection; and when you have completed your lifespan and descend to the shades, there also in that subterranean hemisphere I, whom you now behold, shall be there, shining amidst the darkness of Acheron and reigning in the secret depths of Styx, and you shall dwell in the Elysian Fields and constantly worship me and be favoured by me. But if by diligent observance and pious service and steadfast chastity you shall have deserved well of my godhead, know that I alone also have the power to prolong your life beyond the bounds fixed for you by your Fate.'

The awesome prophecy was ended, and the invincible goddess withdrew into herself. I at once awoke from sleep and arose with mixed feelings of fear and joy, followed by a mighty sweat. Greatly wondering at the way in which the powerful goddess had manifested herself to my sight, I bathed in the sea and, attentive to her august commands, began to con over her instructions point by point. As soon as the golden sun arose to dispel the dark clouds of night, all the streets were immediately filled with bustling crowds. There was a feeling of holy exhilaration in the air; quite apart from my private happiness, everything seemed to me so gay and cheerful that I felt that even the various animals, the houses, the day itself, wore an air of serene enjoyment. Yesterday's frost had been swiftly followed by a calm sunny morning: the springlike warmth had brought out all the songbirds, who in tuneful chorus were propitiating the mother of the stars, the parent of the seasons, the mistress of the whole world, with their pretty greetings. Then the trees too, both the fertile with their yield of fruit and the infertile with only shade to offer, were all bright with budding leaves as they opened out in the south wind, which rustled sweetly in their gently waving branches. The huge roaring of the tempests had abated, the swelling turmoil of the waves had subsided, and the sea was quietly lapping the shore. The clouds had scattered and the sky shone out in all its clear bright luminous brilliance.

7

And now there began to appear the curtain-raiser to the great procession. This consisted of men finely got up, each according to his fancy: one was girt with a sword-belt and represented a soldier; another's short cloak, boots and spear identified him as a hunter; while another, dressed in gilded slippers and a silk gown, wearing expensive ornaments and a wig, swung his hips as he walked in imitation of a woman. Yet another was conspicuous in greaves, shield, helmet and sword, straight out of a gladiatorial school. There was one with a purple robe and fasces playing the magistrate; one

8

who with cloak and stick and sandals and goatlike beard passed himself off as a philosopher; and there were a pair carrying their respective rods, one impersonating a fowler complete with birdlime, the other a fisherman with hook and line. I also saw a tame bear dressed as a lady and being borne along in a litter; a monkey in a cloth cap and saffron-coloured Phrygian dress to look like Ganymede the shepherd-boy and holding a gold cup; and an ass with a pair of wings fastened to him walking along with a lame old man, recognizable as Pegasus and Bellerophon respectively, a comic duo.

9   While these popular sports and diversions were going on all over the place, the saviour goddess's own procession was getting under way. First came women in shining white attire, proudly displaying the different symbols they bore and garlanded with spring flowers, who strewed the street along which the sacred procession passed with flowers from the folds of their robes. Others held shining mirrors behind them to render homage to the goddess as she advanced. Others again carried ivory combs and with movements of their arms and fingers imitated the combing and dressing of the royal hair; and others sprinkled the streets with drops of festive balsam and other perfumes. There was also a large group of both sexes with lamps, torches, candles and every kind of man-made light to do honour to her from whom spring the stars of heaven. Next came tuneful bands of music, pipes and recorders sounding sweet melodies. They were followed by a specially chosen choir of handsome young men resplendently dressed in their best snow-white robes who were singing a charming hymn composed and set to music by a skilful poet favoured by the Muses, its text preluding the solemn prayers that were to come. Then came pipers in the service of great Sarapis, playing on their instruments, which extended to their right ears, the strain belonging to the god and his temple; and a number of others whose role was to call on the crowd to give free passage to the procession.

10   Then came the throng of those initiated in the mysteries, men and women of all ranks and ages in shining robes of pure white linen. The women's hair was perfumed and covered with a transparent veil, the men had their heads clean-shaven and gleaming, and their sistrums of bronze or silver or in some cases gold combined to

produce a clear shrill strain. There followed the earthly stars of the great faith, the priests of the cult, those grandees, clad in tightly-fitting white linen from breast to ankle and displaying the symbols of the most mighty gods in all their glory. The first held up a lamp burning with a bright flame, not one like those which light our dinner-tables at night, but a boat-shaped vessel of gold feeding a more ample flame from its central opening. The second was similarly attired, but carried in both hands one of those altars called Altars of Succour, so named from the succouring Providence of the sovereign goddess. A third came bearing aloft a golden palm-branch of delicate workmanship and a copy of Mercury's caduceus. A fourth displayed an image of Justice, a model of a left hand with palm outstretched: this hand, as naturally inactive and unendowed with cleverness or contrivance, being thought more apt to symbolize justice than the right. He was also carrying a gold vessel rounded in the shape of a breast from which he poured libations of milk. A fifth carried a golden basket heaped with laurel branches, and a sixth a large jar.

Next appeared the gods who deigned to proceed on human feet. 11 First was the dread messenger between the gods above and the Underworld, his dog's head held high aloft, his face now black, now gold: Anubis, holding a caduceus in his right hand and brandishing a green palm-leaf in his left. Hard on his heels followed a cow standing upright, the fertile image of the All-Mother, proudly borne on the shoulders of one of her blessed priests. Another was carrying a chest containing mystic emblems and securely concealing the secrets of the glorious faith. Another carried in his fortunate embrace the worshipful image of the supreme divinity. It was not in the shape of a domestic animal or a wild beast or even a human being, but one that claimed veneration from the very originality of its ingenious inspiration, an inexpressible symbol of a loftier faith to be shielded in profound silence. This was the form it took: a small urn of bright gold, artfully shaped with a well-rounded body and decorated outside with wonderful Egyptian figures; it had a short neck with a long projecting spout, opposite which was fixed a handle which also projected in a sweeping curve. Its finial was a coiled asp with striped scaly neck puffed up and held high.

12   And now the promised beneficence of the ever-present goddess drew near, and there appeared the priest who held in his hands my fate and my salvation. Equipped exactly as she had ordained and promised, he carried in his right hand a sistrum for the goddess and for me a garland – rather a crown, as befitted the victory vouchsafed me by the great goddess's Providence, after enduring so much suffering and surmounting so many dangers, over the malignant onslaughts of Fortune. However, deeply moved though I was with sudden joy, I did not press forward roughly, fearing that the abrupt incursion of an animal would disturb the peace and order of the ceremony. Moving cautiously at an even, almost human, pace, I gradually insinuated myself sideways into the crowd, which made way for me as if (as indeed it was) divinely prompted.

13   The priest, mindful, as I could tell from his actions, of last night's prophecy and marvelling at how exactly everything agreed with his instructions, at once stopped and of his own accord held the garland to my lips. Nervously, my heart pounding, I greedily took the plaited wreath of lovely roses in my mouth and in my passionate longing for the fulfilment of the promise gulped it down. The goddess was true to her word: in a moment my hideous beastly shape fell away. First there vanished my rough coat, then my thick hide became thin skin, my swelling belly drew itself in, fingers and toes emerged from my hooves, my hands were feet no longer but, as I stood up, extended to perform their proper function, my long neck contracted, my face and head became round, my huge ears reverted to their former size, my boulders of teeth returned to human proportions, and – what had been my chief cross – my tail was no longer there. The people were amazed, and the faithful bowed down before this public manifestation of the power of the great goddess, the ease with which the transformation was accomplished and its miraculous conformity with the nocturnal visions; and raising their hands to heaven, loudly and with one voice they bore witness to the goddess's marvellous beneficence.

14   As for me, I stood transfixed in silent stupefaction. My mind could not take in this sudden overwhelming joy, and I did not know what I ought to say first, how I should begin to use my new gift of speech,

which would be the most auspicious expression with which to
celebrate the rebirth of my tongue, what were the most suitable
words in which to utter my thanks to so great a goddess. However,
the priest, who had been apprised through the divine revelation of
the whole tale of my misfortunes and who was himself greatly
affected by this signal miracle, silently indicated that I should be
given a linen garment to cover me up; for from the moment that I
was stripped of the ass's hateful integument, I had kept my legs tightly
closed and my hands clasped carefully in front of me, maintaining
decency, so far as I could being stark naked, with this natural covering.
At once one of the crowd of worshippers took off his outer tunic
and quickly wrapped me in it. That done, the priest, gazing intently .
at me with a benevolent expression and the air of one inspired,
addressed me as follows.

'Many and various are the sufferings you have endured, and fierce   15
the tempests and storm-winds of Fortune by which you have been
tossed; but at last, Lucius, you have come to the harbour of Tranquillity and the altar of Pity. Neither your birth, nor yet your rank, nor
even your pre-eminent learning were of the slightest help to you,
but in the unsteadiness of your green youth you lowered yourself
to servile pleasures and reaped a bitter reward for your ill-starred
curiosity. But in spite of all, Fortune in her blindness, all the while
that she was tormenting and cruelly imperilling you, has by the very
exercise of her unforeseeing malignity brought you to this state of
holy felicity. Now let her go, let her vent her mad rage elsewhere
and find some other subject for her cruelty; against those whose
lives our sovereign goddess has claimed for her service mischance
cannot prevail. Brigands, wild beasts, slavery, journeys hither and
thither along rugged roads, the daily fear of death – of what avail
were these to her malevolence? You have now been received into
the protection of Fortune, but a Fortune that can see, whose shining
light illumines even the other gods. Put on now a happier look in
keeping with the bright dress you wear, and with exultant step join
the procession of the saviour goddess. Let the infidels behold, let
them behold and know their error: see, delivered from his former
tribulations by the Providence of great Isis, here is Lucius rejoicing

and triumphing over his Fortune. But for your greater safety and protection, enrol yourself a soldier in this sacred service to which you were just now called to swear allegiance; dedicate yourself now to the discipline of our faith, and submit yourself as a volunteer to the yoke of our ministry. For once you begin to serve the goddess, then you will really experience the enjoyment of your liberty.'

16   Having uttered this inspired speech, the worthy priest, exhausted and breathing heavily, fell silent. I then joined the throng of the devotees and escorted their sacred charge, the cynosure of the whole city, as they all pointed me out to one another. Nobody could talk of anything else: 'That's him, the one that the august power of the goddess has just restored to human shape. Happy man indeed, and thrice blessed to have deserved such glorious favour from heaven! It can only be the reward of a blameless and pious life; no sooner is he, as it were, born again than he's pledged to the sacred service.'

During all this, amid a roar of joyful invocations, our gradual progress had brought us to the seashore, to the very spot where as an ass I had been stabled the night before. The images of the gods were first set out as the ritual prescribed. There stood a ship, a triumph of craftsmanship, its sides decorated with marvellous Egyptian paintings: the high priest, after first pronouncing a solemn prayer from his chaste lips, with the utmost ceremony purified it with a flaming torch, an egg, and sulphur, named it, and consecrated it to the great goddess. The resplendent sail of this happy vessel displayed letters embroidered in gold repeating the prayer for the new sailing season and successful navigation. The mast, shaped from a pine-trunk, was already stepped and towered aloft, a splendid sight with its distinctive top. The poop was curved in a goose-neck and was plated with shining gold, and the whole hull was of citrus-wood, highly polished to a glowing finish. All the people, initiates and uninitiated alike, then vied with each other to pile up on board baskets heaped with perfumes and other similar offerings, and also poured libations of milk-porridge into the sea. At length, stowed full with this wealth of gifts and propitious offerings, the ship was cast off from her moorings and put out to sea before a gentle breeze. When she had sailed too far for us to be able to make her out, the bearers of the sacred objects took up again what each had brought and returned happily to the temple in the same orderly procession.

When we arrived there, the chief priest and those who had carried   17
the images of the gods and those initiates who were allowed to enter the holy of holies went into the chamber of the goddess and restored the living images to their proper places. Then one of their number, whom the rest addressed as the Scribe, took up his stand outside the door and summoned the Pastophori – this is the name of the sacred college – to a sort of formal assembly. There, on a raised dais, he first read out from a written text auspicious prayers for the Emperor, the Senate, and the knights and all the Roman people, for the seamen and ships under the rule of our worldwide empire; and then with Greek ceremony and in Greek announced the opening of the sailing season. His words were greeted with a shout from the people proclaiming their gladness at the good omen. Transported with joy and bearing green twigs and branches and garlands, they kissed the feet of the silver statue of the goddess on the temple steps and then dispersed to their homes. As for me, I could not bear to think of stirring an inch, but with my eyes fixed on the goddess's image I thought over my past adventures.

Meanwhile swift Rumour had not been slow to take wing and   18
had already spread abroad in my homeland the story of the foreseeing goddess's worshipful beneficence and my remarkable good fortune. Accordingly my friends and household and all my closest relatives at once left off from the grieving occasioned by the false reports of my death, and overjoyed by the unexpected good news came hurrying, all with different gifts, to see for themselves one who had returned from the Underworld to the light of day. Never having expected to set eyes on any of them ever again I was greatly cheered and gratefully accepted their generous contributions, my friends having very considerately thought to provide me with the wherewithal to clothe and maintain myself in comfort.

When therefore I had done my duty by greeting all of them and   19
giving them a summary account of my past tribulations and my present happiness, I returned to what really gave me most pleasure, contemplation of the goddess. I rented a lodging in the temple

precincts, where I set up house for the time being, joining privately in the service of the goddess, constantly associating with the priests, and incessantly adoring the great divinity. No night or snatch of sleep passed without her appearing to admonish me. Again and again she laid her sacred commands on me: I had long been singled out for initiation; now, she decreed, I must take the plunge. Though for myself I was eager and willing, I was held back by religious scruples. I had made thorough inquiries and knew that compliance with the requirements of her worship was not easy, that the practice of chastity and abstinence was very hard, and that a life that was subject to so many mischances had to be surrounded with a rampart of careful precaution. As I repeatedly thought all this over, impatient as I was, somehow or other I went on putting things off.

20   One night I dreamed that the high priest appeared with a pocketful of something which he offered me. When I asked what it was he replied that these were some 'portions' that had been sent me from Thessaly, and that a slave of mine called Candidus had also arrived from there. When I woke up I puzzled for a long time over what this vision might portend, more especially because I was sure I had never had a slave of that name. However, be the event of this dream-prophecy what it might, I thought the offer of 'portions' could only signify a sure prospect of gain. So in high expectation of a fruitful outcome I waited for the morning opening of the temple. When the white curtains were drawn apart and the venerable image of the goddess was revealed, we all adored her; the priest meanwhile was making the rounds of the various altars, worshipping and offering the customary prayers at each, and pouring from a special vessel a libation of water fetched from the innermost shrine. When all this had been duly performed, the voices of the faithful were raised to salute the dawn and announce the first hour of a new day. Then, at that precise moment, there arrived from Hypata the servants I had left behind after Photis' disastrous mistake had embridled me, they having of course now learned what had happened to me. With them they brought back my horse; he had been sold on from one owner to another, but they had traced him by the brand on his back and reclaimed him. So I was left marvelling at how neatly my dream

had worked out, not only the fulfilment of its promise of gain but the recovery of my horse, which was indeed a white one, symbolized by the slave Candidus.

This event caused me to devote myself even more attentively to my religious duties, seeing in these present benefits an earnest of more to come. My desire to be admitted to the mysteries was growing with every day that passed, and I constantly applied to the high priest with urgent prayers that he would finally initiate me into the secrets of the sacred night. He however, a man of great discretion and renowned for his strict religious observance, gently and kindly, as parents restrain the immature impulses of their children, kept putting off my importunities, soothing my anxiety with the consoling hope of better things to come. He pointed out that the day on which any individual might be initiated was declared by the will of the goddess, and the officiating priest was also chosen by her Providence; even the expenses of the ceremony were likewise regulated by her decision. All this he counselled me to bear dutifully and patiently; for I must, he said, do my utmost to guard against excess of zeal on the one hand and obstinacy on the other, both faults to be equally avoided, neither delaying when called nor chafing when not called. None of their company was so abandoned or indeed set on his own destruction as to dare to perform this ceremony unless personally ordered to do so by his mistress; that would be a reckless act of sacrilege and a crime carrying sentence of death. For the keys of hell and the guarantee of salvation were in the hands of the goddess, and the initiation ceremony itself took the form of a kind of voluntary death and salvation through divine grace. Such as might be safely entrusted with the great secrets of our religion, when they had passed through life and stood on the threshold of darkness, these the power of the goddess was wont to select and when they had been as it were reborn return them to a new lifespan. Thus I too should acquiesce in the bidding of heaven, even though long named and marked out by the clear and conspicuous favour of the great goddess for her blessed service. Meanwhile, like her other votaries, I should immediately abstain from unholy forbidden foods so that I might the better attain to the secret mysteries of this purest of religions.

22   The priest having put it like this, I did not allow my impatience to affect my obedience but, calmly and quietly and maintaining a commendable silence, I devoted myself in earnest to the sacred worship for some days. However, the mighty goddess in her saving beneficence did not disappoint me or torment me by prolonged delay; one dark night she gave the clearest possible orders, warning me plainly that the day I had always longed for, in which she would grant my heartfelt prayer, had arrived. She told me how much it would cost to provide for the ceremony, and she decreed that her own high priest Mithras should conduct it, he being, as she told me, linked to me by a divinely ordained conjunction of our stars. Encouraged by these and other kind admonitions from the sovereign goddess, before it was fully light I aroused myself from sleep and went straight to the high priest's apartments, where I met him and greeted him just as he was leaving his room. I had resolved to put my request for initiation more pressingly than ever, as being now my due; but the moment he saw me he anticipated me. 'Fortunate Lucius!' he exclaimed. 'Happy man, to be so greatly honoured by the august goddess's grace and favour! But come,' he added, 'why do you stand there idle, yourself your own delay? The day is here that you have longed and prayed for so incessantly, the day on which by the divine command of the goddess of many names you are to be inducted by these hands of mine into the most holy mysteries of our faith.' And holding my arm affectionately the old man then and there took me out to the doors of the great temple, and after the solemn ritual of opening them and the performance of the morning sacrifice he brought out from the holy of holies some books written in unknown characters. Some of these represented various animals and were shorthand for formulaic expressions, and some were in the form of knots or rounded like a wheel or twisted at the ends like vine-tendrils, to guard their meaning against the curiosity of the uninitiated. From these he read out to me what I needed to procure for my initiation.

23   This I at once proceeded to buy as directed and without counting the cost, partly from my own resources and partly with the help of my friends. Then, when the priest said the moment had come, he

led me to the nearest baths, escorted by the faithful in a body, and there, after I had bathed in the usual way, having invoked the blessing of the gods he ceremoniously aspersed and purified me. Next I was taken back to the temple, the day being now two-thirds over, where he made me stand at the goddess's feet and privately gave me certain instructions which are too sacred to divulge. Then with everybody present he ordered me to abstain from the pleasures of the table for the next ten days and not to eat the flesh of any animal or drink any wine. This abstinence I observed with reverential restraint as instructed. Then the day came which was fixed for my pledged appearance before the goddess. Towards sunset there came flocking from all sides crowds of people, all bearing different gifts in my honour, according to the ancient practice of the mysteries. Then the uninitiated were all made to leave, I was dressed in a brand-new linen robe, and the priest took me by the hand and conducted me to the very innermost part of the sanctuary.

I dare say, attentive reader, that you are all agog to know what was then said and done. I should tell you if it were lawful to tell it; you should learn if it were lawful to hear it. But then your ears and my tongue would both incur equal guilt, the one for sacrilegious loquacity, the other for importunate curiosity. But since it may be that your anxious yearning is piously motivated, I will not torment you by prolonging your anguish. Listen then, but believe; for what I tell you is the truth. I came to the boundary of death and after treading Proserpine's threshold I returned having traversed all the elements; at midnight I saw the sun shining with brilliant light; I approached the gods below and the gods above face to face and worshipped them in their actual presence. Now I have told you what, though you have heard it, you cannot know. So all that can without sin be revealed to the understanding of the uninitiated, that and no more I shall relate.

Morning came, and, the ceremonies duly performed, I came forth 24 attired in the twelve robes of my consecration, a truly mystical dress, but nothing prevents me from mentioning it since a great many people were there and saw it at the time. For in the very heart of the sacred temple, before the statue of the goddess, a wooden platform had been set up, on which I took my stand as bidden. I was a striking sight, since though my dress was only of fine linen it was colourfully embroidered, and from my shoulders there fell behind me to my ankles a costly cloak. Wherever you looked, I was decorated all over with pictures of multicoloured animals: here Indian serpents, there Hyperborean griffins with bird-like wings, creatures of another world. This is what initiates call an Olympic robe. In my right hand I held a flaming torch and my head was encircled with a beautiful crown of palm, its bright leaves projecting like rays. Equipped thus in the image of the Sun I stood like a statue while the curtains were suddenly pulled back and the people crowded in to gaze at me. Following this I celebrated my rebirth as an initiate with enjoyable feasting and good-humoured conviviality. The third day too was celebrated with similar ceremonies and a sacramental breakfast, marking the formal conclusion of my initiation.

For a few days I remained enjoying the inexpressible pleasure of contemplating the image of the goddess, bound as I was to her by a boon I could never repay. At last, at the bidding of the goddess herself, having paid my debt of gratitude to her, not indeed in full but as fully as my means allowed, I set about preparing my long-delayed return home, though it was hard for me to sever the bonds of my ardent yearning. Finally I prostrated myself before her, and repeatedly kissing her feet and weeping profusely, my words constantly strangled by sobs and my voice choking in my throat, I prayed.

25 'Hail, holy one, eternal saviour of the human race, ever cherishing mortals with your bounty, you who extend a mother's tender love to the sufferings of the unfortunate. Not a day, not a night, not a fleeting second passes in which your goodness is not at work, safeguarding men on land and sea, quelling life's storms and holding out that rescuing hand which can even unravel the inextricably tangled threads of the Fates, calm the tempests of Fortune, and check the baleful motions of the stars. The gods above worship you, the gods below revere you; you make the earth revolve, you give the sun his light, you rule the universe, you trample hell under your feet. Obedient to you the stars rise and set, the seasons return, the

powers rejoice, the elements perform their service. At your bidding the winds blow, the clouds nourish, the seeds germinate, the buds break and grow. Your majesty is held in awe by the birds that fly in the heavens, the beasts that roam in the mountains, the snakes that slide over the earth, the monsters that swim in the deep. As for me, my talents are too meagre to recite your praises and my means too slender to offer you sacrifice; and my eloquence is too poor and barren to express what I feel about your majesty – for which indeed a thousand mouths and as many tongues and a flow of words that never tired and lasted for ever would not suffice. And so I shall faithfully do all that a man can who is a devotee, though a poor one: I shall keep and contemplate your divine countenance and your holy power in the secret recesses of my heart for ever.'

Having thus propitiated the great goddess, I embraced the priest Mithras, now my father, and hanging on his neck and repeatedly kissing him I asked him to forgive me for not being able to recompense him properly for his many kindnesses. Then, after expressing my gratitude at great length, I finally parted from him and made haste to revisit my ancestral home after my long absence. However, after a few days, at the prompting of the mighty goddess, I hurriedly packed and took ship for Rome. After a prosperous voyage with favourable winds I arrived safely at Ostia; from there I took a fast carriage and reached the holy city on the evening of the twelfth of December. My most urgent desire was then to offer my prayers daily to the supreme power of Queen Isis, to her who from the site of her temple is called Isis of the Field and is the subject of special veneration and adoration. I was from then on a constant worshipper, a newcomer it is true to this shrine but no stranger to the faith. 26

Now the great Sun had traversed the zodiac and a year had passed, when the tranquil course of my life was once more interrupted by the unsleeping concern of the beneficent goddess, warning me of a second initiation and a second set of ceremonies. I could not imagine what she purposed or what she was foretelling, since I quite thought that I had been completely initiated some time ago. These conscientious misgivings I pondered in my own mind and I also took advice from other members of the cult. I was surprised to discover that 27 though I had indeed been initiated, it was only into the mysteries of Isis, and I had yet to attain enlightenment in the mysteries of the great god, supreme father of the gods, the invincible Osiris. Though the nature and cult of the two deities was closely connected, indeed one and the same, yet the process of initiation was quite different. I should therefore understand that the great god too was calling me to his service.

I was not long left in doubt. The very next night I dreamed that there appeared to me one of the faithful dressed in linen and carrying a wand tipped with ivy and other things I may not mention. These he put down in my lodging, and sitting in my seat announced a banquet in honour of our great faith. To furnish me with a sure sign by which I should know him again, he had a slightly deformed left ankle, so that he limped a little in his walk. With so clear an expression of the will of the gods the dark cloud of uncertainty at once lifted and vanished, and after my morning prayer to the goddess I eagerly asked all the others whether any of them had a limp as in my dream. Confirmation was soon forthcoming: I immediately spotted one of the college who not only limped but whose appearance and dress exactly matched that of the previous night's apparition. I later found out that his name was Asinius Marcellus, very apt in view of my transformation. I lost no time in getting hold of him, and found that he already knew what I was going to tell him, he having already been likewise instructed that he was to initiate me. The previous night he had dreamed that while he was garlanding the statue of the great god he had learned from that very mouth which announces every man's destiny that there was sent to him a man from Madaura, quite a poor man, whom he was at once to initiate into his faith. For that man literary renown and for himself a great reward were prepared by the god's Providence.

28   Though thus pledged to initiation and eager as I was, I was held back by the slenderness of my means. My modest patrimony had been used up in paying for my travels, and the cost of living at Rome was much higher than in the provinces where I came from. With my poverty interposing its veto I found myself sorely perplexed, caught, as they say, between the devil and the deep sea. The god

continued to press me relentlessly, and his repeated goading, which in the end became a command, was most distressing to me. Eventually by selling my wardrobe, such as it was, I scraped together the small sum that was needed. This in fact I did by his express orders. 'Come,' he said, 'if you were planning some scheme for mere enjoyment, you wouldn't have any scruples about disposing of your clothes; now, when you are about to undergo so important a ceremony, do you hesitate to commit yourself to a poverty you will have no cause to regret?' So therefore, everything being properly prepared, I once more went for ten days without eating animal food and once more had my head shaved. Then, enlightened by the nocturnal mysteries of the supreme god, I began in full confidence my devotions in this twin faith. Doing so consoled me a great deal for having to live in foreign parts and afforded me a more ample living into the bargain: for the favouring breeze of Success brought me a small income from pleading in the courts in Latin.

However, it was not very long before the gods once again inter- 29 vened with the unexpected and startling order that I must undergo yet a third initiation. I was extremely worried and in great perplexity asked myself anxiously what the gods might mean by this new and unlooked-for demand. I had been initiated twice: what was there left to do? 'Those two priests,' I said to myself, 'must have given me bad advice or overlooked something' – and I actually, I must admit, began to entertain suspicions of their good faith. While I was in this agitated state, driven almost insane with worry, I was visited one night by an apparition which gently imparted the following revela- tion: 'You have no cause to fear this sequence of initiations or think the first two defective. Rather you should rejoice in this constant favour of the gods and take an exultant delight in it: what is granted once if at all to others, will be yours three times, and you can be sure that this threefold initiation will render you forever blessed. Moreover, this third initiation of yours is necessarily called for, if you remember that the goddess's holy symbols which you received at Cenchreae are still in the temple there where you left them, so that here in Rome you cannot wear them to worship in on feast days or receive illumination from that happy attire when ordered to do so. So, as the great gods command, you must with a glad heart be initiated once more; and may happiness and prosperity and salvation attend your consecration.'

30   With these words of majestic eloquence the divine apparition declared what needed to be done. I did not put the matter off or idly procrastinate, but at once told the high priest what I had dreamed. At once I submitted myself to abstinence from animal food, and indeed in my voluntary continence I considerably exceeded the ten days prescribed by the immemorial law; and I provided lavishly for the ceremony on a scale dictated by my pious ardour rather than my limited means. Not that I regretted this expenditure either of labour or money – had I not through the bountiful Providence of the gods made a very pretty thing of my practice in the courts? So after only a few days the god who is the most mighty of the great gods, highest of the mighty, greatest of the highest, and ruler of the greatest, Osiris, appeared to me in my sleep, not transformed into some other shape but face to face, and deigned to address me in his own august voice. I was, he ordered, to continue confidently my distinguished practice as an advocate and I was not to fear the slanders put about by ill-wishers, provoked by my learning and my application to my profession. Furthermore, not wishing me to serve his cult as one of the crowd, he admitted me to the sacred college of the Pastophori and indeed enrolled me in the order of quinquennial decurions. So, with my head once more completely shaved and not covering or veiling my baldness, I entered joyfully on my duties as a member of this ancient college, founded in the time of Sulla.

Appendix

The Onos *and* The Golden Ass

(See Introduction, §4)

Onos		The Golden Ass
1−3	Arrival at Hypata. Hospitably received/ bored and starved by Hipparchus/Milo	1.2, 21−4, 26
4	In quest of witchcraft. Warned by Abroea/Byrrhena against Hipparchus' wife/Pamphile	2.1−3, 5
5−10	Intrigue with Palaestra/Photis	2.6−7, 10, 15−17
11−15	Metamorphosis	3.19−26
16−26	With the robbers	3.28−4.5, 7−8, 22−3, 6.25−32
26−7	The robbers captured by soldiers/drugged and slaughtered. Lucius well treated by the captive girl/Charite	7.12−14
27−8	At pasture and in the mill	7.14−16
29−33	The abominable boy. Threat of castration	7.17−23
34	Death of the captive girl/Charite and her husband. The establishment decamps	8.1, 15
35−41	Arrival at Beroea/'a certain large and famous city'. Sold to Philebus. With the priests	8.23−9.4, 8−10
42	With the baker	9.10−11
43−5	With the gardener	9.32, 39−42
46−7	With the cooks	10.13−16
48−52	With Menecles of Thessalonica/Thiasus of Corinth	10.16−23
53−5	The games. Lucius regains his shape/ escapes	10.34−5

The stories, episodes and significant amplifications which in all probability were not in *Met.* and were added by Apuleius are then:

Aristomenes' story	1.3–20
The trampling of the fish	1.25
Byrrhena's house	2.4
On hair	2.8–9
Diophanes	2.12–14
Thelyphron's story	2.18–30
Encounter with the 'robbers'; the spoof trial; Photis' explanation	2.31–3.18
Thwarted attempt to eat roses; first beating	3.27
The robbers' lair	4.6
First robber's story	4.8
Second robber's story	4.9–21
Charite's story	4.24–7
Cupid and Psyche	4.28–6.24
Third robber's story	7.1–3
Tlepolemus' story	7.4–12
Death of abominable boy	7.24–8
Story of Charite, Tlepolemus and Thrasyllus	8.1–14
Adventures on the road	8.15–22
Inserted story (i): the delinquent slave	8.22
Inserted story (ii): the lover and the jar	9.5–7
Lucius meditates on his situation	9.12–13
Inserted story (iii): the baker's wife	9.14–31
Inserted story (iv): Barbarus' wife	9.16–21
Inserted story (v): the fuller's wife	9.24–5
Inserted story (vi): the downfall of a house	9.33–8
Inserted story (vii): the wicked stepmother	10.2–12
Inserted story (viii): the condemned woman	10.23–8

A Note on Money

The relative values of the sums of money that change hands in the course of the narrative can be calculated from the table

1 gold piece (*aureus*) = 25 denarii = 100 sestertii.

However, it is clear that Apuleius habitually manipulated and exaggerated prices for comic or dramatic effect or indeed on occasion for no apparent reason at all (see R. Duncan-Jones, *The Economy of the Roman Empire*, Cambridge, 1974, pp. 248–51). For instance, the fluctuations in the price of Lucius-as-ass as he is sold on from one owner to another do not seem to follow any discernible pattern or make any implicit point. It follows that any attempt to relate these sums of money to contemporary economic reality or translate them into modern equivalents is bound to be fruitless.

Notes

1.1 *this Milesian discourse*: see Introduction, §1.

amusing: this renders *lepidus*, from *lepos*, a word connoting charm, grace, wit. Lucius repeatedly uses this adjective to characterize the stories he hears and tells. Their true significance and their relevance to his own case invariably escape him.

an Egyptian book: papyrus came from Egypt. It is only in book 11 that the story takes on an explicitly Egyptian colouring. However, the fact that it is an ass into which Lucius is transformed then takes on its full significance. See Introduction, §9.

with the sharpness of a pen from the Nile: the pen, of Nile reed, is both literally and metaphorically 'sharp', a hint that the book may after all prove to be something more than the 'amusing gossip' promised here.

Attic Hymettus, the Isthmus of Corinth, and Spartan Taenarus: Mount Hymettus stands for Athens, where Lucius had been a student (1.24). Corinth, as later emerges (2.12), was his native place. Taenarus figures only as one of the traditional entrances to the Underworld (6.18); there may be an allusion to the symbolic Catabasis (descent to Hell) which formed part of the ritual of Isiac initiation (11.23).

mastered the Latin language: Apuleius himself had learned Latin as a boy in North Africa; this is Lucius speaking. At the end of the story he will be abruptly elbowed aside by his creator (11.27 and note), who is very far from being 'an unpractised speaker' (11.28). However, see also 9.39 and note.

the trick . . . of changing literary horses at the gallop: a graphic image of the kaleidoscopic variety of content, models, tone and treatment in this unique novel, but referring more particularly to the author's linguistic versatility. See Introduction, §1.

a Grecian story: see Introduction, §§1, 4.

1.2 *Plutarch and his nephew Sextus*: the connection is alluded to again by Byrrhena (2.3). The implication is that Lucius ought to know better: his unenlightened curiosity and degrading involvement in sensual pleasures with Photis are a betrayal of his philosophical heritage. It is only towards the end of the novel that this is brought home to him in the words of the priest of Isis. The attentive reader is supposed to be equipped and alert to grasp the significance of such apparently casual allusions. Sextus was tutor to Marcus Aurelius and Lucius Verus. Descent, real or fictitious, from Plutarch was something for a philosopher to boast of (C. P. Jones, *Plutarch and Rome*, Oxford, 1971, pp. 11–12). On Plutarchan elements in the novel see Introduction, §9.

a pure white animal: later to take on a symbolic significance (11.20).

thirsting as always for novelty: inopportune curiosity will be his, and Psyche's, undoing. The well-informed reader would remember that Plutarch had written a treatise *De curiositate*, in which there is much that is relevant to Lucius and his behaviour (Introduction, §9).

1.3 *milked of her dew*: it was believed that dew was produced by the moon.

1.4 *the Painted Porch*: the Stoa Poikile, a portico decorated with paintings by famous artists and the meeting-place of the sect called after it, the Stoics. The contrast of the setting, with its stern philosophical associations, and the speciously miraculous nature of the spectacle with which Lucius couples it, again hints at his wilful neglect of his advantages. He should have been in the Porch imbibing wisdom, not gawping at mountebanks outside.

twining sinuously round it: Aesculapius (Greek Asklepios) was the son of Apollo and god of medicine. His emblem was a ragged staff and a serpent, symbolizing renewal.

1.5 *Aristomenes, from Aegium*: a rather grand name for a commercial traveller (*aristos*, 'best', *menos*, 'might'), borne by, among others, the addressee of one of Pindar's victory odes (*Pythians*, 8). See below on Socrates. Aegium was a city of some importance on the south shore of the Gulf of Corinth.

on the wrong foot: proverbial for doing something inauspicious at the outset of a journey or undertaking, left being as now the unlucky side.

Lupus: 'wolf'. See next note.

1.6 *Socrates*: the bearer of this name turns out to be no more distinguished for wisdom than Aristomenes for courage. Such 'speaking' names were a feature of epic, and Apuleius employs them freely.

1.7 *a gang of bandits*: brigandage plays a prominent part in the plot of Apuleius' novel, as it does in the Greek romances. It appears to have been a feature of life in the remoter provinces; but Lucius' world is in general a lawless place. See Introduction, §6.

Meroe: there was a famous temple of Isis on the island of Meroe in the upper Nile, but it is perhaps more likely that her name puns on *merum*, 'neat wine'.

1.8 *bring down the sky ... illuminate Hell itself*: a typical catalogue of the feats commonly attributed to witches, and precisely the kind of phenomena discredited by Aristomenes' sceptical companion.

both lots: 'the Aethiopians, that last race of men, whose dispersion across the world's end is so broad that some of them can see the Sun-God rise while others see him set' (Homer, *Odyssey*, 1. 23–4, trans. T. E. Lawrence).

the Antipodeans: the idea of men 'with feet opposite' (*antipus*) on the other side of a spherical world is first attested in Plato's *Timaeus* (63a).

1.9 *biting off their balls*: they were supposed to be aware that it was for the sake of a medicinal oil (*castoreum*) extracted from their testicles that they were hunted (Pliny, *Natural History*, 8. 109, 32. 26–31).

as if it was an elephant: the period of gestation for elephants was popularly supposed to be ten years (in fact, just under two).

1.10 *Medea*: the witch *par excellence*. When her husband Jason proposed to take a new wife she contrived the destruction of the bride and her father Creon, king of Corinth, by the gift of a poisoned robe and a self-igniting crown. The story was familiar from Euripides' classic treatment in his play *Medea*.

into a trench: like Odysseus (Ulysses) summoning the ghosts from Hades (Homer, *Odyssey*, 11. 35–6). According to Heliodorus this was a common necromantic practice in Egypt (*Ethiopica*, 6. 14. 2).

1.12 *Panthia*: 'all-divine'.

Endymion: a beautiful shepherd with whom the Moon (Artemis, Diana) fell in love. At his own request Zeus (Jupiter) granted him eternal life, eternal youth, and eternal sleep.

Ganymede: a beautiful Trojan boy, abducted by Zeus to be his cupbearer and bedfellow.

his wily Ulysses: Calypso was the nymph with whom Odysseus (Ulysses) spent seven years of the ten that it took him to get back home from Troy (Homer, *Odyssey*, 5. 1–269). In the later tradition, Homer's 'man of many resources' (ibid., 1. 1) became a byword for unscrupulous cunning.

1.13 *like Bacchantes*: who tore wild animals apart in their frenzy.

1.15 *Cerberus*: the three-headed dog that guarded the entrance to Hades; see 6.19.

1.16 *Now, now . . . my dearest bed*: with the substitution of *grabatule*, 'bed', for *frater*, 'brother', the opening words of this prayer are identical with an apostrophe put into the mouth of the Numidian Adherbal by Sallust in his *Jugurthine War* (14. 22). This paratragedic appeal to a broken-down bedstead forms an ironic contrast to the real prayers addressed by Lucius to Isis later in the novel.

with which it was strung: the mattress rested on a network of cords stretched across the frame, as in an Indian charpoy.

1.19 *waxy pale*: literally 'with the pallor of boxwood', a recurring poetic comparison.

1.20 *delightful*: *lepidus* (see 1.1 and note).

1.21 *Milo*: the name of (1) a famous Greek wrestler of the sixth century BC; (2) a Roman politician defended by Cicero in a famous speech, the *Pro Milone*, on charges of political violence. In this case there seems to be no particular relevance to Milo's character, which is that of a miser.

his ruling passion: there seems to be a pun on the literal and transferred senses of *aerugo*, 'verdigris' and 'canker of the mind'. Horace writes of avarice as 'this craze for coppers, this verdigris . . . on our hearts' (*Art of Poetry*, trans. Niall Rudd, 330–31).

Demeas: the name of the severe brother in Terence's play *Adelphoe*; again it is difficult to see any significance in the choice.

1.22 *his wife sitting*: the old custom by which men reclined at table and women and children sat had become obsolete, at least as regarded women, at Rome nearly two centuries before Apuleius' time. If this passage (which reproduces the *Onos*) is reliable evidence it survived much longer in the provinces.

1.23 *old Hecale's frugal hospitality*: Theseus, on his way to fight the Bull of Marathon, took shelter from the rain in the cottage of an old woman called Hecale. The episode was the subject of a famous and influential short epic poem by Callimachus of which only fragments survive: see Callimachus, *Hecale*, ed. A. S. Hollis (Clarendon Press, Oxford, 1990).

Photis: her name derives from Greek *phos*, 'light', as Lucius' does from Latin *lux*. In this sense she is an *ignis fatuus*, beckoning him away from the true light, who is Isis, with the allurements of purely sensual pleasure. See 3.22 and note.

1.24 *for our supper*: i.e. for himself and his slaves, whose presence is taken for granted (2.15 and note). Insouciance about such details is an Apuleian hallmark.

Pytheas: Apuleius' manuscripts and modern editors and translators spell him Pythias, which is a woman's name. Again the choice of name seems to have no special significance.

Lucius: here first identified by name.

Clytius: a name borne by several characters from myth and legend; *klutos* in Greek means 'famous'. However, the name here is a conjectural restoration of the manuscript reading *adstio*.

an aedile: aediles were magistrates in charge of various aspects of public order, including supervision of the markets.

1.25 *completely bemused*: as well he might be; the episode has perplexed scholars too. Rather than a gratuitous stroke of satire at the expense of municipal officialdom, always admittedly fair game (Schlam, 1992, p. 33), it seems more likely that it carries some symbolic implication. The fish was an important symbol both in the cult of Atargatis, whose discreditable priests Lucius will later encounter (8.24 and note), and for the early Christians (see *OCD* s.v. fish, sacred), and there is evidence for an Isiac ritual intended to avert inimical influences which involved trampling fish underfoot (Schlam, ibid.). For the possibility that it is Christianity which is glanced at here, see 9.14 and note. The immediate outcome is that at the end of his first day in Thessaly Lucius goes to bed tired out, hungry and bewildered; and it may be that Apuleius inserted the episode, which was almost certainly not in his original, to provide the end of the first book of his novel with an effective conclusion. If that was his intention, the effect remains elusive.

BOOK 2

2.1 *a new day*: and a new book, as with books 3, 7 and 8. This is characteristic of epic narrative, as is the ending of a book with the hero's retiring to rest (1, 2, 10; similarly book 4 ends with Psyche in a deep sleep). It is also in the epic manner to ring artful literary changes on the theme of daybreak.

the cradle of magic arts and spells: the reputation of Thessaly as mother of witches goes back at least to Aristophanes (*Clouds*, 749–50).

2.2 *Salvia*: the name for a medicinal herb (Pliny, *Natural History*, 22. 147), but probably chosen here for its etymological connection with *salus*, 'safety', 'life', 'salvation'; it is Lucius' salvation that, as the reader eventually discovers, the book is all about, and his mother's name is another reminder of the advantages he had enjoyed which ought to have helped him to avoid the pitfalls into which his curiosity is to lead him. The hint is reconfirmed by Byrrhena's allusion to the family connection with Plutarch.

eyes grey: the word used here, *caesius*, is variously rendered 'grey', 'blue-grey' and 'green'; the precise meaning of terms of colour in Greek and Latin is often open to argument. Though this was the colour of Minerva's (Athene's) eyes, it was evidently not as a rule admired in people; in Lucretius' famous catalogue of lovers' euphemisms a man with a grey-eyed girlfriend is advised to pass her off as 'a miniature Pallas [Athene]' (*De rerum natura*, 4. 1161).

2.3 *Byrrhena*: perhaps 'Ginger', *burrus* being the Latin spelling of Greek *purrhos*, 'red-haired'. It has, however, been ingeniously suggested that the allusion is to Greek *bursa*, 'leather', and that her reference to rearing Lucius with her own hands implies that she was a strict disciplinarian; if so, he evidently failed to profit from her attentions. Dickensians will remember Pip's rueful reflections in *Great Expectations* on his upbringing 'by hand'.

2.4 *There was a magnificent entrance-hall*: set-piece descriptions, of which this is the first example in the novel, were a stock feature of poetry and oratory, and Apuleius clearly enjoyed the opportunities that they offered for virtuosic writing. Some of those in *The Golden Ass* have no other justification, as is admitted in the case of the robbers' lair (4.6 and note). This example, however, as will appear, is a significant exception.

a statue of Victory: these statues, so precariously poised, hint perhaps that Lucius' eventual victory over Fortune (11.15) will not be easily won.

Actaeon: while out hunting he came on Diana bathing with her nymphs and was turned by her into a stag and torn to pieces by his own hounds. As a symbolic warning against inopportune curiosity the message could hardly be clearer, and it is immediately reinforced by the ironical implications of Byrrhena's formal words of welcome, 'everything you see is yours' (ch. 5), and her adjuration by Diana, who is also the Underworld goddess Hecate and the Moon, both avatars of Isis (11.2, 5). The story of Actaeon would have been familiar to any educated Roman from Ovid's *Metamorphoses* (3. 138–52), and the subject was favoured by artists.

2.5 *by Diana there*: as Hecate she was goddess of witchcraft and magic.

Pamphile: 'all-loving'; another Meroe. However, in the event it is the involvement with Photis that is Lucius' undoing.

2.7 *to vote with my feet*: the usual phrase when the Senate divided on a motion, which they did by walking to one side or the other of the Senate House.

a succulent stew: there follows another dish, but the text is hopelessly garbled.

stood in amazement . . . stood to attention: Apuleius spices his naughty joke by echoing the words used by Virgil to describe Aeneas' consternation at the apparition of Creusa: 'I was paralysed. My hair stood on end' (*Aeneid*, 2. 774, trans. David West).

witty: *lepida* (see 1.1 and note).

2.8 *this preference*: there is more to this than a personal obsession. This description of Photis' hair is picked up in the epiphany of Isis (11.3), lending weight to the suggestion that Photis is a sort of anti- or false Isis: see the notes on 1.23, 3.22.

her cestus: the love-charm lent by Aphrodite (Venus) to Hera (Juno) in a famous passage of Homer (*Iliad*, 14. 211–23); probably a breast-band rather than a girdle or belt.

her Vulcan: the Latin is nicely ambiguous: *suo*, 'her own', need mean no more than 'her dear', but some translators take it as 'husband', as he is in Homer and the classical poets. However, later on (5.30) Venus by her own account turns out to be married *en secondes noces* to Mars (Ares), who in the usual version of events was her lover. Apuleius may well have known the pre-classical genealogy in which Ares was Aphrodite's husband (Hesiod, *Theogony*, 933–4).

2.10 *a bittersweet morsel*: a literary stereotype deriving from Sappho's famous description of Eros as 'a bittersweet irresistible creature', but again irony is at work. Photis' light-hearted prophecy will turn out to be all too accurate.

2.11 *Venus' supporter and squire*: an allusion to the proverbial sentiment, first met with in Terence's play *Eunuchus* (732), that 'Without food and wine Venus lacks warmth'; but the word translated by 'squire', *armiger*, contributes to the warlike imagery which Apuleius substitutes for the wrestling metaphors of the original in the subsequent description of their amatory encounter.

plenty of oil in the lamp: '. . . moving blind spoils love-making; In love it's the eyes that lead'; so Propertius (2. 15. 11–12, trans. A. G. Lee), expressing a traditional view. Aristophanes' play *Ecclesiazusae* begins with a famous address to the lamp as the accomplice and confidant of lovers, and the theme constantly recurs in the poets. See 5.22 and note.

the bottomless pit: in the Latin, Lake Avernus in the Bay of Naples, traditionally one of the entrances to the Underworld; another is Taenarus (6.18 and note).

2.12 *sharing consciousness with it*: Lucius trivializes the Stoic identification of God (Nature, Fate, Providence) with fire.

a Chaldean: the Chaldeans (Babylonians) were famous for their skill in astronomy and astrology. By Apuleius' time 'Chaldean' often simply meant 'astrologer'.

a legend, an incredible romance in several volumes: the Latin says *historiam . . . et fabulam et libros me futurum*, i.e. I shall be the *Metamorphoses*, the book now in the reader's hands. This is an early hint of the forthcoming identification at the end of the novel of Lucius as 'a man from Madaura' (11.27), the revelation, that is, that this narrative is in some sense confessional and autobiographical. Apuleius peeps out again from behind the *persona* of Lucius at 4.32 and 8.1 (see notes).

2.13 *Diophanes*: 'god-revealing'.

Cerdo: 'profiteer'.

2.14 *both her rudders*: ships were steered by two oars, one on each side of the stern.

Arignotus: 'well-known'.

2.15 *irrelevant anecdotes*: another warning obtusely ignored: if Diophanes cannot foresee his own future accurately, why should his prediction of Lucius' be any more reliable? True, it is correct as far as it goes, but it leaves much unforetold.

the slaves: Lucius'; Photis was the only servant in Milo's household. This is one of the numerous loose ends in Apuleius' conduct of the story; we hear again (11.20) of 'the servants' left behind at Hypata, but elsewhere (2.31, 3.27, 7.2) only one is mentioned. See Introduction, §5.

only waiting to be diluted: wine was generally drunk mixed with water, sometimes, as here, warm.

2.16 *garlanded me*: garlands, it has been observed, were the ancient equivalent of evening dress. Roses were especially associated with Venus, but their appearance here will prove ironic.

without any diplomatic overtures: in the Latin 'without waiting for the Fetiales to do their stuff'. The Fetiales were a college of priests responsible for the formalities of making treaties and declaring war. Not a very plausible witticism in the mouth of a native Greek, but one of many such specifically Roman and often anachronistic allusions in the novel. See below, 2.18 and note.

2.17 *to protect her modesty*: there was a famous painting by Apelles of Venus rising from the sea (Venus Anadyomene), of which Apuleius could have seen a copy at Rome. However, the pose provocatively and self-consciously adopted by Photis recalls rather Praxiteles' equally famous and much-copied statue of the Cnidian Aphrodite (M. Robertson, *A History of Greek Art*, Cambridge, 1975, I. 391–4, II. Plate 127).

2.18 *take the auspices*: the practice of taking the auspices before battle had fallen into disuse long before Apuleius' time. By alluding to Photis' decision in these terms Lucius implicitly accords her divine status.

2.20 *Thelyphron*: 'womanheart'.

amusing: lepidi (see 1.1 and note).

2.21 *like a man making a formal speech*: gesture was an important part of rhetorical technique; the various deployments of fingers and thumb to suit what is being said are elaborately analysed by Quintilian in the *Institutio Oratoria* (11. 3. 92–106).

2.23 *Harpies*: monsters with a bird's body and a woman's head.

Lynceus or Argus: Lynceus was one of the Argonauts renowned for his keen sight; Argus had a hundred eyes. Thelyphron forgets or has never learned that both came to an untimely end, Lynceus killed by Pollux in a brawl about some rustled cattle, and Argus by Mercury, who lulled him to sleep while he was guarding Io (Ovid, *Metamorphoses*, 1. 713–23).

2.26 *Philodespotus*: 'master-loving'.

Pentheus or Orpheus: in the Latin pretentiously paraphrased as 'the proud Aonian (i.e. Theban) young man' and 'the Pipleian (i.e. Pierian, dear to the Muses) bard'. Both were torn to pieces by Bacchantes (1.13), Pentheus for defying the power of Dionysus (Bacchus), Orpheus for shunning the love of women. Neither illustration is particularly apposite; Thelyphron likes showing off his schoolroom acquaintance with classical literature, in this case Euripides' *Bacchae* and Ovid's *Metamorphoses* (11.1–66) respectively.

2.28 *divine Providence*: on the part played in the novel by Providence see Introduction, §11; and on Fortune see 7.2 and note.

Zatchlas: a unique and exotic name, variously interpreted by scholars; it may or may not have been correctly transmitted in the manuscripts. The episode is generally seen as a demonstration of the beneficent power of Isis as contrasted with the malevolence of the witches and as a further warning to Lucius, disregarded like all the others, not to meddle ignorantly with magic. However, it should be noted that the Isiac priest in Heliodorus' *Ethiopica* specifically rejects necromancy as corrupt and unclean: 'the prophetic powers of priests proceed from legitimate sacrifices and pure prayer' (6. 14. 7; see also 3. 16. 3). It looks as if Apuleius got carried away, perhaps by reminiscence of one of the most famous necromantic scenes in Latin literature, the performance of the witch Erichtho in Lucan's *Pharsalia* (6. 507–830). On Apuleius' reliability as a witness to the details of Isiac cult, see 11.16 and note.

with his head shaved bare: as Lucius' will eventually be (11.28, 30).

Coptos . . . Memphis . . . Pharos: centres of Isiac worship.

the risings of Nile: always in antiquity and indeed down to modern times a subject of wonder and speculation. See, for instance, the elaborate exposition by Kalasiris, priest of Memphis, in Heliodorus' *Ethiopica* (2. 28).

sistrums: rattles used in Isiac ceremonies; see the description at 11.4.

2.31 *the god of Laughter*: apparently invented by Apuleius, along with his festival, as the peg on which to hang another cautionary episode.

some suitably lavish adornment: literally 'some material that the great god could flowingly wear', a rather laboured play on the two senses of *materia*, 'literary material' and 'fabric'. Lucius thinks that he is being invited to write an ode or speech in honour of Laughter; in fact he himself will be the material for the jest, and his (for everybody but himself) mirth-provoking speech will be in his own defence. Byrrhena's words 'provide some witty diversion' turn out to be highly ironic.

2.32 *Geryon*: a giant with three bodies; Lucius implicitly equates himself with Hercules, who killed Geryon as one of his twelve Labours.

BOOK 3

3.1 *Rosy-fingered Dawn*: Apuleius exploits a Homeric cliché. On his epicizing descriptions of daybreak, see 2.1 and note.

3.2 *at the bar of the court*: on the relationship, or lack of it, between this trial and that at 10.7–12 to contemporary legal realities, see Introduction, §6.

the coffering of the ceiling: the details of Apuleius' descriptions are sometimes hard to pin down. He evidently envisages a theatre on the Roman pattern with a roofed stage backed by a high wall elaborately embellished with columns, pedimented niches, and statuary.

the orchestra: the space, circular in Greek theatres, semicircular in Roman, between the stage and the front row of seats.

3.3 *ran off drop by drop*: the water-clock (*clepsydra*) was a familiar device; it is typical of Apuleius to provide this careful description of it, not so clear what he thought was the point of doing so.

3.7 *second father*: the word used, *parens*, is often used to describe relationships other than the strictly paternal (compare French *parent*); Hanson renders 'uncle', Walsh 'patron'. At 7.3 Lucius refers to his alleged crime against Milo as parricide (see note).

3.8 *by torture*: the evidence of slaves was routinely taken under torture in the classical period. Roman citizens were legally exempt from torture, but by Apuleius' time this rule was not infrequently breached (J. A. Crook, *Law and Life of Rome*, 1967, pp. 274–5). The point here, however, is that by his conduct Lucius has degraded himself to the level of a slave and this treatment is no more than he deserves. This is clear to the thoughtful reader and ought to be clear to Lucius himself; the townspeople of Hypata are intent only on their sadistic fun.

3.9 *Greek-style*: the wheel was a characteristically Greek instrument of torture; it crops up again at 10.10. The victim was stretched on it while the fire or the scourge was applied.

Proserpine . . . Orcus: Proserpine (Greek Persephone) was queen of the Underworld, Orcus (Greek Hades, Pluto) its king.

3.11 *author and actor*: Lucius has been both plot and protagonist of the play.

among its patrons: in the real world a *patronus* was a sort of ambassador, a man of substance and influence appointed to watch over the city's interests at Rome. Lucius' appointment, like the statue which he tactfully declines, is purely honorific. Apuleius records that he himself received similar honours from more than one city (*Florida*, 16).

3.13 *resulted in your humiliation*: Photis is not made to explain the sequel to her part of the story; the reader is left to infer that the subsequent performance must have been set up by Milo when he discovered what had happened. This is typical of Apuleius' often cavalier way with the details of his narrative.

3.15 *initiated in several cults*: nothing more is heard of these previous initiations, but Apuleius himself had indeed been initiated in more than one Greek cult (*Apology*, 55). This is another hint of the eventual quasi-identification of Lucius with his creator.

3.17 *plaques inscribed with mysterious characters*: i.e. spells and curses. Many examples of such lead tablets have survived; Pamphile's would no doubt mostly be intended to bind her love-victims.

3.18 *like another Ajax*: enraged by the award of the arms of the dead Achilles to Ulysses instead of himself, he set out to kill him, but being driven mad by Ulysses' protector Athene slaughtered a flock of sheep instead. The story was familiar from Sophocles' play *Ajax*.

an utricide: *uter* = 'a skin bag'.

3.19 *even with women of my own class*: the Latin is *matronalium amplexuum*, 'the embraces of matrons'. A young bachelor of good family in search of sexual satisfaction had, for practical reasons, to choose between resorting to household slaves or prostitutes or intriguing with married women. Though Augustus' *Lex Iulia de adulteriis* had made adultery a criminal offence, married women, as in most ages, frequently took lovers. Lucius had hitherto high-mindedly set his face against yielding to sensuality even to the extent of what was generally condoned by society. His total enslavement to Photis, herself a slave, represents abrupt and catastrophic moral degradation, as the priest of Isis eventually tells him (11.15).

3.20 *offered herself to me like a boy*: the idea of this as a stimulating extra is evidently borrowed from Martial: 'All night long I enjoyed a wanton girl, whose naughtinesses no man can exhaust. Tired by a thousand different modes, I asked for the boy routine; before I begged or started to beg, she gave it in full' (9. 67. 1–4, trans. Shackleton Bailey).

3.21 *an owl*: Bubo, the eagle-owl, proverbially a bird of ill omen. It was a common belief (like the more modern fantasy about broomsticks) that witches transformed themselves into birds.

3.22 *a boon that I can never repay*: *irremunerabili beneficio*, the identical phrase later used by Lucius to characterize the 'unspeakable pleasure' with which as an initiate he contemplates the image of Isis; another hint of Photis' role as anti- or false Isis (1.23 and note).

the local wolf-pack: *lupula* means both 'she-wolf' and 'whore'.

3.25 *an ass*: as in English, so to the ancients 'ass' connoted stupidity; so Lucius at 10.13, 'I was not such a fool or an actual ass . . .'. But asses have also always been proverbial for their obstinacy; and Lucius continues to be as resolutely deaf to admonition after his metamorphosis as he was before it. The moral of the tale of Cupid and Psyche, for instance, is completely lost on him.

3.26 *this vile and infamous creature*: this, apart from a handful of maledictions in passing (7.14, 9.15, 11.20), is the last we hear of her. Though her role in the story is, strictly speaking, symbolic, Apuleius has gone out of his way, building it is true on her original, Palaestra, to depict her by no means unsympathetically; her affection for Lucius is genuine enough and without ulterior motives. This can be seen to lend force to the argument: false pleasure does not immediately proclaim its falsity.

the red-carpet treatment: in the Latin a technical term for the entertainment accorded to ambassadors.

3.27 *Epona*: goddess of beasts of burden, worshipped by their drivers.

'*How long, for God's sake*': *Quo usque tandem*, the famous opening words of Cicero's denunciation of Catiline in his first Catilinarian oration; see 8.23 and note. This is the first of several abortive attempts on Lucius' part to eat roses (3.29, 4.1–2, 7.15) and also the occasion of the first of the many merciless beatings he endures. The whole episode is a foretaste of the long series of privations, frustrations and torments which the violent entry of the robbers is about to set in motion. As usual, Apuleius handles the details cavalierly, ignoring the problems which he set himself when he decided to graft this episode on to his Greek original; the reader is left to wonder where the groom was when Lucius was introduced into the stable and why, never having set eyes on him before, he talks as if he were an old offender.

3.28 *Suddenly*: *nec mora, cum*; a favourite phrase of Apuleius', here heralding the first of the many violent and more often than not unmotivated peripeties on which the narrative hinges. On the part played by brigandage in the novel, see 1.7 and note.

they were not checkmated: this renders a technical term from a board-game, possibly that called *ludus latrunculorum*, 'Bandits'.

BOOK 4

4.2 *that festive flower*: the rose, as now, was associated with love and pleasure; Achilles Tatius calls it 'Aphrodite's go-between' (2. 1. 3).

Success: Bonus Eventus, 'Prosperous Outcome', was one of the many abstractions forming the subject of Roman cults; Lucius does not finally encounter him until 11.28. His counterpart, 'Ill Success', appears at 4.19.

laurel-roses: oleanders.

4.4 *a discharge on medical grounds*: Apuleius uses the technical military term, *missio causaria*.

4.5 *threw him still breathing off the edge of the cliff*: this was still the way in which donkeys that had met with an accident or had otherwise outlived their usefulness were disposed of in the Spanish village where Gerald Brenan lived in the 1920s (*South from Granada*, Harmondsworth, 1963, pp. 114–15).

4.6 *The subject and the occasion itself demand*: a stock formula used by historians, orators and poets to underline the significance of a topographical description.

Unlike the passage on Byrrhena's house (2.4 and note), this elaborate treatment of the robbers' cave, on the narrator's own admission, serves no purpose except to display his descriptive talents. As often in Apuleius, the details are not always easy to visualize precisely; it is the general effect that is impressive.

as I later discovered: as will appear, he does not have very long to become acquainted with the robbers' routine. See 9.41 and note.

4.8 *the Lapiths and Centaurs all over again*: another display of rather superficial erudition. The Lapiths were a Thessalian people. At the wedding of their king Pirithous to Hippodamia, to which the Centaurs were invited as the bride's kinsmen, one of them tried to carry her off and a bloody battle ensued. Ovid had told the story in the *Metamorphoses* (12. 210–535), and the subject was much favoured by poets and artists.

Lamachus: one of the generals in command of the Athenian expedition to Sicily in 415 BC, killed in action. The name means 'Fighter for the people'.

4.9 *seven-gated Thebes*: the Homeric epithet lends mock dignity to his exordium.

Chryseros: 'lovegold'.

the expense of public office: wealthy citizens were expected, and might be compelled, to take on offices which entailed considerable expenditure on games and other entertainments. Demochares (4.13) and Thiasus (10.18) are cases in point.

4.10 *into the keyhole*: we are not well enough informed about the locking mechanisms of Roman doors to assess the plausibility of Lamachus' attempt; the likelihood is that Apuleius, as often, was more interested in creating a dramatic denouement than in technical detail. The episode was later gruesomely exploited by Charles Reade in ch. 33 of *The Cloister and the Hearth*. See 9.37 and note.

the safety of them all: Chryseros was indeed crafty; an alarm of fire in a crowded city was the surest way to bring everybody out on to the street to help, whereas the prospect of encountering armed robbers would have been a deterrent.

4.11 *a whole element as his tomb*: this resounding flourish is designed to recall the words attributed by Thucydides (2. 43) to Pericles: 'the whole earth is the sepulchre of famous men'. Thebes is only some fifteen miles from the sea, so that the necessary detour is not perhaps as glaringly implausible as some commentators make out; the real oddity is the choice of the sea as a hero's grave. Burial for the ancients meant burial on land; the idea of being abandoned to the fishes to devour was regarded with horror.

4.12 *Alcimus*: 'stalwart'. Text and interpretation of this sentence are uncertain.

His rib-cage . . . from deep inside him: these details are lifted from epic descriptions of the deaths of warriors in battle; though Alcimus' end is ignominious he dies with some literary dignity.

4.13 *Demochares*: 'people-pleaser'.

an elaborate timber structure: the text is too uncertain to allow a clear idea, if he had one himself, of what exactly Apuleius is describing. Compare the elaborate staging of the pantomime at Corinth (10.30, 34).

4.14 *Envy*: Fortune in another guise.

Eubulus: 'good counsellor'.

4.15 *Thrasyleon*: 'lionheart'.

4.18 *our appointment with plunder*: Apuleius is fond of playing with the legal term *uadimonium*, a promise to appear in court. Isis uses the same terminology when pledging Lucius to her service (11.6 and note). Here the bandits' proceedings are dignified by this veneer of legal language and the preceding reference to professional practice, *disciplina sectae*.

4.19 *Ill Success*: Scaevus Eventus, 'Unlucky Outcome', the opposite of Bonus Eventus (4.2 and note), Fortune in yet another guise.

4.21 *his life . . . his glory*: the conceit, repeated and varied at the end of the chapter, can be paralleled from actual gravestones; the form of the expression is redolent of the declamatory exercises on which Apuleius would have cut his rhetorical teeth.

gone to live among the spirits of the dead: a variation on a theme which goes back at least to Hesiod, who laments that Shame and Righteous Indignation will quit the earth in disgust to dwell among the gods (*Works and Days*, 199–200). In picturing Good Faith (Fides) as taking refuge in hell rather than heaven Apuleius had been anticipated by Petronius (*Satyricon*, 124. 249–53).

mourning the loss of three comrades: another epic touch, an echo of the Homeric formula 'We sailed on grieving at heart, glad to have escaped death, but having lost our dear comrades' (*Odyssey*, 9. 62–3, *al.*).

4.22 *a real Salian banquet*: the lavish repasts of the College of Saliares, priests of Mars, were famous.

4.26 *a Son of the People*: *filium publicum*; the official conferment of such titles is attested in inscriptions.

Attis and Protesilaus: she too has had a classical education. Attis was a vegetation god associated with Cybele about whom many legends clustered; Apuleius appears to be referring to one said by Pausanias (7. 17. 5) to be the best known, in which he went mad and castrated himself at his wedding. The newly-married Protesilaus was the first Greek hero to be killed at Troy; his wife Laodamia is the writer of the eighth of Ovid's *Letters of Heroines* (*Heroides*). Unless the allusion is to a version of the story in which the marriage was not consummated, it does not seem especially apt.

4.27 *the opposite of what actually happens*: so Artemidorus (*Onirocritica*, 2. 49–51), and still conventional wisdom. This dream, however, turned out to be false (8.5).

pretty: *lepidus* (see 1.1 and note). Lucius predictably receives the story in this spirit (6.25 and note).

4.28 *putting right thumb and forefinger to their lips*: a ritual gesture of adoration.

drops from heaven: a delicate allusion to the story of her birth told explicitly by Hesiod (*Theogony*, 176–200): Cronus, having castrated his father Uranus (Heaven), threw his genitals into the sea, where they engendered Aphrodite (Venus), while from the drops of blood which fell on the earth there sprang the race of Giants and other superhuman creatures. The story has already been discreetly hinted at (2.8), and when Venus visits Olympus, Heaven, her father, opens to receive her (6.6). For another version of her parentage see 6.7 and note.

4.29 *Paphos . . . Cnidos . . . Cythera*: important centres of her cult.

4.30 *nurturer of the whole world*: she characterizes herself in terms which recall the Lucretian Venus, the great originating principle of the universe. The rhetoric and tone of her speech, however, recall Virgil's Juno and her implacable persecution of Aeneas and the Trojans (*Aeneid*, 7. 308–10). Her words also foreshadow the epiphany of Isis, who is the true, celestial, Venus (*caelestis Venus*, 11.2; cf. 11.5). This Venus, at least at this stage, is firmly earthbound. See Introduction, §9.

the shepherd: Paris, ordered by Jupiter to adjudicate the prize of beauty claimed by Venus, Juno and Minerva. The episode will be depicted in the pantomime elaborately described at 10.30–32. The reference to his 'impartial fairness' is ironical; all the goddesses tried to bribe him, and Venus won because her bribe, marriage to Helen, was the most attractive.

that winged son of hers: Cupid (Eros, Love) makes his first appearance in his familiar literary guise as a mischievous boy, irresponsibly using his arrows and his fire to vex gods and mortals alike. He is not named until Psyche finally sees him, to her undoing (5.22 and note).

4.31 *the honeyed burns*: a typically Apuleian variation on the age-old idea of love as bittersweet (2.10 and note).

open-mouthed and closely pressed: like those of Photis (2.10) and those promised as the reward for informing on Psyche (6.8). This is very definitely not *Venus caelestis*.

her enemy the Sun: she had three reasons for disliking him: (1) ladies in antiquity, let alone the goddess of love herself, did not cultivate sun-tan; (2) fire and water (her native element) were incompatible; (3) it was the all-seeing Sun (1.5) who had given away her affair with Mars (Homer, *Odyssey*, 8. 302; Ovid, *Ars amatoria*, 2. 573–4, *Metamorphoses*, 4. 171–4, 190–92).

the retinue that escorted Venus: this description is heavily indebted to literary models, especially Homer (*Iliad*, 18. 39–48), Virgil (*Aeneid*, 5. 240–42, 823–4), and the Hellenistic poet Moschus (*Europa*, 115–24). Nereus was father of the sea-nymphs; Portunus was the god of harbours (*portus*); Salacia was an old Roman marine goddess connected by etymologists with *salum*, 'sea'; Palaemon, often depicted by artists astride a dolphin, as here, was originally Melicertes, changed into a sea-god by Neptune (Ovid, *Metamorphoses*, 4. 531–42); Tritons, human above the waist, piscine below, were Neptune's traditional escort.

4.32 *replied in Latin:* Apuleius goes out of his way to shatter the dramatic illusion with this arch reference to the literary character of his story (1.1 and note) and the fact that, though purporting to be told by a native Greek speaker, it is written in Latin. As well as being in the wrong language, the god's reply is in the wrong metre, elegiac couplets; Apollo always answered in hexameters. Apuleius is not alone in this last delinquency; in Heliodorus the Pythia similarly delivers herself in elegiacs (*Ethiopica*, 2. 26. 5, 2. 35. 5). See also 9.8 and note. It was generally considered a breach of literary decorum to mix Greek and Latin in the same book, at least if it had pretensions to literary status; Apuleius indicates his respect for this 'rule' at 9.39, where he translates the soldier's Greek. He allows himself once to use a Greek technical term in an Isiac ritual (11.17). He has no such inhibitions in the *Apology*, which is full of Greek quotations. By Apuleius' day the Pythia was delivering her oracles in prose.

4.33 *For funeral wedlock:* the punishment of Psyche's involuntary offence is to be exposed on a rock for a monster to carry her off. This recalls the fate of Andromeda, made to atone in the same way for her mother's boasting of her own beauty. The story was popular; it was the subject of a lost tragedy by Euripides and would have been familiar to Roman readers from Ovid (*Metamorphoses*, 4. 670–739). The detail that Andromeda was dressed as a bride had been exploited by Manilius (*Astronomica*, 5. 545–8); and Achilles Tatius describes a picture of her 'in a wedding dress like a bride adorned for Death' (3. 7. 5). In what follows Apuleius goes on to exploit the conceit in terms of a favourite paradox of Hellenistic epigram, the bride who dies on her wedding day.

regards with fear: no ancient reader could have been in doubt for a moment over the identity of this 'monster'. Its attributes, wings, fire (torches) and steel (arrows) have already been alluded to (4.30), and Love was the only power in the mythological universe of whom all the other gods, the river Styx included, went in dread.

4.34 *herself encouraged them:* Psyche's speech is that of a tragic heroine such as Iphigenia or Macaria or Polyxena, doomed to be sacrificed for the people. A similar disregard for superficial plausibility (aside from the fact that this story is supposed to be told by a presumably illiterate old woman) is evident in her elaborate prayers to Ceres and Juno (6.2, 4).

NOTES

my spirit rather: the idea of a shared soul is most familiar in the context of
erotic love, but Euripides had used it of family ties (*Alcestis*, 882−4) and Ovid
of the love of husband and wife (*Metamorphoses*, 11. 388). Compare Charite's
speech at 8.12. In the first of several plays on Psyche's name Apuleius exploits
the ambiguity of *spiritus*, meaning both 'breath (of life)' and 'soul'.

4.35 *Zephyr*: the West Wind, harbinger of spring and so apt for the service of
the son of Venus; in some genealogies he was Eros' father. Winds were in the
business of abducting girls, and Ovid had cast Zephyrus in this role (*Fasti*, 5.
201−4). Perseus was airborne when he rescued Andromeda.

BOOK 5

5.1 *What she now saw*: the description of this divine stately home belongs to a
literary tradition which goes back to Homer's depiction of the palace and gardens
of Alcinous (*Odyssey*, 7. 84−132) and which is represented in the novel by the
gardens which figure in Longus (*Daphnis and Chloe*, 2. 3. 3−4, 4. 2−3) and Achilles
Tatius (1. 1, 1. 15). Apuleius also borrows from Ovid's bravura description of the
palace of the Sun (*Metamorphoses*, 2. 1−18). In real life, description of fine houses
almost constituted a genre in its own right, as in the *Silvae* of Statius (1. 3, 1. 5,
2. 2) and in Pliny's letters about his villas (*Epistles*, 2. 17, 5. 6).

5.2 *there is nothing that was not there*: the Latin can also mean 'what was not there
is nothing', i.e. does not exist, an allusive reminder that Love, in its true and
highest form, is universal and all-sufficient. Psyche does not learn this truth
until it is almost too late.

All of it is yours: an ominous echo of the words of Byrrhena to Lucius (2.4
and note) in an identical setting, the wondering examination of a marvellous
house. Like Lucius, Psyche will be the victim of ignoble curiosity.

5.4 *her unknown husband*: this is the primary meaning of *ignobilis*, but it also not
uncommonly means 'humble', 'base', an ironical allusion to the outcast wretch
to whom Cupid had been ordered to marry her (4.31). By this time it will have
become clear to any moderately perceptive reader that he has flatly disobeyed
those orders.

5.6 *obey the ruinous demands of your heart*: the *animus* (Greek *thumos*) which she
is resignedly told to obey is the appetitive part of the soul (*anima*, Greek *psuche*);
the expression recalls Plato's description of the man 'who is ruled by desire'
(*Phaedrus*, 238e). The image of enslavement to the passions occurs in Apuleius'
description in the *Apology* of Venus Vulgaria as 'binding the bodies of all living
things in servile bondage' (12). Lucius, who is listening intently to this story,
of course fails to take the point.

NOTES

impious curiosity: the first overt reference to the failing which, along with her naivety (5.11), is to be her undoing.

whoever you are: under the surface irony of this speech a deeper and fundamental layer can be detected. Psyche has yet to learn, the hard way, what Love really is. What she thinks she loves is not Love itself but physical pleasure.

5.9 *the blindness . . . of Fortune*: see 7.2 and note.

shut up with bolts and bars: in contrast to the palace inhabited by Psyche (5.2), but in this context it sounds as if she is complaining at being kept locked up, whereas it is clear that she can come and go freely. The style of these complaints stereotypes the sisters as middle-class housewives such as those figuring in the series of inserted stories later in the novel rather than royal consorts. Nor is the tone of Venus' haranguing of Cupid quite what one would expect of a goddess (5.29–30).

5.11 *you will not see it*: i.e. he will disappear, but the paradox has a deeper significance: she will not recognize him, i.e. even when face to face with Love itself she will not comprehend its true nature. See 5.6 *whoever you are* and note.

he will be mortal: this son will turn out to be a daughter (6.24). If this is simple carelessness on Apuleius' part, he almost goes out of his way to draw attention to it by making Cupid refer in the next chapter to 'this little son of ours'. If it is a 'deliberate mistake' it is difficult to see the point of it. For down-to-earth common sense it would be hard to beat the explanation of Louis Purser: 'Cupid did not necessarily know the future in every respect. Parents always assume that their first-born will be a boy; and when the sex is unknown, it is allowable to use the masculine.'

5.12 *the Sirens*: half women, half birds, they lured sailors to destruction by their song.

5.17 *an immense serpent*: for the details of this horrific description Apuleius is heavily indebted to Virgil (*Georgics*, 3. 425–39; *Aeneid*, 2. 204–8). Psyche of course knows from experience that in the dark her husband's shape is human; the unspoken premiss of the plot is that it is only by day that he is a serpent. When the sisters instruct Psyche to do the murder in the light they evidently expect an instant transformation; and this suggests that, though they themselves refer to their story as a fabrication (*fallacias*, 5.16), they believe it to be true. The scenario as a whole more or less hangs together and the narrative moves so quickly that the reader is not given time to think about the details, which, as often in Apuleius, do not stand close scrutiny.

the Pythian oracle: it was the one at Miletus (4.32), but in this context the cult-title 'Pythian' is appropriate. The Python was the dragon which guarded the Delphic oracle until Apollo killed it and took over.

5.20 *Take a very sharp blade . . . cut them apart*: in the Latin a single long and continuously flowing sentence; the instructions are framed by the instrument, *nouaculam*, and the act, *abscide*, 'cut'.

5.21 *the savage Furies who harried her*: the irresolute heroine, agonizingly poised between equally dire alternative courses of action, is a familiar literary figure; Apuleius' chief indebtedness is to Ovid's portrayals in the *Metamorphoses* of such women as Procne, Althaea, Byblis and Myrrha.

5.22 *cruel Fate*: as not infrequently, the distinction between Fate and Fortune, the usual instrument of malignant supernatural intervention in the novel, is blurred.

was gladdened and flared up: because it could now fulfil its traditional role, of which it had hitherto been cheated, of confidant and voyeur: see 2.11 and note, 5.23, 8.10.

dripping with ambrosia: here a perfume, at 6.23 a drink (see note).

the gracious weapons of the great god: what at his first appearance had been depicted as the toys of a naughty unbiddable child and what his mother later claims as her 'gear' (5.29) are now transformed into the awe-inspiring attributes of a mighty god. It is this Cupid, Amor I (Introduction, §9), who from now on controls the action.

5.25 *to scorch even water*: Apuleius may well have in mind Ovid's catalogue of amorous rivers at *Amores*, 3. 6. 23ff.

Pan: as a country god and a veteran of many amorous exploits he is naturally an expert on love; when Philetas instructs Daphnis and Chloe in the art of love it is Pan on whom he calls for help (Longus, *Daphnis and Chloe*, 2. 7. 6). With his list of symptoms compare that at 10.2; such inventories were a commonplace of poetry and romance from Sappho onwards.

aware no matter how: clearly briefed by Cupid (Amor I); the first hint that he is at work behind the scenes.

5.26 *take your chattels with you . . . in due form*: another intrusion of specifically Roman references, particularly jarring in this timeless fairytale. Psyche reports Cupid as using the technical legal terminology of divorce and marriage, the latter in its most ancient and solemn form, *confarreatio*, virtually obsolete long before Apuleius' time. See also 5.29 and note.

5.27 *fell to a similar death*: attempts have been made to invest the deaths of the sisters with symbolic significance, but the perfunctory manner in which the episode is handled suggests that Apuleius' principal preoccupation was to get them out of the way once they had served their turn and to gratify the normal human wish to see villains come to a sticky end. He makes no effort to mitigate the inconsistency in characterization by which the naive and credulous Psyche suddenly and briefly becomes as crafty and vindictive as her wicked sisters.

5.30 *your father's estate*: more legal language (5.26 and note), suggesting a divorce or judicial separation from her husband; see below on 5.30.

expose . . . abuse . . . battering me: he behaves like a typical spoilt child, but the words also imply that he turns his weapons on her and 'strips' her (the word is *denudas*), i.e. leaves her defenceless by constantly making her fall in love. Venus was usually depicted naked by artists. This tirade is indebted to Aphrodite's complaints about Eros in Apollonius' *Argonautica* (3. 91–9). See also 5.31 and note.

your stepfather: her husband was Vulcan (Hephaestus), Mars (Ares) her lover, at least in the version most generally familiar. The idea that she had somehow disposed of Vulcan and remarried seems to have been borrowed from Ovid, who is the only other writer to refer to Mars as Cupid's stepfather (*Amores*, 1. 2. 24, 2. 9. 48; *Remedia amoris*, 27).

his infidelities: they were many and various.

groomed with nectar from my own breasts: sense uncertain.

5.31 *Ceres and Juno*: the following scene is loosely modelled on the episode in Apollonius' *Argonautica* in which Hera and Athene approach Aphrodite to enlist the aid of Eros in their schemes (see above on ch. 30). Hera there assures Aphrodite that his behaviour will improve.

BOOK 6

6.2 *There is Venus in her rage*: though in her funeral speech Psyche had implied that she was the victim of Venus' jealousy, this is the first explicit revelation of the fact vouchsafed to her.

an elaborate prayer: too elaborate and learned, like that to Juno, to be plausible in Psyche's mouth. The allusions (see next note) to the rape and rescue of Proserpine foreshadow her own Catabasis (6.16 and note) and the symbolic death and resurrection of Lucius in the first of his three initiations (11.23 and note).

the furrows of the Sicilian fields . . . conceals in silence: Ceres' (Demeter's) daughter Proserpine (Persephone) was carried off from Henna in Sicily down to the Underworld by Pluto (Dis, Hades). Ceres secured her return by preventing the crops from growing, but as Proserpine had eaten some pomegranate seeds (the number varies) during her imprisonment, she was obliged to spend a part of every year underground. In this ancient nature-myth Proserpine represents the regenerative power of the seed-corn, which must be buried each year and lie in darkness during the winter, to be reborn each spring. Ceres' most famous cult-centre was at Eleusis near Athens, where every year the story was symbolically re-enacted for initiates in conditions, supposedly, of strict religious secrecy. Apuleius probably expected his readers to remember Ovid's treatment of the story (*Metamorphoses*, 5. 341–571), in which it is at Venus' instigation that Pluto is shot by Cupid and so inspired with love for Proserpine. Ceres therefore has good reason to be wary of crossing this pair.

6.3 *a thoroughly good sort*: after the lofty tone of Psyche's invocation, Ceres' reply is chillingly matter-of-fact. Venus is a relative and a crony, and Ceres must keep on her right side. Juno's reply is similarly prosaic (6.4 and note).

6.4 *Samos . . . Carthage . . . Argos*: a good example of syncretism, the fusing of originally distinct deities and their cults. Juno is identified with Hera, whose chief cult centres were at Samos and Argos, and also with the Carthaginian Tanit, represented as riding on a lion. Psyche artfully associates these places with the chronology of the goddess's life as child, young girl, and wife and mother. The form of her prayer reflects actual usage.

Zygia . . . Lucina: *Zygia*, 'Yoker' renders in Greek her Latin title *Iuga* or *Iugalis* (*iugum*, 'yoke'), symbolizing her role as goddess of marriage; Lucina is more usually identified with Diana (Artemis) as goddess of childbirth because, according to the ancient etymology, she brought the new-born to light (*lux*). It is appropriate that the pregnant Psyche should invoke Juno in this capacity.

prevented by the laws: by this anachronistic reference to specifically Roman legislation Juno, like Ceres, brings matters down to earth with a bump.

6.6 *Heaven . . . Aether*: her father and grandfather. On Uranus and the circumstances of her birth see 4.28 and note.

6.7 *the loud-voiced god*: so called as herald of the gods, now impressed as town-crier (6.8 and note).

Arcadian brother: he was born on Mount Cyllene in Arcadia. Venus' greeting presupposes an alternative genealogy in which she was daughter of Jupiter and Dione. Mercury's (Hermes') mythological character is that of, among other things, an accomplished liar, which makes him an appropriate assistant in amatory intrigue.

6.8 *Passing far and wide among the peoples*: a discreetly learned allusion, playing on the Stoic identification of Mercury as the divine *logos* (word) and on the etymology of his Latin name as *medius currens*, 'because speech (*sermo*) runs about among men' (Varro, *Antiquities*, fragment 250). This is the sort of ploy which helps to tell against the assumption that the ancient novel had a mass readership.

made proclamation: it is clearly modelled on a well-known poem by the Hellenistic poet Moschus, 'Love the runaway', in which the reward is promised by Venus herself (1–5); but the form of the announcement, beginning with the formula *si quis* . . . , 'If any man . . .', is taken from such advertisements in real life, as surviving inscriptions show.

the South turning-point of the Circus: where the shrine of Venus Murcia was situated. Another anachronistic allusion, in this case, however, far from gratuitous. The Circus Maximus was a notorious haunt of prostitutes; and the description of the promised reward implicitly reduces Venus (Venus II: see Introduction, §9) to precisely that level, the level of Photis and the servile pleasures to which Lucius succumbs.

Habit: Consuetudo; that love was a creature of habit was a traditional idea (Lucretius, *De rerum natura*, 4. 1283; Ovid, *Ars amatoria*, 2. 345, *Remedia amoris*, 503; Chariton, 5. 9. 9; Achilles Tatius, 1. 9. 5). Psyche herself had experienced the truth of it (5.4), as Thrasyllus will (8.2).

6.9 *laughed shrilly*: ironical; her Homeric epithet was 'laughter-loving'.

it will be born a bastard: more anachronistic legalism, possibly embodying a sly allusion to Apuleius' own brush with the law; it was one of the charges against him that his marriage to Pudentilla took place in the country, *in uilla* (*Apology*, 67, 88). These words are picked up by Jupiter at 6.23.

6.10 *the great god's bedfellow*: this is the first overt indication that it is indeed Cupid who is helping Psyche behind the scenes.

6.12 *source of sweet music*: because used to make the panpipes.

6.13 *Styx . . . Cocytus*: Underworld rivers. Venus' house, it seems, is not, as one would expect, on Olympus, but somewhere in the Peloponnese, within easy reach of Taenarus (6.18 and note). It is not clear what she wants with this water. Its traditional role was that of a lie-detector: it was the Styx by which the gods took their oaths (6.15), and the consequences of perjury were dire (Hesiod, *Theogony*, 793–804).

6.15 *the Phrygian cupbearer*: Ganymede (see 1.12 and note).

6.16 *to the Underworld*: in the last of Psyche's ordeals Apuleius exploits a familiar literary theme, the Catabasis or Descent to Hades. Homer (*Odyssey*, 11. 568–635), Aristophanes (*Frogs*; see next note), Virgil (*Georgics*, 4. 467–84, *Aeneid*, 6. 268–899) and Ovid (*Metamorphoses*, 4. 432–80) had all been there before him; it is Aeneas' visit to the Underworld in *Aeneid*, VI which he chiefly lays under contribution.

6.17 *for a certain lofty tower*: the idea that jumping off a tower is the most convenient route to Hades can only have been suggested to Apuleius by Heracles' sarcastic advice to Dionysus in Aristophanes' play *Frogs* (127–33). Visitors to Hell need a guide, Circe in Homer, Heracles in Aristophanes, the Sibyl in Virgil; a tower in this role – Cupid's other intermediaries are all living things – gives a new and unexpected turn to this old theme.

6.18 *Taenarus*: Cape Matapan, the southernmost point of the Peloponnese and one of the traditional entrances to Hades; another was Lake Avernus (2.11 and note).

a lame donkey . . . with a lame driver: the significance of this encounter, which sounds as if it should in some way relate to the adventures of Lucius-as-ass, has never been satisfactorily explained. See also 11.8 and note for a similarly enigmatic pair.

to haul him aboard: this 'temptation' was evidently suggested by the episode in the Virgilian Catabasis in which the dead Palinurus begs Aeneas for a lift across the Styx and is refused, because as an unburied corpse he is ineligible to enter (*Aeneid*, 6. 337–83).

6.19 *some old women weavers*: this reverses a common theme; such old women were apt to turn out to be goddesses in disguise, to whom it was advisable to be helpful.

a huge dog: Cerberus.

the empty house of Dis: an allusion to Virgil's 'empty halls of Dis and his desolate kingdom' (*Aeneid*, 6. 269, trans. David West), 'a world of phantom dwellings, homes of hollow men' (R. G. Austin).

ask for some coarse bread: considering the fate of Proserpine herself (6.2 and note), one would expect a total prohibition of eating.

6.20 *in private*: necessarily so, since she could not be allowed to see the trap that was being set for her. The theme of the message which is the death-warrant of the bearer is familiar from the stories of Bellerophon (Homer, *Iliad*, 6. 166–95), Uriah the Hittite (2 Samuel 11:14–27), and Hamlet; but how is Proserpine or whoever fills the box supposed to know Venus' real wishes? This is another of the numerous loose ends in Apuleius' rapid narrative.

6.22 *became himself again*: Cupid is now abruptly transformed from all-powerful god to ailing apprehensive child, Amor I reverting to his first appearance as Amor II. Given the need to end the story on a light-hearted note – it is meant to cheer the captive Charite up – it is appropriate that the last scene should be played as high comedy in the setting of a traditional Olympus, but this denouement inevitably compromises the fundamental symbolic function of the tale as an allegory of the human soul in quest of love in its highest, divine, guise – which of course makes it all the easier for Lucius to miss its application to his own case.

the Lex Julia: passed in 18 BC, it made adultery a criminal offence.

into . . . base shapes: this catalogue draws on Ovid's list of Jupiter's disguises in the *Metamorphoses* (6. 103–14).

you are bound to pay me back: perhaps to be read as an aside; Jupiter is not only incorrigible but unrepentant.

6.23 *to summon all the gods . . . to assembly*: the Council of the gods is a stock feature of epic from Homer onwards and a favourite subject of burlesque. The idea of making the gods follow the procedures of the Roman Senate seems to have been first hit on by the satirist Lucilius (second century BC) and was further exploited by Seneca in his *Apocolocyntosis* and by Ovid in the *Metamorphoses* (1. 167–76).

in accordance with the civil law: see 6.9 and note. A prosaic conclusion to a reassurance which had begun on a lofty note with a reminiscence of his great speech to Venus at the beginning of the *Aeneid* (1. 257–8).

brought by Mercury: now in his role, here reversed, of conductor of souls to the Underworld (Psychopompus).

a cup of ambrosia: more usually a food, but occasionally a drink, as here, or a perfume (5.22 and note). At the banquet they drink nectar, as one would expect.

6.24 *Liber . . . Vulcan*: Bacchus pours himself out in the shape of wine, Vulcan cooks the dinner in the shape of fire, an example of the common figure of speech called metonymy.

whom we call Pleasure: Apuleius springs a surprise (5.11 and note). The idea is a leitmotiv of the novel. In its immediate context the birth of this divine child can be read both as an encouragement to Charite to hope for a happy outcome to her own sufferings and as a restoration to the world of the true pleasure of love of which it was deprived by the joint secession of Venus and Cupid (5.28). In the larger context of the book as a whole it foreshadows the 'inexpressible pleasure' which Lucius is to experience in contemplating the image of Isis after his initiation (11.24), which effaces and replaces the false 'servile pleasures' offered by Photis (11.15). In the writer's syncretistic vision of Venus–Isis can also be detected the lineaments of Lucretius' Venus (4.30 and note), identified by him in the first line of the *De rerum natura* as 'pleasure of gods and men', the Epicurean *hedone*.

6.25 *such a pretty story*: *bellam*, a variation on *lepidus* (see 1.1 and note), the old woman's description (4.27 and note); Lucius of course takes the story at (her) face value. The author puts in a momentary appearance to remind us that the story will eventually indeed be written down – for it now has been. See also 6.29 and note.

6.27 *Dirce*: she was tied to a wild bull by Zethus and Amphion as a punishment for her cruel treatment of their mother Antiope. The story had been dramatized by Euripides in his lost play *Antiope*.

6.29 *immortalized in the pages of the learned*: another reminder (2.12, 6.25 and notes) of the off-stage presence of the author.

Phrixus . . . Arion . . . Europa: Phrixus escaped across the Hellespont from his stepmother Ino on the back of the ram with the golden fleece; Arion was rescued from his murderers by a dolphin; Europa was abducted by Zeus (Jupiter) in the shape of a bull.

apportionment of the road: another of Apuleius' legal pleasantries, using technical language; compare the miller at 9.27.

6.30 *Pegasus*: the winged horse born from drops of blood from the head of the Gorgon Medusa, cut off by Perseus; ridden by Bellerophon when he killed the Chimaera. Compare 7.26, 8.16 and notes.

from a branch of a tall cypress tree: not the obvious choice of tree for this particular purpose (see 8.18 and note), but the cypress was a symbol of death.

6.31 *burned alive . . . thrown to the beasts . . . crucified*: all, ironically, punishments prescribed for banditry.

aiding and abetting: in the Latin more technical terminology, *sequestro ministroque*, 'trustee and agent'.

BOOK 7

7.2 *his slave*: see 2.15 and note.

portrayed Fortune as totally blind: the blindness of Fortune was proverbial (5.9, 8.24), but the idea is especially significant in *The Golden Ass*, where she is the antitype of provident and beneficent Isis, identified by her priest with 'a Fortune that can see' (11.15). On Fortune and Providence see Introduction, §11.

7.3 *parricide*: the contemporary legal definition of parricide embraced murder of a kinsman or even a patron (3.7 and note).

7.5 *Haemus*: a mountain range in Thrace, perhaps recalling poetic comparisons of warriors to mountains (Homer, *Iliad*, 13. 754; Virgil, *Aeneid*, 12. 701–3), perhaps also suggesting Greek *haima*, 'blood'.

Theron: 'hunter'.

7.6 *a two-hundred-thousand man*: on the various types of post held by *procuratores*, see *OCD* s.v. procurator. They were ranked in terms of their pay: 200,000 sesterces per annum was the second highest grade.

Plotina: possibly intended to recall the exemplary wife of the emperor Trajan; Apuleius might have seen her commemorated on the coinage and she had a temple at Rome.

Zacynthus: modern Zante, an island off the north-west Peloponnese; islands were often used as places of exile, as being easier to keep under surveillance.

7.7 *Actium*: a promontory on the coast of Acarnania, made famous as the place of Octavian's victory over Antony and Cleopatra in 31 BC.

7.8 *a mere donkey-woman*: rather conspicuously dressed for the part, one would think.

7.10 *Treasury Pleader*: the office of *advocatus fisci*, according to the evidence, for what it is worth, of the *Historia Augusta* (*Life of Hadrian*, 20. 6) had been established by Hadrian; the fiscus was the Imperial, as distinguished from the State, Treasury.

7.11 *whoever he is*: this apparently gratuitous qualification ironically hints at Lucius' ignorance of what will shortly be revealed, Haemus' true identity.

7.12 *Tlepolemus*: 'hardy warrior', the name of the commander of the Rhodian contingent at Troy, a son of Heracles (Homer, *Iliad*, 2. 653).

Charite: 'grace'.

7.13 *manfully*: the idiomatic sense of the phrase *pro uirili parte* is 'to the best of my ability', but here the literal sense of *uirilis* is also felt; Lucius displays human awareness of the occasion.

7.16 *deeds of valour at home and abroad*: this has the ring of a quotation or parody of an official citation, but exact parallels for such a formula are lacking.

the king of Thrace: Diomedes; Heracles' eighth Labour was to capture these horses. In the most familiar version of the legend they were mares, but that would have spoiled the comparison.

7.20 *this salamander of an ass*: text and interpretation uncertain. The salamander (actually a completely harmless amphibian) was reputed to be poisonous and invulnerable to fire.

7.21 *while Venus looks away in horror*: *auersa Venere*, a play on words which resists translation; the phrase can also mean 'in the reverse position', which would naturally be that attempted by an ass.

7.23 *the next market*: they were held at fixed intervals, usually of eight days; the delay is plausibly motivated.

a lover's . . . his manhood: the words used are ironically appropriate to the man hidden within the ass. Compare 7.25, 'the butchery of my virility'.

7.26 *My Bellerophon*: Lucius as Pegasus again (6.30 and note).

7.27 *antisocial behaviour*: the principle to which she appeals, *boni mores*, 'honest behaviour', did in fact have some legal standing (A. Berger, *Encyclopedic Dictionary of Roman Law*, Philadelphia, 1953, p. 374).

7.28 *Meleager . . . Althaea*: he was fated to die when a particular piece of wood was burnt. His mother Althaea, enraged by his killing of her brothers in the quarrel after the hunting of the Calydonian Boar, thrust it into the fire and destroyed him. This is another story familiar to Roman readers from Ovid (*Metamorphoses*, 8. 445–525).

BOOK 8

8.1 *the gift of literary style*: another authorial intrusion into Lucius' narrative; see 2.12, 6.29 and notes. The implication is not merely that the tale itself is remarkable but that Apuleius has taken especial pains in combining, elaborating, and embellishing his several literary models.

Thrasyllus: 'Rashman'; see 8.8.

8.4 *the nets*: they would have been set up round the edge of the thicket to catch the game flushed by the hounds; Apuleius does not bother in this instance (contrast the water-clock at 3.3) to elaborate a detail which would have been familiar to most of his readers.

8.6 *like a Bacchante*: the whole scene is pervaded with Virgilian echoes. Dido, when Fame brings the news that Aeneas is preparing to depart, 'raged and raved round the whole city like a Bacchant' (*Aeneid*, 4. 298–303); and Amata, maddened by the Fury Allecto, 'ran through the middle of the cities . . . [and] flew into the forests' (7. 383–7) (trans. David West).

8.7 *nobody is immune*: this was the commonest of the standard consolatory commonplaces, exploited to great effect by, for instance, Lucretius (*De rerum natura*, 3. 1024–52). Thrasyllus is ostensibly behaving exactly as a friend in these circumstances was supposed to.

as the god Liber: the Latin equivalent of Bacchus/Dionysus. This reflects a real custom, alluded to by, for example, Statius (*Silvae*, 2. 7. 124–5, 5. 1. 231–6). Apuleius may also have had in mind the story of Laodamia, who cherished a portrait of her dead husband Protesilaus (4.26 and note); he would have read of this in Ovid (*Heroides*, 13. 151–8). Bacchus is chosen as young and ideally beautiful.

8.8 *his unspeakable treachery*: his pretence of disinterested friendship; she learns of the murder from Tlepolemus' ghost.

8.10 *my nurse*: from Homer onwards a stock character, confidante and go-between.

8.11 *to lay him to rest*: the verb used, *sepeliuit*, literally 'buried', anticipates Thrasyllus' fate.

8.12 *that shed my blood*: see 4.34 and note.

Your matrons of honour shall be the avenging Furies: an echo of the ill-omened marriage of Dido and Aeneas, conveyed through a conflation of allusions to Virgil and Ovid: Juno as *pronuba*, matron of honour (*Aeneid*, 4. 166), and a chorus of Furies (*Heroides*, 7. 95–6).

8.16 *the fire-breathing Chimaera*: a tripartite monster, a lion in front, a goat in the middle, and a dragon behind, with three heads to correspond, killed by Bellerophon (6.30 and note).

8.17 *not so much memorable as miserable*: *non tam . . . memorandum quam miserandum*; the alliteration and assonance underline Apuleius' literary versatility. Encounters with fierce dogs are a recurring feature of his narrative (4.3, 4.19–20, 9.36–7); the changes that he rings on this theme recall the analogous treatment by historians of stock battle motifs (P. G. Walsh, *Livy: his Historical Aims and Methods*, Cambridge, 1967, pp. 197–208); and for the idea of a battle or its aftermath as a spectacle one may compare, for instance, the scene in which the Carthaginians view the battlefield of Cannae (Livy, 22. 51. 5–9) or Vitellius' visit to Bedriacum, described as 'a loathsome and dreadful spectacle' (Tacitus, *Histories*, 2. 70).

8.18 *from the top of a cypress*: like Cupid reproving Psyche (5.24). It is difficult to see any significance in the choice of a cypress; almost any other tree would be easier to climb. See 6.30 and note.

8.20 *by your Fortunes and your Guardian Spirits*: *per Fortunas uestrosque Genios*, an apparently unique combination in appeals of this kind. The idea of a Fortune peculiar to an individual recurs at 8.24, 11.15. The *genius*, a word which resists translation, is 'the entirety of the traits united in a begotten being' (*OCD* s.v. genius).

8.21 *a monstrous serpent*: though the reader is expected to accept witchcraft and transformations such as Lucius' as part of an ostensibly realistic depiction of contemporary life, serpents or dragons such as this are fabulous creatures (cf. 11.24), an intrusion from the fairytale world of Cupid and Psyche.

8.22 *to put it on record*: the inserted stories in the earlier part of the book were cautionary, warnings to Lucius not to persist in his degraded conduct. Those after his metamorphosis point the moral by way of commentary on what his folly has brought him to (Introduction, §§2, 4, 6). The suspension of disbelief required from the reader as to how Lucius-as-ass is supposed to have learned all the details that he recounts is for the most part taken for granted; the mock apology at 9.30 really explains nothing.

his consort: *conseruam coniugam*, 'fellow-slave-wife'; slaves could not legally marry but were often allowed to form near-conjugal connections. In what follows Apuleius uses the terms *maritus* (husband) and *uxor* (wife) without qualification.

8.23 *a certain large and famous city*: identified in the *Onos* as Beroea in Macedonia. Apuleius is studiously vague about Lucius' itinerary between Hypata, where he is transformed, and Corinth, where he makes his last and successful bid for freedom.

How long . . . : another allusion to the famous exordium of Cicero's first oration against Catiline (3.27 and note).

a sieve on four legs: compare 3.29; but the conceit is here elaborated in an obscure and untranslatable pun on the word *ruderarius*, which occurs nowhere else. It is formed from *rudus*, 'rubble', but is perhaps also meant to suggest *rudo*, 'bray'. For once a translator may resort to paraphrase.

8.24 *the Syrian Goddess*: Atargatis–Derceto, a type of Near Eastern mother- and fertility-goddess represented also by Aphrodite–Astarte and Rhea–Cybele. Their cults had many features in common, including that exploited in Apuleius' description of eunuch priests and devotees. See *OCD* s.v. Atargatis. His unflattering account of the conduct of her priests follows that in the *Onos* quite closely but adds a number of picturesque details; the comment at the end of ch. 27 in particular may suggest that he is portraying the goddess as an anti-Isis: see the commentary of Hijmans *et al.* on book VIII, appendices III and IV. On an earlier possible symbolic allusion to Atargatis see 1.25 and note. His treatment of the episode also plays up to the traditional Roman distaste for passive male homosexuals.

a genuine Cappadocian: Cappadocians were proverbially strong and virile.

his tax return: the information required at the census included the citizen's age.

the Cornelian law: such an act was undoubtedly illegal, but this law appears to be a jocular figment. Of course this is precisely what the auctioneer is unwittingly doing; the irony is discreetly underscored by the human overtones of 'good and deserving servant' (*bonum et frugi mancipium*) and 'at home and abroad' (*et foris et domi*).

8.25 *the extent of his patience*: the ass's equipment is large enough to satisfy any demands likely to be made on it by his new masters; the 'patience' (passivity) will, however, be on their part.

Sabadius . . . Bellona . . . the Idaean Mother . . . Venus with her Adonis: Sabadius, or Sabazius, was another fertility deity; Bellona was the Roman goddess of war; the Idaean Mother is Cybele; Adonis was a god of vegetation and fertility, in myth a beautiful young hunter beloved of Venus and tragically killed by a boar. See on all these *OCD* s.vv. The variety of deities invoked is typical of the syncretism of such cults; it is even more strikingly in evidence in Lucius' prayer to Isis and her epiphany (11.2, 5).

its unfortunate guardian: here, as in his address to the 'girls' in the next chapter, he uses the feminine gender.

Philebus: 'lover of youth'. Exceptionally, a character's name is retained from the *Onos*.

8.26 *a hind substituting for a maiden*: to secure a favourable wind for the Greek fleet bound for Troy, withheld by the offended Artemis, Agamemnon was forced to sacrifice his daughter Iphigenia; in one version of the legend Artemis substituted a hind in her place. The phrase was apparently proverbial, but happens to be particularly appropriate here.

8.27 *with lowered heads*: had Dickens read *The Golden Ass*? 'Suddenly they stopped again, paused, struck out the time afresh, formed into lines the width of the public way, and, with their heads low down and their hands high up, swooped screaming off' (*A Tale of Two Cities*, book III, ch. 5). Of this description of the Carmagnole George Orwell singled out 'that touch, "with their heads low down and their hands high up"' for 'the evil vision it conveys' (*Critical Essays*, 1946, p. 16).

8.29 *Romans, to the rescue*: *Porro Quirites*, an old formula of appeal to the people. In the *Onos* (38), 'O Zeus!'; compare 3.29.

8.30 *a certain important city*: see 8.23 and note.

BOOK 9

9.1 *Fortune . . . divine Providence*: here, confusingly, identified, or at any rate apparently for once cooperating. See 9.31 and note.

9.2 *Myrtilus . . . Hephaestio . . . Hypnophilus . . . Apollonius*: humorous 'speaking' names. Myrtilus was Pelops' charioteer; Hephaestio, after Hephaestus, god of fire, is as obviously apt for a cook (6.24 and note) as Apollonius, after Apollo, god of medicine, is for a doctor; and Hypnophilus ('sleep-lover') is, as far as the sense goes, a plausible restoration of what the manuscripts offer (*hypatafium*), though it lacks the literary resonances of the other names.

9.3 *recorded in the ancient authorities*: true, and clinically accurate.

9.4 *amusing*: *lepidus* (see 1.1 and note). The manner of its introduction is calculated to draw attention to the fact that the story has little if any ostensible relevance to the main narrative; see 8.22 and note.

9.5 *her dashing blade of a lover*: *temerarius adulter*, an Ovidian tag (*Fasti*, 2. 335); it is used again of Philesitherus at 9.22.

with your hands in your pockets: in the Latin 'with your hands in your bosom', i.e. in the fold of the tunic which served for a pocket.

9.8 *one all-purpose oracle*: in iambic senarii, not the usual hexameters (4.32 and note). However, this metre too is occasionally attested (e.g. Herodotus, 1. 174; Cicero, *De divinatione*, 1. 81).

9.10 *the local Clink*: in the Latin the Tullianum, the state prison at Rome, a noisome place with a very sinister reputation. The name of the Clink, a prison in London, has passed into the language as a word for prisons in general. So Kipling: 'And I'm here in the Clink for a thundering drink and blacking the Corporal's eye'.

9.11 *blindfolded*: this was commonly done to prevent vertigo; see 9.15 and note.

wandering but never deviating: Apuleius relentlessly milks the paradox that all this walking never gets the walker anywhere.

had often seen . . . in operation: and had, as ass, operated it (7.15), as the narrator of the *Onos* (42) explicitly acknowledges. Unless he is simply being careless, Apuleius appears to go out of his way to underline the asininity of Lucius' behaviour.

9.12 *with a kind of pleasure*: because of the artistic opportunity it afforded for the pathetic description that follows.

the furnaces: the miller, as often, was also a baker.

sprinkle themselves with dust: for a better grip. This alludes to the pancratium, a combination of boxing and all-in wrestling, rather than boxing proper, in which holding was not allowed.

9.13 *a consummately wise man*: Odysseus (Ulysses), so characterized by Homer in the opening lines of the *Odyssey*.

no wiser, I must admit: a rueful gloss by Lucius, recollecting his experiences in tranquillity, on his failure at the time to draw any conclusions from them bearing on his own case.

9.14 *a prettily polished production: fabulam . . . suaue comptam*, a variation on *lepidus* (see 1.1 and note).

the One and Only God: whether this identifies her as a Jew or a Christian is debatable; see the commentary of Hijmans *et al.* on book IX, appendix IV. For the latter possibility, see the episode of the trampling of the fish (1.25 and note).

9.15 *enabled me to follow everything that was happening*: though blindfolded while at work (9.11 and note). Another sop to the sceptical reader (8.22 and note); see also 9.22.

9.16 *Philesitherus*: 'love-hunter'.

9.17 *Arete*: 'virtue'.

Myrmex: 'ant'.

busy with her woolwork: spinning was the traditional occupation of the dutiful Roman housewife.

to the baths: as is clear from the frequent mention of them in the novel, public baths were an indispensable feature of urban life under the Empire; as a rule only very grand houses would have had their own. They afforded obvious opportunities for intrigue, as Ovid notes in the *Ars amatoria* (3. 639–40).

9.18 *will force open even gates of steel*: the thought is proverbial, the expression pointedly recalls Horace on Jupiter's finding his way into Danae's tower in the shape of a shower of gold: 'gold can pass through the midst of attendants and break through stone with greater power than a thunderbolt' (*Odes*, 3. 16. 9–11).

9.19 *his purpose driven this way and that*: like a distraught heroine (5.21 and note).

like all women: the Latin is ambiguous: *genuina* can mean, and is so taken by some translators, 'natural to her', sc. individually. However, the notion that frailty is endemic in the female sex was old and persistent (compare the jaundiced view taken by Lucius at 7.10); the old woman who is telling the story naturally takes the cynical view. There is a similar ambiguity at 9.23.

9.20 *Love the Raw Recruit*: *Amori Rudi*; though each is individually experienced in love, they are recruits in a new service so far as this relationship is concerned. For the military metaphor, compare 2.10, 2.15−17.

9.21 *in the baths*: the theft of clothes from bathers was a common crime, so Philesitherus' inspiration is not implausible.

9.22 *the dashing adulterer*: the phrase is repeated from 9.5 (see note), but with ironic effect. Apuleius seems to go out of his way to draw attention to the fact that in combining two originally distinct stories into one, with the same protagonist, he expects the reader to accept without demur Philesitherus' metamorphosis from a man of the world, equal to coping with the formidable Barbarus, to a pretty boy who needs (as the old woman's speech indicates) a good deal of encouragement to come to the scratch and is then thrown into total panic by the arrival of the wronged husband. See below, 9.27 and note.

9.23 *the cunning of her sex*: *ingenita . . . astutia*, the same ambiguity as at 9.19 (see note).

by holy Ceres over there: a mill-cum-bakery would naturally house a shrine of Ceres, as a stable would one of Epona (3.27).

9.25 *bless you*: he would have said *salue*, 'be well'; sneezing could be lucky or unlucky as it came from the right or left respectively.

9.27 *I'm no barbarian*: *non sum barbarus*, also meaning 'I'm not Barbarus'; nor is this Philesitherus (above, 9.22 and note).

I shan't sue: more legal pleasantries (6.29 and note).

9.30 *let me tell you*: a tease; he never does so. See 8.22 and note.

9.31 *her stepmother's crimes*: only now do we learn that she is typecast in this archetypally malevolent role.

Fortune: here again (9.1 and note) implicitly identified with divine Providence, who set this chain of events in motion by providing Lucius with the opportunity to avenge his master (9.27).

9.32 *the subject demands*: see 4.6 and note.

9.37 *leaving his body balanced in mid-air*: a specifically epic touch (Ovid, *Metamorphoses*, 5. 126−7, 12. 330−31; Lucan, *Pharsalia*, 3. 601−2, 7. 624); compare the fate of Alcimus (4.12 and note). This and other details of the fighting invest a sordid brawl with literary dignity.

9.38 *you will always have a neighbour*: a proverbial idea, but hardly calculated to crush this aggressor.

9.39 *the vine-staff*: the centurion's emblem of rank.

couldn't understand what he was saying: how could Lucius? In taking over this episode from the *Onos* (44) Apuleius seems to have overlooked the fact that it was only later that he learned Latin (1.1 and note).

calling him 'mate': *commilito*, 'fellow soldier'.

9.41 *as I learned later*: we are not told how; compare 4.6 and note.

a sacrilegious breach: because the oath was sworn by the Emperor or, as here (see below), by his genius.

9.42 *the common proverb*: in fact an Apuleian conflation of two proverbs. 'The peeping ass' put his head into a potter's shop and broke the pots; the potter sued his owner. 'The ass's shadow' is a story supposedly invented by Demosthenes to shame an inattentive jury: a man hired an ass and took a nap in its shadow, and the owner sued him because he had only rented out the beast and not its shadow. Both stories in different ways satirize frivolous behaviour.

BOOK 10

10.2 *the sock . . . the buskin*: the low shoe (*soccus*) and high boot (*cothurnus*) worn by comic and tragic actors respectively. This is an Apuleian tease: the story of the stepmother who falls in love with her stepson was familiar in particular from Euripides' play *Hippolytus*, but here it turns out to have a happy ending. The literary texture is enriched by echoes of Virgil, Ovid and Seneca.

Alas, th' unknowing minds of − doctors: an adapted quotation from Virgil's comment on Dido's attempts to invoke the blessing of the gods on her ill-starred love for Aeneas (*Aeneid*, 4. 65); in the original, 'of seers'. Compare these symptoms with those at 5.25.

10.3 *It is his likeness*: lifted from Seneca's play *Phaedra* (646−7).

hasn't happened: this has a proverbial ring: 'What's hid's unknown, and what's unknown's unsought' (Ovid, *Ars amatoria*, 3. 397, trans. A. D. Melville). Compare Psyche's sister: 'You aren't really rich if nobody knows that you are' (5.10).

10.5 *buried before his eyes*: to be predeceased by one's children, more especially by a son, was looked on as a terrible misfortune; the theme had been eloquently exploited by Juvenal in his tenth Satire (250ff.).

10.6 *a parricide*: see 3.7 and note. So at 5.11 the sisters' plot against Psyche is described in the Latin as parricide.

10.7 *the council*: in this case the court apparently consists of the town councillors (*patres*) acting as a jury, with the magistrates presiding. See Introduction, §6.

the court of the Areopagus: this very ancient court was still in being in Apuleius' time; that these prohibitions were still in force in provincial courts may be antiquarian fantasy.

I don't know and am in no position to report to you: after his report of the stepmother's *ipsissima verba*, a belated concession to plausibility. Apuleius may have felt, reasonably enough, that another pair of full-dress forensic speeches after those at 3.3−6 would, even by his standards, be overdoing things. He has, however, no compunction in reporting the doctor's speech verbatim.

with a show of nervousness: this, in terms of transcriptional probability, is a more convincing correction of the manuscript text than the reading preferred by some editors, 'without the slightest trace of nervousness'. The fact that two readings diametrically opposed in sense are from the literary point of view almost equally plausible is a salutary reminder of the difficulties that sometimes confront critics of Greek and Latin texts.

10.8 *to be sewn up in the sack*: another antiquarian flourish. The ancient punishment for parricides was to be enclosed in a sack with various animals and drowned. It had been abolished in the mid first century BC.

10.10 *as usual in Greece*: see 3.9 and note.

10.11 *improper for one of my profession*: as contrary to the Hippocratic Oath: 'I will not administer poison to anyone if asked, nor suggest doing so'.

mandragora: a decoction of the mandrake. Seneca records a similar incident when a slave, ordered to give his master poison to save him from death at the hands of Caesar, substituted a narcotic; there as here the story ended happily (*De beneficiis*, 3. 24). The theme was also exploited by the Greek novelists Xenophon of Ephesus and Iamblichus, and long afterwards by Shakespeare in *Romeo and Juliet*.

the extreme penalty of the law: in this case crucifixion (10.12), but a slave convicted of conspiring against his master was liable to be burned alive or thrown to the beasts.

10.12 *famous, indeed fabulous*: *famosa atque fabulosa*; in introducing the story Apuleius had announced it as 'a tragedy, no mere tale', *tragoediam non fabulam* (10.2). A 'tale' is of course precisely what he has made of it.

10.13 *a pastrycook . . . a chef*: a slave might be allowed to own and manage property or conduct a business on his own behalf. Technically the profits or savings – the 'nest-egg' (*peculium*) referred to at 10.14 – belonged to the master; in practice they were often used by the slave to purchase his freedom, as is evidently the case with the freedman mentioned at 10.17, referred to as *satis peculiato*, having set himself up well. See *OCD* s.v. *peculium*; J. A. Crook, *Law and Life of Rome*, 1967, pp. 188−9.

10.14 *doing an Eteocles*: Oedipus' sons Eteocles and Polynices died at each other's hands while fighting for the kingship after his death. Their conflict was the theme of Aeschylus' play *The Seven against Thebes* and the background to Sophocles' *Antigone*.

10.15 *the Harpies*: see 2.23 and note. They persecuted the blind Phineus by fouling and plundering his food. Apuleius' readers would have been familiar with Virgil's description (*Aeneid*, 3. 209–69).

10.16 *silphium*: a kind of asafoetida, used for both medicinal and culinary purposes. It was a purgative and perhaps an acquired taste.

10.17 *upwards for 'no' and downwards for 'yes'*: still the regular gestures of dissent and assent in Greece.

10.18 *Thiasus*: 'revel'.

the capital of the province of Achaea: and also Lucius' native place (2.12), something one might have expected him to allude to. In the *Onos*, the scene of this last episode is Thessalonica (49). Another loose end; see also 11.18, 11.26 and notes.

the quinquennial magistracy: as municipal censor; see *OCD* s.v. municipium.

10.19 *Pasiphae*: wife of Minos, king of Crete; she fell in love with a bull and mated with him concealed in a wooden cow made by Daedalus. Their offspring was the Minotaur, half bull, half man. The story had been told with mock-revulsion by Ovid in the *Ars amatoria* (1. 289–326).

10.21 *even the band*: often shown in pictures of lovemaking as kept on.

10.23 *put to death at birth*: by exposure. In law the Roman father of a family (*paterfamilias*) had the absolute power of life and death over its members. By Apuleius' time it was rarely exercised except on unwanted new-born infants, a practice which continued in spite of attempts to outlaw it.

10.25 *many victorious battles and many notable trophies*: doctors who killed their patients were a favourite target of satirists; there is a similar conceit to this in an epigram ascribed to Lucian (*Greek Anthology*, 11. 401), in which a doctor boasts that he has sent many souls down to Hades in an adaptation of a famous line of Homer referring to the exploits of Achilles (*Iliad*, 1. 3). This one evidently does it on purpose.

Lifegiver . . . Lifetaker: literally (but the text is uncertain) 'sacred to Health . . . sacred to Proserpine'.

10.28 *from a child prematurely deceased*: text and interpretation uncertain.

10.29 *holy matrimony*: matrimonium confarreatum; see 5.26 and note.

the very pretty sight inside: once more Apuleius indulges his love of elaborate description. However, this is not pure embellishment. The mythical Venus portrayed in the pageant, who offered Paris pleasure as the price of his Judgement, with proverbially ruinous consequences (10.33), can be seen in retrospect as an ironic contrast to the true Venus, subsumed in the all-embracing godhead of Isis (11.2, 5), in whose service Lucius will find the high and pure pleasure which, like Psyche, he has hitherto failed to recognize. That the reference to the fatal verdict of Paris is blunted of its point by being made to form part of a general diatribe on corrupt juries can also be seen as ironic: once again Lucius fails to grasp the real significance of what he sees and of his own reactions to it. His revulsion from what awaits him in the arena is grounded, not on moral principle, but on a distaste for criminal associations and fear for his own skin. These are the motives for his escape; he finds salvation not because he has come to deserve it but because he desperately needs it.

a pyrrhic dance in Greek style: a war-dance, properly performed by men and boys in armour. If Apuleius knew the etymology which derived the name from *pyra*, 'funeral pyre', i.e. that of Patroclus, round which it was first supposed to have been danced, its performance before a re-enactment of the events which led to the Trojan War is doubly appropriate.

10.30 *the wand he carried*: his herald's staff (*caduceus*).

with a nod: a pointed piece of mime, representing the nod with which in epic Jupiter irrevocably confirms his decisions.

10.31 *her descent from heaven . . . her connection with the sea*: see 4.28 and note.

egg-shaped helmets with a star for crest: their mother Leda bore them to Jupiter, who had mated with her in the shape of a swan, in an egg; as the constellation Gemini (the Twins) they protected sailors.

the Ionian pipe: a quiet ladylike mode for the most ladylike of the three goddesses.

Terror and Fear: the Homeric Deimos and Phobos, Athene's (Minerva's) attendants in battle (Homer, *Iliad*, 4. 440).

a Dorian piper: the martial mode; Milton, *Paradise Lost*, 1. 549–51:

> Anon they move
> In perfect *Phalanx* to the *Dorian* mood
> Of Flutes and soft Recorders; such as rais'd
> To highth of noblest temper Hero's old
> Arming to Battel . . .

10.32 *sweet Lydian harmonies*: the softest of the modes.

10.33 *you gowned vultures*: lawyers as a class have never been popular, and complaints about justice being sold to the highest bidder are as old as Hesiod (*Works and Days*, 37–41). 'It was a widespread conviction in antiquity that all arts and artefacts must have been invented by somebody' (R. G. M. Nisbet and Margaret Hubbard, *A Commentary on Horace: Odes Book I*, Oxford, 1970, p. 49); so the invention of the lamp is ascribed to a lover (5.23). Lucius credits Paris, on top of starting the Trojan War, with the additional distinction of being the first corrupt judge. He himself later on is not ashamed to boast of doing well for himself as an advocate (11.30).

Palamedes . . . Ajax: both victims of Ulysses' unprincipled cunning. Palamedes unmasked Ulysses' deception when he feigned madness to escape service in the expedition against Troy, and was subsequently framed by Ulysses and executed on a trumped-up charge of treachery. Ajax was defeated by Ulysses' sophistical rhetoric in the contest for the arms of the dead Achilles, and in his humiliation committed suicide. Both stories would have been familiar from Ovid's treatment in the *Metamorphoses* (13. 1–398); and both are mentioned in the speech ascribed to Socrates by Plato in the other case cited by Lucius as 'men of old who lost their lives through an unjust judgement' (*Apology*, 41b). See next note.

An old man of godlike understanding: Socrates, condemned to drink hemlock on a charge of corrupting the youth of Athens.

10.34 *a shower of wine mixed with saffron*: spraying perfume over the stage was a standard refinement. Mixing saffron with wine is expressly recommended by Pliny (*Natural History*, 21. 33).

10.35 *the famous colony of Corinth*: it had been destroyed by Mummius in 146 BC and refounded as a Roman *colonia* in 44 BC.

BOOK II

11.1 *by her Providence*: the divine Providence so often referred to is now identified with the goddess herself.

her light and might: *luminis numinisque*.

godlike Pythagoras: a reminder of the philosophical background that ought to have stood Lucius in better stead (1.2 and note). The mystic properties of the number seven were widely venerated in Greek and Oriental cults; Venus in her anti-Isiac guise offers seven kisses as the reward for informing against Psyche (6.8 and note).

my silent prayer: Lucius throws himself on the divine mercy. The ensuing chain of events calls forth the most sustained display of Apuleius' rhetorical and descriptive powers in the novel. His invocation, like those of Psyche (6.2, 6.4 and notes), follows the traditional forms and conventions of ancient prayer and is constructed with great elaboration (see the analysis by Gwyn Griffiths, *Isis-Book*, pp. 119–22). It and the following description of Isis' epiphany also reflect ancient catalogues (aretalogies) of the goddess's powers and attributes (Walsh, 1970, pp. 252–3).

11.2 *Phoebus' sister*: Diana (Artemis), though in classical (Homeric) myth a virgin goddess, was worshipped at Ephesus as a fertility goddess and as Lucina (Ilithyia) presided over childbirth. She was also identified with the moon, as Phoebus was with the sun.

of the fearful night-howling and triple countenance: not here the courteous hostess of Psyche, but the Underworld goddess identified with Hecate, whose coming is heralded by the howling of the dogs (Theocritus, *Idylls*, 2. 35–6; Virgil, *Aeneid*, 6. 257–8). She too is identified with the moon in the all-embracing figure of Isis.

if I may not live: van der Vliet (1897) added *hominem*, 'as a man', which is more logical and pointed: the escaped Lucius-as-ass is not now confronted with imminent death.

11.3 *First her hair*: as in the description of the sleeping Cupid (5.22) he follows the rules of classical rhetoric by starting at the top. The emphasis on hair, though brief, is pointed (see 2.8 and note).

11.4 *a bronze sistrum*: a rattle made of rods loosely fixed in a metal frame (two examples are depicted on the cover). See 11.10.

the blessed perfumes of Arabia: blessed as coming from Arabia Felix, Arabia the Blessed; as usual, Apuleius scouts the obvious turn of phrase.

11.5 *first-born of mankind*: as claimed by Herodotus (2. 2. 1). Pessinus was an important provincial centre in Asia Minor.

the native Athenians: they boasted that they had always lived in Attica.

Dictynnan Diana: the Cretan goddess Dictynna was identified with Artemis/ Diana.

the triple-tongued Sicilians: they are not elsewhere so described, and it is not clear what third language after Greek and Latin Apuleius may have in mind. Elsewhere *trilinguis* means literally 'three-tongued', e.g. of the three-headed Cerberus, and the allusion may be to the triangular shape of Sicily, often so characterized; *lingua* can mean 'promontory'. Compare 'the island-dwelling Cypriots' preceding.

Rhamnusia: i.e. as Nemesis, worshipped at Rhamnus in Attica.

both races of Ethiopians: see 1.8 and note.

11.6 *that has always been so hateful to me*: see Introduction, §8.

make spiteful accusations against you: similar considerations had deterred Lucius from seizing an earlier opportunity of release (3.29).

solemnly promised: she uses the technical term meaning 'legally bound over to appear'; see 4.18 and note.

that subterranean hemisphere: in the pseudo-Platonic dialogue *Axiochus*, and apparently nowhere else, the gods and 'those below' are described as inhabiting the upper and lower halves of a spherical universe (371b).

beyond the bounds fixed for you by your Fate: a striking claim: the gods of the pagan literary tradition were powerless to override the decrees of Fate. Perhaps, as suggested by Gwyn Griffiths, 'fate' is used here to mean 'what the astrologers predict'.

11.7 *wore an air of serene enjoyment*: Lucius' lyrical description recalls the Lucretian

NOTES

Venus, at whose coming 'the creative earth puts forth sweet flowers, the broad ocean smiles, and heaven is appeased and glows with diffused light' (*De rerum natura*, 1. 7–9). See Introduction, §7.

11.8 *Pegasus and Bellerophon*: see 6.30 and note. It is tempting to see some symbolic significance in these masqueraders, especially since it is an ass that brings up the rear, but no really convincing interpretation on these lines has been offered; see 6.18 and note. As Lucius carefully distinguishes between this popular buffoonery and the goddess's procession proper, the description may be intended to throw the true significance of the following spectacle into relief by contrasting it with the uncritical and uncomprehending enjoyment of the uninitiated.

11.9 *Sarapis*: the Greek spelling; he is more familiar as Serapis. Here identified with Osiris.

which extended to their right ears: a periphrasis for the transverse pipe (*plagiaulos*, *tibia obliqua*). The *aulos* or *tibia* was a reed instrument, and the 'flute' of some translators and commentators gives a misleading idea of its tone, which was more calculated to excite than soothe.

11.10 *the earthly stars of the great faith*: these words were transposed to this position in the text by van der Vliet (1897); in the manuscripts they characterize the body of the initiates.

a copy of Mercury's caduceus: see note on Anubis at 11.11 below.

more apt to symbolize justice than the right: this interesting idea seems to be otherwise unattested and may be a flight of fancy on Apuleius' part. It is hazardous to trust him implicitly on such points; see next note.

a golden basket heaped with laurel branches: text and interpretation are disputed, but most modern versions (Butler's is an honourable exception) do violence to the Latin or the sense or both. Laurel is not elsewhere mentioned as playing a part in Isiac ritual, but see previous note. The *vannus* doubled in cult as a winnowing-fan and a receptacle for sacred objects.

11.11 *his face now black, now gold*: perhaps as symbolizing the Underworld and heaven respectively; but whether one statue with particoloured face is meant or two different statues is not clear from the description. Anubis, like Mercury, is a shepherd of souls and shares his attributes.

the All-Mother: Isis herself, figured as a cow or with a cow's head.

11.15 *a Fortune that can see*: it is one of the unresolved paradoxes of the revelation finally granted to Lucius–Apuleius that it should be blind Fortune (7.2 and note) that places him in the end under the protection of a seeing Fortune in the shape of Isis. It was probably the paradox itself and the opportunity it offered for rhetorical exploitation that primarily interested Apuleius rather than its theological implications. The priest's characterization of Lucius' persecuting Fortune owes at least as much to literary as to religious conceptions.

you will really experience the enjoyment of your liberty: an idea familiar to Anglicans in the words of the Collect for Peace: 'whose service is perfect freedom'; not found in this pointed paradoxical form in the New Testament. It goes back through the early Fathers at least to Seneca: *De vita beata* ('How to be happy') 15. 7, 'Liberty is obedience to God'.

11.16 *the reward of a blameless and pious life*: the remark is prefaced with a word which Apuleius often uses as a nudge to the reader, *scilicet*, 'obviously' but also ironically 'no doubt'. Taken at its face value it is flatly at variance both with what the reader knows and what the priest has just said; Apuleius is slyly indicating that the idea that salvation is earned by works rather than faith is a popular misconception. See Introduction, §10.

an egg, and sulphur: though sulphur and eggs figure separately in other allusions to purificatory rituals, they are otherwise mentioned in combination only by Ovid in the *Ars amatoria* (2. 330). Apuleius knew his Ovid, and this may be another detail that owes more to literary reminiscence than to accurate observation. See next note.

11.17 *the Pastophori*: 'shrine-bearers'. Here and subsequently Apuleius writes of them as if they had priestly status, which does not appear to have been the case. See 11.30 and note.

in Greek: ta Ploiaphesia, 'the Ship-launching'. These are the only words actually written in Greek (slightly garbled but plausibly restored) in the novel; see 4.32 and note.

11.18 *in my homeland*: Rumour did not in fact have far to go, or his visitors to come, for he was now only a matter of a few miles (10.35) from Corinth, where he was born. The implication that he was a long way from home is a hangover from the Greek original, in which the narrator's native city is several days' sail from the place of his restoration to human shape (*Onos*, 55).

11.20 *some 'portions'*: partes, suggesting 'shares' in an enterprise of some kind, but the modern connotations of the word render its use misleading here.

after Photis' disastrous mistake had embridled me: cum me Photis malis incapistrasset erroribus, i.e. turned me into an ass, but the words can also mean 'had trapped me in my unhappy wanderings', a good example of Apuleius' linguistic versatility. *incapistro* is found nowhere else and was evidently coined by him, as was a good deal of his vocabulary.

11.21 *return them to a new lifespan*: in this world or the next? The ambiguity reflects that of Isis' promise at 11.6. But initiation is clearly, as the case of Lucius himself shows, not reserved exclusively for those at death's door.

11.22 *her own high priest Mithras*: Mithras seems to have been a not uncommon personal name, but it is striking to find a high priest of Isis so called. All the mystery religions shared certain features, and it is on record that people were initiated or held priesthoods in more than one. If Apuleius is hinting at an affinity between the cults of Isis and Mithras he does not develop the point. On Mithraism see *OCD* s.v. Mithras.

a divinely ordained conjunction of our stars: again a literary echo, here of Horace addressing Maecenas: 'our horoscopes agree in a marvellous manner' (*Odes*, 2. 17. 21–2).

unknown characters: in the hieroglyphic and hieratic scripts.

11.23 *my pledged appearance*: again the legal phrase connoting being bound over to appear in court (11.6 and note), almost 'to answer to my divine bail'.

the other for importunate curiosity: this phrase is a supplement added by van der Vliet (1897); curiosity is not a vice of the tongue.

that and no more I shall relate: what exactly initiates in the mystery cults experienced has been the subject of much speculation. So much is clear, that an ordeal by darkness and terror culminated in a brilliantly lit revelation of divine beneficence. The pattern has survived in the rituals enacted in *The Magic Flute*.

11.24 *Hyperborean griffins*: fabulous monsters that lived in the far north guarding stores of gold (Herodotus, 4. 13. 1).

an Olympic robe: the epithet has not been convincingly explained. *Olympiacam* means 'Olympic', not as in the translations 'Olympian'. Perhaps a symbol of victory?

a boon I could never repay: see 3.22 and note.

11.26 *my ancestral home*: Corinth, just the other side of the Isthmus, an hour or so away on horseback. Lucius makes it sound as if he had a long way to go: see 10.18, 11.18 and notes.

Isis of the Field: Isis Campensis; her temple was in the Campus Martius, the Field of Mars. Like other Isiac temples, it was notorious as a lovers' rendezvous (Ovid, *Amores*, 2. 2. 25, *Ars amatoria*, 1. 77, 3. 393; Juvenal, *Satires*, 6. 489, 9. 22; Martial, 11. 47. 4).

11.27 *the invincible Osiris*: consort of Isis; he had appeared in the procession in the guise of Sarapis (11.9 and note). He is called invincible or unconquered (*inuictus*) because of his restoration to life by Isis (herself also so styled, 11.7) and his victory over his evil brother and murderer, Seth-Typhon.

a wand tipped with ivy: the thyrsus, associated particularly with the worship of Bacchus (Dionysus).

very apt: the cognomen Asinius is derived from *asinus*, 'ass'.

a man from Madaura: attentive readers have been prepared for the revelation that 'Lucius' is a mask for the author himself (2.12 and note), but the way in which it is finally effected is wonderfully offhand. See Introduction, §8.

11.28 *between the devil and the deep sea*: in the Latin *inter sacrum . . . et saxum*, 'between the altar and the flint-knife', sc. of the sacrificing priest. Apparently proverbial, but Apuleius almost certainly picked the expression up from Plutus, who uses very nearly the same words in his play *Captivi* (617).

in Latin: this is Apuleius speaking (1.1. and note).

11.30 *the Pastophori*: see 11.17 and note.

the order of quinquennial decurions: the term and the office belong to the world of provincial administration (10.18); the *decuriones* were municipal senators or town councillors. There seems to be no other firm evidence for the existence of such an office in the Isiac priesthood. See 11.10, 16 and notes.

entered joyfully on: *gaudens obibam*, the last words of the Latin text. The book ends as it began, with an emphasis on pleasure, but ambiguity persists to the last. The verb, in the imperfect tense, may be inceptive, as it is rendered here, 'began to perform', or continuative, 'went on performing'. The reader is left wondering how long ago all this was and what may have happened between then and the 'now' implied in the Prologue.

founded in the time of Sulla: Sulla lived from 138 to 78 BC; it is perfectly possible that an Isiac priesthood was established at Rome during this period, but there is no reason to connect it with Sulla himself. The prosaic chronological formula signals the final emergence of the hero and his story from the colourful nightmare of metaphorical metamorphosis into the light of common day and leaves the reader once more confronting contemporary reality. See Introduction, §3.

Index